M000003079

TWO LANCES OF ENEMY 'MECHS POURED FROM THE JUNGLE.

Aris opened a general line to the company. "Fall back. Repeat, fall back to southern bank. Jumping 'Mechs take to the air. Fire Lance break off now. Yan Lu, take rear guard. You'll have to walk backward in order to keep your good armor toward the enemy."

Yan's *Thunder* had the best armor of any of Aris' Battle-Mechs, and it could sustain hits better than anyone else's. And the machine's autocannon would keep the opposing 'Mechs from following too closely.

His defense laid as best he could, Aris pivoted his *Wraith* and ran to the edge of the riverbank. At a stretch, the 'Mech could jump just over two hundred meters. It's *gonna be close,* he thought, triggering his jump jets for the third time this battle and angling for the far shore.

And then incoming rockets made him realize that getting to the other side of the river had just become the *least* of his concerns. . . .

BINDING FORCE

FASA

BATTLETECH®
HEAVY METAL MAYHEM

THE BLOOD OF KERENSKY TRILOGY
by MICHAEL A. STACKPOLE

The Successor States had lived in peace for three hundred years. Now, an unknown military force of awe-inspiring power is about to change all that. They are a threat from beyond the Periphery, a genetically bred race of warriors possessing technology beyond your wildest dreams and a taste for blood beyond your darkest nightmares. They are powerful. They are ferocious. They are THE CLANS.

LETHAL HERITAGE
THEY ARE COMING

Who are the Clans? One Inner Sphere warrior, Phelan Kell of the mercenary group Kell Hounds, finds out the hard way—as their prisoner and protege.   (453832—$4.99)

BLOOD LEGACY
THEY HAVE ARRIVED

The Clan invaders had chosen their next objective: the capital of the Draconis Combine. While House Kurita desperately fights for survival, Hanse Davion is presented with the perfect opportunity to destroy this hated enemy once and for all. Or, is this the opportunity to reunite the houses of the Inner Sphere against a force inimical to them all?   (453840—$5.50)

LOST DESTINY
THEY HAVE CONQUERED

The Inner Sphere lies in ruins. Heirs are missing. Realms have been overrun. Entire regiments of BattleMechs have been destroyed. The Clans are closing in on their prime objective—Terra, the cradle of civilization and hub of the ComStar network. The only hope for the beleaguered denizens of the Inner Sphere rests in those who betrayed them—ComStar and their untested warriors—the last against total defeat.   (453859—$5.99)

Buy them at your local bookstore or use this convenient coupon for ordering.

PENGUIN USA
P.O. Box 999 — Dept. #17109
Bergenfield, New Jersey 07621

Please send me the books I have checked above.
I am enclosing $_____ (please add $2.00 to cover postage and handling). Send check or money order (no cash or C.O.D.'s) or charge by Mastercard or VISA (with a $15.00 minimum). Prices and numbers are subject to change without notice.

Card #_____ Exp. Date _____
Signature_____
Name_____
Address_____
City _____ State _____ Zip Code _____

For faster service when ordering by credit card call **1-800-253-6476**

Allow a minimum of 4-6 weeks for delivery. This offer is subject to change without notice.

BATTLETECH®

BINDING
FORCE

Loren L. Coleman

A ROC BOOK

ROC
Published by the Penguin Group
Penguin Books USA Inc., 375 Hudson Street,
New York, New York 10014, U.S.A.
Penguin Books Ltd, 27 Wrights Lane,
London W8 5TZ, England
Penguin Books Australia Ltd, Ringwood,
Victoria, Australia
Penguin Books Canada Ltd, 10 Alcorn Avenue,
Toronto, Ontario, Canada M4V 3B2
Penguin Books (N.Z.) Ltd, 182–190 Wairau Road,
Auckland 10, New Zealand

Penguin Books Ltd, Registered Offices:
Harmondsworth, Middlesex, England

First published by Roc, an imprint of Dutton Signet,
a division of Penguin Books USA Inc.

First Printing, June, 1997
10 9 8 7 6 5 4 3 2 1

Copyright © FASA Corporation, 1997
All rights reserved

Series Editor: Donna Ippolito
Cover art by Bruce Jensen
Mechanical Drawings: Duane Loose and the FASA art department

 REGISTERED TRADEMARK—MARCA REGISTRADA

BATTLETECH, FASA, and the distinctive BATTLETECH and FASA logos
are trademarks of the FASA Corporation, 1100 W. Cermak, Suite B305,
Chicago, IL 60608.

Printed in the United States of America

Without limiting the rights under copyright reserved above, no part of this
publication may be reproduced, stored in or introduced into a retrieval
system, or transmitted, in any form, or by any means (electronic, mechanical,
photocopying, recording, or otherwise), without the prior written permission
of both the copyright owner and the above publisher of this book.

BOOKS ARE AVAILABLE AT QUANTITY DISCOUNTS WHEN USED
TO PROMOTE PRODUCTS OR SERVICES. FOR INFORMATION
PLEASE WRITE TO PREMIUM MARKETING DIVISION, PENGUIN
BOOKS USA INC., 375 HUDSON STREET, NEW YORK, NEW YORK
10014.

If you purchased this book without a cover you should be aware that this
book is stolen property. It was reported as "unsold and destroyed" to the publisher and neither the author nor the publisher has received any payment for
this "stripped book."

This story is dedicated to my parents,
LaRon and Dawn Coleman,
who have both contributed much to my career
and my appreciation of family.

ACKNOWLEDGMENTS

I would like to charge the following people with aiding and abetting a known author:

Jim LeMonds, who gave me my initial tools.

Keith A. Mick, for that first invitation. Ray Sainze, wherever he ended up, for sharing his fascination for Battle-Tech—it was contagious. Tim Tousely and Matt Dillahunty, who keep putting my computer back together.

Everyone associated with "the gang"—that is, the Eugene Professional Writer's Workshop. Jon, Jak, and Tom, who first drew me in and made me feel welcome. Jerry, Kathy, Steve, Chris, Ray, Dan, and all the others who I haven't seen recently. Dean Wesley Smith and Kristine Kathryn Rush, who have both done so much for my skills and my career.

Greg Gordon, the man in the know.

Bryan Nystul for my first BattleTech job. Mike Stackpole, Blaine Lee Pardoe, and Annalise Raziq, for their advice. Donna Ippolito, who worked very hard to help me get this story out.

Heather Joy Coleman, a willing partner in my life. My sons, Talon Laron and Conner Rhys, who make everything worthwhile just by being there.

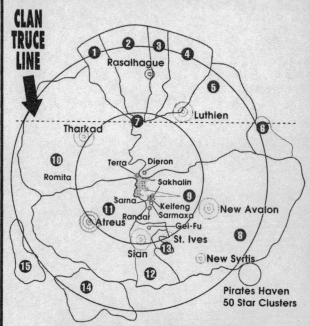

CLAN TRUCE LINE

Rasalhague

Luthien

Tharkad

Terra · Dieron

Sakhalin

Romita

Sarna

Keifeng

Sarmaxa

New Avalon

Randar

Atreus

Gei-Fu

St. Ives

Sian

New Syrtis

Pirates Haven
50 Star Clusters

MAP OF THE INNER SPHERE

1 • Jade Falcon/Steel Viper, 2 • Wolf Clan, 3 • Ghost Bear,
4 • Smoke Jaguars/Nova Cats, 5 • Draconis Combine,
6 • Outworlds Alliance, 7 • Free Rasalhague Republic,
8 • Federated Commonwealth, 9 • Chaos March,
10 • Lyran Alliance, 11 • Free Worlds League,
12 • Capellan Confederation, 13 • St. Ives Compact
14 • Magistracy of Canopus, 15 • Marion Hegemony

Map Compiled by COMSTAR.
From information provided by the COMSTAR EXPLORER SERVICE
and the STAR LEAGUE ARCHIVES on Terra.

© 3058 COMSTAR CARTOGRAPHIC CORPS.

Prologue

Celestial Palace
Forbidden City, Sian
Sian Commonality, Capellan Confederation
21 February 3058

Ion Rush, Master of Imarra, toured the third-floor ballroom of the Celestial Palace, trying to avoid the other guests. He sipped occasionally at a light, dry wine that left the tang of plums on his tongue. Attired simply for the evening, he wore the dress uniform of House Imarra. An ivory-colored suit trimmed heavily in what was commonly called Liao green. Gold buttons decorated the sleeves, and the crest of the Capellan Confederation rode on a patch at his right shoulder. The Imarra uniform did not sport the narrow cape of the regular Capellan Armed Forces, and Ion had chosen to forego his ceremonial katana sword and medals.

The Celestial Palace, seat of government for the Capellan Confederation, was currently hosting its biggest celebration of the year outside of the Chancellor's birthday. The Chinese Lunar New Year. Its fifteen days of celebration and ritual observances gave the normally reserved Capellan citizens a chance to unwind, relax.

If that is so, then why am I so tense? He accepted a *jiaozi* from the tray of a passing server and bit into the spicy meat dumpling, concentrating on its rich flavor rather than the question he'd asked himself.

The ballroom was nowhere near filled to capacity, but still Rush guessed that at least two hundred people milled about the spacious floor, making small talk, drinking wine, eating *jiaozi* or the sweet rice pudding *niangao* that was also a favorite of the New Year celebration. Red bunting and ribbon had been strung everywhere, the bright, cheerful color meant to reinforce the festive mood. The buzz of half a hundred conversations warmed his ears, but none engaged him as he continued his solitary patrol.

Not because he could be easily ignored. Ion Rush was not a small man, nor usually one of quiet disposition. With close-cropped blonde hair and broad Slavic features he was obviously not a member of the Directorship, the Confederation's bureaucratic and administrative caste, which took such pride in breeding themselves ever closer to their ideal of sharp-eyed, dark-haired Asian ancestry. Nor was he a member of the Intelligentsia, the technicians and scientists who made up the other high-ranking caste present at the Chancellor's celebration. Even more than the uniform, it was his strong build, his confident, almost swaggering gait, his way of calmly searching a crowd— blue eyes sharp and piercing, spotting potential allies, enemies—that gave him away as a member of a third group. *Janshi.*

Warrior.

The Inner Sphere, over a thousand light years wide and comprised of hundreds of settled worlds, held few constants. Each world possessed its own resources and needs. Governments were varied, and promoted their own agendas. But one thing did hold true throughout. Warriors were a privileged class.

The five Great Houses of the Inner Sphere, which included the Capellan Confederation, had once united all of humankind under a single government known as the Star League. But the League had collapsed some three hundred years before, and the surviving Successor Houses had been at each other's throats ever since. To fight their wars they used BattleMechs—giant humanoid machines weighing up to one hundred tons worth of armor, weapons, and control components.

Ion Rush was a thirty-year veteran of those ongoing wars, a MechWarrior who piloted one of the ten-meter tall 'Mechs. He was also Master of Imarra, the most prestigious of eight Warrior Houses supplementing the Capellan military. The Warrior Houses lived by special laws, apart from normal Capellan society, each House a world unto itself. Members were hand-picked by the House Master at twelve years of age. They were cared for, taught, and trained by the House Mentors. A Warrior House directed the lives of its members, lives that would be dedicated to service to the Capellan ruler and the state until death. It was one of the greatest honors to which a Capellan citizen could hope to aspire.

It was also the reason Rush remained apart from the festivities. As a protector of the realm, he felt it his duty to remain on guard. Even if the current Chancellor was not. *Especially* if he was not.

"Join me at the window, Ion?"

As if summoned by thought, Chancellor Sun-Tzu Liao suddenly appeared at Rush's side flanked by two large men dressed in black uniforms. The Master of Imarra gave each bodyguard an appraising glance while trying to conceal his surprise. A white death's head pin worn at the collar was the only badge of rank they wore. For most people, that was more than enough to identify them.

They were members of the Chancellor's elite Death Commandos—some of the Confederation's deadliest warriors. Drawn from the regular military and the Warrior Houses, their lives were pledged directly to the Chancellor. But Ion Rush had trained both of these men. Had controlled their lives for six years before releasing them to the Death Commandos. He did not feel the least bit intimidated.

Perhaps that was a mistake. Perhaps not.

Tall and thin, Sun-Tzu was a contrast to the powerful builds of his men and looked even younger than his twenty-seven years, though Rush knew from weekly matches that the young ruler kept himself fit and was a decent student of karate. The Chancellor wore red silk robes traditional to his office, these with black and gold

Bengal tigers cavorting on each breast and around the edges of his wide sleeves. And across the back would be the Chinese zodiac wheel, recently adjusted to reflect the New Year.

Ion Rush shrugged off his discomfort at having been surprised and gave the Chancellor a neutral smile. Sun-Tzu had apparently taken pains to come upon the Master of Imarra unaware, and the Liao was not known for his empty gestures.

"At your service, Celestial Wisdom," Rush said, and gestured the Chancellor ahead of him.

Fully a fourth of the ballroom's eastern wall was constructed of bullet-proof glass, allowing the guests to look out over a large courtyard and the east palace walls to where the lights of the capital stared back. On the way over, Rush plucked a piece of fried dough from a serving plate. It would serve well as a prop to keep his hands busy or his mouth quiet if he needed a pause to think.

Sun-Tzu's walk was slightly staggered, as if the young Chancellor had drunk too much wine, and once he stumbled slightly when passing Jesse Villars, Master of House LuSann. Villars kept his face studiously blank, but Rush could read the scorn in his eyes. He wished Sun-Tzu would take notice and deal with the man's insolence. That might solve a few of the problems worrying the Imarra House Master. But Sun-Tzu apparently had other things in mind.

The Lantern Festival parade was passing by the eastern gate, and nearing its end. Now Rush silently thanked the Chancellor for his timing, and tore off a small piece of the candied bread and chewed on it slowly with something approaching relish. Of all the New Year's festivities, he liked best the parade with its color and energy and high spirits. The Lantern Festival concluded the New Year's celebration, and the citizens of the capital threw themselves into it with limitless vigor.

People wearing colorful, giant lion and dragon masks danced in the street beyond the gate. This close to the glass wall Rush could hear the rhythmic beats of the large drums and crashing cymbals they danced to, sounds that would turn the streets into a barely controlled frenzy. He couldn't hear the staccato string of firecracker explosions, but he knew that the hundreds—the thousands—of flashes around the dancers' feet were just that. Pinwheels carried on poles spun their red and orange fire well above the heads of the dancers and rained down glowing sparks. As Rush watched, a single stilt-walker passed the gate, a dark silhouette against a backdrop of colorful fire.

"So the Year of the Yellow Horse is upon us," Sun-Tzu slurred, his voice carrying to several nearby members of the Directorship, who tactfully took it upon themselves to edge further away from the young Liao.

Without looking, Rush knew that the zodiac wheel on the back of the Chancellor's silk robes showed the Horse in the dominant position and that the entire wheel would be trimmed in gold thread. He'd been born and lived his entire fifty-two years in the Capellan Confederation, where the Liao family proudly endorsed the Chinese culture as part of their ancient heritage, but he'd never entirely understood some of the mysticism.

Though last year *had* been eerily prophetic. *Ding si.* Year of the Red Snake, the year 3057. The red snake was identified with fire, and was characterized as being both soft-spoken and a deep thinker. The red of Sun-Tzu's silk robe sent Rush's thoughts back over the events of the past year.

A few short months ago Sun-Tzu had joined Thomas Marik of the Free Worlds League in a drive to reclaim worlds lost to the Davions and their damnable Federated Commonwealth. The brief offensive had been more successful than anyone could have predicted. The Federated Commonwealth had split back into two states over internal differences brought about by the invasion, while the Capellan Confederation had reclaimed dozens of worlds lost in the Fourth Succession War. Dozens more were assisted in breaking away from Davion rule.

But reclaiming worlds was one thing. Being able to hold them against an invasion was another. For that reason, these planets were listed as being of *strong Capellan influence*. Still other worlds managed to make a clean break altogether, away from both the Federated Commonwealth and House Liao. These fledgling independent worlds occupied space now popularly known as the Chaos March.

Yes, Sun-Tzu could be soft-spoken and a deep thinker, and he had already proved on several occasions that he could accomplish great things. What remained to be seen was whether he had inherited his mother's obsessive streak. Ion Rush knew that was what had truly killed Romano Liao. And it was what could still bring down the Capellan Confederation if Sun-Tzu wasn't careful.

Rush watched as the first lanterns began to pass the gate, oil lamps with colored shades carried by first a few people, and then dozens more. The sight helped to calm his thoughts, reminding him of the serene beauty that was life's mate to turmoil. Yin and yang. Besides, he did not much like thinking of Romano Liao's death, and his part in it, while standing next to her son and heir. "So what does the Yellow Horse signify, Celestial Wisdom?"

"It is a good prophecy," Sun-Tzu said after a moment's reflection, slurring his words only slightly. "Yellow corresponds to the element earth, and could also forecast heat waves. The Horse is cheerful, perceptive, and quick-witted. It has a love of being where the action is."

Sun-Tzu studied the fingernails of his left hand. As with the right, the nails of the last three fingers were ten centimeters long, carbon-reinforced and painted with intricate designs in black lacquer and gold leaf. "It has made me think of perhaps setting a Warrior House against Sarna."

Sarna! Ion Rush controlled his exasperation with several deep breaths. Then he finished chewing his candied bread and swallowed. "Why Sarna?" he asked, already knowing the answer.

"The Sarna Supremacy sits on the Confederation's coreward border, protruding into my realm like a cancer. It is the most stable of all the Chaos March alliances. Reports have them hiring mercenaries, readying themselves to expand their influence to other nearby worlds or perhaps to strike into the Confederation itself." Sun-Tzu studied his right-hand nails. "I cannot allow this."

The Master of Imarra nodded because it was expected of him. He believed the reason Sun-Tzu had failed to secure Sarna in the invasion was because he hadn't sent in a large enough force early on. By the time he could divert the necessary forces, Sarna had liberated nearby Sakhalin for its mineral resources and Kaifeng for its agricultural potential. Sarna's leaders then announced the rebirth of the Sarna Supremacy, an alliance whose original charter had been signed centuries ago, predating the existence of the Capellan Confederation. Yes, the Sarna Supremacy could make trouble, but in Rush's opinion they were nowhere near the threat Sun-Tzu believed.

"And once Sarna is eliminated?" the House Master asked.

Sun-Tzu smiled at their reflection in the glass, his eyes sharp and full of emotion. "Then the rest of the Chaos March, and the disputed territory, is open for the taking. We could free up military forces and sweep up through those systems without opposition."

Free up what forces? Rush knew as well as Sun-Tzu how thinly the Capellan garrisons were stretched. And perhaps it was true that the Capellans would not encounter *local* opposition in a drive through the Chaos March, but Rush would never discount Victor Steiner-Davion so readily. Davion still considered himself prince of the Federated Commonwealth, and was not about to relinquish his claim to these worlds. And Rush saw an even more important problem. "Have you thought about which Warrior House you would use? Which you can trust?" He uttered the questions softly, for the Chancellor's ears alone.

"You refer to your report, that some Warrior Houses may not be as loyal as I would like?"

Ion Rush nodded. "Your mother demanded the utmost loyalty of the Warrior Houses. She proved herself in battle when she stood against the Canopus-Andurien invasion back in the 3030s, then rebuilt those Houses that had been destroyed in the Fourth Succession War. Your actions last year won you some acclaim, Chancellor, but you are not really a warrior."

"As my sister is becoming?" Sun-Tzu asked with a trace of impatience.

Kali Liao was unstable, in Ion's opinion, but not stupid. Also she was ambitious, which made her a greater danger. He knew about the scar on her chest, a vestige of her gruesome initiation into the feared Thugee cult of assassins, whose members believed in personal advancement at *any* price. That should serve as some kind of warning.

"She works hard to improve her rudimentary 'Mech skills. Now she endears herself to some of the Warrior Houses by espousing many of your mother's policies and methods. There are those who think the Confederation would be strong under her."

"The Warrior Houses are loyal to the person of the Chancellor," Sun-Tzu said, as if repeating a maxim.

No, sir, they are not. Ion Rush searched for a diplomatic way to contradict Sun-Tzu, especially on the matter of his own House's loyalty, and failed. The Warrior Houses traditionally pledged themselves to the person of the Chancellor, but their true devotion was to the Liao bloodline, not to any single individual. If the Chancellor were to set himself on a path of destruction, as Sun-Tzu's fixation on the Sarna Supremacy could become, some Warrior Houses might turn openly to support young Kali.

Such things had occurred before.

Again his thoughts turned to the past. Romano Liao, then Chancellor, had ordered the assassination of her sister Candace and Candace's husband Justin Allard. Allard happened to be Prince Hanse Davion's chief advisor. If the Federated Commonwealth hadn't had its hands full with the Clan invasion at the time, Davion might have destroyed both Romano and Sian for her audacity. Ion Rush could still recall his own fury that she had gambled so carelessly with the fate of the Confederation.

But Candace had survived the attempt, if her husband did not. With the help of Ion Rush, among others, she had secretly made her way to Sian, where she exacted vengeance on her sister. When it was all over, Romano and her husband were dead and Sun-Tzu was Chancellor.

And now with Kali Liao making waves, the problem was how to persuade Sun-Tzu that solidarity was the Capellan Confederation's best hope just now.

"Where would you free up military forces?" he asked, hoping to make his point by attacking the argument from the other end. Simply put, the Confederation had ample military might to keep what it had, but not yet enough to take *and hold* the Chaos March even if the Sarna Supremacy no longer existed. Though he had his own thoughts on how that task might be accomplished, he would say nothing of them yet.

Frustration showed on Sun-Tzu Liao's face as he drew some of the same conclusions. "I will find a way," he promised in a whisper.

Past the east gate, the New Year's dragon was finally making its appearance. Constructed in two-meter segments of bamboo rods and colored satiny cloth, the serpent danced and writhed its way up the street. It was more than a hundred meters long, each segment supported by a pair of long sticks. Dozens of people worked these rods to brace the dragon and make it move with lifelike grace. Rush knew that the dragon symbolized fertility and vigor, and he watched with interest this emblem of his own plan for destroying Sarna. He also considered the New Year. The color yellow was associated with the element of earth. Also prophetic?

Sun-Tzu finally broke the silence. "No ruler likes to talk of divisiveness in his realm, House Master Rush."

"*Dangran,* Celestial Wisdom," Ion Rush said. *Of course.* He popped another piece of fried bread into his mouth and chewed it slowly, savoring the sweet taste as he watched the dragon.

"Makes a ruler nervous," the Chancellor continued, voice pitched low enough that only Rush would hear. There was no trace of slurred speech as he continued. "Like, for instance, the way my Aunt Candace made it onto Sian, murdered my mother, and then escaped. She even said— what were the words?—that I would not be far wrong if I imagined that she had more palace people on her payroll than my mother."

The candied bread suddenly lost its taste, and what Rush had already eaten sat heavily in his stomach. As his mouth dried, the simple act of chewing became more difficult. He glanced over at Sun-Tzu and found him staring intently.

"Can you imagine what my mother would have done in my place? No doubt she would have ordered one of those bloody purges by which she consolidated her own power. And Kali? Being so like my mother, as you put it, would probably do the same if she ever took the Celestial Throne. Especially if she had names . . ."

Rush did not doubt for an instant that Sun-Tzu had proof that he, Ion Rush, Master of Imarra, had personally helped smuggle Candace Liao onto Sian. He could also feel the gaze of the Chancellor's two Death Commandos burning into the back of his neck. Suddenly he felt isolated from his House and his warriors. But if his Chancellor was about to call down a death sentence, Rush steeled himself meet it with the dignity of his training and his office. He returned Sun-Tzu Liao's unwavering green gaze.

Then Sun-Tzu turned back to the window, putting on a wistful expression as he watched the tail end of the dragon disappear past the gate along with the last of the lantern-bearers. "Do you know what I like about the New Year, Master Rush?" he asked, his tone now suddenly casual.

"What, sire?"

"According to Chinese custom, it's a time to begin fresh. Not to forget, or forgive. But the troubles of last year are past and it is a time for looking forward."

Ion Rush nodded slowly. Was Sun-Tzu offering him a lifeline? "An admirable sentiment, Celestial Wisdom."

"Besides, are you not Master of Imarra?" Sun-Tzu's voice had again dropped to a confidential pitch. "You share the Chancellor's authority over all the Warrior Houses, do you not?"

In theory, Rush thought. But he wasn't about to disagree at this moment. He simply nodded.

"And since you are a loyal warrior of the Capellan Confederation, and loyal specifically to me, I have nothing to fear, do I?" Sun-Tzu's tone implied that the question was purely rhetorical.

The Master of Imarra considered the unspoken offer. *Pledge myself and my House to Sun-Tzu Liao, and I may continue to serve the Confederation.* Rush believed he would have refused such an offer from Romano Liao, and possibly Maximilian before her. Sun-Tzu, though, was different.

"Hurt them," Sun-Tzu commanded, not making it clear who *them* was. The ghost of a smile played at the edges of his mouth. "I will stumble around a bit more and then retire. It will give Kali and any of her supporters present a bit of courage. Our Maskirovka agents will handle any traitors among the Directorship. You will keep the Warrior Houses in line however you must, and you will find a way to keep Sarna from thrusting a knife deeper into the Confederation's side. Leave the rest of the Chaos March to me.

"That is a riddle for me to solve," Sun-Tzu promised. "It's only a matter of time."

First Interlude

Being tactful in audacity is knowing how far one can go too far.

Jerome Blake, founder of ComStar, 2788

House Hiritsu Stronghold
Randar
Sian Commonality, Capellan Confederation
24 April 3047

A sharp kick just behind his right knee made the leg buckle. Aris Sung fell heavily to both knees just as the main doors were swung open by muscular guards who must have heard their House Master approaching. Then he felt the steel of two katana blades pressing down hard from behind, one on each shoulder, to keep him from trying to rise. The wielder of the blade pressing down on his right shoulder sawed with his weapon, ever so slightly, to cut through Aris' tight-fitting black shirt and into the flesh beneath. Aris clenched his jaw against the pain and kept his eyes focused on the doors, waiting to see the person he had gambled his life to meet.

A woman entered, dressed in silk robes of a green so dark they were almost black. She walked with strength and purpose to her step. Her long dark hair showed a touch of iron gray at each temple, and her high cheekbones and slightly uptilted eyes spoke of her Asian ancestry. Late thirties, he judged, only because he knew how to look. This woman had that ageless quality of so many Asians, though it might have had less to do with genetics and more to do with her indomitable will. It was as if not even time dared presume too much in her presence.

The room was simply constructed and furnished, even though it was part of the largest stronghold on Randar. Aris had had the devil's own time getting over the outer walls, which were built of steel-reinforced ferrocrete and designed to keep out BattleMechs. Then in avoiding patrols and passing through armored doors. Now he was where he'd risked all to be, in this room trimmed in hard-wood polished to such a sheen that the grain seemed to dance in the light of the lamps. Most of the seating consisted of mats of woven rushes. Against one wall, however, was a platform too low to be called a dais, though what sat on it could definitely be construed as a throne. On it was a bench seat, which Aris guessed to be constructed of dark linwood. It was hand-carved with intricate designs and cushioned with pillows of a green satiny cloth.

And on the wall above the seat, an empty sword rack.

The woman stepped up onto the platform and quietly stared up at the empty rack for a long moment. Aris Sung counted thirteen drops of blood seeping beyond the dark cloth of his shirt and trickling down his right side. A good omen, he decided. He had recently turned thirteen years of age.

The woman settled herself onto the bench seat, arranging her robes about her as if in afterthought. Not a word had yet been spoken by anyone. Aris was sure his throat would be slit before he could utter a sound should he open his own mouth. So he waited, meeting her icy sapphire eyes with a determined gaze of his own. He willed himself not to blink, carefully widening and relaxing his eyelids.

Neither one of them moved for half a minute, and then Aris took his first calculated risk. He straightened his back, slowly so as not to invite a deeper cut into his right shoulder. Then he rocked back, jaw set against the pain as he unavoidably forced a deeper cut, until resting comfortably against his own calves. Adjusting his posture from defeated slump to comfortable meditation.

She blinked.

"Lance Leader Non." The woman turned her gaze to stare over Aris' right shoulder. "How does Crescent Moon happen to be missing?"

"House Master, we caught this thief in the outer chambers." The answering voice was proud and firm. An accomplishment for anyone under the direct stare of this forceful woman, Aris thought.

Her expression was inscrutable, but her voice seemed to hint at something Aris almost thought was amusement. "Then why don't I see Crescent Moon lying on the floor where it would have fallen, Ty?"

The pressure eased against Aris' shoulder as the sword-wielder considered this riddle. According to information purchased by Aris at a steep price, the katana sword Crescent Moon had originally been given to the first Master of House Hiritsu by Dainmar Liao, twenty-third Chancellor of the Capellan Confederation, at the time of Warrior House Hiritsu's formation almost two centuries before. Only the current House Master was allowed to touch the artifact. For the past year and a half, ever since his initial failure to be accepted by House Hiritsu, Aris had been planning its theft. Forcing himself to be patient until he knew he would succeed. Were he caught too soon, any Hiritsu warrior would have cut him down on the spot. But the *successful* theft of the sword, that demanded the immediate attention of the House Master.

Lance Leader Non finally came up with an answer. "We searched the outer chambers. He must have cached it somewhere else within the stronghold. Or possibly outside the walls, before returning to steal again."

Time to turn the conversation, Aris decided. If the House Master passed sentence now . . .

He kept his voice even and calm. "And how many times would you say I walked right through Hiritsu security, Ty?"

Aris had discovered many things concerning House Hiritsu in his eighteen months of planning, including their rigid devotion to courtesy. As expected, the familiar use of the lance leader's name infuriated him. In one fluid motion the warrior laid his blade flat against Aris' shoulder and then slid it forward till the point rested just under Aris' chin with his head tilted back. "No one gave you leave to speak, carrion."

"It is a fair question, Lance Leader." Was that the trace of a smile tugging at the right corner of the House Master's mouth? Aris couldn't be sure. *Master of the House,* he thought, for the first time feeling out of his depth.

The lance leader read it as a challenge. "We will find it, House Master York."

"Like hell," Aris spat out.

The point pressed up harder, breaking the skin just under his jaw, but that was only pain and Aris was now confident that this man was too well-disciplined to kill him unless so ordered by his House Master. That was the way of things.

The will of the House Master is the will of the House. If any one maxim defined the Warrior Houses of the Capellan Confederation, it was that one. Aris longed to be a part of this world—of honor and family and service to the Chancellor and the state. But for now his only chance lay in boldness of word and action. "You will never find Crescent Moon without my help," he said quietly.

Now there was no trace of amusement in the House Master's face or voice. "Do you really think so little of us?" she asked, her face like stone.

Careful, Aris warned himself. He bit back on the response that leapt to mind, a boast of his own abilities. That was not the way. "I think that *highly* of House Hiritsu," he finally said. "I spent eighteen months preparing for this night, this moment. I left nothing to chance."

House Master York's eyes narrowed as she studied him. "You are willing to wager your life on that?"

"Will you put up a position in House Hiritsu against it?"

The moment the words left his lips, Aris knew he had made his first real mistake. Over his left shoulder he heard a female voice whisper, "Impudent bastard," and from behind he heard several more oaths at his presumptuousness. Those, however, did not concern him. What did was the way House Master Virginia York's eyes suddenly widened and turned upward in thought, her fingers rubbing together in anticipation. If living on the streets had taught Aris anything—other than the fact that he wanted more than that solitary, meaningless life—it was to read the language of the body. He had just handed the House Master his motivation, his goal, and now she was puzzling it through with the relish of a master gameswoman. Putting herself in his place.

When her gaze began to scan the room slowly, searching, he knew she almost had it. "You're not going to find it sitting on your ass," he said, deliberately forcing some scorn into his voice and trying hard to keep his own fear from showing.

The point disappeared from under his throat and a sharp pain bit into the side of his head, making his ears ring. For a moment Aris thought he was dead, but then realized that Lance Leader Non must have hit him with the flat of his blade. That, more than anything else so far, actually frightened him. He had been a quarter-turn of the wrist away from death.

But the gamble suddenly seemed to be paying off. House Master York was no longer searching the room. Her sharp gaze seemed to pin him to the wall. "What is your name?" she demanded.

"Aris Sung," he said with a dry mouth. He thought about adding more, his home city or name of his father, but then decided it wiser to answer nothing more than she asked. There might yet be a limit to the House Master's patience.

"Aris Sung. I welcome you into House Hiritsu." The blades fell away from his shoulders with those words, though Lance Leader Non at his right shoulder seemed to hesitate ever so slightly. "Does this make you happy?" House Master York inquired almost pleasantly.

You mean, can I die happy? Aris translated. He knew she could order the death of any House Hiritsu member as easily as that of any thief. But the door had opened a crack, and he now had to make sure it wasn't slammed in his face. So he leaned forward and bowed his head in shame, his forehead almost touching the polished wooden floor. "No, House Master York," he said quietly.

"And why not?"

It was time to make amends. "Because this unworthy one has spoken rudely to a highly placed House warrior," he said, voice filled with contrition, "to the House Master herself, and dared to lay hands on Crescent Moon, which is taped to the underside of your seat. I expect and await punishment. I regret that you will have to stoop in order to retrieve the blade." A drop of sweat rolled off his nose and spattered against the wood grain. Aris kept his attention focused on it, not daring to look up. Was that enough?

Virginia York's tone revealed no trace of either anger or acceptance. "I won't have to stoop at all, Aris Sung. After I leave this room, you will return Crescent Moon to its place of rest, voluntarily, and suffer twice the punishment."

Aris felt his hopes rise slightly. He could only die once, so perhaps House Master York had other plans in mind.

"Lance Leader Ty Wu Non," she continued. "You are recognized as this child's Mentor. He is now your responsibility. I want him trained against the day when such audacity might actually be of use. Start with fifteen lashes for touching Crescent Moon, another fifteen for his insult to me, and five for the insult to yourself. Then run him for five kilometers. If he falls, shoot him."

"Yes, House Master."

Aris looked up, not wanting to speak out of turn but realizing that he had to make sure his debt was fully repaid to the satisfaction of the House Master.

"Yes, Aris Sung," she said. "You have something to say?"

He nodded and met her eyes. "The House Master has not sentenced me for the second offense of touching Crescent Moon."

Her gaze was cold and appraising, as if wondering just how much a thirteen-year-old boy thought he could take. Finally she nodded to Aris' new House Mentor. "If he lasts the run, another twenty lashes." Then she gathered her robes about her and left the room with the same proud stride that had brought her in.

Aris smiled grimly. He was right where he wanted to be. Now all he had to do was survive it.

1

The master alarm circuit on the bridge of the Kaifeng Recharge Station *Jodo Shinsa* pulsed out soft beeps at steady intervals while amber caution lights atop several consoles flashed for attention. Conversation among the five Kaifeng SMM officers on duty ceased abruptly, a comment on the latest 'Mech duels from Solaris hanging in the air unfinished and forgotten. Two of the five men and women swung their chairs around to face their panels while a third unbuckled herself and swam across the null gravity to a panel manned only during the main shift or high-traffic periods.

Petty Officer Second Class Shen Dok To swung around too fast, clipping his right elbow against the edge of his panel and cursing as his entire arm went numb with a bone-tingling sensation. Rubbing life back into his arm, he bent over his primary monitor. "We've got a strong electromagnetic pulse," he called out to the watch officer and the other two technicians. "Multiple JumpShips."

He looked over the numbers again as they printed down his screen in a column of amber against black. His was the main control panel, which routinely sampled data from the other stations. It wasn't complete, but good enough for initial readings. Now he amended his earlier interpretation. "Or it could be a single ship, right on top of us."

For interstellar travel, humanity relied on JumpShips. The long, slender vessels were built around the core of a Kearny-Fuchida jump drive that could manipulate energies powerful enough to tear a hole in Einsteinian space and allow a ship to pass through. Leaping up to thirty light years in a single jump, the transition itself was instantaneous. The main drawback was the week or two a starship normally needed to recharge its jump drive by deploying a large sail to collect solar energy.

Recharge stations solved that problem. Or at least offered a better solution. The stations were placed at either the zenith or nadir point of a star system, points far above or below the system's gravity well. JumpShips entered and left from these points to avoid the tidal forces of these gravity wells, which, on a miscalculated jump, could literally tear the vessel apart. Stations such as *Jodo Shinsa* deployed kilometers-wide solar sails that charged massive energy storage banks. This energy could be transferred to a JumpShip in a mere six days or, if the JumpShip docked, could be hotloaded in two to four days if it was worth the risk to the JumpShip's delicate hyperdrive. The recharge stations also fulfilled important secondary roles as cargo way-stations, refueling points for the DropShips used in interplanetary movement, and as maintenance bays for the dry-dock of DropShips or a JumpShip up to a hundred and fifty thousand tons in size.

The station also acted as an early-warning site, using its sensors to detect incoming vessels and identify them as hostile or friendly. In the case of hostile approach, the station could warn the planet, which then had anywhere from a few days up to a couple of weeks to prepare to meet an assault.

Petty Officer Belko, manning his console off to Shen's left, confirmed the primary operator's second guess. "Just one," he said, his normally strong voice weak with surprise. "Merchant Class JumpShip four hundred fifty kilometers off our forward port hull. Her IR signature corresponds with the *Liu*. I'm patching video over to Shen."

Shen didn't understand the other man's concern. The *Liu* was a merchant ship that routinely made runs from Kaifeng, transporting the planet's substantial food surplus to the other Sarna Supremacy worlds of Sakhalin and Sarna and to various other nearby planets. Four hundred fifty kilometers was close, as distances go in space, but he wouldn't have thought Belko could be shaken so easily. Then his primary screen cleared and painted up the Jump-Ship's video image. His mouth dried, leaving behind only the metallic taste of reprocessed air. Shen heard a whispered "Blake's blood" from the watch officer, who was looking at the screen over Shen's shoulder from her own station behind him.

The *Liu* was a wreck. Its hull showed several gaping rents, and a few smaller ones that continued to bleed air into the vacuum. The air froze immediately, forming thin streams of ice crystals that trailed out into space. Debris hung suspended around the JumpShip, any momentum robbed by being pulled through the jump. Shen thought he recognized a few larger chunks as halves of aerospace fighters. *Thrushes*, possibly, ships that might have been just a little too close when the hyperspace field formed around the starship in preparation for the jump. And trailing behind the JumpShip was what was left of its solar sail, now a torn and mangled mass. Jumping with sail deployed was an invitation to get stranded wherever you arrived, and was just one more sign of the wounded vessel's apparent desperation.

"DropShips," Shen said, too stunned to notice much else besides the two empty docking collars.

Petty Officer Davidson had swum over to the console that controlled the tracking and identification equipment. "I've already tagged at least two large pieces of . . . something. Could be off the primary hull of a DropShip."

Shen shook his head as if to clear it, then realized the ringing in his ears was the continued beeping of the master alarm circuit. He brushed a hand impatiently over the mac's cutoff switch, silencing it, while he tried to sort things out in his mind. It didn't make sense. JumpShips were considered inviolate, the supreme example of *lostech*. Centuries of warfare had taken their toll on the Inner Sphere, to the point where the technology to produce these interstellar vessels had become seriously threatened. No JumpShips meant neither trade nor war, two instruments of state policy no government wanted to do without.

"Transponders?" the watch officer, Leftenant Ellen Harris asked, starting to shake off her own surprise.

Shen was already pulling the information through to his console. "IFF transponders are intermittent. Not surprising considering the power fluctuations they must be going through over there. But it's the *Liu*."

"I'm getting voice communication," Petty Officer Davidson said. She threw a few switches and sent the transmission to the bridge speaker. Static rolled across the bridge, punctuated by words robbed of their emotion by the poor transmission quality.

". . . *Liu*. Are you receiving us, Kaifeng Station?"

The watch officer nodded as she spoke. "We receive you, *Liu*. What is your status?"

Her calm response seemed to lend strength to the operator on the other end. "Kaifeng Station. Main bridge is smashed. We're running the ship from out of Secondary Control. Severe loss of atmosphere and energy fluctuations. Main drive is out but under repair."

Leftenant Harris could not restrain herself. "What happened, *Liu*? Who attacked you?"

Shen had visions of some kind of massive strike from out of the Capellan Confederation. The resurrected Sarna Supremacy was still in its infancy, and uncertainty over what Sun-Tzu Liao might try next was a dark specter that hung over everything the Supremacy was trying to build. But Shen didn't fear this so much as he actually felt relieved. No more worry over what the future might hold. The Supremacy would have to stand up to the Liao sooner or later if it was going to survive. Better now, he and most of his comrades thought, while the Capellan Confederation was still rebuilding its power. Hurt them, and make them understand that the Sarna Supremacy was better left alone.

The JumpShip's answer, when it came, was as much a disappointment as a relief.

"*Jodo Shinsa* Station, this is the SMM *Liu*. Raiders from the disputed territories—we think either the planets Menkib or Zaurak—tried to hit Sakhalin. We were on site and holding position for the return of our DropShips. The raiders hit us hard, possibly trying to silence us so we couldn't warn Sakhalin. We jumped—it was our only chance."

Shen had been waiting for a break in the conversation, and now spoke up before Leftenant Harris could digress further from what was clearly an emergency situation. "Watch Officer, recommend we dispatch tugs at once to bring the *Liu* in to the Number One maintenance bay. The DropShip *Annabelle Lee* is there right now, but she can be moved to one of the smaller bays. I also suggest we wake the commander. And double the guards around the station." That last was a standing order in the event the Sarna Supremacy ever entered a situation that threatened war. While this raid might not qualify, Shen preferred to err on the side of conservatism and it was his duty to make recommendations.

The *Liu* came back before Leftenant Harris could respond. "Our engineer just reported engines working. We can start in on our own power, but tugs would be appreciated."

Harris nodded. "Do it. I'll buzz the station commander." She picked up the sound-powered phone and selected the commander's cabin. Before ringing him, though, she turned to the fifth member of the bridge team. The sentry carried an assault rifle and wore the dark gray uniform of the Sarna Martial Academy.

"Better wake your buddies," she told him. "We're going to double the guards, and the rest might be of use down in the maintenance bay to help search for wounded and to recover bodies."

Shen was already hard at work, relaying orders over his own phone circuit, backing them with computer-delivered verification when necessary. One thing was for sure, he thought. No one would be complaining about boring off-shifts for a while.

2

***JumpShip* Liu**
Zenith Jump Point, Kaifeng System
Sarna Supremacy, Chaos March
10 July 3058

The *Liu*'s grav deck held a gallery, two recreation rooms, an all-purpose metal shop, crew berthing, and three staterooms normally reserved for the JumpShip officers. Ty Wu Non had commandeered one of these last, turning it into his office for the operation.

Lance Leader Aris Sung stood just within the doorway, waiting impatiently to be recognized by the elder Hiritsu warrior, who sat at his desk studying internal schematics for an *Olympus* Class recharge station. More out of impatience than concern, Aris checked his watch again. He noted that less than thirty minutes remained before the *Liu* was to dock with the *Jodo Shinsa,* and he clenched his hands into fists so hard that his fingernails dug painfully into his palms. It was thirty minutes he could be using to brief his assault team or to review the internal layout of the recharge station as Ty was doing. A half hour that could be better spent almost anywhere than being ignored or in argument with the second most powerful person in House Hiritsu.

With Ty and Aris, it was usually one or the other.

Aris Sung had not fallen on that five-kilometer run

eleven years earlier. He didn't think Ty Wu Non had ever forgiven him that. The memory always resurfaced when Aris was forced to endure Ty's presence. That long five kilometers—swallowing dust, feet and muscles sore, back whipped raw and stinging from the lash. And Ty running alongside him the entire way, Nakjama laser pistol in hand as he heaped on a stream of verbal abuse the whole way. Aris had never told Ty, hadn't even wanted to admit it to himself, that it was Ty's constant belittling that fueled his own drive to survive the run that first day.

Ty Wu Non had not gone away after that run. As Aris' personal Mentor he remained an active part of his life, teaching him the customs and traditions of House Hiritsu and overseeing all phases of his training. All Warrior Houses were comprised of a battalion of BattleMechs and one of specialized infantry. In House Hiritsu, MechWarrior trainees spent their first four years training alongside the infantry to season them and to develop a stronger bond than normally existed between BattleMech pilots and their unaugmented cousins. Ty had enlisted the aid of the more vicious infantry Mentors, putting Aris through the paces at a faster, harder rate to make up for his late start at thirteen. Aris had learned anti-Mech tactics as well as how to operate as a scout, infiltrator, and assassin. When he'd single-handedly stopped an enemy 'Mech from killing Virginia York—only sixteen years old but already a full infantryman—the House Master had praised Ty's work as Mentor and promoted Ty to her BattleMech honor guard.

Aris was granted the right to begin his higher education, including training in 'Mech operations and tactics. Which suited him at the time. Everything in its place.

At twenty Aris again defeated House Master York in simulated BattleMech combat. That earned him his katana, the sword carried by all House warriors. It also earned Ty another promotion, this time to company leader. Virginia York assigned Aris to Ty's company, and thereby continued the pattern. When Aris accomplished anything, he also strengthened Ty's position in the House. Aris' promotion to lance leader was followed hard by Ty's to senior company leader, which placed him next in line as House Master.

Aris was willing to bet that Ty was already cogitating how he could take full credit for the assault on Kaifeng.

It had been Ion Rush, Master of House Imarra, who'd identified Kaifeng as the weak point in the Sarna Supremacy's armor. Kaifeng was not heavily populated, nor of great strategic value. What it did have were thousands of square kilometers of some of the best agricultural land to be found anywhere. Sarna relied heavily on Kaifeng's food surplus, as did Sakhalin, the third Supremacy world, which was a frozen waste and was only able to grow crops in expensive greenhouse environments. Remove Kaifeng, and the Sarna Supremacy could feed itself only by digging deep into its budget, including military spending, or it would starve.

Either result served the Capellan Confederation.

When House Master Virginia York returned from a conference on Sian with orders to assault Kaifeng and deny the Supremacy its breadbasket world, Aris had taken it from there.

He was recognized within House Hiritsu as an innovative tactician, and when the final recommendations were made Virginia York endorsed his plan. That plan had two parts. The first was to take control of the Kaifeng recharge station and deny the surface of the planet advance notice of the assault. Using the *Liu* as a Trojan horse would accomplish that. The second part was a surprise attack that would leave the Capellan Confederation in control of the world. Should leave the Capellan Confederation in control of the world. Might leave the Capellan Confederation . . .

Still waiting by the door, shifting from foot to foot, Aris frowned. As he turned the situation over in his mind, it bothered him even now. The Kaifeng SMM, First Battalion of the Sarna Martial Academy regiment, garrisoned the planet. Regular troops, and extremely loyal to their fledgling state. Aris Sung had heard good things about the Sarna Martial Academy. And while the academy couldn't possibly match a Warrior House in training, the fact remained that the Kaifeng SMM was far more battle-experienced. Blooded warriors, that was the old term. House Hiritsu consisted mostly of green troops, having been held in reserve during the Chaos March fighting the year before. How did the saying go? Something about the meeting of armies of equal or near-equal strength being a recipe for disaster?

He couldn't help wondering about the rumors he'd heard over the last few months, rumors that Imarra Master Ion Rush was attempting to curb Warrior Houses whose loyalty was suspect by sending them on questionable missions. House LuSann had been sent on an extended campaign into the Chaos March. And House Ijori sent up into the Arc-Royal Defense Cordon. To test themselves, Master Rush had said, against Clan Jade Falcon. To blunt themselves, the rumors whispered. Both Ijori and LuSann were thought to have strong ties to Kali Liao. Was there a similar intent in House Hiritsu's assignment to attack Kaifeng? Aris didn't think it likely. Virginia York was loyal to Sun-Tzu. And the will of the House Master was the will of the House.

The will of the House Master was to take Kaifeng.

Aris Sung shook away his doubts. He owed much to Virginia York, and the thought of failing her now was so alien as to be inconceivable. At age twenty-four he was the youngest lance leader in House Hiritsu since before the Fourth Succession War. And he'd earned his way at every step. House Master York pushed him hard, always testing his commitment and his ability. He didn't even begrudge her repeated placement of Ty Wu Non over him, realizing that was just another of her methods. So he would concentrate on the current task, leaving the broader political issues in her capable hands.

"Report," Ty finally barked out, not bothering to look over his shoulder in even the semblance of courtesy.

Aris stiffened, but a few deep breaths helped calm him. Courtesy was a major element of Hiritsu traditions, following the teachings of K'ung-fu-tzu incorporated into House Hiritsu's vows decades before. Ty's deliberate rudeness was a calculated attempt to make Aris say or do something foolish. Then he could remove the young warrior from the order of battle, which Aris would detest more than anything.

"Everything is proceeding according to schedule," Aris answered crisply. "We still have clearance for the station's maintenance bay, which means we won't have to attempt a space transfer. Contact in"—he checked his watch again—"twenty-two minutes. We'll be dry-docked within the hour."

Finding the *Liu* had been the first step in Aris' plan for the assault on Kaifeng. Because of the sacrosanct status of JumpShips, several officers of House Hiritsu had balked when he'd first proposed his plan. But they'd finally agreed when he showed them how the House could acquire a merchant JumpShip, and that most of the damage would be superficial.

"When will they receive verification from Sakhalin?"

Aris thought about that for a moment. Arranging the raid against Sakhalin had been more difficult, requiring concessions to Menkib and making sure nothing could be traced back to House Hiritsu. That diversionary force should have fully withdrawn from the Sakhalin system by now after creating a lot of confusion. "Sakhalin should have already transmitted news of the attempted raid via ComStar's hyperpulse generator network. Sarna and Kaifeng should both have it. There's roughly a four-hour lag in communications between the recharge station and the planet." Aris did some quick and easy math in his head. "I'd say by the time we dry-dock, the recharge station will have received *some* word of the situation."

Company Leader Non glanced back and gave Aris a once-over with a casual flick of his gaze. "House Master York arrives with our 'Mechs in less than ten hours. Do you see any difficulties?"

Aris shrugged his indifference to the question, which he felt was quite ignorant. "If we aren't in control of the situation within the first ten minutes or so, we lose our advantage."

"Do you see any difficulties?"

"No."

Ty Wu Non swiveled around in his chair, reclining back in a too-casual posture. Aris could read the man's attempt to cover his own impatience. *There's something coming,* he thought. *And it's pointed right at me.*

"I've been thinking about the boarding party assignments again," Ty finally said. "I'm considering some changes."

Aris frowned. Now that was a dangerous game to be

playing. Once the House Master set a plan in motion, changes were only to be made in response to direct enemy actions. Her word was law and her will that of the House. Part of the reason behind that tradition was to maintain the bonds that wove the House into a close-knit family. Another—and perhaps more practical reason—was that the House Master was accountable directly to the Chancellor. When one was only one step removed from the Celestial Wisdom, mistakes were often dealt with at *the* highest level. "Your reason, Company Leader Non?"

"Your advance teams are small in number, five to seven men each." Ty checked his schematics. "We're talking about a station fifteen hundred meters long, with a crew of a hundred and fifty."

Aris nodded. "But only two dozen actual soldiers, most off duty." He took a deep breath and launched into the old explanation, though he was sure Ty Wu Non knew it and was only being difficult for the sake of antagonizing the younger warrior. "Small teams can move faster, and each member is an expert. We need to gain immediate control of the bridge, auxiliary control, any other docked DropShips, and the station communications center. With enough time, any of these will transmit a message back to Kaifeng and then we lose surprise. The secondary teams are larger, and move in to hold the area after we control it."

"Yes, yes." Ty dismissed the explanation with a wave of his hand. "But the bridge team? Five men? The station has been transmitting video along with audio, and there are now at least seven people on the bridge."

"I still recommend no more than five."

Ty paused a moment, as if in deep thought. He then widened his eyes as if enlightenment had struck. "Then I will make only the most superficial change, but one that might make up the difference. I will take your place as leader of the bridge assault team."

Hidden by the way his arms were crossed over his chest, Aris' left hand tightened into the ridge-hand he liked for making a strike. *Step forward, knee bending, and catch Ty Wu Non in the side of the neck.* He felt the shame almost at the same moment as the thought came. First of all, House members were not allowed to fight each other without the direct permission of the House Master. Second, it was not in keeping with the spirit of the family. *So it must be endured.* "And what would the Company Leader have me do instead?"

"Well, I considered placing you in overall command, letting you try your hand at high-level tactics. The basic plan was yours, after all. But then that would be a slight to Infantry Commander Sebastian Jessup. So you will lead the assault team responsible for securing the station's comm center."

Aris forced himself to relax. Infantry Commander Jessup was the highest ranking member of the House infantry and technically the third in overall command, though any MechWarrior could challenge his authority at almost every turn. Having served under Jessup for his first three years, Aris actually felt better than if Ty were in overall command.

It still bothered him that Ty would pull something like this so very close to the operation. And that it was all in an effort to deny Aris what was only his right—taking the bridge. But at least Ty hadn't cut him out of the fighting altogether. The other warrior still did not really understand him. Aris did not truly desire power, nor did he especially want to be in command. House Hiritsu was his home; he had made it such eleven years ago. All he wanted was to serve, and to belong. And it was a pity Ty Wu Non could not grasp such a simple fact.

But he will, Aris promised. Someday, Aris would find a way to make him understand.

3

Kaifeng Recharge Station Jodo Shinsa
Zenith Jump Point, Kaifeng System
Sarna Supremacy, Chaos March
10 July 3058

The station alarm tolled off repeated peals of computer-simulated gong sounds that rang down through the corridors.

A grunt of pain forced its way past Aris Sung's lips as one of the recharge station's technicians swung a wrench and caught him across the shoulder. The force of the blow sent Aris tumbling through the station's low gravity until he fetched up against the corridor wall. He broke his motion with a flat hand-slap against the smooth metal surface, and with a quick tuck and kick rebounded back into the fight.

Two bodies lay further back along the corridor, one already settled onto the floor and the other still shedding momentum as it rubbed along one wall. That left two others still up and moving. The tech with the heavy wrench obviously wasn't used to low-gravity combat. He had forgotten to anchor himself, so his strike had thrown him away just as hard as Aris, but into the opposite wall. His rebound left much to be desired, so Aris counted him out of the fight for a few desperate seconds.

When Aris hit that same wall, he came off at an angle

that placed him between the two remaining techs. The fourth man had produced a screwdriver from within his coveralls, and had learned from his companion's mistake. He had drifted near a life boat hatch, and had now anchored himself by curling one arm into the hatch's large operating wheel. Then he reversed his grip on the screwdriver as if intending to throw it like a knife.

Aris was grateful for the man's stupidity. First of all, you never threw away your only weapon. Better if the tech had launched himself forward, trying for a stabbing attack. Second, the chances of the man throwing hard enough and accurate enough to actually hurt Aris were slim, at best.

Slim did not mean *none*, though, and Aris couldn't afford to take the chance. Especially as he was in danger of failing his House.

The timetable for gaining control of the recharge station had been carefully set. Taking control of the maintenance bay had been easy, the Hiritsu infantry swarming out to surround and disarm the emergency teams that had shown up to assist the wounded JumpShip's crew. That had even netted them the station commander, an unexpected but welcome bonus. Then the advance Hiritsu commandos had begun to deploy through the ship, staggered out in an order depending on who had furthest to travel. Aris' team was first, needing to work their way through almost the entire station to get at the comm center located near the aft end.

The team had first run into trouble when they'd discovered that their planned route to the comm center was sealed off by several decks of long-term storage lockers, a modification to the typical *Olympus* design. That had cost Aris and his party several minutes. And just when they'd managed to get back on track, the alarm sounded. At the intersection for every major corridor a small amber light strobed in time to the deep gongs. The one bit of hope to which Aris still clung was that the alarm was a general one, designed to wake the station crew and put everyone on alert until further notice. That would give him several long and critical minutes before the plan completely fell apart.

But two armed sentries outside the comm center finally

put a halt to their advance. The door to the comm center lay at the head of a T-shaped corridor junction. From the base of the T, Aris' team could see the door and prevent anyone from getting inside. The station sentries, however, carried pulse laser rifles and had taken cover in the side corridors to either side of the door. It was a standoff. Aris left his four infantry troopers to keep the sentries from getting inside the comm center while he backtracked to find a way in behind them. He knew he couldn't afford to waste another minute, but the main thing now was to act, and act fast.

Then he'd run into the four technicians, who came at him with tools and bare hands the instant they saw his uniform and weapon.

Rebounding off the wall, Aris reached out in both directions so that his Nakjama laser pistol was pointed toward the tech preparing to throw the screwdriver and the other hand was directed at the wrench-wielding man. The counteracting forces kept his aim steady, and he caressed the trigger. His first shot hit the technician high in the right shoulder, making him let go of the screwdriver. Then he tracked the second man inward and burned a hole through his temple and into his brain. Then it was time to tuck and absorb another impact. Only this time he simply waited out the bounce, then twisted about to shoot the last surviving tech three times in the chest. The wrench flew and clanged down the corridor on its own path.

Four bodies, a full minute wasted, and Aris was still two turns away from his own men. It was not going well.

"Lance Leader Sung!"

Aris twisted about and saw Infantryman Mikhail Chess flying up the corridor toward him. Aris was hoping his people had managed to take out the sentries, but the grave look on Chess' face told him it wasn't so.

"Report," he called out while Chess was still a good ten meters away, though flying fast.

"All the shouting in the corridor finally got someone's attention." Chess reached out to slap at the closer wall, braking. He ended up a short way past Aris, finally catching himself against the same life boat hatch that the technician had used earlier. "The comm center door opened and someone stuck his head out. He lost it, but there was at least one other person inside."

And from little time, now we're left with none, Aris thought, kicking his brain into overdrive. Biting down hard enough on his lower lip to draw blood, he inventoried their assets. Five House warriors, four with Intek laser rifles and him with a Nakjama pistol. Four dead technicians. Some small tools. He glanced back down the corridor. And one large wrench somewhere down that way that could do a real number on one of the sentries . . . *or the comm equipment.*

He had it.

"Infantryman Chess. Get back to the T corridor and help keep those sentries pinned down. I'll take care of the comm center. Go!"

Without an instant's hesitation, Chess launched himself back down the corridor. Aris didn't waste any more time watching him go. Instead, he grasped the hatch wheel Chess had used for an anchor and began wrenching it open. Any other accessway would have had a remote-operated hatch, but emergency escapes had to be ready to deal with worst-case conditions such as no power.

With a final metallic clang the wheel reverse-seated itself. Aris pulled open the hatch and dove through, then turned and pulled the hatch shut after him and fastened it down. He was in a short tunnel that dumped him out into the small, rectangular life boat. Quickly making his way to the front and sliding into the pilot's seat, he hit the emergency release at the same time he started to bring the engines up. There was a jolt and the feeling of a giant hand pushing him back in his seat as the boat released from the station and was kicked away by the explosive charge. And then complete freedom from even the limited gravity provided by the position-keeping thrusters of the massive recharge station. Aris prayed to the elder gods for another few precious minutes.

The recharge station was theirs—he knew that for a fact. It had become theirs the moment the JumpShip *Liu* had been allowed to dock. A hundred or so technicians and, at most, twenty-four marines against a full company of Hiritsu infantry? No. What was left was to secure the station before someone could get an alert to the surface of Kaifeng. To maintain the element of surprise.

He was gambling again, counting on the station crew to know their jobs and the bridge officer to be more politically than militarily minded. The comm center technicians would try to report to the bridge first, and then auxiliary control. They wouldn't take it upon themselves to send an alert toward Kaifeng. Or they shouldn't, anyway. Aris frowned, remembering the fanatic gleam in the eyes of those four technicians. Once they'd passed their report on to an officer, then it came down to how confident that officer was in himself. A true military man might send an immediate alert, accepting the risk of ending up embarrassed or even reprimanded, if wrong. A career officer would worry about making a mistake. With round-trip communication taking somewhere close to eight hours, and actual help more than a week away, that officer would wait for confirmation. Which would give Aris the time he needed.

Fortunately, life boats were designed for a fast startup. As the chemical engine came up with a low vibration of the boat's hull, Aris used the attitude jets to spin around and the small main thruster to arrest and then reverse his momentum. Shortly, he was thrusting back toward the station and slipping around toward its after end, where he found what he was looking for nestled down between the massive pylons that held the station's immense solar sail.

Ask most citizens of the Inner Sphere how a recharge station sitting out at a system jump point transmits messages into the system and they would probably guess it to be by radio. The more knowledgeable might know that what the ship actually did was to send a video and audio transmission on a microwave carrier. What most didn't realize—and was the one fact that might save House Hiritsu's element of surprise—was that the transmissions were also *directional*. They had to be. Jump points were millions, often billions, of kilometers above or below the elliptic plane. Even the strong electromagnetic pulse of an arriving JumpShip could rarely be detected after a billion kilometers, and radar emissions couldn't be tracked much further than a million.

So the answer was either to build a transmitter so large that it ate up incredible amounts of station space and power, or to focus the transmission into a tight beam that had to be pointed fairly accurately back into the system. Accurate to the tune of a million kilometers. Though that might sound like an incredibly wide margin, taking into account the incredible distances of space actually allowed for less than a single degree of error.

The transmitter was a huge, double-barreled device that looked like some kind of giant weapon. Thirty meters long, it sat on top of an equally large platform and was held almost parallel to the station's hull. Sitting near the base of the transmitter, like some kind of high-powered rifle scope, was a large contraption that looked like a combination radar dish and telescope. It was this last device that allowed the precision aiming back toward Kaifeng.

Aris carefully maneuvered the small life boat nose-first down into the valley formed by two rising pylons. Walls of gray metal rose to either side of him. The transmitter, backed by the main hull of the station itself, filled his entire front viewscreen. Using attitude jets only, he nudged the nose of his craft down against the transmitter barrels until contact came with an echoing clang. Then he kicked in his thrusters.

For a moment nothing happened. There was only the faint, steady roar of the boat's small engine punctuated every few seconds by the creak of protesting metal. Aris began to wonder which would give way first—the transmitter, the actuators that positioned it, or his limited fuel supply. Life boats were supplied with ninety seconds of fuel at full thrust. Aris had already counted over sixty seconds when there was a small shudder as the entire transmitter assembly shifted over a full meter, and he quickly backed off on his thrusters. That would do it, he decided.

He used the attitude jets to back off a few meters and then leveled out the life boat in relation to the recharge station. He had given the Hiritsu warriors their chance. Providing no alert had already been sent, it no longer mattered if the bridge or auxiliary control was captured quickly or not. Or the comm center, for that matter. Only the dry-docked DropShip could make a difference now. Smiling to himself, the amber lights of the boat's control panel in his eyes, Aris engaged the engine on minimal thrust and started the boat moving toward the shuttle bays, where eventually the House Hiritsu warriors would let him in.

His final pass clipped the aiming dish, wrenching it about on its own precision gearing. Just in case.

4

Kaifeng Recharge Station Jodo Shinsa
Zenith Jump Point, Kaifeng System
Sarna Supremacy, Chaos March
11 July 3058

The officer's wardroom, located on the massive grav deck of the Kaifeng recharge station *Jodo Shinsa,* stank of old grease and scented cleaning products intended more to overpower other odors rather than to actually clean. With its narrow tables, hard metal seats, and poor lighting, the room left much to be desired as a meeting hall. Especially with the recent arrival of the House Hiritsu JumpShip *Tao-te,* meaning the Way of Power, whose modern war room was only a quick shuttle flight away.

But Aris Sung knew that House Master Virginia York preferred to be close to wherever House Hiritsu's main interests lay. She had transferred to the station immediately upon her arrival in the Kaifeng system for a personal inspection and to oversee the next, short phase of the operation. Shortly after she'd called this meeting.

And, he had to admit, there was also something to be said for gravity. Aris had spent two years learning the acrobatics of zero-G operations, and took pains to keep proficient, but every 'Mech pilot felt more comfortable with some weight around him. Preferably about fifty-five tons, Aris thought, with a smile. That was the weight of his

Wraith. With only a few things left to tie up on the station, he looked forward to hitting the surface of Kaifeng.

"Has there been any progress in locating the origin of the alarm?" Virginia York asked, drawing Aris' attention back to the here and now. The House Master's once-dark hair was shot through with silvery-gray. And there were a few more wrinkles at the corners of her eyes. Other than that she still carried herself with a strength warriors half her age would envy, and her bright blue eyes could still cut through a warrior's resolve.

Company Leader Lindell, who had been assigned to oversee that investigation, met her gaze evenly. "It came through a remote fire-station panel, two bulkheads over and one deck up from the maintenance bay where the *Liu* is stationed. The crew who responded were caught by our secondary teams."

"Which slowed those teams from reaching the bridge and auxiliary control. It also put everyone on alert. Who do you think turned in the alarm?"

Lindell kept his voice neutral and face blank. The company leader was known for his strict control over himself. "Well, we're guessing that it was a technician who saw one of our advance teams. Both the bridge and aux con teams moved through that area. The tech hit the nearest alarm, and then hid."

Virginia York's face tightened just marginally around the eyes, and her gaze broke from Lindell's and then returned as if to guard some thought she didn't want to reveal. Aris recognized the expression—the faint precursor to an important question, one to which she already knew the answer but had to make sure. He leaned forward, waiting.

"Which team passed closest to that fire station panel?"

Lindell looked nonplused by the question. "Mine."

"And the closest intercom panel that would give them voice communication with the bridge?"

"Well, there's a secure circuit to damage control right there on the fire-station panel. But damage control isn't manned except in an emergency." Lindell thought for a few seconds. "It would have been in main corridor Twenty-one Tach Thirty-two Bravo. But Company Leader

Non's commandos passed that way, and if the tech saw them I doubt he would have risked sticking his head out into a main corridor."

Aris didn't see what the House Master was getting at, but she routinely thought several steps ahead and he couldn't always keep up with her. He did disagree with Thom Lindell, though, on a small point. From what Aris had seen of the Sarnese technicians' fierce response to his own team, he didn't think any of them would have waited for the bridge team to pass before venturing to the intercom. But then people were often braver in groups, so he let it pass.

"All right." Virginia York nodded. "Not entirely according to plan, but everything worked out." She favored Ty Wu Non with a smile and half-bow. "Good work forcing the bridge crew to capitulate, Ty. I wouldn't have wanted to blow the door. Better to keep the bridge in perfect order."

Aris swallowed against a sour taste building at the back of his throat. As far as he was concerned, Ty Wu Non had botched the plan. Granted, he had not been as fortunate as Aris, who'd managed to trap the Sarnese sentries outside of the comm center. Those sentries had retreated back onto the bridge, and locked Ty out. The senior company leader then grabbed a half-dozen hostages and proceeded to eliminate them one at a time until the watch officer on the bridge finally had enough.

But in the meantime the bridge crew had been trying to send an alert back to Kaifeng. If Aris hadn't knocked out the transmitter, the entire operation would have failed. He didn't expect House Master York to mention that. She couldn't praise him without drawing attention to her senior company leader's failings, which would have been inappropriate.

He was surprised, therefore, when Lance Leader Terry Chan spoke up from her seat next to Ty Wu Non with that praise instead.

"House Master," Terry Chan began, then waited to be recognized. "I'd like to extend a commendation to Lance Leader Sung. His timely action may have saved the element of surprise."

Aris missed the setup. Terry Chan was Ty Wu Non's other lance leader, and recognized by Non as his chief lieutenant. If anyone in House Hiritsu treated Aris with less respect than Ty, it was Chan. Caught off-guard by the unexpected praise, Aris actually let himself feel a measure of pride in having served his House. Then Ty spoke up and he realized that Chan's comment had merely been part of a prearranged dialogue meant to expose him to criticism.

"Instead of timely, we could also say rash," Ty said, frowning at Terry Chan as if the two of them had not set this up beforehand. "A lack of message traffic from the station will alert Kaifeng as surely as a warning message would have. If we cannot repair the damage Aris has done to the transmitters and focusing dish soon, this whole plan falls through and we're right back to a standard assault."

Aris felt a warm flush spreading out from the base of his neck and up over his scalp. Normally, only the House Master was allowed to speak out directly with negative comments in regard to a House warrior. But anyone could offer praise. And by Chan expressing false praise for a rash action, Ty stood within his rights in correcting her for praising Aris.

And perhaps there might have been another way. Aris certainly wasn't about to open the subject and invite discussion. It would change nothing, and would only serve to weaken the House—the family. He glanced over at Terry Chan, who looked properly chastened. But Aris caught her gaze flicking from the tabletop to the faces of other House officers, carefully judging reactions to her performance.

Sitting directly across the table from Chan, Company Leader Lindell wore his stone-faced expression that no one, not even Aris, could accurately read. Lindell could be counted on, though, to maintain traditions and not question Ty's methods. Ty Wu Non would be House Master one day, and his will would become the will of the House. Until that time, it was Virginia York's place and the right of none other to hold him accountable.

However, also across the table and one seat away from Aris, the third Company Leader, Jason James, looked ready to leap blindly to Aris' defense. James did not possess the stoic acceptance of Lindell. He had, quite the opposite, a quick temper only held in check by devotion to Virginia York and House Hiritsu. The color flushing James' normally pale features told Aris that the other man also recognized the setup and was prepared to take issue with it. Aris moved his head only fractionally, a slow shake that said he would rather drop the matter. James looked at him for a moment, then nodded slightly to show he understood.

House Master York finally broke the tense silence. "Aris Sung, have you checked into the communications down-time?"

"Yes, House Master." Aris did not meet her gaze. Did not want her to see the anger smoldering in his eyes. Not anger against Ty Wu Non and Chan, though perhaps they deserved some amount of ire, but at himself. Whether or not his action with the transmitter was the best solution, he had acted rashly. And now he was a point of contention, which was the last thing he would ever want for House Hiritsu.

"The transmitter was positioned using myomer bundles and actuators rather than with gears, same as in our Battle-Mechs. Apparently I snapped a few of the artificial muscles and ruined an actuator. Those should be repaired within the next few hours. The focusing dish is being replaced completely out of stores. Faster than attempting to repair the one I damaged, but it still won't be operational for four to six hours."

"So a full twelve hours at most."

"Yes, House Master. And a twelve-hour silence would not be unusual."

Virginia York nodded once. "Good enough," she said to him, and then turned again to the rest of her officers. "I want this next phase to run smoothly. We will delay leaving the station for twenty-four hours or until we're sure that Kaifeng thinks there's nothing amiss up here. That makes reestablishing communications and then faking several transmissions our top priority."

"I would like to oversee those procedures, House Master," Aris offered. "As Company Leader Non said, it is my responsibility."

Ty Wu Non was quick to speak up. "As to the repair of the communications system, I agree. But I will oversee the bridge transmissions, House Master. It was my team that took the bridge intact." He stressed the word as another subtle dig at Aris' damaging the transmitters. "We can handle the bridge crew. This Leftenant Harris already fears me, and with her in line the others would not dare oppose us."

Aris thought again of the four technicians who had faced him, armed with nothing more than a few tools and bare hands. He had seen the hatred naked on their faces. He did not believe these Sarnese would be cowed as easily as Ty Non seemed to think.

"Then let it be so," Virginia York said simply, ending the discussion. "Ty, I want the first bridge transmission ready to be sent as soon as Aris informs me the transmitter is fixed. Recorded messages only. No live transmissions. Everyone else not specifically needed by Senior Company Leader Non report to the *Tao-te*. Infantry Commander Jessup and his infantry can maintain security. Dismissed."

Aris sat where he was as the others filed from the room. Ty Wu Non, first up and out the door, looking very happy with himself, did not notice Aris remaining behind. Thom Lindell did, though his face gave away no reaction and he filed out with the others.

"You had a question, Aris?" Virginia York asked as the wardroom door finally closed, leaving the two of them alone.

"An observation, House Master." Aris bit down on his lower lip, trying to decide how to proceed. "I am concerned over the transmissions to Kaifeng."

Her chin came up slightly in warning. "Aris, I have assigned Ty Wu Non to that chore. It is his command and you may offer recommendations only if he solicits them from you."

As if he ever would, Aris thought, but did not say. If Ty Non could split hairs concerning the traditions, perhaps he could too. And here, before the House Master alone, it did not become a matter of contention. "I would not think to presume upon his wiser judgment, or yours, House Master. My observation concerns the Sarnese who attacked me outside the comm center."

She thought a moment and then nodded carefully. "Very well."

"I wasn't sure if my written report conveyed the level of the resistance they put up. Even facing a trained warrior armed with a laser weapon, they were not cowed nor even visibly concerned for their lives. I would like to believe I seemed at least somewhat threatening."

The joke fell flat as Virginia York merely looked him over, carefully, head to toe before proceeding. "You would judge them as fanatics?"

"Let us say zealots," Aris said carefully. "Fanatics sometimes fight against any odds. Zealots are smarter, more likely to wait and martyr themselves at an opportune moment."

"Such as?"

Careful, Aris, he cautioned himself. The situation was beginning to remind him of his first interview with the House Master, eleven years before. It was like walking through land mines, having to be careful for the least misstep. "Let us say I was able to force my way into the comm center just as a technician was concluding his preparations to send a live message to Kaifeng. With five weapons pointed at him, and given the choice to surrender and live, I believe he would turn the equipment on so it would record his death for the benefit of Kaifeng."

House Master York neither moved nor spoke for several minutes. Aris held her gaze, using the same technique as eleven years ago to refrain from blinking. You have to make the connection, he silently willed.

"I have ordered Ty Wu Non to use recorded messages," she finally said. "No live transmissions."

"Were we talking about Company Leader Non?" Aris asked innocently. "I just wanted to make clear my report. Yes, I cannot think of any way the station crew could sabotage a recorded message." Aris rose to his feet. "With your permission, House Master?"

Frowning at the wall, she nodded.

Aris paused in the doorway and glanced back. The House Master still stood there, staring off into space as if at some problem only she could see while mentally working out all possible solutions. Good enough, Aris thought. Everything would be fine with Virginia York watching over the House.

5

Kaifeng Recharge Station **Jodo Shinsa**
Zenith Jump Point, Kaifeng System
Sarna Supremacy, Chaos March
11 July 3058

The bridge of the recharge station felt unfamiliar and cold to SMM Petty Officer Shen Dok To. Panels with their switches, gauges, and flashing lights intimidated him. The overhead lighting, which twelve hours ago he would have called subdued or even inadequate, now seemed to beat down harshly, stabbing into his eyes and making him sweat. The difference wasn't the House Hiritsu warriors who stood nearby to ensure proper behavior. Not exactly. No, the bridge itself felt different. Because it was no longer theirs—the Sarna Supremacy's. He now sat in Capellan state property—Liao property—and that thought left him feeling disconnected from reality.

Shen sat at the master control panel again, having just relieved one of the Capellan technicians the Hiritsu warriors had brought along specifically for the purpose of running the station. Two other SMM officers were also here. Behind him at the watch officer's station sat Leftenant Ellen Harris, and on his immediate left, working the bridge communications panel, was Petty Officer Davidson. Petty Officer Belko had not been allowed back onto the bridge, his station and presence not required for a transmission, and of course there would be no Sarnese sentry. All the marines were dead.

Belted into his seat against the low gravity, Shen felt trapped and helpless. From the other side of his waist-high console, a House Hiritsu warrior stared down at him like he was some insect waiting to be dissected. He'd learned that her name was Terry Chan and that she was his *minder* for the transmissions. It was her job to make sure Shen didn't get any ideas about trying to get a covert warning to Kaifeng during the transmission. Shen was a primary concern, she explained, because the camera normally used to record the watch officer's reports also captured him and part of his console. What's more, Shen was *her* primary concern. Then she hit him, driving a fist into his stomach and forcing him to double over, then bringing her knee up into his chest. Nothing, of course, that could show up on camera.

Just a reminder of who was in charge.

Shen held no illusions about who was in charge, not at any level. He had met their commander twelve hours earlier, when the arrogant bastard had taken over the bridge after killing four crew members just outside the door. Shen remembered the muffled report of every shot, followed each time by requests from the marine sentries to open the door so they could fire on the Capellans. Leftenant Harris had denied permission to unlock the door, and had held out through four deaths while trying to send an alert to Kaifeng. Finally Petty Officer Davidson admitted defeat, that the main transmitter couldn't be realigned without extensive work, and Leftenant Harris surrendered the bridge.

No, Shen thought, correcting himself, *Leftenant Harris simply surrendered.*

He glanced back over his shoulder to where Ellen Harris sat strapped in at the watch officer's desk, a defeated slump to her shoulders. Her *minder* stood menacingly over her. It was the one who'd ordered them to call him Senior Company Leader Non but whom Shen privately referred to as The Jackal. The man who'd been last to enter the bridge, uniform and face spattered with blood from the messy executions in low gravity, but still moving with the air of one totally in command. Exchanging his slug-thrower for a laser pistol, he had personally executed the two sentries at the door and then threatened to kill the entire bridge crew one at a time for Leftenant Harris' resistance.

Even while cowering in his own seat, wishing there was something—anything—he could do to stop them, Shen had been amazed at how quickly Non dominated the leftenant. Unable to tear his eyes away from the scene, he'd helplessly watched the final push that sent Ellen Harris over the edge. She'd ordered Davidson to help establish communications with the *Liu*. For that, Non had thanked her and reached out almost kindly to trail a finger down her cheek. The blood mixed with her tears left a runny red smear down the side of her face. Shen would never forget the sad half-smile that trembled at the edge of her mouth as her will crumpled completely.

The Jackal was speaking to her now, continuing what seemed a personal crusade to break her without realizing he already had.

"Where do you live on Kaifeng?" he asked her in casual, almost friendly tones.

"Tarrahause."

"Yes." Shen could almost hear the smile in The Jackal's voice. "That is what your station record says. Also that you have children. Two of them. Staying with your husband while you pull duty here?" Shen assumed there was a nod; The Jackal sounded sure of himself. "Do you have holopics?" There was a slight pause and the sound of movement. "Fine-looking boys."

Then Non was beside Shen, having drifted over silently. *If only I had a beltknife,* Shen thought. *Or even a simple pair of scissors or a screwdriver.* A quick thrust into The Jackal's side might have been enough to kill him. But Shen had nothing like that to hand and so he did nothing.

Non handed the holopics across to Terry Chan. "Enter those into the file," he told her. "Possible subversives."

He drifted back to the watch officer's desk, out of view again. Shen wanted to throw up.

"Now, would you care to repeat your instructions to your bridge crew? Let them know that you are determined to assist us."

"This station—"

Non interrupted her with a quiet snarl. "You had better get some life into your voice. If I get the idea that you're holding back, trying to sabotage this transmission, your children will answer for it."

"This station is the property of the Capellan Confederation, in service to his Celestial Wisdom, Chancellor Sun-Tzu Liao." Harris' voice broke off, choked with tears, but quickly strengthened. "Our responsibility, as loyal Capellan subjects, is to assist House Hiritsu with their operation. So we will not make any attempt to communicate, by direct or covert means, the actual military situation on this station."

"Very good," Non said. "I believe we can begin now."

While Leftenant Davidson worked at the communications console under the watchful gaze of her Capellan observer, Shen carefully reached for his noteputer, feeling his hands shaking. Terry Chan glared down at him, and then awarded him one sharp nod of permission when she realized what he was doing. Someone must have briefed her on bridge operations. At least once every hour, the technician sitting at the main control panel was required to log the readings of his few active gauges and to make a written report of bridge events. Shen decided it would give him something to do while Ellen Harris recorded the bogus message.

He scrolled down to the Comments section and then sat there, idly tapping his stylus against the 'puter screen. What could he write? Maybe he could use the opportunity to organize his thoughts. *Zero-eight-forty-five*, he wrote, *became loyal Capellan subject.*

Not citizen. Subject. Shen squeezed his eyes shut, holding back tears of frustration and rage. He'd grown up on Kaifeng a free citizen of the Federated Commonwealth, but always with strong ties to his Capellan—or, rather, his Chinese—ancestry. Reminders of it stared back at him whenever he looked into a mirror. The dark, almond-shaped eyes. Yellow tint to his skin. Thick black hair that he kept well shorn because of his work in low gravity.

And then there was Kaifeng, an agricultural world with a huge belt of farming communities but only four actual cities. Many Chinese traditions remained alive there, even after nearly thirty years of FedCom control. Particularly the traditions dealing with local holidays and fertility rites. So a rebirth of the Sarna Supremacy, joining the freedoms of FedCom rule with the Chinese heritage so well preserved and promoted under the Liaos, had seemed like the realization of a dream for his homeland and his people.

A dream that had lasted less than a year.

There would be no pardons from Sun-Tzu Liao. The three Sarna Supremacy worlds were not among those that had welcomed the return of Capellan rule. In the chaos wrought by the Liao-Marik invasion of Federated Commonwealth territory, the planets Kaifeng, Sarna, and Sakhalin had declared themselves an independent alliance standing in opposition to Capellans.

So Sun-Tzu Liao now arrived as conqueror instead of liberator. And in the Capellan Confederation, subjects acquired as the direct result of war, regardless of former social position or education, were automatically relegated to the Servitors caste. They were slaves, treated as less than human and put to menial tasks in service to the Confederation. Citizenship could be regained, in theory, after five to ten years of loyal service. But in practice it would only be those of the next generation, the ones actually born under Liao rule, who could escape the onus of the Servitor caste.

"Petty Officer Davidson, if you would assist me?" The words were out of Shen's mouth before he could think better of it. It was risky, interrupting her work under the direction of their Hiritsu keepers. Plus, there was still one Capellan technician on the bridge who might recognize his request as being out of order and therefore suspicious.

Fortunately, Davidson herself was not a concern. Her face was turned away from the others on the bridge, and that gave her time to compose her expression before looking around. "Yes," she asked simply, neutrally.

Shen swallowed, his throat suddenly dry and constricted. He was quite aware of the intense study Terry Chan was giving him, and could feel a warmth on the back of his neck that would be The Jackal staring at him as well. "I need the angular deviation to Kaifeng. For the logs." He glanced up at Terry Chan, trying to look both intimidated and just a little dispirited. Her suspicious glare made it easy. "I don't think I should be getting up to take readings just now."

Davidson smiled sadly. "Right," she said, with just a small nod. She checked her screen, then told him, "Holding at four-point-two-nine degrees."

Shen entered that into his logs, thinking furiously all the while. Why had he done that? Just to see if Davidson would back him up? Well, she had. Now what did he plan to do with that information? The simple truth of the matter, which he should have realized before trying something so stupid, was that he couldn't do anything. Shouldn't do anything. Not yet. *Wait,* he counseled himself. *This isn't the time to attempt a warning. Not while these Hiritsu troops are all high-strung and The Jackal himself is here on the bridge.* Kaifeng was more than a week away by DropShip. That gave him plenty of time *after* these people left to organize a warning message.

But with every faked message, Shen knew he would lose his will to resist, much as Leftenant Harris already had. *Cooperation is policy.* He remembered that phrase from courses at the military academy. With planets constantly changing hands during the Succession Wars and all the border skirmishes in between, it had often become easier for people on occupied worlds to simply cooperate rather than resist.

He was still deliberating when The Jackal's sharp voice broke his reverie. "Silence on the bridge. You, Ellen, get ready to record. And don't worry, I know you will do a perfect job. One that will make your new nation, and your family, proud. You, Shen? Continue making your log entries. That should keep you busy. All *minders* fade back, out of the camera angle."

Ty Wu Non and Terry Chan moved off to Shen's left, taking seats at consoles against the wall. On the right-hand side of the room, a Hiritsu sentry drifted over to the starboard wall to find an anchoring position. The Capellan technician remained next to Petty Officer Davidson, whose station would not be in view of the camera. "Recording," Davidson said.

Shen tried not to even hear as Leftenant Harris began the prearranged spiel about taking advantage of low traffic to perform monthly preventive maintenance early. He continued to type comments into the log. *Zero-eight-fifty, cooperation becomes policy.*

Then Shen suddenly hit the Period key at the end of that sentence with a violent stabbing motion that cracked the notecomputer's screen. He picked it up and hefted it and with a mighty throw, sending the 'puter spinning across the short distance between him and the technician overseeing Davidson's work on the communications console. The spinning device caught the man in the ear and threw him completely off-balance for a few precious seconds. Shen was already talking frantically.

"Capellan forces have seized this station and will soon invade Kaifeng. Trust no further transmissions. Inform Sarna. Prepare for—"

The first laser burst caught him in the left shoulder, the second against the left side of his chest. Shen crumpled, sagging to the right in an effort to escape the pain while the stench of his burnt coveralls and scorched flesh made him gag. Behind him Leftenant Harris was screaming at him for being such a stupid, selfish bastard. Shen wanted to cry and laugh at the same time. He settled for several choking gasps while looking over toward Petty Officer Davidson at her station.

Forewarned that Shen might try something, her hands flew over the comm panel in practiced efficiency trying to send out the message before anyone could stop her. She stabbed repeatedly at the Transmit button, paused, threw a few more switches, and then kept hammering at Transmit until the technician finally regained his legs and stopped her with a vicious punch to the side of her head. Then Shen's view changed as Terry Chan grabbed him by the hair and hauled him about, placing her Nakjama right up to the side of his head. Well behind him he heard the bridge door cycle open as more Hiritsu personnel entered the bridge.

Doesn't matter, he thought. *I beat you. Zero-eight-fifty-five, defeated House Hiritsu.*

"Did it go out?" The Jackal asked the Capellan technician. The anger in his voice promised death. "Was the message sent?"

The answer did not come from the technician, but from a voice he hadn't heard before. "No, it was not."

Shen couldn't see much more out of the corner of his eye than the barrel of the laser pistol shoved up to his temple and part of Terry Chan's hand. But the new voice was that of another female, full of strength and authority. He found himself believing it without question, and the despair welled up inside him. He'd failed.

The voice rang out again, chiding. "Foolish to think we would not anticipate such an attempt. The bridge comm station is unable to transmit at all. The message has to be physically carried down to the communications center and transmitted from there. You accomplished nothing."

Shen heard Davidson crying softly, and then realized that tears were spilling silently down his own cheeks as well. With an effort he brought them under control. "We tried," he said, spitting out each word at the unseen voice. "The others will know that we tried."

"And failed," the new voice said in casual dismissal. "Ellen Harris, you will prove your worth by sitting in judgment over these two. They were your people. Make them answer for their crime, or answer for them."

There was a moment of silence in which Shen felt a glimmer of hope that the leftenant would not undermine the sacrifice they had just made. Then his hopes died as he heard her answer without faltering.

"I recommend you gather two bridge crews at the forward docking collar. Let them watch as the disobedient are punished by being ejected into space. That should solve your discipline problem."

"Yes, it should. And make sure everyone understands, Ellen Harris, that even the smallest episode of defiance will be considered a capital offense." A slight pause and then the new voice was addressing the Jackal. "You trained this one well, Ty. I expect no further trouble from these other two, so you may turn this operation over to Lance Leader Sung. I have need of your presence aboard the *Tao-te*."

Shen felt cold and empty, utterly despondent. He would not have believed he could feel more pain, until the unseen woman's next words drove one last spike of hopelessness into him. "Please tell Aris Sung that Ellen Harris may operate the airlock controls herself, as her reward for faithful service."

Aris Sung drifted into the hub of the grav deck. Like a giant spinning wheel some twelve hundred meters in diameter and forty meters thick, the only place one could realistically expect to enter it was through the middle. The eye of the storm, so to speak, where the centrifugal forces were so minor as to be easily dealt with.

Grabbing onto one of the handholds, Aris swung down out from the hub into one of many access tubes that ran down to the outer wheel, where gravity was maintained at one Terran standard gravity. His weight increased the further down he climbed, finally reaching his normal sixty-six kilograms as he stepped out onto the grav deck's outermost level. From there it was a short walk to the station commander's stateroom, appropriated by Virginia York for her stay.

Aris felt pleased with himself. Not for having gotten the better of Ty Wu Non. Inwardly he felt guilty that the senior company leader had suffered a slight loss of face. But it had been necessary to preserve the will of the House Master, which was to maintain the element of surprise. And in the final analysis, Virginia York was still Master of House Hiritsu and Ty Wu Non was only her most senior warrior. Aris had served her well, and so deserved the small pleasure of self-satisfaction.

But the feeling faded quickly as he crossed the short stretch of hallway. In its place came an unease, a gnawing sensation in the pit of his stomach. Where were the House Master's guards? At least one Hiritsu infantryman should have been stationed at the head of the corridor. And as it was too early for the House Master to be sleeping, a junior MechWarrior or MechWarrior trainee should have been posted outside her stateroom in case she had need to send someone on errands.

No, it didn't make sense. Aris drew his Nakjama laser pistol and pressed his back up against the smooth metal bulkhead. He slid forward, passing a door by turning his back out toward the open passage, keeping the laser chest-high and covering the closed door, and then completing the spin to end up with his back to the bulkhead on the opposite side of the door once more. Three of these careful movements later, he stood next to the House Master's adopted stateroom slash office.

Maybe she had returned to the *Tao-te,* Aris thought. Overseeing the preparations for the assault or simply deciding that the recharge station no longer warranted her full attention. The idea was so compelling that he almost dropped his guard and walked into the room.

Almost.

Aris reached across the closed door to thumb the opener and then pulled his arm back before the door actually began to cycle open. He waited for it to close, and then repeated his action. No sounds from the dark room. No sensation of movement. On the fourth cycle Aris swung around and into the room, immediately diving to one side so he would not be framed by the corridor light.

Pressed up against the room's outer bulkhead, he still neither heard nor sensed any motion. The light spilling in through the open doorway was enough to show him that no one occupied the starkly furnished room. No one alive.

Virginia York sat at the desk, slumped over as if asleep. Aris could smell the scent of death, of blood and a body having voided itself in final relief. Off to the right were two other bodies, piled into the corner out of the way. He stood, pistol gripped loosely in his right hand, which hung down impotently at his side. He walked forward a few steps, enough to see by the corridor light Virginia York's staring, unseeing eyes and the pool of blood spilling across the desktop and down onto the floor. He swallowed hard, his throat suddenly dry and scratchy, and he fought the gnawing sensation in his stomach that threatened to sap his strength altogether.

He stood there for several minutes after the door cycled shut, his world again plunged back into darkness.

6

JumpShip Tao-te
Zenith Jump Point, Kaifeng System
Sarna Supremacy, Chaos March
11 July 3058

"The passing of Virginia York is a tragic loss to House Hiritsu. She guided our path for over thirteen years. Many among us have known no other Master of our House. Many among us would not be here if not for her command on the battlefield, or off."

Ty Wu Non paused in his speech, eyes sweeping the faces of the assembled warriors. Aris thought his gaze lingered an instant longer on him, as if once again singling him out. *Yes,* he thought, *it was by Virginia York's wish alone that I managed to join House Hiritsu. Must you belabor that even now?*

Aris felt wooden, detached. He knew the shock would pass, but not quickly. He could vaguely remember giving the alarm, and joining in the search for the assassin. Popular speculation was that it had to be some secret agent posing as a member of the recharge station crew. Sarnese, most likely, but possibly a FedCom operative guarding the latent interests of Prince Victor Davion. Certainly the kill was too clean for an ordinary crewman to have done it.

Whoever the assassin, the fact remained that the House

Master was dead. And that gnawed away at Aris from within.

The thirty-six MechWarriors and a select dozen men and women from among the House infantry had gathered in the war room of the *Tao-te*. The command staff, lance leaders and above, sat belted in at their usual places along the metal conference table. The others crowded the walls or drifted up in the null gravity to catch a handhold near the ceiling. The room felt uncomfortably warm and confining with so many bodies, but no one complained and no one left.

Aris Sung kept his eyes fastened on Ty Wu Non. Despite the possible slur against himself, Aris felt that the senior Hiritsu warrior had delivered a fairly decent service in memory of Virginia York. He wasn't sure why that should surprise him. Had his own feelings toward Non blinded him to the man's devotion to the House they both served? It must have. Aris felt a twinge of shame. He depended on his ability to read people, and that ability had failed him.

The problem was that he'd simply never believed that Virginia York could die. He still found it hard to accept, though he had spent several minutes alone with the body before calling the alert. He had noticed bruises on the back and sides of her neck, nearly hidden by her hair. Strangulation. Then her throat slashed to finish the job properly. It reminded Aris of Hiritsu infantry custom— *the enemy isn't dead until you see blood spill.* Aris had pointed out the bruises to Doctor Hammond, House Hiritsu's chief surgeon. He had only nodded absently, made a note in his private log, and sealed up the body for return to Randar.

Virginia York had always been so full of strength, so able—her unflagging devotion to the House inspiring those around her. He thought back on his acceptance into House Hiritsu. How he had been shunned by the other trainees, treated with utter contempt by his instructors. And everyday, interrupting his training, came a personal summons from the House Master to the inner chamber, where Aris would spend one hour staring at Crescent Moon and contemplating his origins as a thief and his breaking of House law. Aris remembered that daily vigil, being removed from training and then the hour alone with his thoughts, as his most humiliating time in those first months.

Those first six months, to the day, from his eventual acceptance.

Virginia York visited the training field that day, inspecting the training procedures of two infantry Mentors and the progress of their charges. Not an unusual occurrence, except that it was the exact hour when she usually sent a runner with the summons for Aris Sung. She'd walked along the line where the trainees continued their rifle drills, and coming up on Aris' position she asked who was consistently the best marksman among the students over the last month. Aris knew that it has him, but had thought the instructors would surely name someone else. Someone in better standing. He still had not fully realized the real nature of the commitment to a Warrior House by its members.

When the Mentors singled him out, Virginia York's tone registered neither surprise or displeasure. She merely accepted the information, and ordered them to assign Aris an extra hour of training each day until he could compete with House Hiritsu's best marksman.

Aris' time in purgatory was over. The other trainees accepted him. And while his Mentors still drove him hard, as per the directions of Ty Wu Non, they never again showed disdain for what he once had been. Aris had never thanked Virginia York for that, or anything else she had done for him. It would not have been appropriate. But he thanked her now, silently, and pledged himself even more to the will of House Hiritsu.

And he promised both himself and her memory that when this was all over he would find whoever was responsible for her death. Find them, and kill them. He was sure House Master Virginia York would have wanted it just that way.

Aris was last to leave the war room, lingering behind until he felt sure that both Ty and Terry Chan were far enough away. Not that he bore either of them ill will.

Terry Chan, for all her recent antagonizing, was merely emulating her Mentor, Ty Wu Non. And Ty, well, he was Master of House Hiritsu now. Or would be. Chancellor Sun-Tzu Liao would have to recognize him as the legitimate successor to Virginia York. But that was merely a formality, to be accomplished when contact could be reestablished with Sian.

Until that time, House Hiritsu would follow the path on which Virginia York had started them: the taking of Kaifeng. Ty Wu Non had been explicit on that point in closing the service. They would continue to obey the will of the House Master, who could be replaced only in accordance with the wisdom of the Chancellor. Ty Wu Non would take on the temporary title of battalion commander, to signify his acceptance of responsibility for the House forces. Aris found that comforting. It meant that Ty Wu Non was endorsing Virginia York's plan of assault, which was Aris' creation. Ty would have to be careful of any changes he made, since failure at this point made him answerable directly to Sun-Tzu Liao himself.

Aris rose from his seat, pulled himself along to the door by the backs of other chairs, and finally swam out into one of the *Tao-te*'s main passageways. This corridor ran from the war room only a short distance before splitting into a T-shaped junction. From there one could take the lift down to other decks or follow one of the two branches that split off toward either the bridge or the executive staterooms. He took the final launch toward the junction with a push that would leave him ready to catch the handhold next to the lift.

"Last out the door, Aris Sung? That doesn't seem like you."

Ty Wu Non's deep voice startled him, and Aris twisted around to see the battalion commander hanging onto the wall just inside the corridor branch that led away to the bridge. The twisting also put him out of position for his landing. Aris caught the wall at an awkward angle, and he was forced to rebound back toward the passage he'd just left. Recovering, he caught the junction corner and was able to rebound a final time to end up in the same passage as Ty but on the opposite wall.

The battalion commander's smile was thin, but present. Aris even thought he saw a quick flash of admiration in the other's face. "Not a bad recovery," Ty said, though clearly more from a need to cover an otherwise awkward silence. "Sorry if I startled you, Lance Leader Sung."

Aris tried to keep the surprise off his face, unable to remember the last time Ty Wu Non had voiced an apology to him, even one that was more form than genuine. "I should have been paying more attention," he said. "You wished to see me, Battalion Commander?"

"Yes. I wanted to talk to you about tying up some loose ends." Ty paused, but Aris did not give him the satisfaction of asking for clarification. "Your report stated that you were on your way to see House Master York about the transmissions. I would like to hear that report now."

"Of course. I should have done so earlier. My apologies." Aris drew in a deep, steadying breath. "Everything is in place. A message must now be routed through two stations, both monitored by our own Capellan technicians and under heavy guard, before it can pass to the communications center. At each stage it is analyzed for direct or indirect indication of the station's capture. The comm center, of course, is the weakest link. We now have four infantrymen inside and four more stationed directly outside, both teams supported by three two-man roving patrols in the nearby area."

Ty frowned. "That seems excessive."

"We have a possible espionage agent aboard the *Jodo Shinsa*. I would rather find out later that I assigned too many men, rather than too few."

"Point taken. What about the DropShip *Annabelle Lee*?"

"Communications equipment completely removed," Aris said. "In the last six hours prior to transfer to the *Taote*, I personally screened several innocuous messages and flight-controller spiels that can simulate normal station-to-ship message traffic." His report given, Aris waited for Ty Wu Non's judgment.

"Adequate," was the senior warrior's response. High praise for Aris. Then the other man's eyes grew vague, unreadable. "You know, Virginia York's last order concerning you was that you continue overseeing the simulated message traffic between the station and Kaifeng."

Aris bit down on his tongue hard enough to draw blood. Was Ty going to use that to keep him from combat? Leave him behind on the station while the DropShips burned insystem toward Kaifeng? He swallowed, clearing the salty taste of blood from his mouth. "With all due respect, Battalion Commander, I think—"

"Don't worry, Aris Sung," Ty interrupted. "I don't plan to leave you behind. In fact, I am promoting you to Company Leader *pro tem*."

Aris blinked rapidly, then shook his head slightly as if that could clear away the confusion. Ty Wu Non, the man who had been poised behind him for eleven years, ready to shoot him the moment he stumbled, was promoting him? Before Aris could react, Ty enlightened him.

"I don't like you, Aris. I never have. If you think that's why I've treated you as I did, you're partly correct. But it was never my responsibility to like you. It was given to me to oversee your training. Which is what I did. I made sure you were pushed as hard as any. And always I worked myself harder, where you could not see, to make sure that when the time came House Master York would recognize me above you.

"I outlasted four other company leaders who have since been killed or moved into duties as full-time Mentors. Now I will be named House Master. But only after the success of this mission. Virginia York endorsed your plan. Now I must as well. By accepting the post of battalion commander, I forced a vacancy in my old company. However much I think Terry Chan might deserve that position over you, it could later prove self-defeating if your plan does not work. So I promote you. Does this help clarify matters?"

Aris weathered the soft-spoken barrage of brutal truth with greater ease than he had Ty's praise. What the other man said made sense. House Master Virginia York would never have needed to have such a talk with a subordinate, but Ty was just as strong-willed and could yet become a decent House Master. And if he thought it necessary to continue the antagonistic control of Aris' life, then that must be endured. *That which does not kill me, makes me stronger,* Aris told himself. That thought, of course, could not be voiced.

"Yes, Battalion Commander Non," was all he said.

Second Interlude

"To be what we are, and to become what we are capable of becoming, is the only end of life."
—Quote inscribed over the gate to the House Hiritsu stronghold on Randar

Hsien Park, Yushui
Gei-fu
Sian Commonality, Capellan Confederation
8 March 3051

The small riverside park in the center of Yushui wasn't much more than a flat piece of grassy ground that hosted a weekly bazaar or the occasional small carnival. The Nunya River passed nearby, following the ferrocrete bed that had been engineered into the city's design to help accommodate the heavy annual rainfall for which the world of Gei-fu was infamous. A crowd of perhaps fifty people had gathered, all solemn and devoting their attention to the small, hastily constructed stage. The ground they stood on was soft and damp. The overcast sky and damp chill in the air promised more rain before too long.

Aris Sung glanced up at the dark, heavy overhang of clouds as if they might pose some potential threat, and then swept his gaze once again over the gathered audience. Only his eyes moved. Feet slightly apart, back straight, Hollyfeld assault rifle held at port arms—he looked ready to bring the weapon up to his shoulder and begin killing at a second's notice.

Aris wore the simple green and black uniform of House

Hiritsu's regular infantry, though at sixteen he was already a highly trained scout and competent assassin. He stood up on the plywood stage along with five other infantrymen and two House MechWarriors, all a part of the personal guard for House Master Virginia York, who stood not three meters away. She was present to oversee the public execution of the Gei-fu rebel leadership.

Aris was present in the honor guard because Lance Leader Ty Wu Non had assigned him there versus one of the combat teams out hunting down the last of the renegade militia.

The border world of Gei-fu had chosen a bad time to attempt a rebellion. Relying on the planet's Third Militia, which included a lance of light BattleMechs, the planetary director had thought to engineer a quick and complete secession from the Capellan Confederation and join the nearby St. Ives Compact. He had gotten as far as taking military control of the planet before learning that the Compact would not be able to extend any support toward the move. The leadership of the entire Inner Sphere was gathered on Outreach for some big talk concerning the Clan invasion, and no general—no matter how highly respected or trusted—was about to launch what amounted to a military invasion without direct consultation with his sovereign.

But Senior Colonel James Teng and Imarra House Master Ion Rush, in whose hands the Capellan Confederation had been left, felt no qualms about enforcing loyalty within their borders. House Hiritsu had been dispatched to crush the rebellion, which it accomplished in rather short order. Perhaps a single BattleMech and a handful of conventional troops remained to be hunted down. In the meantime Virginia York would preside over the formal and very public execution of the planetary director and his supporters, effectively cleaving the head from the movement.

The select group of Yushui citizens gathered that morning included the new planetary director and her immediate staff. Virginia York had ordered all BattleMechs to the city's perimeter. Sealing off Yushui was a routine precaution, but it was also that she didn't want the gigantic war machines towering over the proceedings to enforce the impression that the Chancellor held power through

BattleMechs alone, and not through the loyalty of warriors such as House Hiritsu and citizens such as the new director.

A single squad of anti-Mech infantry and another of jump troops stood in attendance on either side of the stage, carrying most of their normal weapons but not at-the-ready. Two squads of regular infantry stood guard over the movement's leadership, one trooper armed with a slug pistol for each rebel. When the time came, one by one, each Hiritsu warrior would lead his charge to the front of the assembly and perform the execution by means of a single shot to the head. Aris' squad was the only one with weapons held ready, the assault rifles good crowd-controllers. Besides the Hollyfelds, each infantryman on the stage also carried a full medical kit strapped to his or her right hip, ready to leap to the side of House Master York should the unthinkable happen. It didn't seem very likely, what with the strong infantry presence and the two MechWarriors flanking her and ready to serve as human shields.

But then no one had counted on going up against a BattleMech.

There was little warning. Only a large sloshing sound from the waters of the Nunya as the 'Mech stood and then emerged from the depths like some fabled leviathan. A *Stinger*. Nearly nine meters tall and humanoid in appearance, six of its twenty tons were devoted specifically to armor and weapons. It mounted twin machine guns, carried one on each arm, and an Omnicron medium laser gripped in its right hand like some kind of oversize pistol. Its shoulders and arms were broad and blocky, but its legs were streamlined legs and its head very tiny for the size of its body.

Aris didn't have to be told that the 'Mech must have traveled along several kilometers of river bottom to work its way in so close without being discovered. It was the kind of desperate plan he himself might have come up with in the same situation. Kill the Master of House Hiritsu, free the rebel leadership, and you have a born-again rebellion. And *Stinger*s were fast, so there was even some hope of escape.

The *Stinger* fired before it ever cleared the river, its

machine guns ripping long, broken furrows into the ground as it tracked in on the stage. Aris was already moving, dropping his assault rifle and diving past the two stunned MechWarriors to tackle House Master York and take her off the back of the stage. The long staccato bursts warned him that he would be too late. Should have been too late. He expected at any time to feel the heavy slam of steel-jacketed slugs that would leave him broken and useless. But service to House Hiritsu demanded that he try, and that left no time for useless internal debate.

But the only impact came when he and Virginia York hit the ground behind the stage, Aris' face smashing into the soft earth in his efforts to keep from landing heavily on the House Master.

Spitting out mud and grass, wiping away the blood that poured from his broken nose, Aris quickly rose to his knees and took stock of the situation. From what he could tell, the *Stinger* pilot was still too interested in living. Those first rounds of machine-gun fire had punched into the anti-Mech troops, and now the *Stinger* finished off the only apparent threat with another spray from each arm-mounted weapon. *One more spray at most,* Aris thought. *Then it will come for her.*

Virginia York had risen to a half-crouch. Aris grabbed her by the shoulders and pulled her back down. "You head for the river. Stay low and move fast." She started to open her mouth and Aris shook her, hard. "Don't argue. Just go! The water will carry you away faster than you can run. If it comes for you, try to stay deep as often as you can." Then with another shove he started her on her way toward the river bank and he raced for the corner of the stage. He never looked back. He trusted her to preserve her own life, for the good of the House.

By now the *Stinger* had turned its attention to the milling crowd of Hiritsu warriors, strafing with its machine guns as it searched for the House Master. It was Aris' one advantage, that BattleMechs were built for engaging other BattleMechs. Even a 'Mech as small as a *Stinger* had trouble identifying one particular person out of a crowd. But that confusion might not last long. Aris had to make good use of his time.

The shape of a plan began to form, one that seemed to

guarantee that House Master York never got the chance to punish him for his rude treatment of her. *Act now, think later.* It was a maxim drilled into Hiritsu warriors, the principle that it was usually better to do something constructive immediately rather than wait and think of the perfect response that might then come too late. So before he could talk himself out of it, Aris dashed from his cover behind the stage toward where the shattered bodies of the anti-Mech troops lay.

Anti-Mech troops generally carried heavy laser rifles that could actually inflict some minor damage to a Battle-Mech's thick armor plating. On his own, Aris doubted that would amount to much. No, he had another of their tools in mind. The grapple rod—a meter-long shaft with a foot strap at one end and a ball made of special adhesive at the other. Anti-Mech troops used the device to scale up the side of a BattleMech so they could plant explosive charges at vulnerable places such as knee and hip joints. The dead Hiritsu warriors had turned out with grapple rods on their backs, but no explosive charges. If the *Stinger* MechWarrior had realized that, House Master Virginia York and Aris would likely be dead by now. Working quickly, Aris picked out two grapple rods that hadn't been damaged in the attack.

He planned to get a lot higher than the hip.

The *Stinger* had turned back toward the stage, still searching for its target. Almost in afterthought, it reached out to the side and spat out two large red darts from its right-arm medium laser, straight into the middle of a determined clump of Hiritsu warriors who were concentrating a hail of bullets and laser fire against its flank. The acrid taste of ozone burned in Aris' nose and at the back of his throat, followed by the faint but sickening scent of charred flesh. Then the nine-meter-tall machine was striding straight at him, eating up the ground in huge, four-meter strides. Aris did the best thing he could at that point. He stayed low to the ground and froze.

BattleMechs tracked best on heat and motion. The anti-Mech troops were too recently dead to be much cooler than Aris, and not even the watchful eye of the *Stinger*'s MechWarrior was likely to see Aris crouched there, plac-

ing a foot in each stirrup and tilting the first grapple rod to
take careful aim at the middle torso of the 'Mech.

The ground shook now with each heavy, ponderous
step the giant machine took. Aris waited. A grapple rod
was only good for ten meters at most, and he needed to
get as high up as possible on the first try. When the
Stinger's left foot hit the ground just three meters away,
sinking into the soft earth, Aris thumbed the first control
stud that fired the adhesive ball. It flew out, still attached
to the shaft by ten meters of thin nylon/myomer cable,
and struck the humanoid machine in the center chest.
With the right foot rising and looking as if it would crush
Aris where he crouched, he thumbed the second control
stud, which activated the winding motor.

Suddenly Aris rose swiftly off the ground, pulled in
between the *Stinger*'s legs and up, barely missing the
right leg as it stepped forward and the right heel came
down where Aris had waited. Aris' shoulder clipped the
lower torso as he passed up from between the Battle-
Mech's legs, almost making him lose his grip on the second grapple rod. He clenched his teeth and fought against
the pain, determined to see it through.

The cable finished winding back into the shaft, leaving
Aris dangling against the *Stinger*'s chest. The machine
slowed as its pilot realized what was happening. With images of giant metal hands rising to smear him over the
broad chest like some kind of annoying insect, Aris took
quick aim with the second grapple rod and thumbed the
firing stud. It hit right on target, against the metal overhang that framed the upper edge of the cockpit viewscreen.
Aris abandoned the first grapple rod, and rode the second
up until it hit its limit and he hung there, bouncing against
the high-impact plastic of the viewscreen.

The *Stinger* pilot's eyes widened to see a House Hiritsu
infantryman hanging not a meter away from him. Aris
wasted no time trading gazes, not yet. The metal lip to
which his grapple rod had connected hung down at a
slight angle to partially shield the viewscreen and to
house the external cleaners that would spray off any film
of dust or mud. Hooking his left elbow around the grapple
rod to hold himself, he reached down with his right hand
and pulled the medkit off his hip. The kit was large and

square and dark green, and Aris hoped it looked a lot like an explosives pack. His left hand tore into a side pouch on the kit and pulled out the digital thermometer. Holding onto that, he shoved the medical kit up under the lip and held it there with his right.

From the immediate look of fear on the 'Mech pilot's face, it was obvious he thought the pack was real. Aris held up the thermometer, hand hiding most of it and thumb poised over its end like it was a remote activating trigger. Now he matched gazes with the MechWarrior, riding out the bluff with what he hoped was the zealous expression of a true fanatic. He worked at not blinking, widening his eyes only slightly and then relaxing them. A good unblinking stare could sometimes be as unnerving as facing a bomb.

Aris could read the man's indecision. There was no way to brush Aris off his 'Mech before the supposed explosives were triggered. Then there was the fact that *Stingers* were notorious for their cramped conditions, and that the two-meter by two-meter viewscreen opened up onto the entire cockpit. Most of the blast would be deflected downward, and if the explosives were real, Aris would cease to exist. But thanks to the metal overhang, some of it would likely penetrate the viewscreen and then there was nowhere for the pilot to go. He'd die instantly, if he was lucky, or sit there strapped into his command couch while the cockpit burned around him.

Of course, there was the cockpit ejection feature. Aris caught the pilot's nervous glance toward those controls, the man obviously trying to judge whether he could hope to punch out before the blast caught him too. Aris smiled slowly, daring him to try it. For a moment he thought he'd gone too far, and that the other man just might, but then the MechWarrior's shoulders sagged back in defeat.

The final option was obvious. Surrender. There would be no leniency, not for a renegade. But apparently the man thought it better to gamble that his captors might be somewhat more forgiving than an explosive satchel going off in his face.

Aris never let his elation show, protecting his victory. He kept eye contact with the MechWarrior right up to the point when other Hiritsu infantrymen climbed up and pulled the man from his cockpit. Then he rode the grapple rod back down to the ground and retrieved his assault rifle.

Virginia York met Aris as he came off the stage, handing him a neurohelmet. She was dripping wet, her black hair plastered to her skull, but seemed to project an air of satisfaction all the same. She handed him the neurohelmet.

"You caught it," she said simply. "Now learn to use it."

7

DropShip Lao-tzu
Inbound, Kaifeng System
Sarna Supremacy, Chaos March
19 July 3058

The four House Hiritsu DropShips continued to decelerate, holding their widely spaced diamond formation. Each vessel's aft end pointed toward the area of space the world of Kaifeng would occupy in exactly ten hours. Long plumes of glowing plasma speared out into the darkness of space like some kind of hellish flashlight, marking their path ahead.

The *Dainwu,* an egg-shaped *Overlord* Class ship, was the obvious head of the diamond, painted the Hiritsu colors of green and black and bearing the House insignia of a radiant white katana against a field of stars. The massive DropShip could have easily carried House Hiritsu's full battalion of BattleMechs as well as its six *Thrush* aerospace fighters, but such concentration would also have limited their tactical flexibility.

Twin *Union* Class DropShips anchored the outside points of the diamond, their spheroid shapes two gray teardrops against the blackness of space. Like the *Overlord,* each one held a full company of twelve BattleMechs as well as two fighters. The *Union*s had also crammed a full platoon of infantry with transport vehicles into the bays, allowing a good mix of 'Mech, ground, and air support.

The base of the diamond was supported by a slightly less-massive *Intruder*. Carrying the bulk of the infantry, nearly three platoons, it would drop with the *Overlord* and Ty Wu Non.

Aboard the *Union* Class DropShip *Lao-tzu*, Aris studied the holographic model of House Hiritsu's flight formation while the last of his company filed into the briefing room and took seats. He couldn't find anything wrong with the arrangement or disposition of troops, though Hiritsu's limited aerospace support had always made him uneasy. The twenty-five ton *Thrushes* weren't good for much more than reconnaissance. But Kaifeng didn't have heavy aerospace assets either, and coming in with surprise meant no fighter screen to penetrate. No, he saw nothing particularly wrong. Yet a growing unease kept him from relaxing.

"Where's Lance Leader Chan?" Aris asked. Leaning forward he idly tapped at the controls on the holographic projector. The projector, mounted in the center of the table, went dark.

MechWarrior Justin Loup cleared his throat uneasily. "Lance Leader Chan is down in communications, sending an acknowledgment of Battalion Commander Non's last set of changes. She said to start without her."

Aris forced himself not to frown. Except for critical communications, a transmissions blackout was to have gone into effect at exactly the twelve-hour point. As Aris' second in command Terry Chan could send messages over her own authority, but she should have spoken with Aris personally rather than relay through a junior Mech-Warrior. Aris had no doubt that it was merely another carefully orchestrated show of contempt. One he might be forced to take issue with now that he was her superior, but better to do so in private rather than in front of his people.

"Well, Terry Chan and I have been over this enough in the last few days," he said, brushing off the matter as if it was of little consequence. "For that matter, so have we all. And after this briefing I want everyone in their rooms for down time. See the physician if you need chemicals, but I want everyone rested. We power up in seven hours."

Aris reached out and punched a few more keys on the holographic controls, bringing it back on line but this time with a computer-generated model of Kaifeng floating above the metal briefing table. With a quick nod for Lance Leader Raven Clearwater to take over the controls, Aris rose from his seat and began a slow circuit of the room.

He moved easily, comfortable in the artificial gravity created by the DropShip's constant deceleration. Braking at just under twelve meters per second, the *Lao-tzu* was able to duplicate Kaifeng's heavy 1.1 standard gravity. To acclimatize his warriors, Ty Wu Non had ordered the initial burn toward Kaifeng started at 1.5 standard, trailing off slowly over several days until at the midpoint all DropShips were holding at 1.1. Now all of them moved naturally, comfortably, and on the planet's surface there would be no distraction from combat.

A method I shall remember, Aris thought.

"I would hope by now," he said, "that all troops have familiarized themselves with Kaifeng. Sixty percent of its land mass is heavy jungle, and if we're ever forced into that area we're in trouble. It's dense and wet and we don't know it half as well as the natives. So we avoid it. That simple."

Aris didn't bother to mention that the nearest heavy jungle to their site of operations was over three hundred kilometers away, and that being forced that far off track would mean much greater trouble than simply having to deal with dense undergrowth. Focusing their worries on a distant threat would make any up close and personal dangers, like heated battle with the Kaifeng SMM, seem preferable.

"The rest of the land mass has been cultivated into some of the most productive agricultural land in the Inner Sphere. Kaifeng feeds itself, Sarna, and Sakhalin, as well as some nearby worlds. The farmland is clumped into three large districts, one in the southern hemisphere and two in the northern. Each district is administered by a single large city—Franklin in the south, Beijing and—our target—Tarrahause in the north. The largest city, Mahabodhi, is situated outside the Beijing District. It has the only full-service spaceport on the planet, is the administrative capital, and is the primary garrison of the Kaifeng SMM."

Aris drew in a steadying breath. There had been a lot of debate over this next point, one of the lynch pins to the plan he had developed. "Most assaults would target Mahabodhi, seeking to capture the spaceport and defeat the garrison force. This is precisely what we're *not* going to do." An assault against the capital would be costly to both sides, and was by no means a certain victory.

"Our mission profile specifies the taking of Kaifeng, yes. But what Imarra House Master Ion Rush really wants from us is to deny food to the Sarna Supremacy. So we accomplish both by shutting off the flow of surplus crops into Mahabodhi."

Without needing to be told, Lance Leader Clearwater highlighted each of the four cities involved in the assault plan. Aris continued his circuit. "The three district cities act as gathering points. Surplus food is routed from them to Mahabodhi via conventional transport. House Hiritsu will take control of these three cities, effectively shutting off nearly all export of food supplies. This will force the Kaifeng SMM to leave the protection of Mahabodhi and come after us. We can then deal with them as we see fit."

Justin Loup leaned forward, hands clasped in front of him and staring speculatively at the projection of Kaifeng. "Do we have any more information on mercenary presence?"

Aris nodded. That was a chief concern. The Sarna Supremacy had been hiring mercenaries recently, preparing to expand its influence over other worlds inside the disputed territories. "From intercepted civilian holovid signals, we estimate that there are no more than two companies of mercenaries on planet, likely scattered between the three district cities."

"So the most we should have to contend with is a company of mercs." Lance Leader Clearwater rubbed at the edge of her tanned jaw. "Or maybe a double lance, supported by one lance of Kaifeng SMM troops."

"Right," Aris said, nodding his agreement. "And we'll use the same tactics at company level as at battalion level." He waited while Lance Leader Clearwater pulled up the next map. Just as well Terry Chan wasn't present, he thought. She might have chosen to fight him on this and that wouldn't have sat well with his people.

The model of Kaifeng disappeared, to be replaced by a flat contour map that lay over the center of the briefing table. The area was stripped of almost all detail, with general green and green-brown covering denoting the level of vegetation and grid squares dividing up the territory into one-kilometer sections. What looked like blurry gray foothills occupied one corner, sitting next to a large lake. Aris leaned in to flick his right hand over the spot. "Tarra-hause," he said, fanning the blurry gray projections. "Sitting on Lake Ch'u Yuan." He traced a ribbon of blue that meandered diagonally across the map, connecting at the lake's northeast and southwest corners. "And this is the Jinxiang River."

Aris straightened and allowed the others a few minutes to study the terrain. It wasn't perfectly to scale, but accurate enough to give them an immediate feel for distances and directions. "The farmland surrounding Tarrahause is devoted mostly to the production of rice, vegetables, and fruits. At four hundred million metric tons, rice is Kaifeng's number one export. We are responsible for shutting that down." He looked at Raven Clearwater. "Enlarge the upper river."

What had been a thin blue ribbon widened into a large band surrounded by multiple strands of blue. "Along almost all of the Jinxiang are large rice paddies, fed by tributaries or irrigation. The rice is harvested and moved to large collection sites along the river, where it can be stored. It is then shipped down river by large barges to Tarrahause and from there flown over to Mahabohdi for export. We don't want to ruin the stores or the current harvest, but we will if that's what it takes. Better to take and control the collection sites, denying any further shipments into Tarrahause. That will draw out the Tarrahause garrison. We'll hit them hard once they're outside the city, either destroying or crippling them. Second Company will employ similar tactics at Franklin, but Battalion Commander Non will lead Third Company in a direct assault against Beijing. Beijing has to fall quickly because it's so close to Mahabohdi and could receive immediate support from the Kaifeng SMM garrison."

And that should be that. Aris played his gaze over the network of rivers and streams. The plan felt solid in his mind, but he couldn't shake a feeling of unease over the entire mission. "Questions? Observations?"

Raven Clearwater nodded. Her long black hair was braided on one side into several plaits and tied with wooden beads that clacked together when her head moved. "What about the main road that follows the river's course? Is there a backup transportation system?"

"Only sufficient to supply Tarrahause itself with food. And if they start pressing extra transports into service, we can shut that road down very easily. It passes over too many bridges to be dependable."

"You have us formed into two demi-companies working close together," Justin Loup observed. "Why not break down into our three lances or even two-Mech elements? We could strike along a large section of river front simultaneously."

Aris' muscles tensed, but he forced himself to relax by beginning to walk a slow circuit around the briefing room. Terry Chan had also submitted such a plan, which Aris had rejected, and he wondered now if she was trying to make her point again in front of the company by working through Justin. Possible. Terry Chan had likely reasoned that Aris was being overly cautious, or perhaps that was her standing opinion of him.

He couldn't shake the thought that Ion Rush had recently been ordering Warrior Houses of questionable loyalties into extended campaigns that would thin their ranks. If this was another such mission, then Aris couldn't rely on intelligence supplied by the Imarra Master. But he couldn't explain that, not without undermining the chain of command and sowing suspicion among his own people concerning House unity. That was a sure way to lose the battle before it began.

"Our goal," he said, "my goal, is to make it into Tarrahause without losing one BattleMech or infantryman. I want fast movement down the river, yes, but I don't want us spread so thin that we can't react to a threat. There might be 'Mech patrols, troop garrisons, or other defenses we don't know about. A demi-company running into a standard four-'Mech patrol can hold its own. And by working in close proximity, the demi-companies can support each other should something like that occur."

Aris gave his warriors a thin smile, softening his voice only slightly as he fed them the final hook. "When Battalion Commander Ty Wu Non catches up with us at Tarrahause, I'd like for us to be in control of the city and receiving him with a formation that includes every last warrior we started with."

He saw the silent smiles and private nods around the table as his people all considered that challenge. Flawless victory. That was what he wanted to sell them on. He completed his circuit of the room, coming back to his seat at the head of the table, and he placed his hands on the back of it.

"The will of the House Master is the will of the House," he whispered in near-reverent tones, "and the will of the House Master was to take Kaifeng with minimal losses." He waited a moment for those words to fully sink in, until he was sure that everyone knew that Aris referred to Virginia York as much as Ty Wu Non. Then he straightened.

"Get some rest," he ordered, then turned and went out through the door of the briefing room.

8

The general quarters alarm on the *Lao-tzu* sounded much like the one on the Kaifeng Recharge Station—a harsh, computer-generated gong. It rang out seven times, the first two or three chimes shocking everyone into a few seconds' inactivity. With the DropShip an hour away from entry into Kaifeng's atmosphere and with no indication of being spotted, the last thing anyone expected was to hear an alarm promising such immediate danger.

In the DropShip's lower 'Mech bay, Aris was the first to move—walking briskly toward his BattleMech and yelling, "Stations!" at technicians and other MechWarriors. There was a loud clanging as someone dropped a heavy tool against the metal deck, then everyone was moving as if that sound had shattered the invisible web holding them motionless. No one ran. Running could be dangerous within the narrow corridors of a DropShip and promoted panicked behavior. And there was little speaking except for those few in position to give orders at these times.

Following the seventh gong a high-pitched whistle sounded over the ship's PA system, demanding attention.

One of the bridge officers came on and called for everyone to move quickly to their general quarters station. His deep voice sounded confident, and he gave no indication of the problem. But then the *Lao-tzu* trembled, throwing a slight hitch into everyone's stride as the deceleration-induced gravity fluctuated for an instant, and Aris knew that they'd just been struck by weapons fire.

It seemed the battle for Kaifeng had been joined sooner than they'd expected.

Aris' *Wraith* was berthed in its cubicle next to the main bay doors, looking like a giant armored sentinel that would let pass only those it favored. Aris loved the look of his 'Mech, even though it was a Free Worlds League design instead of Capellan-originated. The smooth, segmented body had a fully streamlined appearance lacking on many BattleMechs. Its head had been molded down into the shoulders, offering better shock absorption, and its narrow, turret-style waist possessed an incredible range of pivoting motion. Twin medium pulse-laser barrels curved out from its left elbow like spurs while the *Wraith*'s main armament, a Tronel XIII large pulse laser, extended out along the outside of the right arm. With an LTV 385 Extra-Light fusion engine at its heart and Curtiss jump jets mounted just behind, the *Wraith* was the fastest, most maneuverable 'Mech design possible for its weight class. Aris and a few techs had painstakingly applied the blued-steel look of a rifle barrel to the BattleMech's armor plating, giving it the polished, deadly look of a weapon.

A chain ladder dangled down from the open cockpit hatch at the back of the *Wraith*'s head. Even as Aris grasped one of the lower rungs, airtight hatches were being slammed shut all around the 'Mech bay with resounding metallic clangs, protecting against loss of atmosphere in case of a breach of the DropShip's hull. Aris scaled the ladder to the cockpit, climbed in and then immediately shut and dogged the hatch behind him.

He settled into the command couch and pulled a wireless headset out from a small, tilt-open storage space beneath the *Wraith*'s communications system. He clipped the transceiver onto his belt, then donned the headset, which consisted of an earplug and thin-wire microphone.

It was similar to the device built into a BattleMech neuro-helmet, but there was no need to put the bulky helmet on until he was actually ready to pilot the 'Mech. With the belt transmitter, he could leave his 'Mech immediately if need be, but any use of the comm system still required some basic security checks. He switched his computer to battery-augmented power and brought it on-line.

"Proceed with voiceprint identification," the computer said emotionlessly.

"Company Leader Aris Sung."

"Voiceprint match. Confirm authorization."

Because voiceprint identification could be faked, Battle-Mechs were also programmed with another special key. A code word or often a phrase known only to the MechWarrior. Aris smiled. "I am right where I wanted to be, now I must survive it." That thought, from eleven years ago, had never left him. It seemed an especially appropriate reminder whenever battle loomed before him.

"Company Leader Aris Sung on-line," he said, once the computer cleared him. "Requesting status report."

"One moment, sir," a voice replied, sounding tinny and distant. There followed general fumbling sounds as the comm set was passed to someone else.

The radio filtration couldn't fully rob the rich, deep tones of the next speaker. It was the same man who had made the general quarters announcement. "Sir, Bridge Officer Kyle Lee. We have been engaged by a full company of aerospace fighters, mixed *Lightning*s and *Sparrowhawk*s. They slid out from behind Nochen as we pulled inside its orbit."

Nochen was Kaifeng's poor excuse for a moon. From his study of the system, Aris knew that the small planetoid was only barely bigger than a mere asteroid. But it could have hidden a company of aerospace fighters easily enough. *Which means they knew we were coming.*

"One of the escorting *Thrush* fighters is down," Bridge Officer Lee continued. "We were responsible for the alert-ready fighters and have already launched. We sustained minor damage to the number one landing gear on the enemy's last pass."

Aris thought furiously, trying to sort out the mechanics of three-dimensional space combat in his head. "Send to

Battalion Commander Non," he ordered. "Recommend we pull to a tighter diamond formation. It will put their fighters at greater risk on any attack runs."

"Already done, sir. Two, no three, enemy craft disabled or destroyed. Damn. And another *Thrush* down."

Damned light aerospace fighters. As if in agreement, the *Lao-tzu* trembled again as she took more damage. Aris swallowed dryly and began to throw switches on his control panel, bringing the *Wraith*'s engine to life.

"Bridge Officer Lee, I want all 'Mech pilots not already in their 'Mechs and powered up to do so at once. Rig the ship for a hard surface drop." A hard surface drop meant steep atmospheric entry and heavy G-forces all the way to the ground. Not the best way to begin an assault, shaking up your warriors, but better than having your DropShip shot out from under you. "Technicians are to stand by with BattleMech jet packs. If the *Lao-tzu* takes too much damage I want the company ready for high-atmosphere deployment."

"Acknowledged, sir. Battalion Commander Non standing by on auxiliary channel bravo."

Jaw clenched in frustration, Aris spun a dial on the comm gear to select the private channel. "Standing by, Battalion Commander."

"Aris Sung, can you explain this attack?" Ty Wu Non's voice was cold and demanding, losing little of its strength in transmission.

"No, Battalion Commander. I would guess that our approach was detected, but I do not preclude the possibility that a covert message was somehow smuggled off the recharge station."

There was a slight pause, as if Ty Wu Non was deciding whether or not to take issue with Aris over the recharge station messages. "I want your opinion, Aris. How does this attack affect your assault plan?"

Aris was ready for that one. "Short-term effect is negligible, providing we don't take heavy losses from the fighter attack. Perhaps even beneficial. Kaifeng will worry most over Mahabohdi. Possibly they will pull in outpost forces, and they will certainly concentrate efforts on erecting extra defenses. This leaves the district cities and their food production vulnerable. Long-term, we will have to be concerned with the possibility that Sarna has received notification of our attack and will manage to get reinforcements to Kaifeng sooner than planned."

"Don't worry about Sarna," Ty said, surprising Aris. What did Ty Wu Non know of Sarna that Aris did not? There was a moment's pause before Ty continued. "I've ordered our remaining fighter craft to concentrate on the heavier *Lightning*s, drawing them off. We will proceed on a hard drop."

A moment after Ty Wu Non gave the order, Terry Chan's voice came on, startling Aris. He thought he'd been speaking privately with Ty Wu Non. "Company Leader Sung," she said, addressing Aris formally. "With the new time constraints, I would recommend again that we split the company down into two-Mech elements for faster results."

A sudden burst of white-hot anger burned inside Aris, flushing his face with warmth. There was only one place Terry Chan could be in order to eavesdrop on this channel. "Lance Leader Chan," he said, giving his tone an unmistakable hard edge, "you were ordered to mount your BattleMech. You will remove yourself from this channel, from the bridge of the *Lao-tzu*, and follow those orders. If I hear a single word out of you before your *Cataphract* is powered up and ready, I will remove you from the order of battle and promote Justin Loup to command your lance."

That said, Aris forced himself back into calm and waited for either Terry Chan to test him or Ty Wu Non to undermine his authority by overriding Aris' right to discipline a member of his company.

Neither happened, and it suddenly disturbed Aris that he would actually expect such behavior from two members of his House.

After another pause, Ty Wu Non came back on the line. "Your bridge crew verifies that Terry Chan has left. Now, is her point valid, Company Leader Sung?"

"The arguments haven't changed, Battalion Commander. In my judgment, the time saved does not offset the increased risk of spreading ourselves so thin."

"Do you suggest any change to the plan at all then?"

It was obviously the prelude to ending communication, and Aris was about to say no, but then he smiled and nodded inside his cockpit. "Yes, Battalion Commander Non. I would suggest one alteration. Right now we're running under electronic blackout. I say we light up our DropShip IFF transponders, and let Kaifeng know exactly who we are. It should place them more on the defensive."

"I will order that done." Was that amusement in the voice of Ty Wu Non? "It appears the Kaifeng fighters have had enough for now. They're in retreat. We should have a clear run at the planet now.

"I'll see you on the ground, Aris Sung."

9

Jinxiang River Port Terminal 12 North
Tarrahause District, Kaifeng
Sarna Supremacy, Chaos March
20 July 3058

Port Terminal Twelve North spread out along the west bank of the Jinxiang River in a large half-circle, a maze of buildings surrounding the extensive system of docks. The golden, lotus-like flowers from which the Jinxiang took its name clustered in the shallows, sending their perfume into the air. A light wind blew in from the west, helping to stir up dust in between buildings. And the harsh sounds of battle hung over the facility as BattleMechs clashed.

"Mechs on the road," someone shouted over the main battle frequency. "Heavies. Sixty to seventy tons each."

"We have doors opening on the northeast storage vaults and a maintenance depot," said someone else, her voice calm. "A lance of medium 'Mechs. Damn. And Von Luckner heavy tanks. Two . . . six. No, eight total."

"Anyone see where that *Rifleman* went?"

Port Terminal Twelve North was a trap. The thought took a few long seconds to register with House Warrior Justin Loup, the sudden burst of near-frantic comm traffic so startling the young warrior that he couldn't act for a moment. No one had expected resistance. Not this soon.

Not a hundred and twenty klicks outside Tarrahause and on the first day!

The Hiritsu demi-company under Company Leader Sung's command had moved into the port terminal just as they had the two previous terminals, occupying critical positions and keeping obvious threats such as the warehouses covered. Justin's position had been the docks, the ferrocrete and timber constructions used to tie up and load the barges that transported rice and other crops down river to Tarrahause. The plan, which had worked well at the previous sites, called for 'Mechs to take control of the facility. Then Hiritsu infantrymen arrived in hovercraft to shut the place down. The easiest way was to wreck the machinery that brought the produce up from large underground storage vaults and then loaded up the large cargo holds of the barges. Without that, the food shipments could only be brought out and loaded in very small quantities.

The first enemy BattleMechs had come up from those underground vaults—light 'Mechs hitting hard and fast, throwing the House Hiritsu force into a moment's confusion while the heavier enemy units closed the trap. Now as the radio chatter continued—some worried, some calm—Justin Loup shook himself into action.

He walked his *Hatchetman* around a corner of the small dock warehouse that hid him from the rest of the facility. The 45-ton *Hatchetman* was one of only five such 'Mechs Justin knew of in the entire Capellan Confederation, this one a leftover from back in the late 3020s when Richard's Panzer Brigade came from the Lyran Commonwealth to serve House Liao. Justin's grandfather had been part of that mercenary unit, and had come to appreciate, if not love, his adopted nation. When Virginia York accepted Justin into her House, the old man had been so proud that he'd left the 'Mech to Justin rather than his elder grandsons, Justin's brothers, who both served in the Brigade.

Sensors screamed immediate warnings as soon as he left the sensor shadow thrown by the two-story building. Turning his back on the docks and barges he'd been ordered to secure, Justin looked out over the main loading yard. Warehouses and administration buildings ringed the hundred-meter expanse of hard-packed earth, forming what looked like a small arena within the heart of the port terminal. And standing along the far side, turning now to fully face him, was the top-heavy design of a 35-ton *Jenner*.

Justin caressed the main trigger on his right-hand control stick. His *Hatchetman*'s shoulder-mounted autocannon belched gray smoke and a tongue of fire, kicking its right shoulder back. Shells of depleted uranium sped across the open expanse of the loading yard to slam into the left side of the *Jenner*, rocking it sideways as they ripped through one of its stubby, wing-like arms. Justin quickly sidestepped back around the corner, hoping to draw the enemy 'Mech to him. He began a slow count to ten.

A cool killer. That was how Justin Loup normally thought of his *Hatchetman*. Fairly humanoid in appearance except for the trademark elongated head that it shared with its big brother 'Mech, the *Axman*, it carried a large titanium hatchet in its right hand that built up no heat and made the 'Mech a devastating in-fighter. For ranged combat it relied on its LB-X autocannon, again trading off heat for weight. Only the trio of medium pulse lasers and the *Hatchetman*'s jumping ability generated any concern about heat, but the double-strength heat sinks House Hiritsu technicians had installed quickly bled away any buildup. At times, Justin wondered if he could do away altogether with the cooling vest that all MechWarriors wore to survive the killing temperatures that could build up in their tiny cockpits.

His count had barely started when Aris Sung finally broke in on communications. "I want a confirmation on those tanks," he said. "Eight Von Luckners?" Justin could just make out the twinge of concern in his commander's voice. Mounting one of the most destructive weapons available, a large-bore autocannon, Von Luckner tanks were a threat to be reckoned with.

"Affirmative, Company Leader. And they're mercenary. I saw the crest much closer than I'd have liked. Looks like Jacob's Juggernauts. I'm pulling back out of range."

"I want *everyone* out of range," Aris said then. "Someone find us an exit path from the port terminal, *now*."

Justin kept up his silent count. Six Hiritsu warriors against a company were bad odds, not even counting the tanks. Von Luckners were at home in tight confines like the port terminal. No one faced eight 12-centimeter autocannons at close range, not without a death wish. Eight . . . nine . . .

On ten, Justin Loup raised his 'Mech's hatchet weapon high overhead and stepped out from around the corner. The *Jenner* was bearing down on him, not thirty meters away. The *Jenner* pilot's best course of attack would have been to continue his charge and try to slam into the *Hatchetman,* possibly pushing it completely off the docks and into the Jinxiang. The sight of the black and green-painted 'Mech, hatchet held high and ready to strike, was apparently too unnerving. The *Jenner* tried a last-minute change of course, firing off a barrage of six short-range missiles in an attempt to deter the *Hatchetman.*

The missiles pitted the *Hatchetman*'s legs and lower torso, throwing it into a violent tremble, but Justin was too conditioned a warrior to miss the opportunity. He stabbed the thumb-trigger for all three medium pulse lasers, and then brought down the hatchet. The emerald darts stitched their way up the *Jenner*'s side, melting armor over its left and center torso areas. Then the hatchet fell, its titanium edge smashing down and through the *Jenner*'s cockpit, cutting deep into the center torso.

The light 'Mech skidded first to its knees and then sprawled out full length as it tumbled past Justin and out onto the dock. Trailing sparks and gray dust over the ferrocrete surface, it shattered a wooden pylon and then slid head-first into the river, barely missing a low-lying barge. One leg remained draped up over the dock's edge while the upper half of the 'Mech sank underwater.

Justin opened a channel to Aris Sung. "Company Leader Sung, this is MechWarrior Loup. The docks are clear, no enemy. We could simply ford the river here and escape down the eastern bank."

Aris came back at once. "How wide is the river?"

Justin eyed the distance, not understanding why the question was important. It looked to be maybe a hundred fifty meters across, but he knew that the flat, slow-moving surface of the water would make him underestimate.

"Wide," he said. "Maybe two hundred meters. But I doubt it runs very deep. Barges are flat-bottomed, and I see no evidence of dredging."

Silence answered him. Justin stood at the corner of the warehouse, watching as BattleMechs further into the port terminal dodged among buildings and each other in a deadly game. Most were out of his range or appeared and disappeared too quickly for him to get weapons lock. He thought fleetingly about moving in toward the battle, but repressed the urge and forced himself to wait. *I have not been released from my position.* Aris Sung had assigned the docks to him, and right now they might be the only route to safety for the warriors of his House.

Someone yelled for support fire, cursing the Von Luckners. The call for help seemed to make up Aris' mind. "We'll chance it," he said finally. "All units converge on the docks. Set up defensive perimeter. Prepare to ford."

Nearly a quarter-kilometer distant, Justin saw the dark form of a 'Mech rise up above the warehouse rooftops on jets of plasma as it began to angle for his position. A quick glance at his heads-up display indicated that it was Aris' *Wraith.* With a grace that belied its 55 tons, the *Wraith* skimmed over rooftops and the loading yard to finally land with earth-shaking force sixty meters to Justin's left, with the small dock warehouse between them. Justin wasn't sure why Aris Sung was hesitant to ford the river. The *Wraith*'s jump radius would get him across easily, possibly even enough to clear the river without getting his 'Mech's feet wet.

Then Justin understood. Aris' BattleMech was the only one that had even a *chance* of crossing in a single jump. Justin's *Hatchetman* might clear a hundred meters, but then would hit the water and have to walk the rest of the way. And some BattleMechs couldn't jump at all. Wading across, slowed by the water and mud along the bottom, they'd become great target practice for any enemy 'Mechs left on the docks.

And Justin had suggested the route.

The responsibility settled down firmly on his shoulders with the weight of an *Atlas* as two House Hiritsu Battle-Mechs ran into view, followed by three APC hovercraft full of infantrymen. His brothers and sisters, all. Justin stepped aside to let the *Thunder* and *War Dog* pass. The APCs drove right between the legs of Aris' *Wraith*.

"Into the river," Aris ordered as the third APC flew past. The 'Mechs plunged in and began to walk. The first two APCs were already on the river, flying across the surface as easily as they would have solid ground.

Justin didn't have time to follow their progress. His *Hatchetman*'s sensors screamed for attention just an instant before his 'Mech was slammed sideways. He fought for control, the heavy neurohelmet he wore reading the signals from his own inner ear and feeding them to the *Hatchetman*'s large gyroscope, which sat just under the fusion engine. Working the control sticks, he used the 'Mech's arms to help adjust his balance while checking his damage schematic and heads-up display.

A *Rifleman* had broken cover far to the right, coming down the backside of a long, low warehouse. Its large lasers had cored into the *Hatchetman*'s right and center torso, sending armor to the ground in molten rivulets. Now the 60-ton 'Mech held its position and sniped at him, alternating between its two large lasers and its small autocannon. Even as Justin torso-twisted to bring his own autocannon in line, the *Rifleman* scored, shattering armor plates on his right torso and driving through to chip away at the ferrotitanium skeleton beneath. Several shots hit the physical shielding around his fusion reactor, opening a breach that sent his heat monitor soaring high into the yellow band.

Aris' *Wraith* sent a series of scarlet pulses toward the *Rifleman* while Justin thumb-selected cluster ammo for his autocannon, then stroked the main trigger and gave the *Rifleman* something to think about.

Cluster ammo, like the LB-X autocannon itself, was one of the rediscovered technologies that had been lost for so long in the wars following the collapse of the Star League. The ammo fragmented into submunitions shortly after leaving the barrel, working much like an anti-Mech shotgun. As Justin maneuvered his *Hatchetman* to make it a more difficult target, he watched through his viewscreen as the cluster submunitions chipped deeply into several locations on the *Rifleman* and scoured paint off the side of the warehouse behind it. He noticed with satisfaction that a few of the fragments struck the enemy 'Mech's head, which was guaranteed to shake up the pilot inside. The *Rifleman* withdrew behind the corner of the building, and Justin paused to see how things were going.

A fifth Hiritsu BattleMech was just entering the water, and the sixth, a *Blackjack,* held the dockside with Aris. Both it and the *Wraith* would lean out from behind opposite ends of the small dock warehouse, snapping off shots of red and green laser fire and then ducking back behind cover. Occasionally they took a hit, but more often the warehouses absorbed the punishment.

"Into the water, Justin." Aris' order came through just as the wall shattered in front of his *Wraith,* exploding outward in a rain of brick and metal that half-buried his 'Mech.

Justin moved quickly to Aris' side, exposing himself to scattered laser fire. His targeting computer painted threats onto his HUD. Four of the Von Luckner tanks held the opposite side of the loading yard, covering the approach of half a dozen BattleMechs, which were moving to flank the Hiritsu warriors. Grabbing the *Wraith* by one arm, Justin dragged it back into the cover of the warehouse. He knew what had to be done. Aris Sung would never abandon his people. He'd be the last one to cross, and with those damned Von Luckners closing he'd likely pay for it with his life.

Justin would not permit that to happen. He believed in Aris Sung, in his company leader's skill and in the plan he had crafted, which would see the House to victory on Kaifeng. "We have to get across," Justin said, positioning himself so that the *Wraith* was between him and the river.

"Someone has to guard the crossing," Aris replied, moving to return to his position at the dockside entrance. "Get into the water, Justin. Now!"

Conditioned obedience almost forced Justin away. You did not disobey a House superior; you did not even question those orders without invitation. But just as strong was his personal loyalty to his company leader and his fellow warriors. They would need Aris Sung more than they would ever need Justin Loup.

"Someone will," Justin said, though he wasn't sure

whether he said to himself or to Aris. Working the control sticks, he drew in his BattleMech's arms and then shoved the *Wraith* with all the strength the *Hatchetman's* my-omer muscles could give him. The *Wraith* stumbled backward, teetering at the edge of the dock. Then Aris surrendered to gravity and jumped into the river rather than tumble in.

Justin slammed down hard on his throttle pedals, engaging his jump jets before Aris could recover from the push. Rising on jets of plasma, he sailed over the *Blackjack* and toward the advancing mercenaries. He throttled the jump jet output and maneuvered the *Hatchetman* into a landing directly behind the advancing Von Luckners. *Sixty seconds,* he thought, calculating roughly how long it would take Aris' *Wraith* to wade across. *I only have to buy him a minute.*

He slammed his hatchet twice into the turret of the rear-most Von Luckner, caving it in before the others could even react to his presence. Then Justin was moving again, racing about the yard to make himself as difficult a target as possible. He moved in short bursts of speed, pivoting sometimes to run back the way he'd come but never staying still. And when possible, he struck out at any enemy unit in range.

On his first complete circuit of the open yard, he traded laser barrages with an enemy *Cicada* and staved in the side of a second Von Luckner with a kick.

On the second circuit he feathered his jump jets to take him to his far left, and with the hatchet cut off a *Jager-Mech's* left arm.

On his third pass he fired the jump jets again, this time landing directly behind the *Cicada* he'd damaged earlier and driving his hatchet through its weakly armored back and into its gyro housing. The light 'Mech dropped like an unstrung puppet.

Exhilaration coursed through Justin, goading him to greater acts. A burst from his autocannon and lasers savaged a third Von Luckner, and a swipe of his hatchet severely damaged an *Enforcer*. Justin was just beginning to think there might be some hope he would actually fight his way free. Another pass, he told himself. Maybe two. Then into the river and away.

The AC/20 fire caught his *Hatchetman* in its already damaged right leg, severing it at the knee and dropping the hapless 'Mech onto its side. Justin was thrown roughly against the restraining straps of his command couch, the edges of the wide belts cutting into his shoulders and waist as he was wrenched about.

He tasted blood in his mouth, and a sharp pain in his left shoulder promised a dislocation or possibly a broken bone. His primary monitors were out, showing either dark or snow-filled screens. His damage schematic still functioned, listing a wrecked autocannon, missing leg, and a fusion reactor encased by shielding now more myth than fact. He rolled his 'Mech slightly forward and half rose by propping one arm underneath. He shook his head slightly, trying to clear his mind. Through his viewscreen he studied the scene and hung onto a coal of resistance.

Two Von Luckners were closing now, autocannons ready. The *JagerMech* had already passed him, heading for the river's edge, and the *Enforcer* was in the process of doing the same. That they so easily dismissed a warrior of House Hiritsu who still possessed at least a partially functioning 'Mech angered Justin and fanned that coal into flame. The *Rifleman* from earlier already stood at the edge of the docks, perhaps forty meters away, firing its autocannon repeatedly out over the river. That Aris was still in danger snapped Justin fully back to awareness.

There was a final service to perform.

He steadied himself with his other arm, its hatchet impotent against the ground. He couldn't reach the *Rifleman* with any weapon better than a medium laser, but his *Hatchetman* had one final trick left to it. Justin overrode his cockpit stabilizers and then punched the ejection controls.

The *Hatchetman* had one other distinctive feature over most BattleMechs in that it did not eject the command couch through a special blast-away panel in the cockpit ceiling. Instead, it detached the entire head on liquid propellant thrusters. With the stabilizers overridden, control was left entirely to Justin. Jaw clenched and lips skinned back against the G-forces pushing him down into his seat, he worked to keep the assembly sailing nose-down and on a straight course toward the back of the *Rifleman* and its infamous paper-thin rear armor. All he could see was the ground rushing by his cockpit viewscreen, and had to work mostly by instinct.

That was enough.

The impact came with a satisfying crunch of armor plates being crushed. The head assembly of the *Hatchet-man* began a lazy spin as Justin lost control, arcing into the air and then straight for the wall of a dockside warehouse. *Loupin'*, he thought with a sickening rush of cheer, the outside world spinning—looping—by faster as his head assembly finished its short-lived flight. One of the last things he saw through his viewscreen before the expanse of brick and steel filled it was the *Rifleman,* toppling forward into the river with fiery chunks of metal spilling out its back from a fusion reactor overload.

Justin laughed out loud, his voice strong and confident in his own ears. It had been the will of the House Master to take Kaifeng. Aris Sung was essential to that plan. If Justin saved Aris, that made him also essential to his House.

What more was there?

10

Jinxiang Jungle
Tarrahause District, Kaifeng
Sarna Supremacy, Chaos March
20 July 3058

Aris Sung stood on the edge of the river bank, dividing his attention between study of the river and the early afternoon sky. City-born and raised on the streets, Aris found communing with the natural world among his least-favorite things in the galaxy. For him, nature meant little more than bitter wind-chill or heat stroke—something to be avoided. Now, on Kaifeng, it could become an important part of the mission.

The river was wide and slow-moving, clear near the bank but becoming murky within twenty meters of shore. Flowing roughly northeast to southwest, it connected the city of Tarrahause to its largest rice-producing plantations. Kaifeng's moon, Nochen, produced only the smallest lunar tides, so river depth rarely varied. The Jinxiang fed into a large saltwater ocean several hundred kilometers south of Tarrahause. From his recent experience in escaping from Port Terminal 12, Aris knew that in places the river could run at least as deep as twelve meters.

Now he lifted his eyes to the heavens once more. Large, light gray clouds drifted across the late afternoon sky, creating shadows that chilled him, dressed as he was only in a MechWarrior's shorts, cooling vest, and steel-toed boots. It might have been any cool summer afternoon. But darker clouds were drifting in from the west, threatening heavy rains. Rain would turn much of the land they needed to traverse into a soupy mire. That would be a problem, but Aris had no idea how to predict or circumvent it.

"Company Leader Sung?"

He recognized the voice of Raven Clearwater as much for its huskiness as for her perfect courtesy. Her salutation alerted him well enough in advance that her approach would not startle him, yet was pitched low enough as not to be a shout. And he also recognized just the touch of a question in her tone as a way of requesting audience. Aris, too, had studied and learned the House traditions regarding courtesy, and sincerely attempted to honor them, but he knew he would never master their subtlety the way Raven had.

"Yes, Lance Leader Clearwater." He turned from the river after a final cursory glance up and downstream, checking that the APCs were still in place and on guard against any more surprises.

Accompanying Raven Clearwater, though trying to maintain an extra half-step lead, was Terry Chan. Raven's long, straight black hair framed the dark skin and chiseled features of the Navajo heritage she'd left behind in her devotion to House Hiritsu. Terry Chan's skin seemed yellow—even jaundiced—in comparison, her dark hair shorter, finer, and with some curl at the ends. How different were these two women, Aris thought, noticing how Terry Chan's arrogant stride seemed to say she felt superior to the world around her.

"The *Blackjack*'s flooded sections have been drained and repaired to the best of our field ability," Lance Leader Chan said without preamble. "It has lost complete mobility in the right arm, but we managed to save the laser."

Raven Clearwater spoke up after a polite pause. "MechWarrior Lewis locked the arm at a ninety-degree angle, so the laser can still be used in battle."

Aris peered back into the tall, vine-shrouded trees from which the two women had emerged. He could just make out his *Wraith*. The other BattleMechs of his company were hidden further in, taking cover in the kilometer-wide belt of jungle that bordered the river at this point. The Kaifeng government had left such stands at frequent intervals, not wanting to seriously unbalance the planet's ecology. But it also provided the House Hiritsu warriors with reasonably safe hiding places. "So we're ready to move out?"

Terry Chan nodded. "Eleven 'Mechs functional and ready to deploy," she said, her expression carefully neutral as she reminded Aris that he'd just lost a warrior.

Aris was too experienced in minding his own composure to make any sign that her barb had struck home, though inwardly he winced. Justin Loup had traded his life to assure the safety of his company leader and the other House warriors. His sacrifice had bought them precious seconds in which to cross the river. Justin had managed a good accounting of himself, but they'd had to fish the *Rifleman* from the river. Aris credited Loup with kills against three heavy tanks and two BattleMechs. A fine last stand.

But now Justin was dead and House Hiritsu had lost his courage and strength because Aris had walked his people into a trap. He had apparently underestimated the Kaifeng military leaders from the start. They'd been waiting for him at Nochen, and then again at the port terminal. Aris was sure Ty Wu Non would have something to say about that. Well, the next time it would be Aris sitting in wait while Kaifeng forces walked into a battle of his choosing. The enemy had made a mistake, and he planned to exploit it.

"Order our warriors powered-up and ready to deploy," he said. "We move immediately on Tarrahause."

Both women looked surprised, but only Terry Chan spoke up in challenge. "Tarrahause? You're abandoning the plan?"

The same charge Aris had repeatedly wanted to make against Ty Wu Non. It felt strange, being on the receiving end. "The plan has always been to draw the defenders out of the city, to where we could deal with them more easily and then take the city without obstacle," he said. "We've accomplished this. Tarrahause has already sent out a full company supported by armor to stop us. How much more can they have as a garrison force? We move against the city now, before the mercenaries can catch up."

Raven glanced out across the river, at the road bordering the length of the Jinxiang and which would eventually run into Tarrahause some eight kilometers downstream. She voiced her thoughts aloud, as if trying to organize them, but Aris wondered if she was trying to speak up in support of her company leader without directly challenging Terry Chan. "We can be sure that they haven't returned because the road across the river is the fastest route back and they haven't passed. Any other path and we can outdistance them."

Aris nodded. "There's a similar road on this side of the river about another ten klicks downstream. That will allow us to move faster. Also, I contacted the *Lao-tzu*. There's been no indication of DropShip activity, so the mercenaries are on foot."

"But we haven't defeated the garrison force." Terry Chan's tone was barely respectful.

"The primary goal of the assault does not call for their elimination," Aris said calmly. "It calls for stopping the flow of food to Sarna and the capture of Kaifeng. By taking Tarrahause now, we can shut down the entire district. That will put us into an improved position when the mercenaries try to retake the city."

"Did you pass along your new *interpretation* of plans to Battalion Commander Non?" Terry Chan asked, not masking her hostility.

"He was unavailable. Kaifeng SMM supported by mercenaries are holding him out of Beijing. He had to dispatch his DropShip to deal with the surviving aerospace fighters so he's temporarily outside communications range. In fact, only Company Leader Lindell seems to be having an easy time of it with Franklin down in the southern hemisphere."

Terry Chan crossed her arms defiantly, though she was phrasing her words with obvious care. "Battalion Commander Non might consider it premature to strike at Tarrahause with enemy forces in our rear. If we stay at company strength, we could continue to shut down port terminals all along the river. And if the mercenaries come at us again, we'd have the force necessary to crush them."

Aris felt his anger building at Terry Chan's lack of support. First she wanted to break down into units smaller than the plan called for, and now she was arguing to go for company strength. He'd ignored her animosity when they were on equal footing within the House, but that could not be allowed to continue. Had she no respect for the traditions, if nothing else?

"That would slow us down." He tried to be patient. "And with the mercenaries already in the field, what you suggest gives them too much room to maneuver against us. But if we take Tarrahause, it forces them back into a narrow field of operations. It's the same plan, only put into effect from a different direction."

"Better a known enemy in an open environment."

If Aris said the Kaifeng sky was blue Terry Chan would argue. He felt his muscles tightening, drawing the tension across his shoulders like a cloak. "Lance Leader Clearwater, please pass my orders to the company. But tell MechWarrior McDaniels I would like to see her before she powers up."

"Of course, Company Leader Sung." Raven Clearwater turned smartly on her heel as if she sensed nothing of the tension hanging between the two Hiritsu officers.

Aris watched the various expressions that seemed to war on Terry Chan's face. First hostility and then suspicion and finally concern. After Justin Loup, Jill McDaniels was the most accomplished MechWarrior in the company and likely the next in line for position as a lance leader. Terry Chan was probably wondering if he planned to follow through on his earlier threat to replace her.

"MechWarrior McDaniels is a member of my lance, Company Leader."

Aris stood there, watching the river and letting her worry. After the aggravation, studying the calm flow of the river—the swirls and eddies, the slow, majestic force of it—actually soothed him.

"If you have orders, they should be passed through me."

Aris gave her a long, appraising glance, noticing the

slight tic at the edge of her left eye that betrayed her nervousness. "Perhaps I *should* discuss something with you, Terry Chan."

"Yes, Company Leader?"

Amazing what the implied threat of demotion did for her level of courtesy. "Chan, I know you do not like me. It does not matter whether that is due to my history, my methods of command, or my general personality. I do not care one way or another. You do not have to like me, but you will respect my position." *Or I will find someone who will,* he did not say. The look on her face told him he didn't have to.

"Of course, Company Leader Sung."

He nodded. "Dismissed."

She paused, as if trying to word her next statement carefully. "I will see that MechWarrior McDaniels is sent to you at once."

A good way to bring the subject back up without seeming too persistent. Aris relented slightly, hoping she would see it as a gesture of good will. "Thank you. I have heard good reports from Raven Clearwater and others. I thought a personal note of praise was in order."

"Yes. Of course." Terry Chan nodded once and backed away respectfully, then turned and walked briskly for the treeline.

Aris sighed. He doubted that he'd solved the problem, but he'd gotten her thinking and maybe that would correct her attitude for now. In the meantime, Tarrahause lay ahead of him and he had better start devoting more time to the enemy than he was to these petty struggles. He picked up a rock and side-armed it out into the river, watching as it skipped across the flat surface and finally sank from sight.

It only occurred to him then how much he had sounded like Ty Wu Non when giving Terry Chan her dressing-down. He wasn't sure if he liked that.

11

Three kilometers upriver from Tarrahause, the Jinxiang straightened into roughly an east-west course as it cut through the Shé Shan, or Serpent, Hills. On the north bank the thin line of rolling hills turned to follow the river west for more than two kilometers, their green-shrouded, rolling peaks and valley reminding travelers of the way a serpent moved across the ground. On the south bank the hills trailed off south and then southeast in a sort of atrophied Z formation. A causeway-type bridge crossed the Jinxiang, raised just high enough for barges to pass beneath. The river flowed swiftly, restricted to less than two hundred meters by the framing hills, making the bridge the safest path for BattleMechs to cross.

And a good spot for an ambush.

Strapped into the command couch of his BJ2-O *Blackjack,* Major Karl Bartlett raised binoculars to his eyes. Peering through his cockpit viewscreen and an opening left in the camouflage, he scanned the southern bank for 'Mech activity. Major Bartlett commanded Third Company of the Kaifeng SMM. All twelve of his 'Mechs currently stood behind carefully constructed blinds on the north bank, running at low power and waiting in ambush for House Hiritsu. His spotters up in the Shé Shan Hills had reported the invaders within two kilometers. And Jacob's Juggernauts had picked up the Capellan trail and would soon be pressuring them from behind. It couldn't be long now, he thought. *Then maybe I'll show Cyndi Fallon how to properly stop an invasion.*

Leftenant General Cynthia Fallon had assigned Third Company to Tarrahause three days before, in anticipation of the House Hiritsu assault. She had also dispatched the mercenaries into the outlying regions, to soften up the invaders and keep them unbalanced. Her strategy demanded a series of limited engagements.

"Cut into their numbers," she'd said. "Always let them withdraw. We don't force an all-or-nothing confrontation until Sarna can reinforce us." From the way she was talking, it sounded like Sarna troops wouldn't be arriving anytime soon, which was strange. And then this morning Fallon had also passed along a list of primary targets, by 'Mech design.

Bartlett hated having his tactics dictated to him, and to tell him which BattleMechs he should and should not target was especially galling. In the heat of combat a MechWarrior shouldn't have to question whether an enemy 'Mech was on some list or not. Battle was fast and furious, and trying to micromanage was a recipe for disaster.

But Fallon was playing this cautious—scared was Bartlett's word for it—concerned about facing Capellan Warrior House troops. She wanted to keep her intelligence sources happy and the information rolling in, all the while trying to buy time. As far as Bartlett was concerned, you exploited every opening an enemy gave you. Which was exactly what he planned to do and the general's orders be damned. It was hard to court-martial a hero.

Movement caught his attention, and Bartlett refocused his binoculars. Across the Jinxiang and very near the southern head of the bridge, approximately a company of BattleMechs had emerged from the light jungle that bordered the southern riverbank. The 'Mechs trailed vines and branches and were plastered with large, wet leaves. The left torso of each was painted black with a pattern that looked like a piece of the night sky. A radiant white katana was set over the left breast, its curved length like a crescent moon.

House Hiritsu.

Bartlett counted eleven BattleMechs. That confirmed what he knew of the company under Aris Sung. Then he saw the *Wraith* that supposedly belonged to the Capellan company leader striding toward the bridge. *Soon now.* Bartlett switched an auxiliary monitor to weapons availability, checking his 'Mech's configuration for the twentieth time. His *Blackjack* was one of two Inner Sphere OmniMechs in service with the Kaifeng SMM battalion, assigned to them for testing when the unit was still part of the Federated Commonwealth. Bartlett was extremely proud of it, though still a bit uncomfortable with the modular weapons pods.

With two 80mm LB-X autocannons for arms, he could hit the middle of the bridge with either normal or special cluster ammunition. A very handy capability, which he would use to its fullest capabilities. He tied both autocannons into his Target Interlock Circuit, so his main trigger would fire both weapons simultaneously.

"Come to me," he whispered.

The bridge was narrow but heavily reinforced. Aris hated it from the moment he saw it. They would only be able to cross single file, and forward 'Mechs would clutter up the fire lanes of those behind. He assigned Terry Chan and her Fire Lance to the lead, wanting the heavier 'Mechs across first in order to establish a solid presence on the far bank as soon as possible. He led Forward Lance—now down to three medium BattleMechs since the loss of Justin Loup—onto the structure next. Raven Clearwater and her Support Lance of mediums brought up the rear. Aris was halfway across when Chan's *Cataphract* set its massive metal foot on the northern bank.

Then his sensors screamed a shrill warning as four Battle-Mechs suddenly broke from the jungle three-quarters of a kilometer to the north and began to close on the bridge, weapons firing.

Aris' *Wraith* rocked under the impact of autocannon cluster munitions, a few of the fragments striking his cockpit and jostling him hard against the command couch's restraining straps. Fortunately the *Wraith*'s design absorbed much of the impact, leaving Aris with only a slight ringing in his ears. A ringing that was quickly drowned out by rapid, pulsing tones warning of a missile lock on his machine. Through his viewscreen, Aris could see the trails of white smoke arcing out from the long-range missile pack of a *Shadow Hawk*.

It took him less than a second to react. Pinned to the bridge, there wasn't much he could do to maneuver. His own lance blocked any rearward movement. Yan Lu's 70-ton *Thunder* had paused at the head of the bridge to fire off its heavy autocannon, giving Aris only a scant seventy-five meters or so in front of him. Not enough to evade missiles. He could step off the side of the bridge, taking cover in the Jinxiang but abandoning his company. Unacceptable.

Aris slammed his feet down hard on the *Wraith*'s pedals. So hard that he shoved the rod that normally pivoted forward or back to control direction of movement and speed down to the floor, where it hit a limit switch. The BattleMech's computer overrode the normal throttle commands and shunted plasma from the fusion engine through to the jump jets in the *Wraith*'s back.

The 55-ton 'Mech rose into the air on fiery plumes, jumping out of the missiles' path and arcing toward the north bank and battle. While still in the air, Aris snapped off a quick shot from his large pulse laser. He was rewarded with a solid hit against the *Shadow Hawk*'s right torso. Armor melted and ran under the scarlet beam. Not enough to penetrate, but Aris hoped that it would give the mercenary something to think about.

He didn't realize his error until after the *Wraith* landed on the northern bank. Aris had assumed the enemy warriors were mercenary. The four 'Mechs were of medium weight—his computer had tagged them as a *Blackjack,* two *Lineholder*s, and the *Shadow Hawk*. He had a fair idea of the enemy's full strength on Kaifeng, and it made sense to him that this would be an auxiliary lance of the merc company they'd already met, held in reserve in case the initial assault failed. Both were painted the dark and light greens of jungle camouflage, and it was a division of troops that Aris might have made under similar circumstances.

The enemy *Blackjack* changed his mind.

*Blackjack*s were 45-ton machines with a very distinctive outline. Turret-style shoulders and torso, and two large lasers in place of the usual blocky arms. This 'Mech was larger and possessed a blocky, compact outline. The large-bore barrels on each arm could only be 80mm autocannon.

Modular! The word screamed out in Aris' mind as he glanced at his tactical display. The proof was painted right next to the red triangle that designated an enemy 'Mech. Not a BJ-2, as he'd thought. A BJ2-*O*. Omni-Mech. One of the Inner Sphere versions of the advanced technology of the invading Clans.

The presence of this machine did not match the profile of the mercenaries they'd engaged back at Port Terminal 12, those 'Mechs had a more standard design and technology. Not even House Hiritsu had been assigned Omnis yet, though the Warrior House's TO&E did list a good percentage of topnotch 'Mech designs that were virtually hot off the drawing board.

Riding out a few laser hits, Aris punched up a video image of the *Blackjack* on his primary monitor and increased the magnification. There was the clinching evidence, emblazoned across the upper right leg. Three four-pointed stars arranged in a lopsided triangle against a red shield—the emblem of the Sarna Supremacy.

Lance Leader Chan obviously came to the same conclusion as Aris. He could make out the frustration and anger in her voice even over the commline. "Aris, these are SMM troops!" The way her transmissions bled over those of other Hiritsu warriors trying to communicate told Aris she wasn't using her private channel to him. "You walked us into an ambush. I warned you—"

Aris couldn't let that kind of insubordination pass unchallenged. Not over general frequencies. He cut her off. "Lance Leader Chan, you will restrain yourself right now!"

He pivoted the *Wraith* to the right and raced out from the river bank at an oblique angle to the enemy 'Mechs, relying on his greater speed as defense. If he could worry the enemy flank, his heavier machines near the bridge-head would have an easier time rolling over the SMM lance. The Hiritsu warriors still held the advantage. "Concentrate fire on that *Blackjack*," he ordered. The Omni had to be the lance commander. "Support and Forward Lances move across at best speed. Fire Lance move forward and engage."

A half-dozen LRMs peppered the *Wraith*'s right thigh, while autocannon fire and at least another dozen missiles streaked by in near misses. Aris pivoted again, this time to the left, now racing in to directly intercept the *Shadow Hawk*. He had placed the *Hawk* between him and the rest of the Kaifeng 'Mechs, and now he hoped to move inside the effective range of its long-range missiles before they could cycle again.

At two hundred meters he fired off his large pulse and pair of mediums, the scarlet beams all tracking in on their target and shaving more of the *Hawk*'s protective armor off its leg and right torso. A wave of heat washed over Aris, the result of his BattleMech's fusion engine spiking hard in order to provide enough energy to power all three weapons at once. The heat wash stole moisture from his eyes and mouth, and drew sweat all across his body. Aris blinked away the momentary blur to his vision, and then licked salty residue from his lips. Another shot into the *Shadow Hawk*'s right torso and he'd be chewing away at its internal structure. The place where its missile ammunition was stored. Aris grinned, already envisioning the kill.

More warning screams from his sensors and several hard jolts to his *Wraith*'s right side left Aris fighting for control of his 'Mech and wondering what the hell had just happened. He wrestled with the control sticks, trying to use his arms for leverage, while the neurohelmet all MechWarriors wore transmitted signals from his inner ear to the heavy gyroscope located in his *Wraith*'s torso. He managed to avoid a fall, while a quick glance to his damage schematic told him that he'd lost roughly a ton and a half of armor from his right side. No breeches, but a few red areas told him that several spots were close to it.

The HUD was alive with enemy 'Mechs. His computer painted another four red triangles on the tactical screen. Then another four. Aris swung around to put his back to the river and rocked back on the throttles, walking his *Wraith* backward from the threat. The ground where he'd just stood was now pocked and scorched and smoking from missed shots. He suddenly felt very lucky that he'd lost only the armor he did.

Two lances of Kaifeng BattleMechs poured from the jungle. As Aris watched through the viewscreen, missile-carrying BattleMechs like the *Shadow Hawk* and a newly arrived *Orion* launched a wave of missiles that arced out and fell onto the bridge. Those with direct-fire weapons leveled them in his direction. Aris slammed down on his throttles again. Forgotten was the *Shadow Hawk* and its weakened right torso. Right now he only wanted to put as much distance as possible between his *Wraith* and the attacking SMM company before their concentrated fire left his machine a burned-out husk.

"Thunders on the bridge," someone called over the communications net. "Say again, Thunder mines on the bridge."

Aris had just reached the apex of his jump and was beginning to angle for a landing near the northern head of the bridge. He cursed as the news registered. Thunders were special LRM munitions. They detonated over ground, dropping hundreds of small bomblets that effectively mined an area. As the *Hawk* and the *Orion* launched a new wave of missiles, he knew that those, too, would fall on the bridge. They were trying to cut off escape.

Fire Lance was falling back now under the threat of facing an entire company. Aris' Forward Lance was clustered up along the northern run of the bridge. Raven Clearwater and her people were still spread out over the entire bridge span. *And the longer we sit here, the better their chances of sealing us in.* Aris bit down on his lower lip hard enough to draw blood. It was the second time in as many days that he would be ordering a retreat. But he could recognize a losing scenario when he saw it. The Kaifeng commander had stolen the initiative, and Aris was not about to gamble the lives of House Hiritsu warriors to satisfy his own personal desire for glory. He'd already lost one of his. He wouldn't lost another.

Aris opened a general line to the company. "Fall back.

Repeat, fall back to southern bank. Jumping 'Mechs take to the air. Everyone else watch the Thunders as best you can. Fire Lance break off now. Yan Lu, take rear guard. You'll have to walk backward in order to keep your good armor toward them."

Yan's *Thunder* had the best armor of any of Aris' Battle-Mechs. It could sustain hits from Thunder munitions better than anyone else. And the machine's autocannon would keep the SMM 'Mechs from following too closely.

His defense laid as best he could, Aris pivoted his *Wraith* and ran to the edge of the riverbank. At a stretch, the 'Mech could jump just over two hundred meters. *It's gonna be close,* he thought, triggering his jump jets for the third time this battle and angling for the far shore.

He never made it.

Rising steadily into the air, Aris looked out the viewscreen as his people crossed back to the southern shore.

"Once we're across, we blow the bridge," he said. That would force the Kaifeng troops to follow with jump-capable machines only, or else have half their 'Mechs wade over, making them easy targets for his warriors.

"Lance Leader Clearwater, establish a defensive perimeter on the south bank." That was the last command he was able to give. From the fighting on the north bank, a blue-white PPC beam of particles and energy reached out after his 'Mech and caught him a hundred meters from shore. The PPC fire cored into his rear right torso, the weak rear armor disintegrating as the beam carved away at the endo-steel of his internal skeleton. It also ruined two of his three jump jets mounted in that location.

Fifty-five tons of metal and myomer fly about as well as anyone might expect. Suddenly losing half its capability, in the middle of a jump, was more than a match for the *Wraith*'s gyro. The 'Mech pitched over violently to the right, unable to regain its balance. Aris fought the controls the entire way, but there was no correcting it.

The *Wraith* skimmed low over the bridge, barely missing Richard Smith's *Vindicator,* and then slammed into the river fifty meters downstream of the bridge. The impact threw Aris forward, his restraining straps digging into his shoulders and abdomen, and then bounced him repeatedly against the back of his command couch.

Sometime before the *Wraith* hit the bottom of the river, Aris Sung finally blacked out.

12

Aris entered quietly through the open window. He cut himself free of the rappelling line and stepped down onto the hardwood floor. His target, one Captain James Luange, sat at his desk just steps away, his back to the window. Aris kept his breathing light and forced himself not to swallow against the dryness in his mouth. A swallow could be heard. From inside the right cuff of his tight-fitting sweater he pulled a length of thin wire, a metal peg the size of his finger fastened to one end and a metal ring on the other. By slipping the peg through the ring he formed the garrote into its deadly loop. Now all he had to do was throw the loop over the victim's neck and pull tight on the peg. Aris had already killed this man exactly this way once before.

He didn't expect a problem the second time.

A strong arm slid around Aris' chest from behind, enveloping him in a bear hug. Then another hand clamped itself over his mouth and nose, and he couldn't breathe. *Came in through the window, just as I did.* The thought paraded through his mind has he struggled against the encircling grip that seemed as strong as a steel band. This hadn't happened before. Something was very wrong here.

No one—no one not a member of House Hiritsu—should have known he was coming.

Aris' vision began to swim, blurring his view of the office. The room dimmed but for a few hazy patches of light. His chest burned from a lack of air and he felt his muscles going numb. He tried to grab hold of the other's hand, the one that remained pressed into the center of his chest, but had trouble getting a grip on it. Frantically, he slapped and clawed at it, trying to find some purchase. Then he was falling forward. His right shoulder was wrenched around, still in the other's grip, but the hand did fall away from his face and he could breathe.

Barely.

Aris woke to find himself hanging from his right-side restraining straps, dangling over his cockpit controls. The view his viewscreen was pitch black. He tried to suck in a deep breath of air, and felt a burning sensation grab at his lungs. *I'm in the river,* he realized. *And using up the last of my air.*

Even though the haze that was slowly burning away but still clouded his thoughts, Aris understood what had happened. He'd been knocked unconscious when the *Wraith* had slammed into the Jinxiang River, and now his cockpit viewscreen was face down in the river's muddy bottom. How long he'd been out he wasn't sure. *Long enough to use up most of my air, though, even with recyclers still scrubbing it.* The air recirc system that constantly drew in fresh air from the outside—properly filtered, of course—had shut down automatically on entering the water and he hadn't been able to activate his backup air supply.

Then the strange dream he'd had before coming to. The difficulty with breathing. And the pressure against his chest, which had been him dangling from the restraining straps. Somehow, when he'd clawed at the "hand" pressing into his chest, he must have actually hit the left-side release of his harness' quick-release buckle. And something else . . . Something important that he couldn't recall now . . .

Setting his feet on the edge of his control panel, Aris quickly released his right-side restraints and then unfastened his neurohelmet. With a quick pull he yanked the sensor pads away from his thighs and chest. Then he disconnected his cooling vest from its coolant supply tube and was finally able to move about freely.

With the cockpit turned on its face, so to speak, it took Aris a second to coordinate his thoughts and locate the air-supply valve. Twisting the first ball valve ninety degrees reopened the air recirc system on its underwater setting. The second valve started the fresh air bleeding into the cockpit at a controlled rate from tanks of compressed air stored in the 'Mech's torso. Aris dialed this one up for a few minutes, flushing out the stale air of the cockpit before returning it to the constant feed-and-bleed routine that could support him for several hours if need be.

BattleMechs weren't originally designed for underwater use, but they *were* designed for limited operations in vacuum and harsh atmosphere environments, and the same principles applied. A MechWarrior depended on the BattleMech's armor to maintain air integrity, and a built-in air reserve system and the normal recyclers provided a breathable atmosphere in the cockpit. Regulated through the computer, that air could keep a warrior alive and well for some time. Also, in case a warrior wanted to don an environmental suit and venture outside, there was a built-in safety margin that would allow the cockpit to be vented to vacuum and repressurized twice.

Underwater, a warrior had a few more concerns. For one thing, loss of integrity could be a problem in any location, not just the cockpit. Aris crouched over his control panel and began to check systems. His luck held; the 'Mech had maintained complete hull integrity. Next was to decide on a course of action, which brought up a second problem with underwater operations—there was no way to tell what was going on above him.

According to the computer, he'd been on the river bottom for over three hours. Early evening. His last order to the company had been to fall back into the jungle. Terry Chan would certainly have taken control of the company soon after, but how she would have played out the situation from there was beyond Aris. He remembered the tactical situation, and felt sure that she would have withdrawn. Maybe they would have held the southern bridgehead for a few minutes, waiting for him, but certainly not for an hour. Not with the mercenary force unaccounted for and a full company of the Kaifeng SMM holding the northern bank.

That raised another question. What had happened to the Kaifeng SMM company? If they'd followed Terry Chan and the rest of his warriors, the two sides might be in the middle of a battle thirty kilometers away by now. If they hadn't, they could be standing up on the bridge or along the riverbanks. Perhaps even searching for him. He didn't dare try to break the surface here. He'd have to move downstream at least a half kilometer or so before trying.

Better a full kilometer.

Even better, two.

Aris put his neurohelmet back on and carefully worked his *Wraith* into the middle of the river where he could stand up without fear of being spotted from the bank. Strapping himself back into his command couch, he began the slow and arduous task of walking down river. Along the way he placed his air recycler under strict computer regulation.

The journey gave him time to think. Walking two kilometers through murky water—paying particular attention to staying in the deepest part of the river and moving slowly enough that he didn't disturb the surface—took him nearly forty-five minutes. By then Aris realized his unique position. He was fit. His *Wraith* had suffered only light damage, the destruction of two jump jets notwithstanding. *And he was behind enemy lines.* It reminded him of Gei-fu, when that *Stinger* had positioned itself to do great harm to House Hiritsu and been stopped only by Aris' bluff. One 'Mech showing up where the enemy least expected it could be decisive. Why hadn't they thought of this before, walking the entire company into Tarrahause underwater?

In the end, Aris' indecision made the difference. He couldn't say for sure whether Ty Wu Non would want him to rejoin his company. It was just as likely that his commander might order him to maintain his position near

Tarrahause. So the only answer was to secure his *Wraith* in a hiding place and then attempt to contact the battalion commander.

And why secure the Wraith *near Tarrahause,* he suddenly thought, *when I can place it in Tarrahause?*

13

K'ung-fu-tzu Park, Tarrahause
Tarrahause District, Kaifeng
Sarna Supremacy, Chaos March
20 July 3058

K'ung-fu-tzu Park was popular in the early evening. Shaded from Kaifeng's sun by the park's tall, leafy trees, people lounged on the wood-slat benches or strolled along the gravel paths. Along the southern side, a two-lane road separated the park from the sandy beaches of Lake Ch'u Yuan. The crosswalks were busy with those heading lakeside for a picnic dinner and those returning from an afternoon at the beach.

Li Wynn stood near the park's southern border, leaning up against one of the evergreens. Its rough bark scratched at the young man's right shoulder through his light cotton shirt. He pretended to stretch and enjoy the cool breeze that blew in off the lake. Every few seconds his eyes flicked left and then right as he habitually searched for marks. And the Djing-cha, the Kaifeng police. Already it had been a profitable day: three wallets and a camera left on towels along the shore of Ch'u Yuan. Profitable enough that he'd taken time off his work to satisfy a twinge of curiosity.

Why does a man go swimming in the lake, but not bring along towel or sandals?

Li was, by nature, observant. You had to be in his line of work, unless you wanted to get pinched. He had noticed the other man stumbling from the water as if tired from a long day of swimming. He looked older than Li by perhaps five years, making him twenty-four or twenty-five. Asian, and very fit. A quick shake of the head, flinging away the excess water that clung to his shoulder-length black hair, and the man strolled off the beach as if in no particular hurry. Just like any number of others. Except all he wore were shorts. Missing were the sunglasses and beach towel. No shirt or sunscreen. Not even a pair of thongs to protect his feet from the hot sand or, a few minutes later, the hot sidewalk.

Now the man rested on one of the park benches, doing a bit of girl-watching, as if nothing could be more natural. Except Li couldn't see anyone else who strolled the gravel paths barefoot. It bothered Li, like he'd overlooked something obvious.

The man had developed an interest in a passing redhead. She too was fresh off the beach, wearing a sarong and bikini and carrying a net bag casually over her shoulder. She passed by the bench, seemingly oblivious to the man who swiveled around to follow her progress. There was a moment when Li thought the stranger might get up and go after her, followed by a pursed-lip expression that spoke of second thoughts, and finally a nod of resolution as the man rose quickly from the bench with his goal in sight.

Only to collide with another couple who by this time were passing the bench seat.

There followed an exchange that Li could only assume was the standard round of apologies. The man gestured up the path at what had been the object of his attention. Li smiled to see the quick flash of disappointment as he realized the redhead had vanished down one of the side paths. A final gesture of apology, and the man sank back down onto his seat with slumped shoulders. The couple linked arms again, the female smiling her sympathy to the seated man, and continued on their way.

The man was still shaking his head in disappointment. Then he rose again, more careful this time, and began to walk along behind the couple. A moment later he turned up a side path, a purposeful movement to his stride as if he might yet catch up to the object of his desire.

Li shrugged. There didn't seem to be much else involved in this game. He took sunglasses out of his shirt pocket and slid them on, then shoved himself away from the tree. Gravel crunched under his sneakers—when you might have to run, better to be wearing something with a little more protection than sandals. He walked past the bench where the man had been sitting, noticing the damp mark against the wood from the other man's wet shorts.

"Djing-cha!"

Li Wynn started at the yell, instinctively seeking the fastest path of escape and searching for the source of the call. He saw the young couple from a moment before, the man pulling his girlfriend along by the hand as he raced back along the path toward the bench. "You," he yelled, pointing at Li. "Did you see a man sitting here? Asian? Wearing shorts?"

Li forced a calm over himself. He'd nearly bolted when pointed at. Now that people all around were beginning to take notice, the odds were better for talking his way out than for flight. "Yes," he said. *Never lie if the truth can be misleading.* That was a rule you learned early on the streets. "Something wrong?"

"Stole my damn wallet," the guy snapped back, searching around for the pickpocket. "You see which way he went?"

Li didn't have to fake his surprise. The guy had picked a mark and executed a perfect grab right in front of him! The natural urge to cover for the other thief, to lie, rose in him and Li had to suppress it. If anyone else had noticed, being contradicted would focus attention back on himself. So tell the truth. Sort of.

"Don't know exactly where he went," Li said, choosing his words carefully and masking it by scratching at his jaw and pretending to concentrate. "But I recall he didn't have no shoes. Don't think he'd have walked far on gravel." Li kicked at the path, scattering a few small rocks. "I'd guess he slipped back over to the beach."

The other man looked across the road and searched what he could see of the beach. At least a dozen men of the same general build and features were within sight.

"Thanks, buddy." Pulling his girlfriend along after him, he jaywalked the road and began looking carefully at nearby faces.

Li nodded, shrugged, and then slowly walked along the gravel path. After taking the same turn as the pickpocket had, he stepped up his pace and began his own search for the man. Curiosity drove him more than common sense. You shouldn't pressure a thief. Things could turn ugly real fast. But the fact that the guy had been so smooth, yet so ill-prepared in his choice of dress, told Li that the man might be in trouble and in need of a little help.

Twenty meters up, another path crossed his. Now there were three directions the guy could have gone, and Li found himself trying to second-guess another professional. If it were him, he'd have gone straight ahead, putting some distance behind him. To the left would risk a run-in with the mark. To the right led back toward the grab, the area where the police would first begin a search. Then he recalled the smooth calm with which the guy had followed the mark after the grab. That took nerve, chancing that the mark wouldn't discover the loss until after the pickpocket had turned down another path.

Li turned to the left, brushing past a hedge that grew to the right of the path. He increased his step to a brisk walk. Running might seem like he was chasing the man, not searching for him. A subtle yet important difference. He was still trying to figure out how exactly to approach when he felt a hand on his shoulder, clamping down like a vise. It spun him around. For the second time in less than five minutes, Li Wynn had been surprised.

His first thought was that he'd guessed the right path.

His second was that the pickpocket had known all along that he was being watched, and had anticipated *him*.

"I admire persistence," said Aris Sung. "Unless I'm mistaken, you have a proposition for me. Yes?"

14

K'ung-fu-tzu Park, Tarrahause
Tarrahause District, Kaifeng
Sarna Supremacy, Chaos March
20 July 3058

So far, it was getting out of his BattleMech that had given Aris the most trouble.

He'd spent an hour working his way down the Jinxiang River. He only broke the surface once, and that by accident at a point where the river widened and became shallow. Fortunately it was also a remote point, and Aris had quickly resubmerged his machine only to move even slower and more carefully than before.

Changes in water temperature and the slope of the river bottom eventually told him that he'd worked his way into Lake Ch'u Yuan. From what Aris could recall from memory, the great lake was over ten kilometers across at any point and shaped rather like an inverted L. The Jinxiang fed into it at the northeastern tip, and then continued on its way from the southwest. Tarrahause framed the outside angle. If he'd wanted to, Aris could have walked his *Wraith* straight into the heart of the city.

But that wasn't part of the Hiritsu plan. Not yet. First Aris had to find a way to confer with Ty Wu Non. So he'd walked his machine to where he was fairly sure he stood less than half a kilometer off Tarrahause and at a spot only fifteen to twenty meters deep.

Then came the problem of getting out of his 'Mech without flooding the cockpit.

BattleMechs could be opened to vacuum, to be sure. All that was involved was replacing the spent air. Vacuum didn't short out electrical circuits. Water, however, was another matter, and Aris' cockpit hatch was set into the back of the *Wraith*'s head. If he were to open the hatch now, the water would come pouring in.

The solution—well, part of the solution—was for Aris to lay the *Wraith* on the lake's muddy bottom with his cockpit viewscreen facing up. This would put the hatch at the lowest point of the 'Mech cockpit. Then he could simply open the hatch and slip into the water. There was no path for the air to escape. So with the surface a faint rippling blue patch far above, he'd undogged the hatch and forced it open a crack against three atmospheres of water.

He had then let it close as fast as he could, the pressure difference still in his favor. Approximately two to three gallons of water had rushed in during those first few seconds, washing over his combat boots and putting the lie to his reasoning up to that point. Aris felt like hitting something. He'd forgotten that air would compress.

And that had been the other half of the solution. Over the course of a few minutes, he pressurized his cockpit by shutting down the modified recirc system and manually adding more air from the reserve tanks. He had to guess at the pressure, but after having to equalize his sinuses four times, he figured he was close enough. This time the hatch opened easily, dropping down into the cold lake water as some of the cockpit air forced its way down through the water to bubble up around the outside of his *Wraith*'s head.

Compared to all that, rigging a marker seemed simple. Like most BattleMechs, the *Wraith* carried emergency gear. Aris tied together two 10-meter lengths of nylon cord, one end of which he fastened to the outer hatch wheel. Then he emptied two bottles of a sports drink popular with MechWarriors for replenishing electrolytes lost in the cockpit heat and tied them to the other end of the rope. Taking a deep breath, he slipped into the Ch'u

Yuan's cool embrace and pulled the marker rope with him. He fastened the hatch from outside, and swam to the surface, bottles in tow.

Treading water, Aris eyeballed a few landmarks on shore to give him a basic idea of where he'd left the *Wraith,* and then set out for the nearest shore. The half-kilometer swim was a fair stretch, but Aris was in good shape. He'd rested up in the park, aware all the time of the youth shadowing him, then picked up some traveling money, and moved on. He'd waited just the other side of the hedge to see how persistent, and how competent, his shadow was.

Now he sat on a slab of cool concrete in the center of the park, leaning back against the base of a statue of K'ung-fu-tzu. The great Chinese scholar-sage rose above him dressed in simple robes carved from granite. His face was wrinkled and wizened, and he seemed to be reading aloud from a book held at chest level in one hand. The other hand was raised as if to draw the masses forward to hear his oration.

Whether K'ung-fu-tzu or Confucius, it was still Master K'ung, and Aris knew all the sage's speeches and writings. Many of those teachings were at the heart of House Hiritsu, as important to its way of life as the Lorix Order. Teachings that defined the cardinal relationships, whether between superior and inferior, and those that dealt with relations between equals. To know your place in life was the core of Confucianism. Obey superiors. Treat inferiors virtuously. And always, always, be respectful of another's station in life, regardless of its level.

Aris had vowed to live by those codes the day he joined House Hiritsu. They acted as a good check on his other vows, those of the Lorix Order that drove him to excel at being a warrior. Between the two, war was justified but tempered with reason. Those vows and others helped to define the Warrior House, both within itself and in relation to its place in the Capellan Confederation.

The cotton shirt Li had loaned Aris was too small for him, and it pulled at his shoulders, but Aris shrugged away the discomfort. The boy would return to the park soon, with newly purchased, or stolen, shirt and thongs. Aris couldn't help of thinking of him as almost a child, though Li Wynn was at least nineteen or twenty Terran Standard years of age. Li seemed to be the person Aris would have been destined to become had he not managed to become adopted into House Hiritsu. That had made him grow up fast. Li hadn't been given that benefit, and Aris doubted that Li had ever known anything other than the streets.

He heard the soft, rasping brush of sneakers against concrete a moment before he noticed a wavering in the statue's shadow. Someone was trying to approach from behind, using the statue to mask his own shadow. Aris couldn't be sure if Li Wynn was trying to impress him, or if the street raff routinely tested himself this way. He wanted to believe the latter, but either way it wouldn't do to let it pass unnoticed.

"Too anxious, Li Wynn. You can never let impatience get the better of you."

A pair of black thongs dropped to the concrete beside Aris, and he looked up. Li Wynn stood behind him, a dark shirt clutched in his right hand. He gave Aris a reluctant nod. "Sorry it took so long."

Aris stood and quickly pulled off the shirt Li had loaned him and handed it back. "I'm in no position to be choosy. Again, I appreciate your offer of assistance." Aris took out the wallet he'd liberated from the couple on the beach and pulled out two twenty C-bill notes. "This should cover the purchase."

Li Wynn never mentioned that the amount certainly tripled the purchase cost, and it raised Aris' estimate of the younger man another notch. What wasn't said could sometimes be as important as what was. "Where will you go now?" Li asked.

"Into town," Aris answered vaguely. "I've got some other purchases to make. I was"—he paused and forced a grin—"*forced* to leave most of my belongings elsewhere."

"You're new to Tarrahause."

Aris' grin faded. The kid was pushing for information, and Aris still wasn't sure how far he should go with Li Wynn. Then again, a street contact was nothing to throw away lightly. "What makes you think so?"

It was Li's turn to grin. "If you were *connected* around here, I'd know you."

He probably would at that. Aris remembered his own days on the street, when survival meant recognizing by face who was an undercover dick and who you could turn to for advice—advice properly paid for, of course. "Okay, I'm not from around here. But I might be here for awhile, which means I'll have to get settled in and bone up on any local . . . customs." *Meaning whose toes am I likely to step on?* Aris was properly concerned. If there was any organized criminal activity in Tarrahause, they could be onto him faster than the police. They wouldn't automatically turn him in, but they would do what they considered the best for themselves. Aris would do well to get on friendly terms.

Li pursed his lips, as if trying to decide how far *he* should trust Aris. "Well, for starters you're in prime hunting ground. The beaches are easy pickings, but this area is also fairly well patrolled by the local Djing-cha. And before long we might be under martial law, which is never good for business."

Aris nodded his understanding. Martial law meant that thieves could be shot on the spot. It meant curfews and a military presence on the streets. "I heard about all the trouble. Any idea how long it might last?"

"Franklin has already fallen. Beijing don't look good, according to the Mahabohdi news station." Li shook his head. "This General Fallon—she leads the Kaifeng SMM—she's already ordered communications cut off between the three district cities. We can only get news directly through Mahabohdi now."

That wasn't good. A communications blackout would seriously hinder Aris' ability to get in touch with Battalion Commander Non. "I imagine that doesn't apply to ComStar stations, though."

"Not directly," Li Wynn said. "But ComStar has instituted one of their infamous rate hikes."

That figured. *So I'll need to acquire some extra funds first, but then I should be able to reach someone in House Hiritsu through Franklin.* A day. Maybe two. "Got any clue where I can find a cheap place to lay low for a couple days?" he asked. Aris felt himself falling easily into the intonations and language of the streets.

"Grab an uptown bus. Once you cross Fiftieth Street, you're in the Zone."

Aris didn't have to ask what that was. Every city had its poorer section, always given some almost affectionate nickname by those who had no choice but to live there. "Thanks again, Li. I owe you."

Li hesitated, again as if trying to read how much he should tell Aris. "Look. If you're needing some action, find a place called Monte's. I gotta run some errands, touch some bases. If anything pans out, maybe I can cut you in."

Aris thought the younger man too trusting by half. But he wasn't about to give him a lecture this time. "Monte's. I'll remember that." He pulled the wallet out of his pocket, removed a handful of bills, and then handed the wallet to Li. "Do me a favor and ditch this somewhere, will you?"

"You got it."

Aris moved off then. He'd left another twenty C-bill in the wallet, a fact Li would certainly discover before throwing the billfold away. Loyalty couldn't be bought on the streets; anyone who'd ever lived on them knew that. But nothing generated enlightened self-interest like a generous hand-out. Aris was sure he'd see Li Wynn again. Maybe by then he'd have a better idea of the situation on Kaifeng. Because if he couldn't solve the communications problem soon, he'd be forced to act on his own.

And that frightened Aris more than anything else that had happened to him on this planet so far.

═══ 15 ═══

Beijing Aerodrome, Beijing
Beijing District, Kaifeng
Sarna Supremacy, Chaos March
22 July 3058

The administrative building adjoined the main hangar of the Beijing Aerodrome. The *Dainwu,* or Great Tiger, House Hiritsu's *Overlord* Class DropShip, sat on a ferrocrete pad outside the hangar, its thirty-six-story height dwarfing everything around it. Six BattleMechs patrolled the airfield's perimeter. Closer in, two platoons of Hiritsu infantry surrounded the hangar and admin building.

The building's small conference room could seat only six people. Battalion Commander Non, Infantry Commander Jessup, and the three BattleMech company leaders—now including Terry Chan—sat at the table. Each company leader had also brought one lance leader, but since the table couldn't seat them all, they stood behind their respective commanders. Terry Chan had brought Jill McDaniels, recently elevated to lance leader with Aris' disappearance. An interesting choice, in Ty's opinion. Technically, it should have been Raven Clearwater. But, then, perhaps Terry Chan hadn't wanted to leave the bulk of her company, even in a stand-down, under the command of her most junior lance leader.

Ty stood behind his chair, having already ordered the

others to be seated. He leaned on its back, hands pressing into the vinyl covering. There were congratulations to be handed out and admonishments to be made, neither of which he particularly wanted to deal with now but knew were expected of him in his role as House Master. The first order of business, though, was to ascertain the status of a missing son of the House.

"Company Leader Chan. Your report said that Aris Sung was lost crossing the Jinxiang, but there was no positive evidence of death. Is Aris Sung missing or deceased?"

Terry Chan raked fingers back through her short hair. "I would have to say missing, Battalion Commander. Several of us saw his *Wraith* enter the Jinxiang, but it seemed to be caused by a failed jump rather than from a killing blow. We held the bridgehead as long as seemed safe, and then pulled back, as per his final orders. One lance of the Kaifeng SMM linked up with the mercenaries and kept pushing us further away. If Aris survived, I would surmise that he was either captured or no longer has a BattleMech. Either way, of little use to us at this time."

Ty Wu Non kept his face carefully neutral. He had always resented Aris Sung, first for the way the younger man had entered service to House Hiritsu and second for his superior performance in his duties. If Ty had not been assigned as Mentor to the street urchin—if, say, James or Lindell had—it could just as easily have been one of the other company leaders who'd risen to the position of House Master. Ty would prefer to think he had reached this position through his own ability, but Aris was a constant reminder that he'd had help. That he'd needed that help.

But Ty Wu Non *would* be House Master now, barring incident, and a House Master could not afford the petty jealousies and rivalries that raged quietly among younger members of the House, just as between the members of any family. Virginia York had taught him that. Not in so many words, but by the even-handedness of her leadership. Ty swore he would try to live up to her standards.

"All right, Aris Sung is to be considered missing in action. If he's still alive, no doubt he will attempt to communicate with us. Everyone"—he paused, making direct eye contact with Terry Chan—"*everyone* is to remain alert for any such attempt." Ty ignored the slight flush that rose to Chan's face. He didn't like singling her out, but he also knew how strong the temptation might be to ignore any signal from Aris. *Would I have done that?* No, he did not want to believe he would.

"Status report," he snapped out, forcing his mind away from such thoughts and drawing the immediate attention of his command staff. "The plans laid out by Aris Sung have worked reasonably well, perhaps even commendably considering the early loss of House Master York and Kaifeng's obvious preparations against us. Company Leader Lindell has effectively shut down Franklin District and taken control of the city, all according to our original schedule. Thom?"

Thom Lindell rocked his chair back on two legs while studiously blanking his face. Ty knew the report would be dry and almost monotone. He could appreciate the other's personal control, but was always left with the impression that something important could be left out and no one would ever know it.

"We had to contend with a single lance of the Kaifeng SMM, supported by a lance of mercenaries and a strengthened armored company," Thom Lindell began, each word delivered with the same precise intonation. "Aris' plan predicted their actions perfectly. We took control of the major shipping routes for their major crops of rice, fruits, and vegetables. When those stopped flowing into the city, it drew out the mercenaries. From interrogations we knew that only a single SMM lance held the city of Franklin. We forced the confrontation and seized it in a single day."

"Company Leader Lindell's detailed report on tactics employed by both sides is on disk," Ty informed them. "I suggest you all review it on your way back to your commands." He looked to Lindell again. "Force disposition?"

"I do not expect Leftenant General Fallon will try to retake Franklin," Lindell said. "We are well-established behind the city defenses, and she has problems closer at hand to consider. I left six of my BattleMechs and an infantry company to hold the city. The rest await reassignment."

Ty nodded his acceptance of the report. "Well done, Thom." He was glad Lindell was not overly ambitious. Such rock-steady competence could have placed him above Non, Aris Sung or no.

"The Beijing assault has not proceeded according to schedule," Ty continued, "but as of eleven hundred hours this morning we are finally in control of the district. By using the *Dainwu* for air control, we were able to push those damn aerospace fighters back into Mahabohdi. Our 'Mech forces knocked out two Kaifeng lances and re-pelled a full mercenary company, which we believe has also fallen back into Mahabohdi. The Kaifeng SMM lances were waiting for us along the shipping routes, which suggests they knew where we planned to strike."

Ty glanced over at Company Leader Jason James. "Quick action on the part of Company Leader James saved us from taking severe losses. He tricked three enemy units into jumping toward swampy terrain, where they got mired down. Good work, Jason."

James nodded, one side of his mouth twitching up in a smile. Then he sobered as an earlier comment finally hit home. "How did they know we were coming?"

"That is the question. Terry Chan reports a similar oc-currence in Tarrahause, and of course there's the matter of the aerospace ambush that hit us as we passed Nochen. Anyone have an answer?"

Terry was quick to respond. "Whoever assassinated House Master York had to be a professional, possibly FedCom MIIO still in place when Sarna went independent. They could have gotten a message through that we missed."

Ty Wu Non nodded. "That has been considered. I sent a message up to the station last night. They're reviewing all transmission logs. And SMM prisoner interrogations all say the same thing, that order came directly from General Fallon. So no help there. Any other ideas?"

"Well . . ."

Ty turned to Lance Leader McDaniels. "Yes, Jill? You have something?"

The newly promoted lance leader shifted uncomfortably from one foot to the other. Then she seemed to become conscious of her hesitant attitude and quickly snapped herself to a more dignified posture.

"This is based on little more than rumor," she said. "But there are those *questionable* assignments given out by House Master Ion Rush in the last few months." McDaniels glanced around, saw that she had everyone's attention. "I mean, there's speculation that these were designed to weaken Warrior Houses whose loyalty to the Chancellor might be in doubt."

Ty picked up on her train of thought. "And you think perhaps the esteemed Ion Rush has set us up?" He shook his head slightly. "I wouldn't put such tactics past him, Jill, but I don't think he'd play a game like that in this situation. We're not involved in a mere exercise here. This is a well-defined military operation with a goal that is important to the state."

Thom Lindell leaned forward almost imperceptibly. "Regardless of where the betrayal came from, have we taken the early warning into account when predicting Sarna reinforcements?"

Ty felt himself tense up as he considered how much he should tell them. Then he decided not to hold back. "Two days ago, if all went according to plan, three of the Confederation's new warships came out from under wraps and jumped into the Sarna system. Their DropShips are carrying fighters only. Sarna is under a blockade that will be tightened over the next week. House Master Ion Rush promised House Master York a full month. It would take Sarna that long to organize any kind of break-out attempt against warships."

Several people started to speak at once, then all fell back into silence rather than continue the discourtesy of trying to talk over some else. After a suitable pause, Company Leader James leaned forward and continued for all of them. "Three warships? That's almost everything the Confederation's got. Isn't that risky?" Several others around the room nodded agreement with the question.

"The risk was deemed minor. These ships needed a proper test of their abilities. They have ample fighter cover to help protect them, and all three are continuously updating jump solutions. They're under order to abandon their fighters if necessary to ensure their survival." Ty paused, hoping for the proper dramatic effect. "I've reviewed the plans, and I believe the blockade will work."

He watched as the faces of his people visibly relaxed, and an inner glow warmed him. As it had been with House Master York, his assurance was enough for his people. He thought he saw some small flicker of doubt in the eyes of Terry Chan, but wrote that off to what she knew was coming.

"Next order of business," he said, his voice stronger, "Tarrahause." He let a harsh note bleed into his tone. "Company Leader Terry Chan, what is going on over there?" Ty wasn't looking forward to this part. No matter what was said, he was sure he was going to have to reprimand Chan. The daughter of two House Hiritsu warriors killed in battle, she'd been an able and worthy protégé over the last several years. Ty had sponsored her adoption into the House, and if not for Aris Sung, would have taken her as his personal student. But Ty could no longer maintain such an active interest in one person's career, and her assumption of command in the Tarrahause District made her responsible for the failure to secure it.

Terry Chan knew how to accept that responsibility. Back straight and shoulders squared, she faced her battalion commander. "We have failed to take the initiative in Tarrahause. As mentioned earlier, they seemed to know what we were about. Mercenary forces supported by Von Luckners hit us at the port terminal. Then a full Kaifeng SMM company ambushed us at the river crossing. Our 'Mechs were torn up by concentrated fire and Thunder munitions, so I fell back into the jungle rather than continue to push what had become a bad position.

"We never got the chance to retake the offensive. The SMM commander knew he had us, and pressed his advantage. A Kaifeng SMM scout lance hooked up with the mercenary force that had been following our backtrail and pressed us well outside our field of operations. That was when I called in the *Lao-Tzu* for pick-up. Since then we've been rearmoring and rearming."

Ty Wu Non fixed her with a penetrating stare. "A direct assault against Tarrahause, before the elimination of defending forces, deviated from the House plan." He did not elaborate, wanting to see how she would handle the politically treacherous ground.

"Company Leader Aris Sung re-interpreted the plan due to the unexpected presence of garrison troops in the field. He believed we could reach Tarrahause ahead of them and defeat what was sure to be a small garrison force in the city. He was mistaken." She paused. Hedged. "To be fair, I would not have expected a full Kaifeng SMM company either. Especially sitting outside the city. And the basic thrust of the plan, after all, *was* to pull forces from the city so we could take it with less opposition."

Good. Ty Wu Non was pleased. Terry Chan could have taken the opportunity to launch a scathing indictment of Aris' tactics. But instead she offered some amount of support for her previous lance leader. By lessening Aris' mistake, she lessened the eventual punishment that would now fall on her, in his place.

"Tarrahause might well become the key to this operation," he said. "Company Leader James and I are still evaluating the cost of a direct assault against Mahabohdi, but the initial estimates are not acceptable. We assume at least one company of Kaifeng SMM, Leftenant General Fallon's command company, will remain in the city for its defense. We know of one mercenary company that has pulled back into the city, and there could easily be another waiting in there as well. And as long as foodstuffs continue to flow into Mahabohdi from Tarrahause, the enemy has no reason to force a confrontation with us. They will sit and await reinforcement from Sarna, whether it takes one month or six. We don't have the aerospace assets to shut down the shipping. We must take Tarrahause."

Now that he had everyone focused on the goal, it was time to reorganize what had effectively become a stalled offensive. "Company Leader Lindell, take your demi-company and link up with Terry Chan's forces in Tarrahause. Company Leader Chan, you are to consider yourself reprimanded. You will continue to lead your company, but Thom will be the senior officer present and you will report directly to him." Terry nodded curtly, accepting the rebuke without argument. He decided to overlook the naked anger that flashed in her eyes.

Ty nodded back. A few days ago, he would have followed that with an *Is that clear?* Now he no longer felt the need. He was learning. If he was to be House Master, he couldn't be relying on such clarifiers to remind the others of his authority. He either had it, or he did not. He remembered the confrontation with Aris Sung, so soon after Virginia York's death. Ty had been heavy-handed there, bringing too much of his personal feeling into the conversation. He hoped that he knew better now.

"Lance Leader James and I will continue to strengthen our defense around Beijing. We're quite close to Mahabohdi here, so a counterattack is a real threat. Also, I want at least a full company on station and ready to take advantage of any weakness in Mahabohdi's defenses."

He paused, eyes sweeping the room. "Now, I have one final piece of business that might affect everyone's strategies." *So listen up.* Again, he didn't feel the need to say it.

"There is a major holiday only three days from now. The Dragon Boat Festival. Those of you who follow the Chinese lunar calendar will know that, according to the Terran Standard calendar, the official holiday is some weeks off. Kaifeng has a shorter year than Terra, though, and this holiday is based in old fertility rites. Kaifeng has adjusted the date in accordance with their own crop-growing season. In three days, yang and yin begin to change over, and Kaifeng asks for a seventy-two-hour cease-fire to conduct their ceremonies, beginning at midnight tomorrow night. The request came in six hours ago from Planetary Governor Teresa Larsen, on behalf of the people of Kaifeng.

"Let me explain why we will honor this request," Ty said, forestalling any questions. "The Liao family takes great pride in its Chinese heritage. And while they have not actively fostered the old religions, you all know that every Chancellor has encouraged the celebration of the traditional Chinese holidays. That is because the people need a periodic release. Now, part of our goal here is to pacify Kaifeng and return it to the Capellan fold. We must show the common people that their lives will not suffer dramatic changes under our rule." Ty smiled. "This gives us that opportunity.

"However, I believe we can also find further advantage

in this event. So here is what I propose. We organize a major offensive against Tarrahause, to commence at nineteen hundred hours tomorrow night. That gives us five hours before the start of the cease-fire. If we're in luck, the enemy commander won't be expecting an attack so close to the cease-fire."

Ty paused, waiting. Thom Lindell picked up on the idea first. "The offensive couldn't hope to take the city in so short a time, but it could hurt the defenders immensely." He nodded, an uncharacteristic gesture of approval from him, then he looked straight at Ty. "We time our attack to stop just short of midnight?" Ty nodded. "And if their troops fire at us while we're withdrawing?"

Ty's earlier smile returned. "I'm hoping for exactly that. If they fire at us after zero-hundred, then they've broken the cease-fire and we can press the offensive right into the city. And we can lay the blame on the Kaifeng SMM or their mercenary friends."

Everyone nodded their admiration of the plan and the meeting was dismissed. Ty Wu Non held Thom Lindell and Terry Chan to their places by eye contact alone. After the others had filed out, he gave each a single nod. "I expect that offensive to press in after midnight. I don't care how," he said, voice almost a whisper, "but this could be the chance we need. Find a way to make them break that cease-fire."

The Zone, Tarrahause
Tarrahause District, Kaifeng
Sarna Supremacy, Chaos March
23 July 3058

Aris slumped back in his seat, one hand curled tight around his glass and the other hidden conspicuously under the table as if he had a weapon concealed. He stared down into the dark liquid. Every minute or so his eyes lifted briefly to scan the room, looking for danger or opportunity and never inviting company. It was both an appearance and an attitude, neither of which was unfamiliar to the patrons of this bar. That was the kind of place Monte's was, and Aris was beginning to feel much too comfortable there.

It had surprised him how quickly he was able to fit in among the residents of the Zone's downtrodden but streetwise citizens. The place and people were eerily reminiscent of his early life on Randar. He still felt alone, unused to being separated from the family of House Hiritsu. But he no longer felt afraid or out of place.

Aris searched the dimly lit bar again. From his booth he had a clear view of both doors and most of the room. This was a hangout for the younger crowd, and as the clock ticked away into late afternoon, business was beginning to pick up. Still no sign of Li Wynn, though Li had promised to return within two to three hours. Had to check on some business prospects, he'd said. Aris saw a few others he'd been introduced to over the last few days, but they went about their business and left Aris to his.

Three days. Aris had spent that first day picking up spending money and acquiring something other than beach clothes. He had also discovered that something so simple as a visiphone call wasn't going to get through to Franklin or Beijing, so scratch that plan. The next day he'd tried amateur radio, only to discover that anything with the power to reach Beijing was monitored. And of course no local radios would be configured for the Hiritsu radio net. Trying to buy radio crystals that covered the appropriate frequency bands, those reserved for military use, would raise way too much suspicion. Aris would have to steal them, or else have Li hook him up with whatever passed as the local black market.

ComStar had washed out yesterday afternoon. With House Hiritsu in control of Franklin and Beijing, the fate of Kaifeng no longer seemed certain. ComStar had opted out of the conflict, determined to remain neutral for fear of angering whichever was the final winner. Oh, they still provided off-world communication, the rates for HPG messages appropriately adjusted for what they called Hazardous Area Transmissions. But they refused to provide any inter-city communication. Aris could try relaying a signal to Randar and back to Franklin, but that would take more time and, of course, more money.

He cursed softly into his drink. He remembered when ComStar had been a little more confident—a bit more aggressive. Now Word of Blake apparently had them worried, especially since the Blakists had recently taken Terra away from them. With HPG communication no longer a ComStar monopoly, it was better for business to remain neutral than back the losing side. Aris remembered all the old complaints about ComStar arrogance, and everyone's wish that someone would provide some competition and put ComStar in their place. Now they'd gotten their wish.

He'd decided to wait one more day. Possibly he could purchase an amateur radio transmitter and modify it himself. If Li could get the crystals for any kind of reasonable price. If not, Aris would have to steal a vehicle and leave

Tarrahause in order to search out warriors of his House. He'd almost left today. Would have, in fact, except for the news that both the Kaifeng SMM company and Jacob's Juggernauts—the mercenary forces assigned to Tarrahause's protection—had returned from the field.

Li had explained why. Told him all about the seventy-two-hour cease-fire that went into effect at midnight this night. Preparations for the festival were underway. Aris had seen people hanging the bright red banners always used for Chinese festivals around the city. He wasn't exactly sure why Ty Wu Non would agree to such a cease-fire, but if he had, then House Hiritsu would honor its agreement. But it wouldn't surprise him at all if Ty was planning to launch some kind of special strike tonight, timing it very close to the start of the cease-fire.

Lost in these thoughts, Aris didn't spot Li Wynn until the youth was halfway across the floor to his booth. Aris sat up straight and answered Li's easy nod with one of his own. He kept most of his attention over the younger man's left shoulder, watching the front door and the rest of the bar while trusting Li to keep watch over the other half.

"Sorry that took so long, Aris. Things were a bit hectic at the office."

Aris smiled at the thin attempt at humor. "You said there might be work available. Better than working the crowds tomorrow at the lake?" He needed money and thought he might find good pickings when people flocked to the lakeside for the dragon boat races.

"Much better." Li's eyes were wide and alive with excitement, his nostrils flaring, mouth twitching at the corners. Aris read him easily, and knew that the kid believed what he was saying. Also, that he had something major in mind, perhaps a bit out of his league. "Maybe enough to get me off this backwater world. And there's room for others."

Aris caught the offer, but paused a moment to consider. He still didn't know much more about Li Wynn than he had two days ago. "I'll want to know more about the job," he said, finally making up his mind.

Li slid out of the booth. "C'mon. Gotta move on this now. We'll talk as we ride."

There were three others besides them, already waiting

in a car out front. All young, and all nervously excited.
Li introduced the driver as Kyle, *just* Kyle. Aris understood. First names only, probably because he was new. Li
didn't offer the names of anyone else as the car pulled
away from Monte's and turned onto a major street that
would quickly take them out of the Zone. Aris noticed a
lot of traffic moving the other way. "What's the score?"
he asked.

"The word finally came down," Li explained. "These
Hiritsu warriors are going to launch a raid against the city
within a few hours. We've been expecting them to do
something before the cease-fire, and had almost given up
on it. Apparently they expect to catch us napping."

House Hiritsu raiding Tarrahause? Aris wanted to howl
his frustration. If he'd known this earlier, he could have
timed it with bringing his *Wraith* up from the lake bottom.
Now there was no time. "How sure are you of this information?" he asked.

"Got it straight from a 'Mech jock's mouth. Normally
someone hangs out at this little club they all go to, the
Gold Pavilion, eavesdropping on the conversations.
That's how we keep in touch with what the military's up
to. Well, since we knew this one was coming, I had a little
talk with a technician who works for those mercs, the Juggernauts, we got in the city right now. She hooked me up
with a 'Mech jock who clued me to the plans. All for a
price, of course." Li reached forward and slapped Kyle on
the shoulder. "Hey, turn here."

The car swerved onto a side street, heading into a
business district along the west side of town. Again the
traffic was heavier moving in the opposite direction, but
Aris paid that little attention. He was trying to figure out
how to get a message to his people. Contacting the infantry might be possible—if they were part of the operation and if he could find the incursion point. But the
borders of Tarrahause included a dozen kilometers of
lakefront and a couple dozen more stretching out into
the nearby farmland.

"So anyway," Li continued, "we'll let the metal mon-
sters kick open a few businesses for us and then it's
shopping time."

Aris raised an eyebrow. "That's great, if you can find

the assault point fast enough, and then keep from getting yourself killed."

"Find it?" Li laughed. "Aris, we're there."

Aris looked around. Other than some heavy traffic heading deeper into the city, he saw nothing amiss. Standard two-way street with two- to three-story buildings to either side. Businesses were closed, though it seemed a bit early. "I have to say, this is the quietest battle zone I've ever"—he paused, about to say *been in*—"heard about."

"Well, they ain't here yet, my friend. This is where they'll make the diversionary attack. I guess the Capellans are hoping to pull off any active patrols around the 'Mech yards. Meanwhile, their main thrust will try to hit the 'Mech yards and the Tarrahause aerodrome at the northeast edge of the city. Hey! There's one of our rustbuckets now."

Aris followed the pointing finger. At the next intersection, a 30-ton *Hermes II* stood astride the cross street. It showed the crest of Jacob's Juggernauts and its head turned slowly from side to side as if searching for something. Apparently making up its mind, the 'Mech stepped into an alleyway that ran behind a four-story parking garage and then kneeled down out of view. *Looking for a parking spot,* Aris thought. *Setting up another ambush? But how?* "I don't understand," he said, mostly to himself, though Li picked up on it.

"What's not to understand?" He clapped Aris on the shoulder. "One of the mercenary lances is hiding nearby, ready to pop out and tag the Capellans in the middle of the diversionary raid. We'll hide in manholes until the fun has passed us. Then we crawl out and hit 'targets of opportunity,' as the 'Mech jocks say."

Li leaned into the front seat. "See if you can find a *Vulcan* around here," he told the driver. "It's this real ugly thing with a round head, skinny body, and barrel-like arms. If it's not within, say, two or three blocks, we'll come back and stake this beastie out." Li settled back into his seat. "The *Vulcan* belongs to our mercenary friend," he explained to Aris. "He's been paid off to kick in the side of jewelry stores and the like."

Aris grabbed his young associate by the arm, hard. "Li, what's going on? It's one thing to expect an attack. Maybe scouts or air patrols can clue you that one's imminent. But it's quite another thing to know exactly where the diversionary attacks will be staged." Aris' mind swam. Could it be intercepted transmissions? Aerial reconnaissance?

Li's answering chuckle drove those thoughts from his mind. "Man, you are out of touch. The Kaifeng SMM knows hours or even days in advance every move the Capellans make around Tarrahause. Maybe even Beijing. The MechWarriors have been talking about little else."

"But how is that possible?" Aris unconsciously tightened his grip.

Li pulled his arm away and rubbed at the sore spot in the middle of his bicep. "What's wrong with you? The Capellans got an informer among them, of course. One of their MechWarriors." He read Aris' stunned expression and laughed again. "Yeah, it's a riot, huh?"

═══ 17 ═══

Tarrahause
Tarrahause District, Kaifeng
Sarna Supremacy, Chaos March
23 July 3058

By the yellow glare of the street lamp, the interior of the parking garage looked like the gutted ruin of a building, its ferrocrete walls the white-gray of old bones. A waist-high wall was all that separated each of the four parking levels from the street outside.

Aris eased Kyle's car up the last ramp of the garage. He was running without lights and had kept well back from the north side of the building, the alley side where the *Hermes II* crouched in hiding. Next to him on the front seat, five large glass bottles rolled and clinked together. Aris could smell the paint thinner-soaked rags that stoppered each molotov cocktail, the caustic scent stabbing into his sinuses and making his head ache.

Kyle and Li Wynn had been unable to find the *Vulcan* quickly, and so had abandoned the car just down the street from the *Hermes II*. Each person was handed a metal tool suitable for pulling a manhole cover, and then sent to different intersections where they could hide. The drill was a simple one. Wait for the noise to pass, then pop out and do some discount shopping.

Aris had his own plans. He had doubled back to the car

and hot-wired it, then quickly driven to a nearby hardware store and on to a small market. The glass bottles had held vinegar before being emptied. Industrial-strength paint thinner mixed with liquid detergent made a poor-man's napalm. A roll of duct tape, a disposable lighter, and a broken broom handle completed his shopping. He hurried as much as possible, worried that House Hiritsu might start its attack before he could get into position.

Aris planned to join them on the battlefield.

The fourth level of the parking garage was actually the roof, a flat open expanse save for the thin concrete wall that ran all around its edge. None of the nearby buildings were quite so high except the one just across the alley, which presented a brick face and billboard for a locally produced soft drink. Aris turned the car around, so that it faced back down the ramp.

He smashed the car's dome light with his elbow, wincing as a piece of the glass bulb jabbed him through his light jacket, then opened the door and got out. Nothing seemed amiss. He strained his hearing, trying to detect the telltale thundering footfalls of approaching BattleMechs. He heard only the usual noises of a city at night, including a few horns honking in the distance. Late-night stragglers on their way home perhaps.

Or maybe some more midnight shoppers waiting for the bargains to start.

Aris grabbed one of his cocktail creations and set about preparing the car. He opened the trunk and jammed a small piece of the broom handle into the hinge to prop it open, then used duct tape to hold it in place. Then he pulled out the cloth stopper and splashed half of the foul-smelling and sticky liquid onto the tires and the underside of the vehicle's gas tank. Then he shoved the cloth back into the bottle and left it resting in the trunk. The last thing he did was remove the gas cap and leave it on the ground. Aris glanced around again. He listened. Nothing. Now all he could do was wait and hope he'd done enough.

He didn't have to wait long. It wasn't five minutes before he heard a distant crunch of concrete cracking under the weight of a BattleMech's foot. It was part of a Mech-Warrior's training in House Hiritsu to know what could announce an approach. Stepping on sidewalks was always a sure giveaway. Done deliberately here, Aris was sure. This was a diversionary attack. They wanted to alert the city to their presence and pull BattleMech patrols away from the 'Mech yards. *They don't know that the patrol is already here.*

As if to underscore Aris' thoughts, there came another crashing sound. This time of glass and brick as a 'Mech kicked in a building wall. Bells rang in the distance, like a bank alarm. *Li Wynn and his friends ought to like that,* Aris thought as he finally located the direction of the noise. Coming straight down the street, only two blocks away, a *Huron Warrior* stepped intentionally on a parked car. The squeal and snapping of bending metal and crushed glass echoed down the street.

Raven Clearwater, Aris thought, *or Lynn Trahn.* They were the *Huron Warrior* pilots in his company. Whichever it was, one of them was heading directly down the street and into the ambush. Just before it reached the intersection, the 'Mech would pass the alley mouth and the waiting *Hermes II.*

Where a moment before Aris seemed to have all the time in the world, now it was a race where seconds could count. He jumped back into the car and rolled it down the ramp to the third level, then sought out the longest run he could find that pointed him at the *Hermes'* head. Most of the other vehicles in the parking garage were on the first level, so Aris was able to squeeze into the southeast corner and point Kyle's car almost directly northwest for a full run across the floor. He took his four full cocktail surprises and set them well away from the path of the car, close to the west wall, and then returned and smashed the half-full one into the rear of the trunk.

Now Aris could hear each footfall as the 50-ton Hiritsu 'Mech made its way down the street. Every few seconds it paused to do some deliberate damage to a nearby building or vehicle. Aris checked that the tires had been straightened, and then liberally applied duct tape to the car's steering mechanism. He taped the wheel to the dash, and wrapped the roll of tape several turns around the pivoting point on the column. Hurrying, he ran around the car, setting the tires, gas tank, and trunk on fire with the disposable lighter.

Sitting on the edge of the seat, holding the car door open with one foot, Aris put the car in gear and checked his alignment as the vehicle began to move forward. Then he jammed the broken broom stick down onto the accelerator and fixed the other end against the car's seat so it held the gas pedal to the floor. The car leaped ahead, and Aris had no time for last-minute corrections. He threw himself out of the car.

Elbows tucked in tight, one fist at each temple, Aris rolled as he hit the pavement of the parking garage. The back of his head slammed down harder than he'd intended, taking away a patch of hair and skin and threatening to plunge him into unconsciousness. Aris stopped himself with a flat hand slap against the floor. Shaking off his dizziness, he half-ran half-stumbled over to his four cocktails just as the car smashed through the third level's safety wall.

Aris never got to see the direct result of his handiwork. The restraining wall was only a few centimeters thick, meant to take a glancing blow but not a vehicle slamming into it at high speed. The car burst through the wall, and arced out away from the building, dropping directly onto the *Hermes II*. Aris had aimed for the head, and would have been happy if the car hit the ground within ten meters of the 'Mech. As it was, the car struck it from behind, just above the left hip joint. Shoved slightly off balance, the pilot was just beginning to react when the car struck the alleyway pavement right behind his machine. The gas tank burst, as Aris had hoped it would, and the flames already burning in the trunk and in the tank itself quickly ignited the fuel. The tank exploded, flipping the car back into the air and into the *Hermes II* yet again. The *Hermes* didn't fall exactly, but it did stumble from the alley and drop to one knee in an effort to steady itself.

Aris lit the cloth stoppers on two of the bottles as the explosion shattered the night and flames leapt skyward from the alley north of the parking garage. Picking the burning bottles up, he ran to the shattered safety wall and looked down. The *Hermes II* was just picking itself up. Aris sent one cocktail in its direction, and then the second. The first exploded against its shoulder. No real damage—Aris had intended them as markers for House

Hiritsu warriors, a warning beacon in the dark night. But then the second shattered against the side of the 'Mech's head, flames bursting across the cockpit viewport.

Aris knew that one of the things a MechWarrior most feared was being caught inside a burning 'Mech. It was bad enough to be attacked by a flamer weapon or inferno rockets. But to be threatened by fire from an obvious infantry source?

When the *Hermes II* stepped back into the alley, Aris was running before its left arm ever started to come up. The 'Mech carried a 50mm autocannon in its right torso and a medium laser on its right arm. But you didn't waste weapons like that on unarmored infantry. *Fight fire with fire.* Its left-arm flamer shot out a jet of plasma-fueled flame, washing over the side of the parking garage and streaming through the open-walled design into the second and third levels.

Aris felt the rush of heat that preceded the rolling flames that chased him, and dove behind one of the level's few parked vehicles. He had ruined the *Hermes II*'s surprise, maybe done a bit of damage to it, and even drawn its first attack. He wasn't sure what else he could do for the *Huron Warrior* outside. He curled himself into a ball as the first licks of flame washed over him. He'd better have damn well done enough.

Raven Clearwater staved in the side of a building with another strong kick. For the briefest moment she imagined Terry Chan being inside, and then immediately felt ashamed of her thoughts. She did not care for Terry Chan's method of command or her disrespectful attitude toward Aris Sung when he was company leader, but that did not give Raven the right to wish harm to another House warrior. She was probably feeling uncharitable simply because Terry had assigned Raven's lance to the diversionary raid and not Jill McDaniels.

By normal House doctrine it should have been the most junior officer leading what basically amounted to an ineffective strike. A ruse. But Company Leader Chan had stressed the important timing. Then there was also Company Leader Lindell's directive that the mission be undertaken by a full lance, and Jill only commanded three

'Mechs. So it really wasn't anyone's fault that she was here and not attacking the 'Mech yards. Unless she wanted to blame herself for not being able to protect Company Leader Sung. Aris might have been able to retake the initiative after the ambush at the Jinxiang crossing, and events would be proceeding far differently.

Now Raven and her lancemates were spread out in a widely spaced line, advancing into the city from the northwest. Thom Lindell had chosen this spot because it was one of the few areas bordering the city that wasn't primarily residential. No MechWarrior wanted to make war on civilians, and a business district was certain to be fairly abandoned this time of night. And he'd been right. She hadn't seen a single body yet, and didn't expect to. Any Tarrahause citizens still in the area would certainly be moving in the other direction just as fast as possible. Hopefully one of them would call in an alert to the city defenders, and soon. She stepped on another car, feeling the slight resistance before the metal twisted and compacted beneath fifty tons of compression.

Then came the explosion just up the street, not sixty meters ahead. A single, rolling cloud of flame blossomed up from behind one of the buildings to her left. Shadows danced in the street, cast by the unsteady light of the fire in an alleyway. So close did the explosion follow her crushing the car that for a second her brain tried to form some kind of connection.

Then her sensors screamed a shrill alert. There was more than dancing shadows in the street. Her targeting and tracking system locked onto a BattleMech that had stumbled halfway out of the alley. Just enough for her magscan to pick it up and her computer to identify it as a *Hermes II*. Splashes of fire suddenly blossomed on the other 'Mech's left shoulder and head, and the 40-ton machine straightened and turned its attention to a building that bordered the alley. Looked like a parking garage to Raven. She brought up the Gauss rifle that was her right arm and leveled it at the *Hermes II*'s back.

Raven didn't have time to think about how this 'Mech had arrived on the scene so quickly. That it had approached so close was not unusual, not in an urban setting where the buildings would block visual sensors and foul up the ones like magscan. At that moment she only knew that the enemy was before her and it was the will of her superiors that she engage and hold this area of the city for as long as possible. The golden target reticule on her main screen floated over the enemy 'Mech. She pulled back on her main trigger, and then also brushed one of her thumb triggers to fire her medium pulse laser as well.

The Gauss rifle's capacitors discharged, creating an incredibly strong magnetic field that accelerated a slug of nickel-iron metal. The silvery ball caught the *Hermes II* in the left rear torso, cracking and shattering armor plates all along the broad back of the 'Mech as if they were brittle eggshells. The slug chewed through the entire left torso, crushing the 'Mech's foamed-titanium bones until the entire left side sagged in on itself. The pulse laser continued the job, its red pulsing beam slicing through what was left of the center torso armor and stabbing into the physical shielding that surrounded the fusion engine at the Battle-Mech's heart.

The *Hermes II* rocked forward as if shoved, but its fall was broken by the parking garage. Before Raven's weapons could cycle for another shot, the enemy 'Mech stepped deeper into the alley and out of her line of sight.

She grinned savagely. The *Hermes II* was hurting. If the pilot was smart, he would try to slip away down the alley. But Raven had no intention of letting him off so easily. She cranked her Warrior up to full walking speed that brought it quickly to the mouth of the alley. "This is Support Leader to Support units," she said, clearing a channel to her lancemates. "Have made contact with the enemy. Converge on my location. Damn!"

The *Hermes II*'s right-arm medium laser caught her in the head, splashing emerald light across her cockpit viewscreen and momentarily dazzling her vision. Fortunately it wasn't enough to penetrate. Raven operated more by instinct and the memory of what she had just seen outside her 'Mech and triggered off a burst from the *Warrior*'s left-arm large laser.

She blinked away the spots swimming in front of her eyes. The *Hermes II* was crouched back within the alley, trying to find some cover behind a delivery truck that had been left there. The alley dead-ended thirty meters behind it, which explained its lack of an escape attempt. Scorched pavement and a hole cored through the cab of the truck told her where her laser shot had hit.

Ah, but we both know the painful truth, she thought, bringing the extended-range large laser to bear on the enemy 'Mech again. The ruby beam lanced into its exposed right leg, flaying off armor in molten pieces. *The* Hermes *stores all its autocannon munitions in the left torso, which my first Gauss shot must have ruined. You're out of ammo, my friend.*

The return fire from the *Hermes II*'s right-arm medium laser was a pitiful comeback. Raven waited for her laser to cycle and fired it again, this time with the medium pulse in accompaniment. There was no sense wasting Gauss ammo on such an easy target. The medium carved into the right torso, while the large burrowed into the center and burned off a half ton of armor.

The *Hermes II* pilot seemed to realize his situation at last. It couldn't jump, had no avenue of escape, and obviously couldn't survive trading shots with a fully functional *Huron Warrior*. The pilot brought the 'Mech to its feet and started off at a run down the alley and then immediately swerved into the side of the parking garage, thinking to burrow his way through the structure and escape out the other side. But the open-air garage looked less sturdy than it actually was, and the *Hermes II* bounced off the wall and back into the center of the alley.

Raven caught it on the rebound, hammering the center torso again with her large laser. The pilot had apparently damaged the front of his machine in the failed attempt to smash through the garage, because now the ruby beam easily sliced through armor and penetrated into the BattleMech's interior. Structural supports were cut away, and the beam bored into the 'Mech's gyro. The *Hermes II* dropped like an unstrung puppet, arms and legs flailing.

The pilot tried to regain his feet at once. A big mistake. As Raven watched, the hapless 'Mech rose to its knees and then crashed back down on its already mangled left side. Another attempt rolled it onto its back. Raven added to the pilot's misery by slicing another half-ton of armor off the *Hermes II*'s left leg. On its third attempt to stand the 'Mech fell back onto its left side again, this time knocking an internal support loose, which skewered the remains of the 'Mech's gyro.

There was no further movement after that, and the *Hermes II* shut down its engine.

Raven backed her *Warrior* out into the street. Her grin had faded. Watching a 'Mech die so ingloriously was never something to laugh at. It reminded any MechWarrior that battle was a lot more than glory or even survival. She checked to be sure her commline was still open.

"Count one *Hermes II* down and out," she said softly, in warning. "Be wary of his buddies."

Movement caught her eye then. Through her viewscreen. A dark shadow raced along the western edge of the parking garage, heading for the nearby intersection. The shadow moved low to the ground and in starts. From shrub to lamppost to parked vehicle. Good standard infantry tactics, Raven thought, recognizing the drill from her own days in the Hiritsu conventional forces. She selected her medium laser, the smallest thing she had for what MechWarriors referred to as "crowd control."

The dark-clothed figure darted to another parked vehicle, moving away from Raven and toward the intersection. *Probably trying to regroup with friends, and doesn't think I'll notice him.* Raven floated the golden targeting reticule over the car behind which the figure was hiding. She was easing into the shot when the figure fled cover and crossed the street.

There were several ways to cross open ground in the middle of combat conditions, none of them good. Usually, it was just get across as fast as you can. But some were acceptable, providing you had some friendly fire support. And that the fire support could tell you from the enemy. House Hiritsu had solved that problem by some simple choreographing of open ground movement. There was a standard way you approached a hostile building, or covered a retreat, or moved while under fire. There were even several hand signals, so infantry could communicate with the MechWarriors without having to rely on comm systems.

There was also a set procedure for crossing neutral ground in front of one of your own BattleMechs. House infantrymen were to cross crouched over keeping their

weapon hand tucked in—to show they were no threat—
and the other hand held about knee level and parallel to
the ground. That was the "crossing clear" signal.

And a very surprised Raven Clearwater was watching
the dark figure do exactly that.

Tarrahause
Tarrahause District, Kaifeng
Sarna Supremacy, Chaos March
23 July 3058

Aris slipped over the low concrete wall and crouched
down next to some shrubs growing around the perimeter
of the parking garage. The leaves were aromatic, like the
eucalyptus trees common to Randar, burning his throat
and making his eyes water. He moved over to a car parked
along the street and paused there, his back against the rear
tire, to catch his breath.

The *Hermes II*'s flames had passed over him for the
most part, shielded from the worst of it by the vehicle
he'd been hiding behind. Singed hair was the only damage to speak of. Aris collected his remaining two molotov
cocktails, and quickly made his way to the parking
garage's ground level. He'd lost his footing on the ramp
when the *Hermes* pilot slammed his 'Mech into the
garage, trying to burrow through. One bottle had slipped
from his grasp, shattering against the concrete ramp and
splashing a bit of the homemade napalm against his right
pants leg. Once on the ground level, it had been a short
run to the west-side concrete wall.

Aris looked toward the alleyway behind the garage,
where he could see part of the *Huron Warrior* standing

just inside the mouth of the alley. By the flickering light of Kyle's still-burning car, he noticed that the sensor array—often referred to as the bonnet—was painted a dark, solid color. That told him it must be Raven Clearwater in the *Warrior*'s command couch, for her 'Mech was painted a dark green. The bonnet of Lynn Trahn's *Huron Warrior* was black with light, almost-bilious green striping. Even in the poor light conditions Aris could tell there was no accenting color.

Then Aris thought he heard the distant cracking of concrete. He sat forward and held his breath, waiting for some further sound. From the south, maybe southwest, came a squeal of protesting metal, and there was no doubt it came from deeper within the city. Aris placed his fingertips lightly against the paved street, and could just barely feel the light but steady tremors that warned of nearby BattleMech movement. It had to be another member of the mercenary lance, searching for the Hiritsu force. The sounds had a hollow quality, as if echoing from out of a side street—and the next intersection wasn't more than thirty meters away. That could mean trouble.

Harder tremors and heavy footfalls shook Aris' attention away from the approaching threat. Raven's *Huron Warrior* backed out of the alley, turning to face south and continue its mission. Aris exhaled in pained exasperation. This was one of the problems of city 'Mech warfare, he thought. MechWarriors, strapped into their command couches, were forced to rely on sensors and visual data. In the narrow confines of a city, buildings blocked line of sight and severely limited those sensors. Unless the enemy was on the same street or you had a spotting unit, combat could easily take place at an intersection, with one or both warriors disagreeably surprised. Infantry could prevent that. *Aris* could prevent that.

Aris headed toward the intersection. He moved in brief runs, always dashing toward a new spot with cover he could exploit. He wanted to signal Raven—wanted to get into the safety of her cockpit, for that matter—to warn her about the other 'Mech approaching and the trap being set at the 'Mech yards. But there wasn't time to approach safely, in a manner that would keep her from burning him up with her lasers. And—dammit!—he was the only Hiritsu warrior on the ground and right now Raven needed a spotter. He ran from the cover of a lamp post, back to the street and another parked car.

Now all he had to do was make sure she didn't target him as a possible enemy infantry threat.

With a deep breath, he abandoned the relative safety of cover and darted into the street. He kept himself crouched low, right hand tucked in and cradling his last cocktail bottle against his chest. His left hand was held near his knee, palm facing down and parallel to the pavement. It had been a long time since Aris had done infantry work. Over seven years. He'd forgotten how exposed you could feel, running out in front of the monolithic death machines. After so many years inside a BattleMech, the thought of those massive weapons tracking him was unnerving.

Reaching the other side of the street, Aris edged up toward the corner while breathing a silent prayer of thanks for Hiritsu infantry training techniques. He glanced back, saw the *Huron Warrior* still paused near the entrance to the alley. From his new position, he could distinctly hear the plodding, pavement-crushing thuds of BattleMech footfalls. Risking a quick glance around the corner, he saw a *Vulcan* moving cautiously down the street toward the intersection. Every few paces it would pause, checking nearby buildings and alleys for possible ambush.

Aris knelt and quickly lit his last cocktail. The idea of trying to signal Raven entered his mind. But he couldn't be sure she was even watching him right now, and he didn't have much time. *Hopefully this will get her attention.*

When the cloth ignited, Aris rose and ran around the corner. He allowed himself five paces to build up momentum, and then threw the bottle with every last iota of strength he possessed. It arced out, sailing a good thirty meters before smashing down against the *Vulcan*'s right knee and splashing fiery liquid down the giant leg.

That got the pilot's attention. The *Vulcan*'s left-arm machine gun spoke first, sending a stream of bullets into the pavement only steps away from Aris. He quickly about-faced, dodging back around the corner. Behind him he heard again the now-all-too-familiar throaty roar of a BattleMech flamer being set off. The fiery jet slammed into the corner of the building, flames licking around as if still trying to reach the fleeing Hiritsu warrior. A rush of warm air brushed at the nape of his neck, encouraging greater speed.

Aris balled his right hand into a fist and brought it up to touch the top of his head. It was an automatic response, drilled into him during his years in the infantry. It warned of an approaching enemy 'Mech. He thrust his hand into the air then, with one finger held out. *One enemy BattleMech.*

Glancing up, he saw the *Huron Warrior* tracking him with its head movement. Damn! Wasn't Raven paying attention? This was the second time he'd drawn fire, quite literally, from a BattleMech in order to warn her. She should be getting ready to strike at the approaching *Vulcan.* What was she thinking? *She's thinking what the hell am I doing in Tarrahause.*

Aris knew he had her attention, but there was no way to warn her of the trap set at the Tarrahause aerodrome and 'Mech yards. No direct way.

He slowed and then stopped. It wouldn't be more than a few seconds before the *Vulcan* came round that corner, but he had to try. He held out his right arm, and then with his left hand made chopping motions against it. An infantry-scout signal to others. Counting off enemy lances. He hoped Raven remembered her infantry training. He stopped at a count of six lances. Next he placed a balled right fist in his left palm and inscribed a circle in the air. *DropShip.* Finally he slashed his left hand across his chest and then pointed it back up the street, toward the center of town. *Abort! Get the hell out of here!* There was no signal for *trap* or *ambush*, a deficiency Aris would correct if he ever made it back to Randar.

He heard the violent rush of the flamer, still burning and growing louder, and glanced back. The *Vulcan*, flame unit still operating, was coming around the corner and sending a wall of fire straight down the walk toward Aris. There was no time to run and no cover available. Aris had one way out and took it. Covering his head protectively with his arms, he dove through a window of the building he stood next to.

The shattering glass cut through the sleeves of his light

jacket and into both arms. Another shard stuck into his calf about two centimeters and broke off. Pain lanced through his body as he hit the floor inside.

Aris rolled to his feet, teeth clenched against the pain, and counted himself lucky as the flame tracked away from the building and toward the *Huron Warrior* in the street. He limped deeper into the building, which was filled with offices of some kind. Then the building shook with violent force, knocking Aris off his feet. Chunks of plaster fell from the ceiling, and he heard wood and brick giving way behind and above him. He scrabbled into the next room, a conference room, and dove underneath some kind of large hardwood table.

Most of the roof fell in on top of that a moment later.

Aris Sung! Raven tightened the video image, shocked at the sudden appearance of her company leader and needing further reassurance that it was indeed him. She watched him light a rag sticking out of the neck of a bottle, and then run around the corner.

And just as quickly he came running back into view, a reddish-orange cascade of fire chasing him. She tracked him, relieved to see that the flames were sufficiently blocked by the edge of the building. Suddenly the events surrounding the *Hermes II* made sense. Aris must have blown up that burning vehicle, and thrown more of those bottles—filled with gasoline, or something similar—in an effort to warn her of the enemy BattleMech's position. And the *Hermes II* had been hiding in a dead-end alley, which meant it must have been in place before she ever arrived. Either this was shaping up to be an extremely unlikely coincidence—Aris and an enemy 'Mech in this section of the city—or . . .

A chill washed through her, and it had nothing to do with the circulation in her cooling vest. *They knew we were coming?* But that couldn't be. Not after all of Ty Wu Non's security precautions. Then Aris stopped and signed to her using Hiritsu infantry signals. *Two companies of BattleMechs. A DropShip. And the abort/fall back signal.* Raven put it together quickly enough. The only DropShips nearby were the SMM DropShips at the Kaifeng aerodrome. A trap. Another blasted trap! Aris was warning House Hiritsu out of the city!

Then her sensors screamed a warning as an enemy *Vulcan* walked into the intersection, and Aris dove through a nearby window to escape the flames.

The *Vulcan* pilot's reactions were slightly faster than the *Hermes II*'s had been. Immediately the flamer swung up to wash its flames over Raven's 'Mech. It triggered its large pulse laser almost simultaneously with Raven firing off her extended-range large and medium pulse lasers. Sapphire darts chewed into the *Huron Warrior*'s left torso, melting valuable protective armor. The flamer did little except drive her heat up, but levels in the yellow band of the heat monitor were no cause for alarm. Not yet. Her return fire savaged the *Vulcan*'s left leg and lower left torso, but both 'Mechs were far from hurting.

Then Raven Clearwater brought her Gauss rifle into play.

The large-bore rifle spat out one of its nickel-ferrous slugs, catching the *Vulcan* in its right arm and tearing it clean off at the shoulder. Her large laser stabbed deep into its left leg again, this time melting the last of its armor and cutting into the endo-steel frame. She weathered the light return fire, absorbing the damage against her right leg.

The combination of both the *Huron Warrior*'s large weapons and a possibly ruined actuator in the left leg threw the *Vulcan* off-balance. It stumbled, almost falling, but managed to right itself. Then the second Gauss slug punched into its left leg right where it joined the torso, and the hapless 'Mech lost its second limb. There was no saving it this time. The *Vulcan* stumbled forward, listed to the left, and fell into the very building where Aris had taken cover. The wall gave way under forty tons of BattleMech, and the *Vulcan* went down amid a cloud of crushed plaster and brick.

"Nooooo!" Raven yelled in frustration, not realizing she'd left her commline open to voice-activation. Her three lancemates were on the air fast enough, asking what was wrong and promising they were closing fast on her position. Raven clenched her jaw against any other outbursts. Weapons poised to fire on the *Vulcan* again, she hesitated as she searched the rubble for any sign of Aris

Sung. Even when the *Vulcan* began shifting about, trying to bring its laser to bear on her *Warrior,* Raven waited.

The first weapons to reach her did not come from the building, though. Her sensors alerted her to a third enemy 'Mech, and then a fourth. Checking her head's-up display and primary monitor, she found both of the new machines further south along the street she where she stood. A *Vindicator* and a *Hunchback,* according to the tags her computer painted up on the tactical display. The *Vindicator* fired from extreme range, its PPC lancing into the *Warrior*'s center torso and robbing her of half the armor there. Then the *Vulcan* was able to free at least one of its weapons, and its medium pulse laser stabbed into her right arm.

Raven fired in automatic response, her heat levels spiking high into the yellow band as she triggered all three of her weapons. The Gauss slug was only a fraction of a second behind her large and medium lasers, and all three found the *Vulcan* where it nested in the cavity it had carved into the building. The enemy 'Mech thrashed about, trying to escape certain death and causing more destruction. One more Gauss slug breached its center torso and tore through its fusion engine, effectively gutting the 40-ton 'Mech. It was small consolation to Raven that the engine did not explode and level the rest of the building.

As a second PPC beam missed high, a green circle tagged Apollo One appeared on her HUD, to the rear. Brion Lee, one of her lancemates. She had the enemy 'Mechs evenly matched now. She wanted to tear into them, but a desire for vengeance gave way to a higher calling. Aris had warned her away from the city. Warned her of the trap, possibly at the cost of his own life. She could not disregard that warning. With one final look at the ruined building, half of which now lay in rubble, she turned back to the north and took advantage of the *Warrior*'s speed.

"This is Lance Leader Clearwater to command," she said, after dialing in the battalion's general frequency. "We have hostiles in hiding at the northeast edge of the city. They were waiting for us. Repeat, they knew we were coming."

"Confirm that, Raven Clearwater."

Even through the filtering, Raven could recognize Ty Wu Non's voice and it lent her strength. The battalion commander had flown in to direct this operation personally, leaving Beijing with Company Leader James.

"Confirmed, Battalion Commander. This is a trap and we are disengaging. I was warned off by Company Leader Aris Sung. He was in the city. He indicated to me that there was also a trap waiting at the aerodrome."

Ty Wu Non was silent for a brief moment. When he returned, his voice was as composed as ever. He confirmed Raven's retreat, and then calmly ordered the withdrawal of Hiritsu forces closing on the aerodrome and 'Mech yards. The situation had to be eating at him, Raven knew, but no commander leads troops into a known trap unless he is very desperate. His immediate orders given, Ty Wu Non's attention returned to Raven Clearwater. "Aris Sung is still alive?" he asked.

Raven selected one of her auxiliary monitors to a rear view. The *Vindicator* was almost up to the fallen *Vulcan*. "I hope so, Command," she said, forcing a practiced calm into her voice. "I hope so."

Third Interlude

"There is no such thing as Society. There are individual men and women, and there are families."
—Margaret Thatcher, Prime Minister of Great Britain,
Terra, circa 1984

Pr'ret Forest
Sarmaxa
Sarna March, Federated Commonwealth
2 August 3057

What had burned down this area of the Pr'ret Forest Aris couldn't say. Lightning maybe, or a carelessly tended campfire. The decimation was new enough that the ground still had a scorched look to it, and terrain maps loaded into his *Wraith*'s computer did not show the destruction. It was, however, old enough that life was already returning in the form of sparse grass and very small saplings. The ruined area stretched several kilometers, through flatlands and over a few small hills—forming a natural arena in which the Sarmaxa Militia had decided to implement another rear defensive action.

Aris' *Wraith* rocked under the explosions of a half dozen missiles. He counted himself lucky as nearly another dozen of the solid-fuel projectiles chewed into the ground around him and a flurry of medium laser-fire passed by harmlessly. The *Quickdraw* and *Crusader* that had squared off against him both tried to backpedal out of optimum range while waiting for their weapons to cycle. Too late. Aris cut into the *Quickdraw* with his large pulse laser and both of his mediums, drawing molten lines across its barrel-like torso.

Kicking his 'Mech up to its top speed of nearly one hundred twenty kilometers per hour, Aris raced in at an oblique angle. He had to stay under the effective firing range of the enemy's long-range missile racks, but their close combat ability could also overwhelm him, which meant he had to keep on the move. He noted that, half a klick away, Ty Wu Non had not yet come to that realization as he took almost a full barrage from an older *Archer* variant and a standard *Thunderbolt*. His *Charger*'s armor absorbed the damage and remained on its feet, this time, but Aris doubted that Ty Wu Non could take that kind of punishment for very long.

In fact, no one in the unit could, which had been Aris' point from the start of this assault.

The Liao-Marik Offensive against Victor Davion's Sarna March was in its second month. Several star systems had already fallen, Warrior Houses such as Matsukai and Ijori spearheading a successful drive into the territory taken from the Capellan Confederation in the Fourth Succession War. Meanwhile, what should have been a main thrust through Sarmaxa, Sarna, Sakhalin, and beyond was stalling. Stapleton's Grenadiers and the Tooth of Ymir mercenary unit had failed to take Sarna, as Aris and several others among House Hiritsu, including House Master York, had predicted. And the bulk of House Hiritsu continued to sit on their stronghold world of Randar, held in reserve by Sun-Tzu and Ion Rush. Only one company under Ty Wu Non had been given permission to advance, and then only to the nearby world of Sarmaxa.

Sarmaxa's defenders consisted of six older Battle-Mechs piloted by the planet's standing militia. Hardly a match for a Warrior House in a stand-up fight, and the defenders knew it. Those six 'Mechs had successfully frustrated Company Leader Non's strategic planning and bogged down the entire assault by playing a hit-and-fade game that Aris had warned his commander about right from the start. The defenders would give up ground in return for pulling the faster Hiritsu 'Mechs out of formation, then turn and nip at the leaders. Li Quan Noh's *Snake* and Lynn Trahn's *Huron Warrior* were already sidelined, one with gyro damage and the other now missing a leg. In return, the defenders had lost their *Ostroc*. A great trade, for them.

But Ty Wu Non would not listen. Determined to run the defenders to ground and put an end to the only form of resistance on Sarmaxa, he repeatedly ordered his company in pursuit of the Federated Commonwealth-trained warriors. Aris never questioned the order again. Ty Wu Non was his superior, and had rejected his advice. Now Aris and his company leader had caught up with four of the remaining five militia BattleMechs in this open area.

Aris held no illusions as to who held the advantage.

Taking the corner sharply, he once more threw off the tracking of the missiles that hounded him. Only three reached their mark, chipping away at his still-strong armor. He was not so fortunate with the enemy laser fire. As Aris fired off his own lasers, ruby and emerald darts scored against his left arm and leg. Nearly a full ton of armor was burned away, leaving his left arm especially vulnerable but still without a breach.

The enemy *Quickdraw* was not so well-favored. The scarlet beam of Aris' large pulse laser struck into its left-side, already weakened by his medium lasers a moment before. The beam cut through the last of the armor and into the *Quickdraw*'s internal structure, coring through the loading racks for the 'Mech's long-range missile system and then finally into the ammunition itself. No protective CASE feature for this older 'Mech, the ammunition bay ruptured and spilled incredible explosive force throughout the torso. The explosion of the BattleMech's fusion engine followed on the heels of the ammunition, and the machine simply ceased to exist. An arm flew through the air and slammed into the *Crusader*, crushing a few armor plates over its left leg. No other pieces were large enough to accurately identify.

A thrill of elation shot through Aris Sung, as he once more pivoted inward and fought to keep optimum range against the *Crusader*, which fell back toward his other two companions. That elation quickly cooled and settled into the pit of his stomach like a block of lead, however, as Aris saw Ty Wu Non's *Charger* take another barrage of missile and laser fire. The *Archer* and *T-Bolt* moved in to finish it off.

It never mattered to Aris that Ty had brought this on himself. What he saw was a fellow member of House Hiritsu and his superior officer, fallen. House Hiritsu was his home, these people his family. Any personal difficulties between him and Ty Wu Non did not belong on the battlefield. Aris locked his T&T system onto the enemy *Archer*, judging it the more deadly of the pair. His tactical screen placed the enemy 'Mech at a hair under three hundred meters.

Aris brought the *Wraith* up to its top speed again and rapidly closed the distance. He had to angle away and then turn back in once, avoiding a pile of half-burned logs that could have tripped him up. He didn't waste time trying to fire weapons, concentrating fully on the task at hand. His *Wraith*'s XL engine allowed him to close in less than ten seconds, just as the *Archer*'s large missile systems cycled.

Far too late to do much beside panic, the *Archer*'s pilot noticed Aris' approach at better than one hundred kph and coming in from behind. Only the *Archer*'s rear-facing medium lasers could be brought to bear, and they stabbed out, trying to deter the Hiritsu warrior. The green beams splashed over the *Wraith*'s torso, melting armor but not seriously hindering the 'Mech in any way. The *Thunderbolt* twisted its torso to bring its weapons to bear on Aris, but the *Archer* blocked a direct line of sight and the Sarmaxa pilot could only watch and wait for the shot.

Aris' BattleMech slammed into the rear of the *Archer* with incredible force. Armor plates on the front of the *Wraith* shattered and dropped away, but that was next to nothing compared to the damage wrought against the hapless *Archer*. Its left arm suffered a crushed shoulder actuator and its left leg lost over half its armor from the jarring impact. Its rear-torso armor tore away as if made of paper. The titanium supports that made up the BattleMech's internal skeleton bent inward. Physical shielding around the reactor was ruptured and the gyro knocked off balance.

One of its long-range missile systems was destroyed, though the ammunition inside did not detonate in the launcher.

But that was to be a fleeting sense of luck. The force of the impact threw the *Archer* forward. Unable to keep the 'Mech upright under such an attack, its pilot abandoned it to gravity. The 'Mech tumbled and slid for thirty meters over the blackened ground, tearing large furrows and leaving behind even more of its precious armor plating. As the *Archer* flipped around for the last time, it came down on its back. A weakened support bent further inward, piercing the ammunition storage bay in the *Archer*'s right torso. Fuel cells ruptured, spilling solid propellant among the missile racks. A shower of sparks from the support beam scraping the ammunition storage casing set it off. The *Archer*'s torso jumped into the air, launched by the powerful explosion beneath it. As the left-side ammunition detonated, followed quickly by the fusion engine, the *Archer* followed its companion *Quickdraw* into obscurity.

That was enough for the other two Sarmaxa 'Mechs. They withdrew, turning their fire on Aris to keep him at bay. Aris had barely controlled his *Wraith* after the impact, keeping to his feet by the slimmest of margins. Shaken and bruised from where his restraining straps had cut into his shoulders, he decided not to give chase. Instead, he ran his 'Mech back toward Ty Wu Non's *Charger,* which was regaining its feet with shaky control. He helped his company leader back into the cover of the trees. The armor on Ty's *Charger* was more memory than reality. Gray smoke poured out of a rent in the front torso, and green coolant leaked down the front in tiny rivulets to drip onto the ground below.

"I'm on my feet, Aris Sung," Ty's voice whispered through the communication gear, as if sensing Aris' thoughts. Aris was willing to bet the other warrior was studying a damage schematic of the 'Mech and finding it to be mostly outlined in red.

"Shall we pursue, then, Company Leader Non?" Aris kept his tone respectful, as if seriously broaching the idea. They both knew the *Charger* was in no shape to pursue, and Ty would not send Aris forward alone. Ty was a natural leader, Aris could recognize that in him. He had the aura of command about him. But he was not a tactician. And his dislike for Aris biased him against any advice the younger warrior might offer. "May I make a personal observation, sir?"

"An observation, yes."

Aris carefully phrased his next few sentences. Ty had rejected his advice once, which closed the issue. But if he could bring up a new factor . . . "Company Leader Non, not burdened with your responsibilities, I have noticed something. The enemy 'Mechs have kept to the forest's denser areas, which slows them down. They stop and fight only in clearings or when they can gain a hillside and use the height to their advantage. Doesn't this suggest predictability?"

Ty Wu Non's voice was a calm neutral. "You still believe we could slip 'Mechs in front of them. Using the DropShip, no doubt?"

"That is certainly one possibility, sir."

"Name another."

Was that a crack in the normally impenetrable wall? "My *Wraith* is the fastest 'Mech we've got. I could try to place myself in their way long enough for a coordinated strike force to come at them from the rear."

There was a long pause, as if Ty was considering the possibility. When he came back, though, it was as if Aris had never spoken. "I have Terry Chan on another frequency, Lance Leader Sung. She's only a few moments away. You will await her here, and then pursue the enemy. Pursue, harass, engage if they stand and fight again. Do you understand?"

Aris nodded to the empty cockpit. "Pursue, harass, engage—yes, sir." Answer: no; subject closed. Aris turned his 'Mech and walked back into the burned-out clearing. The Sarmaxa machines were just fading off his scanners, and he plotted in their course in preparation for setting off after them again. Ty Wu Non was determined to win this his way. And if Aris could, he would win this for his company leader. Thoughts of how it could be won—how it should be won—were no longer relevant, so Aris dismissed them from his mind.

That was the way of House Hiritsu, and Aris was a devoted son of the House.

═══ 19 ═══

Tarrahause
Tarrahause District, Kaifeng
Sarna Supremacy, Chaos March
24 July 3058

Aris sat on the sidewalk, resting up against an intact wall of the ruined building where he'd dived for cover against the *Vulcan*'s flamer. To his left the lower torso and remaining leg of the blasted *Vulcan* stuck out of the building. Its other leg and an arm lay a short distance away. Across the street Kyle's car still burned, throwing dancing shadows over the area.

Aris had crawled out of the building covered in dust, bleeding and bruised, his hair and clothing singed. From his jacket he cut strips to bind his arms and thigh to control the bleeding where the shards of the window he'd crashed through had sliced him. The big hardwood table had saved his life when the side of the building caved in. One side had collapsed under the weight of falling debris, but the other remained solid, the strong hardwood top deflecting away the rain of bricks and beams. A clock, miraculously intact in the midst of all that damage, had told him it was after midnight and so the cease-fire would be in effect. Aris hadn't been able to find any evidence of a destroyed *Huron Warrior,* and so decided that Raven Clearwater had gotten safely away to warn House Hiritsu of the trap laid at the aerodrome. A welcome thought, since there obviously wasn't anything more he could do about that.

Headlights swept into the intersection. Aris debated whether or not he should hide, and decided not to bother. Private citizens wouldn't trouble him. The Djing-cha he could handle. And soldiers . . . Aris adjusted the Nakjama laser pistol he'd salvaged from the *Vulcan*'s cockpit and stuck it into the waistband of his pants at the small of his back. He had special plans for any soldiers.

With the excitement over and the pressure off, Li Wynn's statement that a Hiritsu warrior had turned against the House twisted in Aris' stomach like a cold steel blade. Aris didn't doubt him; Li had believed what he was saying. And why wouldn't it be true? There'd already been so many proofs of betrayal. The aerospace raid near Nochen. The trap at the port terminal, and again at the Jinxiang Bridge. The set-up tonight. Blind devotion to his House has prevented him from seeing the truth. The thought so alien . . . But who else besides a House warrior could have provided that kind of information to the Kaifeng SMM?

The assassination of House Master York?

A cold chill spiked into Aris' heart and shook him almost to the core of his being. *No!* He wanted to shout, to rail at the heavens. A House warrior couldn't have been involved in that. And especially couldn't have performed the deed him or herself. That violated precepts at the heart of House Hiritsu. The Lorix Order, which taught that the highest and most important ideal in any MechWarrior's life is loyalty . . . to the chief executive of the state, who is the MechWarrior's commander-in-chief. And the teachings of K'ung-fu-tzu stressed that filial piety, obedience to parents, is one of the most important virtues. Aris didn't want to believe it possible that a warrior of the House had struck off the family head.

But he did believe it. That shook his confidence more than anything else, that he was able to think it not only possible but likely. He remembered his first hours in the Kaifeng system, his thoughts aboard the JumpShip *Liu* of striking out at Ty Wu Non. Was that so far off from actually doing it? And at that point, how much further to out-right betrayal?

A ways, Aris answered himself. But the seeds of failure and betrayal were present in everyone. If they were nur-tured with the right amount of hate and jealousy—

"Aris? Is that you? Man, you look wasted."

Li Wynn looked out of the car window, then opened the door and got out. "We've been looking for you everywhere."

Aris relaxed. Besides Li, he saw the other three young thieves he'd met earlier. "I think I got greedy," he lied. "Came up too soon and got caught in the fun."

Li looked over at the destroyed *Vulcan*. "That was our contact. Damn. No wonder. We haven't found hardly any-thing opened up like we'd hoped. And Kyle's car is gone. One of the metalheads probably picked it up and threw it at something. We had to *borrow* another."

"So you didn't find anything?" Aris asked, rising to his feet.

"Nothing worth talking about. Maybe enough to pay for Kyle's car and the bribes it took to set things up with the mercenary."

Aris limped over to the car. "Maybe I can help you do something about that. What if I could make good your losses tonight?"

That got Li's attention. "How?"

"We'll give things the day to settle down. Then tonight, let's you and me take a trip over to that club you men-tioned, the one where all the MechWarriors hang out." And there, the fates be kind, Aris would find a clue to who the House Hiritsu traitor was.

$=$ **20** $=$

Jinxiang River Port Terminal 5 South
Tarrahause District, Kaifeng
Sarna Supremacy, Chaos March
24 July 3058

Battalion Commander Ty Wu Non sat at the head of the cafeteria table, surrounded by the rest of his command staff. Silently, he let his gaze travel over the faces of his company leaders and lance leaders—studying them even as they waited for him to speak first. Raven Clearwater, near the far end of the table, stared at the cream-colored tabletop and appeared lost in her own thoughts. Terry Chan, at his immediate left, also looked troubled by her thoughts, but was almost able to hide it. Everyone else met his gaze with a strange mixture of uncertainty and expectancy, unsure of the next step but trusting their commander to provide guidance. Everyone except Thom Lindell, who sat stone-faced at the table's far end. Ty squared his shoulders against the weight that seemed to press down on them. Back straight and face set against emotion, he tried to project strength to his people while inwardly his thoughts swirled in turmoil.

Aris Sung was alive. It shouldn't have surprised him. The younger warrior had pulled off a number of feats of survival in the eleven years Ty had been his Mentor, and luck just seemed to follow him around. With the possibility

Aris was dead, Ty's dislike of him had mellowed over the last few days. He no longer thought of Aris as a threat to his position, nor even a challenge to his own ability. Aris was an asset, a son of House Hiritsu, and Ty would be doing his family a disservice not to accept that. The boy was bright and quick-witted. And always, it seemed, where the action was. *Year of the Horse,* Ty thought. He had never followed the older Chinese customs—House Hiritsu running strongly toward the philosophy of Confucius—but this once it made him wonder.

Ty blinked away those thoughts, not wanting them to show on his face. Aris Sung would certainly come up in the discussion, but was not the first order of business this time. The repeated ability of the Kaifeng SMM to predict House Hiritsu movements had gone beyond being merely a hindrance; it now threatened the entire assault. If Aris had not warned off the raid against Tarrahause, Ty could have lost half of his warriors. Such losses might be considered acceptable to Ion Rush and even Chancellor Liao, provided Kaifeng was taken and held according to the plan, but the losses were unacceptable to him. He expected to lose warriors, but he would not sacrifice them.

"Very well," he whispered, more to himself than his people, though they would hardly know that. "As of this day, I am declaring the original plan of assault against Kaifeng fully dissolved. The record will show no fault against anyone, especially since the strategy worked so well in the south and partially up here on the northern continent. But we can no longer attribute the ability of the Kaifeng SMM to predict our movements to anything other than advance knowledge of our plans. Comments?"

Jill McDaniels was first to speak. "Can we be sure about that, Battalion Commander? We saw no sign of a trap near the aerodrome. We only have some vague hand signals from Aris Sung that *could* be interpreted in that manner."

"Are you questioning my ability to read infantry signals, MechWarrior McDaniels?" Raven Clearwater asked, locking eyes with McDaniels. "Or is it Company Leader Sung's warning itself you doubt?"

There was no anger, no hint of recrimination in Raven's voice; she was much too skilled in the ways of the House for such a breach of courtesy. But the questions were inappropriate. Ty Wu Non understood Raven's frustration—she had seen her company leader go down and then was forced to abandon him a second time in pursuit of a higher-calling—but he could not condone any form of disunity. Especially in front of him.

"Lance Leader Clearwater," he said, voice flat and toneless to communicate his displeasure, "I believe the question was meant for me to answer."

Realizing her error, Raven's face pinched in shame, and she nodded lightly. "My apologies, Battalion Commander, and to you Jill McDaniels. I spoke out of turn."

Ty allowed his voice to soften. "We understand how you feel, Raven Clearwater. We will discuss Aris Sung in a moment." He turned back to Jill. "Now, to your question, Tarrahause had 'Mechs in hiding, ready for Raven's lance. Since the area of the city possessed little strategic value, we can only assume that the 'Mechs were there specifically to counter our diversionary raid. This gives extra weight to Aris Sung's warning. I believe they were waiting for us at the aerodrome. The question is, how?"

Company Leader Jason James rubbed at his square jawbone. "Could they be tapping into our communications?"

Ty shook his head lightly. "We have never broadcasted or plans over the airwaves. Such intelligence-gathering would have to be done through the use of listening devices, and our technicians assure me that this could not be the case."

"Satellite observation," Thom Lindell said from the other end of the table, his voice measuring out each syllable. "Or high-flying aerospace observation craft."

Ty paused, considering. "I do not see how. I have kept either the *Dainwu* or the *Lao-tzu* in orbit above us. There have been no aircraft or direct satellite passes. And, besides, that would be visual information only."

"Battalion Commander," Terry Chan said, drawing his attention, "it seems we're grasping in the dark when there's an obvious solution to our problem."

"Go on, Chan."

Terry Chan drew in a deep, steadying breath. "Aris Sung. I've given this much thought." She held up three fingers and ticked each one off as she counted her reasons. "He is in Tarrahause. He is an accomplished scout. And he obviously has some knowledge of their military activities since he was able to place himself on the battlefield before Raven's arrival. If he does not yet know the source of Kaifeng's clairvoyance, he will know where to get it."

"You're suggesting an extraction mission?" Ty was surprised, but couldn't decide if pleasantly so. He wouldn't have thought Terry Chan would ever suggest they recover Aris Sung, since that would automatically demote her back to lance leader. And if there was anyone he should be able to read, it was Terry Chan. But perhaps the animosity she'd shared with him for Aris Sung was mellowing along with his own. He considered the idea. "We do have two days before hostilities resume, per the cease-fire agreement. But Aris could be anywhere in the city, if he still lives after that last battle."

Raven Clearwater sat forward, hands clasped in front of her on the table. "But there's a chance, Battalion Commander Non, and we should avail ourselves of it. I volunteer for the mission. I was forced to leave him there, it's my responsibility."

"No, Raven," Terry said kindly. "I was Aris Sung's second in command, responsible for his safety. Losing him to the Jinxiang was my fault. Don't forget that I started out as infantry. I've been specifically trained to infiltrate an urban environment. I should go in, alone."

Ty Wu Non worked to not let indecision show on his face or in his movements. Sending Terry Chan in after Aris Sung would create a situation that he could not control, and so should not allow. But then Terry really was the most qualified to operate in that environment, and Aris could indeed have the answers they needed as well as precious military intelligence on the Kaifeng SMM. He decided to test her reasoning. "Lance Leader Chan, have you considered your responsibilities to your company?"

Her reply was well-prepared. "Yes, sir. Over the last half hour. But the truth is that my company currently answers directly to Company Leader Thom Lindell, as per your instructions, and so I operate more in the function of lance leader anyway. The minor disruption in our chain of command is offset by the potential gain."

She had him there. Ty felt a twinge of uncertainty in his gut, but could not pin it down long enough to analyze. So he could find no reasonable argument against Terry Chan's idea. "Very well," he said, nodding. "You will infiltrate Tarrahause as you see fit. But regardless of success, I want you back no later that twenty hundred hours day after tomorrow. Understood?"

Terry Chan nodded back. "Understood, Battalion Commander. But I expect to be back well before then."

"Why is that?"

Terry smiled. "I believe I know right where to look for him."

The main warehouse of Highway Terminal Number Two West had been filled recently. Not with sacks of rice or crated fruit and vegetables, though one corner of the large building was stacked high with such food items. What occupied the spacious building was a pair of Battle-Mechs. A *Raven,* with its hallmark beak-like nose, and a *Blackjack.* Jungle camouflage covered the *Raven,* and the Kaifeng SMM shield rode on its upper right leg. Only the *Blackjack*'s left arm still showed any sign of camouflage, the rest having been painted over with a black base. Two technicians worked up on a hydraulic lift, paint guns wafting a black spray back and forth as they ate up the last of the camouflage.

SMM Major Karl Bartlett walked through the partially open main doors, leaving behind the humid jungle heat of Kaifeng for the immediate relief of the warehouse's shaded interior. Paul Harris and Kevin Yang, two of his most trusted leftenants, *Linebacker* pilots in his own lance, followed close behind. Their eyes were wide with curiosity. Bartlett knew they had questions, but they were good enough soldiers to wait for his briefing.

He stopped walking when the paint fumes began to sting at his nose. "Okay," he said calmly, "here's the deal. Our *friends* in House Hiritsu are willing to up the stakes. If we can arrange to severely discredit House Hiritsu, they'll deliver their battalion commander and his most loyal warriors into an ambush."

Bartlett smiled at their wide-eyed looks of shock, enjoying the surprise he'd generated. He'd been working toward a grand play such as this ever since General Fallon had given him direct access to the Hiritsu traitor, something that would vault him into the limelight as the man who defeated a Capellan Warrior House. It would get him out of Cyndi Fallon's shadow. Almost certainly he would be sent to Sarna. And if the Sarna Supremacy ever did fail—*and let's face it,* he thought, *even the Solaris bookies only give us a one in five chance of making it to the year 3060 as an independent state*—that kind of reputation followed a man. Karl Bartlett would be able to get a command anywhere, except maybe in the Capellan Confederation.

Kevin Yang's surprise melted into a puzzled frown. "What are our *friends* getting out of this? Seems kind of one-sided to me."

Paul Harris answered before Bartlett could speak. "Obviously they're working to take down the upper leadership so they can take control of their precious House. From what I understand"—he looked to Bartlett for confirmation—"they've never asked for anything except that we fight a series of limited engagements. They don't want the House destroyed, just weakened."

Bartlett nodded. "There might also be some other political considerations back in the Confederation as well, but those don't concern us."

The two leftenants looked at each other and then back at him. "What's the plan?" Harris asked.

"These two machines"—Bartlett jerked a thumb over his shoulder at the *Raven* and *Blackjack*—"are going to be painted the green and black of the House Hiritsu. The *Raven* is Trufeau's, from our own scout lance. He thinks it's down with actuator trouble. The *Blackjack* we borrowed from Jacob's Juggernauts. Both are standard Liao designs that have been seen in the Hiritsu assault force.

"Tomorrow, during the Dragon Boat Festival, you two will take them through our picket line and raze the lakeshore area where the festival is taking place. Breaking the cease-fire, violating the fertility rites festival. The people of Kaifeng will turn rabid against the Capellans. Hiritsu wouldn't be able to hold the planet then even if the SMM packed up and shipped out, handing over the keys to the world." He chuckled, obviously amused with the plan.

"Walk through our picket lines?" Paul Harris looked doubtful. "Do they know we're coming?"

"And what do you mean by raze?" Yang added.

"Of course they don't know you're coming," Bartlett said. "I want this kept to as few people as possible. But I've positioned the watch stations to leave a good-sized hole in the southwest sector. That gives you clear access to Lake Ch'u Yuan's western shore. The festival is on the north shore, so you'll have to walk around part of the lake.

"As for what I mean by *raze*," Bartlett said, looking hard at Kevin Yang, "is heavy property damage. Kick in buildings, step on cars, throw a medium laser or two into a *zongji* stand—disrupt the festival."

Kevin's eyes widened further, as if unable to believe what he was hearing. "Two words, Karl. Ares Conventions. Ever hear of it?"

Bartlett turned a withering glare on Kevin Yang. Of course he'd heard of it. The Ares Conventions were a system of regulations designed to keep war to the battlefield and spare the civilian population as much as possible. The rules had been intended to keep war from plunging the Inner Sphere back into the dark ages. But dammit, he wasn't asking them for a Kentares Massacre. "We'll pad the report later to indicate massive casualties," he explained. "We don't target our own people."

He didn't mention the real casualties that would occur simply from collateral damage. By the look in Harris' eyes, Bartlett saw that he already realized and accepted that. With his wife in Hiritsu hands on the recharge station, it was doubtful the man would balk.

Yang shifted uncomfortably from one foot to the other. "The general know about this?"

"No!" Bartlett barked, then softened his tone into a low growl. "And she's not going to either. Cyndi Fallon would never go for this because she can't make the hard decisions. She'd rather sit here and pray for reinforcements and allow our *friends* to dictate our strategy to us. Well, guess what, gentlemen? Sarna is under blockade. Three Liao warships—warships! two frigates and a destroyer—with an impressive fighter screen, have Sarna closed up tighter than a Lyran merchant's purse. And Sarna jump points are swarming with marine assault craft. Any JumpShip not willing to risk a pirate point has to risk boarding parties. They've already repulsed three Sarna attempts to break out and get us reinforcements."

"Why haven't we been told this before?" Paul Harris asked, clearly upset. "I would call this affecting our strategy."

Bartlett smiled thinly. *Because I withheld it for the shock value, here and now.* "Fallon doesn't want it widely known that we're cut off from Sarna." Which was true enough. He let his voice turn cold. "Current estimates from Sarna predict a break-out within the next few weeks."

"Weeks?" Harris shouted, then continued more quietly. "That means we can't hope to see help for at least a month."

Bartlett nodded. He could see he had their attention. "Or we can end this matter ourselves."

Kevin Yang still had reservations, but Bartlett could see his resolve cracking. "You trust these people? I mean, Capellan Warrior Houses have never been known for harboring traitors."

"That's true," Bartlett acknowledged. "But I guess times change, even in the repressive Capellan Confederation. Our *friends* have been right several times now, at the cost of Hiritsu lives and equipment. I'd say they've bought their credibility."

Not only that, Bartlett thought, but tonight he would be meeting the go-between who had passed along all the information so far. Face to face. That would give him a chance to double-check the particulars and iron out any wrinkles. Especially this Aris Sung who was supposedly at large in Tarrahause; he could be a problem. The only thing that confused him was why the informant wanted to meet in a public place. That wasn't typical for such a sensitive meeting.

Paul Harris suddenly spoke up. "You think people will believe a Capellan Warrior House intentionally targeted civilian targets?"

Bartlett was ready for that question. "Look at the Hiritsu strategy. They're concentrating on shutting down our food production, preventing our exports. You'll be coming in from the west. The main docks that receive shipping off the Jinxiang are on the southeast lakeshore."

"So we're merely heading for the docks, and the festival is in the way," Harris finished, the reservation gone from his voice. He was obviously sold.

Kevin rubbed at his chin. "I'd feel better if they were the ones actually committing the crime, though. Their battalion commander, huh?"

"I've been guaranteed that their commander and several of his most loyal supporters will be present." Bartlett leaned forward. "I believe we can take out a full company along with their higher-ranked officers, and force them to abandon their efforts against Kaifeng. Even if they tried to mount a full assault against Mahabohdi then, they wouldn't have a strong enough force to take it." He paused for effect, then continued. "What do you say, gents? Either of you want to be known for decimating a Liao Warrior House?"

More glances between the two men and around the warehouse, then after a quick nod from Kevin Yang, Paul Harris answered for them both. "All right. What *exactly* do you want us to do?"

The Gold Pavilion, Tarrahause
Tarrahause District, Kaifeng
Sarna Supremacy, Chaos March
24 July 3058

The Gold Pavilion was loud and obnoxious. The newest video games on Kaifeng lined an entire wall, challenging the reflexes and, occasionally, the intelligence of the patrons. Most of their noise was lost to the two jukeboxes that competed with each other from opposite sides of the large, open room, holo images of the musical performers dancing on top. The bar was set in the middle of the room, an island amid a small, dimly lit sea of dark carpet, tables, and bodies. Just the kind of place that would be popular with Kaifeng's MechWarriors.

Aris had cut his dark hair short, having shaved it over the ears to remove the singed hair and imitate one of the latest styles. Li Wynn stood a loose guard outside, supposedly watching the dark streets for Djing-cha troops, but mostly to keep him out of Aris' way. Right now he was wandering about the place, sipping at the four C-Bill soft drink he'd picked up at the bar. He doubted that any other warrior of House Hiritsu would ever voluntarily enter such an establishment. The discordant music and smoky atmosphere assaulted the senses, a harsh contrast to the austere, House-controlled life.

Kaifeng MechWarriors had taken over one corner of the large room, packing chairs tightly around a cluster of three tables as if setting a defensive perimeter around some important facility. Apparently the Kaifeng SMM got on well with their mercenary cousins. Aris counted three military regulars and four mercs as he walked past, with two whose affiliation he wasn't sure of. For the most part they made it easy, wearing jackets or shirts with unit insignia on them. There were of course other tells as well, like military haircuts and shaved areas of the head for better contact with neurohelmet sensors, but those couldn't always be trusted.

The main target of Aris' little scouting mission sat against the wall, chair rocked back on two legs while he enjoyed a cigarette and kept a close eye on activity throughout the club. He wore a utility jacket made from the lightweight but strong fabric favored by FedCom MechWarriors once they left the steamy confines of their cockpits. The red and black Kaifeng SMM patch rode on one shoulder, and another patch on his left breast gave his rank and name as Major Karl Bartlett. Aris figured him to be a FedCom defector who'd stuck around when Sarna went independent. The man had a snobbish air about him as he listened or spoke to his fellow warriors, like he was superior to the average Sarnese. Every few seconds he would tilt his head up and exhale smoke from his cigarette toward a ceiling fan, watching it get cut into thin ribbons and then finally disperse.

The MechWarriors had appropriated chairs from several nearby tables. Now Aris grabbed one of those that stood empty and spun it back to its former position so he could sit. Taking a seat, he set his drink down on the table and pretended to search the crowd for friends. One of the mercenaries took notice of him, but shrugged it off when Aris nodded to a nonexistent comrade on the other side of the bar and motioned to the captured table as if signaling that he'd found a place for them.

Spies did many things in the holovids, Aris thought. But one thing they didn't do was draw attention to themselves. Especially when taking up a position where they could eavesdrop on their target. The way Aris just had.

Ipso facto, as far as the Kaifeng warriors were concerned, Aris couldn't be a spy.

Conversation among the Kaifeng MechWarriors drifted back and forth among topics ranging from old war stories to the latest 'Mech bouts on Solaris. Aris picked up little through his first two glasses of soft drink. He started to plan a new approach, deciding his waiting-for-friends cover must be wearing thin, when his luck turned. A new arrival to the group, who pulled up a chair from another table though several still sat vacant among the other warriors, led the discussion back to the previous night's activities.

"So what's the news?" he asked. "We know yet what happened to our guests last night?"

There were several derogatory comments concerning various aspects of House Hiritsu competence. One warrior, a mercenary, suggested that the main assault force must have gotten lost in the jungle on the way to Tarrahause.

"Yeah, so what happened to Phineas' lance?" asked a younger member of the group with a strong outback accent. "I heard a single CapCon 'Mech took 'im and one of his mates apart."

The mercenary glowered. "They had infantry support. Popped on us before we could ambush the 'Mechs. We were told there'd be no infantry."

"Wasn't no infantry," another merc said. "Not unless the Capellans have turned in SRM-packs for molotovs as their standard anti-Mech weapon."

"Any news on that, Major?" the new arrival asked. "We got dissidents crawling out of the Zone maybe?"

Aris took a sip of his drink, leaned forward and with a large wave attracted the attention of a waiter. He ordered another, loudly. This one with alcohol in it, though he never intended to drink it.

Karl Bartlett shrugged in response to the question. "Maybe," was all he said.

"You okay, Karl?" another MechWarrior asked. "You seem kinda edgy tonight."

"Yeah," chimed in the outback accent, "has there been some word from our *friend,* Major?"

It required a bit of self-control for Aris not to lean in, trying to hear better as the Hiritsu traitor was finally mentioned. Bartlett leaned forward and stubbed his cigarette out against the tabletop. "Nothing," he said curtly. *He's lying,* Aris thought as the Kaifeng Major ham-handedly changed the topic. "I can tell you that our scouts found out where the Hiritsu force is holed up, though. Port Terminal Five South."

Many of the warriors sat up at that news. "Fifty klicks from here? That's a bit close, isn't it?" asked a nervous-looking member of the group. Aris thought he'd heard someone call him Kevin earlier.

"Maybe a bit," Bartlett said. "They could launch a fast strike against us, that's for sure. I've got to tell you, I'm a little concerned that they might not wait out the entire cease-fire."

Aris couldn't help the frown. The line sounded rehearsed, staged. Was there a reason Karl Bartlett wanted his people nervous? Aris couldn't see it. But the fact remained that if Ty Wu Non gave the word of House Hiritsu, then the cease-fire would not be broken by the Warrior House.

Others didn't share Aris' trust. The outback warrior nodded his agreement of Karl Bartlett's assessment. "Damn Cappies are sneaky as Dracs, but ain't half as honorable."

"What would you know about the Draconis Combine, Martin?" It was the new arrival again. He leaned over and punched his friend lightly in the shoulder, adopting a mocking version of the other's accent. "Back hills trailrunner. Ya haven't been off-planet any more than us, and I bet you kin count your years off the southern continent on one hand."

The other warrior saluted his friend with his middle finger, joining in on the laugh. Aris rose, slurping down the last sip of his soda. He searched about for the waiter, just another impatient customer. So intent on maintaining his cover, he actually didn't recognize her until she yelled out.

"Aris! Aris Sung!"

Aris couldn't have been more surprised and froze where he was, standing next to his chair. Terry Chan approached his table, drink in hand and weaving a bit drunkenly. She smiled and licked her lower lip, slowly. When she reached the table, she slammed her glass down hard and threw her arms around his neck. Paying no attention to the looks they were getting, she planted a hard kiss on his lips and gyrated her body up against him. Aris maintained enough presence of mind to circle her waist with his hands and tried to look like he was enjoying himself. Truth being that he was completely off-guard, and that made him nervous.

Terry broke from the kiss. "Aris Sung," she slurred, turning it into one name, "you bad boy. I been looking for you everywhere."

"Well, you found me," he said, recovering his wits. Smiling an invitation to her, he sat back down. She slid into the chair opposite. "I thought you were seeing Ty these days." Aris tried not to look anxious as Karl Bartlett and two of his buddies passed by their table, heading for the front of the club. He wanted to follow, but now he would have to maneuver around Terry Chan's adopted role or risk drawing suspicion from the MechWarriors still seated nearby.

"Ty, Ty, Ty," she waved her hand through the air as if brushing away each repetition of the name. "He has other things on his mind these days. You know, though, he did ask about you recently. I think he kind of misses the old days."

Aris wasn't sure how to take that. By now his brain was starting to catch up with the situation, and he could only assume Ty Wu Non had sent Terry in to extract him. But there was his *Wraith* to consider, as well as the need to pass along news of a Hiritsu traitor. They needed to talk more openly. "Look," he said, hedging as if struggling with an uncomfortable shyness, "I was about to head out, maybe try another club. You wouldn't want to come with, would you?"

Terry's smile was truly award-winning. "I thought you'd never ask."

They stood together, Terry slipping one of her hands into Aris' back pocket and walking with her head lying half against his shoulder. Aris circled her waist with his right arm and steered her toward the front of the building. They looked like any of several other couples, and Aris was finally beginning to feel comfortable again.

That comfort lasted all of ten seconds.

His only warning was a slight tensing in Terry Chan's

muscles as they passed through the front door. She was expecting something. Aris barely had time to consider the thought when he found himself staring at the barrel of a .44 caliber slug-thrower.

Karl Bartlett stood outside the door, leaning back against a car parked on the street. His weapon was held at arm's length, centered directly on Aris' chest. A quick glance left and right placed Bartlett's two friends, both with their sidearms out and held ready. The realization hit him as Terry Chan slipped away from his side and left him standing on the walk alone.

She had led him into a trap!

Tarrahause
Tarrahause District, Kaifeng
Sarna Supremacy, Chaos March
24 July 3058

The realization hit Aris like a PPC blast. Terry Chan is the traitor! Calling his full name out in the club alerted Karl Bartlett, and she had held him up just long enough for the SMM major and his two friends to get in position outside. A nice, clean trap, and he'd walked right into it.

Aris' first impulse had been to fasten his hands around Terry Chan's throat and choke the life out of her. It was a knee-jerk reaction more than a thoughtful response. She represented an incredible danger to House Hiritsu—threatening not only the success of the assault but the very foundation of the House itself. Aris' life would be a small sacrifice to protect that. He tensed, ready to spring forward, but his reason prevailed at the last moment. Three weapons aimed at him made for too long of odds. He clenched his hands into impotent fists, willing himself to wait.

As Terry Chan moved further from Aris' side, Bartlett's gun shifted to keep both Hiritsu warriors threatened. "Not so fast, you. I appreciate the tip-off on our warrior friend here, but let's just verify who you are." He smiled thinly. "Thus have I heard . . ." He let his voice trail off speculatively.

Terry Chan nodded. "That a MechWarrior has the right to exact personal retribution," she said, staring at Aris Sung.

"Without fear of reprisal," Bartlett finished.

Aris fought to keep his face passive, and met Chan's gaze evenly. She was obviously expecting some kind of reaction, quoting the Lorix Order out of context in a very self-serving manner. Aris denied her that small sign of victory, though disgust for what she was roiled within. Terry Chan was a traitor to her House, a breaker of the vows and oaths that bound the warriors together. The acidic taste of bile stung at the back of his throat, and Aris swallowed against it.

Bartlett, for his part, seemed satisfied with the response, and the cavernous barrel of the .44 swung back in line with Aris' heart.

"Drop to your knees," he commanded, very calm, very casual, as though sending a messenger for coffee. Aris complied.

"Cross your legs at the ankles and sit back on your calves. Hands behind your head."

Aris knew the drill, one of the classic positions used by law enforcement for centuries to render a subject non-threatening. People on the street stopped to stare at him, and then quickly moved on at the sight of the Kaifeng SMM soldiers with guns drawn. Aris scanned the passing faces for one in particular, but saw no sign of Li Wynn. If the young thief possessed any sense of survival, he was back in the Zone by now.

Bartlett crouched down and leaned in close, the .44 held easily in his right hand but still level with Aris' chest. "So, you're the one who ruined our little surprise last night. A shame, that."

Aris stared over Bartlett's left shoulder, his gaze locked onto Terry Chan. "Why?" he asked simply, voice hard. There was no disbelief, no further moral outrage. It was as if all that had been burned out of him. He simply demanded an answer.

Terry Chan half-smiled, her disdain for him twisting her lips into a sneer. "Why? A predictable question, I suppose, coming from someone who I doubt has ever understood the true potential of a House warrior."

She paused as if she might stop there. But then with a

victorious smile, the air of someone who believes she has won, she continued. "We could be so much more if the House Mentors did not stifle us with all those House laws and traditions. You know the words, Aris."

Her eyes tightened into cold slits as she concentrated on quoting the Lorix Order. " 'MechWarriors must be afforded the opportunities to advance their various skills and expertise to the highest possible level.' Do you see that happening within the Warrior Houses? We used to be considered the elite. Now the Capellan Armed Forces ranks half the Houses as regular or even green troops. Green!" She threw up her hands in a gesture of disgust. "And we are courteous and polite and say 'thank you, sir' just like our traditions demand."

Aris eyed Karl Bartlett, but the man seemed willing to let the conversation take its course. And why not? He was the one holding the weapons, and he probably thought the argument might give him tactical insight into the ways of House Hiritsu. Aris doubted the man could ever understand the inner workings of a Warrior House, especially with Terry Chan as his guide, someone who saw the strength of the House as a mere limitation. "Hiritsu laws and traditions teach discipline, Terry Chan. They are the binding force that holds together the warrior family."

"Will you listen to yourself? Hiritsu laws? The warrior family?" Terry shook her head. "Aris, you distance yourself from the family even as you speak. Aren't they your laws and traditions, your family?"

Aris visibly flinched away from her gaze because deep within himself he was afraid she might be right. Not that House Hiritsu stifled its warriors—man for man the Warrior Houses turned out some of the best troops in the Confederation, in the entire Inner Sphere. No, what he feared was that even after all this time he did not truly belong. That he was still an outsider, playing at having a family.

Chan's voice dropped in volume but increased in intensity, whipping at Aris in a savage whisper. "Some among the House are no longer content with being Sun-Tzu Liao's lap dogs. His, and the ever-faithful Ion Rush's. House Hiritsu has been kept on too short a leash ever since the Fourth Succession War. We were not even allowed a proper place in the Liao-Marik Offensive last year. Our leaders have abandoned their duty to us. That will change. We will change it. Advancement by any means necessary—dogma that can govern the group as well as the individual."

Aris' gaze snapped up to Terry Chan's face, reading her determination and confidence but not finding the fanatical gleam he'd expected. "Advancement by any means? You are a Thugee?" The brutal Thugee cult had gained power in the Confederation and even some measure of respectability with first Romano Liao's backing and then Kali Liao's. But the doctrine was so alien to the ways of House Hiritsu that Aris could not conceive of how a House warrior could even be tempted to join them.

Terry laughed at him, sharp and brittle. "No, Aris Sung. I am not of the Thugee cult. But I do admire their drive to become all they are capable of becoming."

"And their methods?" Aris asked. "Is that what happened to House Master York? Thugees would not hesitate to assassinate their leader if it meant advancement."

A frown stole over Chan's face, and she licked her lips nervously. Obviously the conversation no longer amused her. "I never raised a hand against any member of our House." Aris wasn't sure if she was trying to convince herself or him. "By lending tactical assistance to the Kaifeng SMM, I created situations in which the survival of certain warriors depended on their own combat skills. And if I directly betrayed you to the enemy, then apparently you failed in your advance planning for tonight."

Words someone else has fed to her, Aris thought. So Terry Chan was not the leader. Could it be Ty Wu Non? Aris found that difficult to believe, that the battalion commander would hurt the House over which he was about to assume control. Aris needed more information. "Place any name on it you wish, Terry Chan. House Hiritsu will never follow a renegade."

"Always the loyal son of the House, aren't you, Aris?" Terry asked with a sad expression. "I wish you could see the possibilities that open before us. You came to the House an outsider, and conformed to the traditions better than many. I wish that had not blinded you."

"Is that why you dislike me?" Aris asked. "Because I am content, while the simple truth is that you are merely an oath-breaker and a traitor to your House? I think you give too little credit to our Mentors. House Hiritsu is strong, and it will survive your attempts to force change on it."

The roundhouse kick caught Aris on the right side of his head. There was no time to evade, and his kneeling position precluded any strong actions even if there'd been time. Pain exploded against his right cheekbone and ear, making his vision swim. Aris caught himself before his body could fall hard against the sidewalk, but his torso was still twisted around and his balance was slow in returning. Bartlett had backed up a pace to survey his handiwork, and seemed surprised that Aris had not gone down.

Terry Chan looked on without emotion. She stopped Bartlett with a touch to the shoulder, like a master to her faithful dog. When she spoke, it was like someone explaining a lesson to a child. "You underestimate House Hiritsu, Aris Sung. You of all people should realize that change, even radical change, is built into the core of our philosophy. The will of the House Master is the will of the House. Remember that? And House Masters change."

Aris wasn't allowed to respond. With another touch Terry Chan released her hold on Major Bartlett, who laid a second kick up against his head, and blackness overcame him. In his final thoughts, he cursed Terry Chan for her twisted visions and himself for failing his House by not being better prepared.

As Aris had requested, Li Wynn had loitered around the front of the club to watch for any sign of trouble. The young thief had positioned himself near the side of the building where he could watch the entire front entrance without appearing too conspicuous. The Gold Pavilion's neon sign cast a yellowish glare over the sidewalk and street, cut only briefly by the headlights of passing vehicles, and Li worked at keeping his face in the shadows.

Trouble was a very non-specific term, he thought. Usually it meant Djing-cha troopers, but something told Li that Aris wasn't worried about the local authorities. After seeing Aris' condition the previous night, after the raid, Li wasn't sure he wanted to know what did make Aris worry. Then three men had exited the club. Two wore utility jackets with the Kaifeng SMM insignia, and the third had one of those die-hard military haircuts that left his scalp thinly frosted with small blonde hairs. The first man, one of those in a utility jacket, had spun around and walked backward away from the door until fetching up against a parked car at curbside. The other two broke to either side of the door. All three drew weapons.

Li had decided that this constituted trouble, a thought that was instantly confirmed when Aris stepped out onto the street and was trapped.

The car parked in front of the Gold Pavilion was an old ground-style car with just enough clearance for Li to crawl under. He walked around to the street side, like he was looking for a cab in the light traffic, then dropped to his stomach and wormed under quickly. The scent of tar and oil clogged his nose, and the blacktop scraped at his forearms and face. He couldn't see much: Aris' legs and waist, the feet and pants legs for everyone else. But he could hear. He listened, first for any indication of what they would do to Aris and how Li Wynn might be able to help, then in growing unease as he learned who Aris was.

Li Wynn could not be described as a patriot. As with most residents of the Zone, he felt little more than contempt for the present state of affairs and his greatest dream was to get away from it through any means possible. Aris was a member of the enemy, or so it seemed. That most likely meant imprisonment and later there might be a trade, Aris for a captured Kaifeng warrior. That was how the game was played in the vids. But there was another term, one that could apply to the aid Li had given Aris. Treason. For treason, Li Wynn could be put up against a wall and shot. Not for the first time since meeting Aris, he felt slightly out of his league.

What should he do? Not an easy question to answer. The safest thing would be to hightail it back into the Zone and find a deep dark hidey-hole. But what if they made Aris tell them who had helped him? Li Wynn held no illusions about his chances of remaining hidden. Kaifeng could be a big place, full of hiding places, so long as you were small-time. Aiding an enemy spy? They would tear Li out of whatever crack he crawled into. But what else could he possibly do? The internal debate was still raging when Aris toppled over, his head hitting the walk with a sickening thump.

"Yang," a hard voice commanded from far above Li Wynn's line of sight, "go get my car." A pause. "Harris, you drag our friend here off to the side and watch him, will you?"

Hands reached down to fasten around Aris' ankles, and then dragged the unconscious man face down over several meters of paved walk. That left the one Kaifeng Mech-Warrior alone on the sidewalk with the Hiritsu traitor—the woman Aris had referred to as Chan.

"When can you deliver the battalion commander?" the same male voice asked. "After tomorrow, I'll need to wrap this up quickly before Leftenant-General Fallon can ask too many questions."

The responding voice was airy and distant—almost snobbish. "Not the most private place to discuss these matters," it observed. To Li, she sounded like any one of the stuck-on-themselves women in the Zone who rated a man on his job and the price of his car. What would it be with this one? Rank and the weight of his BattleMech?

"You picked the location," the man reminded her.

"Because I knew that Aris Sung would be dogging your heels by now," she said in a scoffing tone. "I needed to take him in a public place. He can be slippery."

"Well, thanks for the identification." There was a slight pause. "Makes me wonder how much he heard, eavesdropping on us in the club there."

Her voice dropped lower, into a more reasonable tone. "If you're worried about tomorrow, don't be. If Aris knew about that, he wouldn't have been hanging about. He would've killed himself getting the information to Ty Wu Non, or even General Fallon."

"Fallon?" Bartlett looked a bit taken aback.

"I told you," she said, obviously enjoying the other's discomfort. "He's slippery."

Twice now they had referred to an event planned for the morrow, and Li Wynn felt an uneasy churning in his stomach. That the Kaifeng SMM would deal with a Hiritsu traitor didn't shock him too much—that was a favorite part of any good war movie on the holovids. But this sounded more like a private deal. It reminded him of another conversation he'd overheard one time, listening to a messenger make private book on the Solaris matches, but then not reporting it to the bookie. Worked out fine, until one of the betters hit it big and the man couldn't cover the win.

"Whatever," the man said, obviously brushing aside the matter. "Our friend won't see another morning, so problem solved. I'll squeeze whatever information I can from him tonight, then drop him in a hole somewhere. Good enough?"

"He's been out of the loop for days. You won't get much of use out of him, but suit yourself. As for when we can deliver Battalion Commander Non, I'll have to let you know over our private frequency. And of course this is all contingent on your men smashing the festival tomorrow."

Li drew in a deep breath, inhaling dust and the scent of road grime while trying to steady the sudden contractions in his chest. Smashing the Dragon Boat Festival? He stifled a cough as the dust tickled the back of his throat. That couldn't mean what he thought it did.

"The 'Mechs are painted up and ready," the man assured her. "I'll deliver the incident, you just handle your part."

Or maybe it did mean what he'd thought. Li's head swam with the implications. Members of the Kaifeng SMM were going to attack their city, and then blame it on the Warrior House? What would that accomplish, other than make the citizens of the Sarna Supremacy even more anti-Liao? It didn't make sense, but then Li was far out of his element here. He needed Aris to talk to. Perhaps the Hiritsu warrior could help.

Li Wynn didn't really give a damn about politics or nationality—he usually lived independent of such matters. In fact, the Capellan assault on Kaifeng had opened up possibilities he'd never had before. But tomorrow he'd have lots of friends out there along Lake Ch'u Yuan— some at work, others actually a part of the festivities— and they might get hurt. Honor among thieves? No, not really. But friendship was a treasured value, even more so among those who normally lived their lives alone.

So the decision was actually made for him; he had to

rescue Aris Sung. Li Wynn crawled back out from under the car, on the street side, his mind racing desperately.

Kevin Yang throttled down as he drove Major Bartlett's hovercar up to the front of the club. The Tempest slowed and then jolted slightly as the skirting that protected the large fans underneath bumped up against the curb. He checked that the car's gyro, a very limited piece of equipment when compared to the massive gyro at the heart of a BattleMech, was holding the car steady, and then he popped the side doors, which swung upward in gull-wing fashion. Kevin slid out, leaving the car running. Smooth, he thought, silently complimenting the car on its appearance as well as its ride.

"Yang, give Harris a hand," Major Bartlett ordered. "Throw our friend into the back seat." Then he resumed his private conference with the Hiritsu traitor.

Nodding, Kevin Yang walked over to help Paul Harris haul the unconscious Hiritsu warrior to his feet. He didn't like any of this. Not when Major Bartlett had first recruited the two of them for their "mission" tomorrow, and not the major's casual use of the Hiritsu traitor, Terry Chan. It seemed to him that Bartlett was ignoring his own advice of several days ago about placing too much emphasis on the requests of the traitor. Was what she was promising really worth the cost? Yang knew he was placing a lot of trust in Karl Bartlett to know what the hell he was doing. He helped Paul manhandle Aris' body into the back of the Tempest. Quite frankly, he was tiring of the intrigue and wished it would just go away.

When the Tempest immediately pulled away from the curb and entered traffic, Kevin's first thought was a hearty good riddance. His second was realizing that Karl Bartlett still stood off to his left, near the parked car and Terry Chan.

"What the hell?" Bartlett yelled, and rushed into the street to stand next to Harris and Yang.

There was no chance to catch the car, which careened off another as it raced at breakneck speed down the street. Kevin Yang's pistol was out only a fraction of a second ahead of the others. The thunderous sounds of firing echoed in the narrow street as all three men hoped to arrest its flight with a few chunks of well-placed lead. That kind of luck was not with them, however, and the Tempest was quickly lost among the cars it left behind.

The echo of the last shot died with a hollow sound that gave way to the street noises again. All three Kaifeng MechWarriors stood in the street, dumbly, until Terry Chan joined them. Her voice was a quiet whisper, directed to no one in particular. "It would seem, gentlemen, that we have a problem."

Kevin Yang looked to Karl Bartlett, who nodded, a hard mask settling over his face as he stared after the retreating taillights of his car.

23

The late morning sun sparkled across the waters of Lake Ch'u Yuan, scattering brilliant points of light among the deep blue of the reflected sky. Twelve dragon boats floated serenely on the calm water, each one twenty to thirty meters long, holding as many as sixty rowers. Each sat within thirty meters of shore, bow facing out toward the middle of the lake. The boats were slender, hand-carved of a light wood, and brightly decorated with the five elemental colors—red, azure, yellow, white, and black. An intricately detailed dragon's head rose from the prow of each vessel—some open-mouthed and spewing tongues of flame, others with clenched teeth and lips skinned back in a snarl—while a scaly tail came up off the stern to wave in the air behind.

The richer boats used carved and painted wood for the dragon, while others, for reasons of money or weight, turned to plastic or even a glazed papier-maché. One boat, to the embarrassment of its rowers, had not glazed its dragon properly and the waters of the lake had worked their way through at the base of the tail to wet the plaster beneath. There was a half-hearted effort to save the drooping stern decoration as rowers from other boats and some spectators on the shore took to jeering, calling them *rwan wei*—the soft, or limp, tail rowers.

Aris twisted around in his seat on one of the dragon boats, shading his eyes with his right hand against his brow as he scanned the crowded beach. Banners and streamers hung everywhere. People wore ribbons of the five elemental colors around throats and wrists, the ends trailing behind them and snapping in the light breeze. Musicians played sprightly tunes while people wearing large dragon masks more appropriate to the New Year celebration danced about. There were some fireworks being lit off in scattered areas—mostly colored smoke and small firecrackers, again probably left-overs from the New Year. Other areas had been roped off, creating small islands within the crowds from which food servers could sell various forms of *zongzi*, a traditional rice dumpling stuffed with any of several sweet fillings. The one Aris had breakfasted on had been filled with honey-roasted duck and walnuts.

House Hiritsu did not embrace the Confederation's Chinese heritage. A Warrior House was a world, a nation, a family all unto itself and steeped in its own history and traditions. But every warrior was well-versed in history, so Aris knew something of what was going on. The Dragon Boat Festival was bright and colorful and usually full of energy. That energy was lacking in Aris just now, though, as he fearfully scanned the lakeshore for the arrival of Kaifeng BattleMechs painted the colors of House Hiritsu.

Waking up to Li Wynn's tale of what the young thief had overheard in front of the Gold Pavilion had left Aris cold inside. There seemed to be no end to the horrors Terry Chan was willing to commit. He'd had Li recount what he'd heard in several different ways, including talking it out and putting it in writing to be sure of pulling out every last scrap of information.

Chan's arrangement with Bartlett made sense to Aris, in a perverted way. At least he could see what each side gained. The Kaifeng SMM would be able to claim that House Hiritsu had violated the cease-fire, which could create a political nightmare for the Warrior House once

Sun-Tzu Liao learned of it. Especially as it was a flagrant violation of the Ares Conventions. The attack would also turn the common people heavily against the Capellan Confederation, which would not make House Hiritsu's job here any easier. And there seemed to be some plan to turn Ty Wu Non over to the SMM, a loss that would strike deeply into the fighting spirit of House Hiritsu, which had already suffered from the loss of Virginia York.

Terry Chan's reward was a little less obvious. From the conversation last night, it seemed as if she wanted to weed out the rolls of House Hiritsu through attrition in combat. Also there was that last reminder, that the will of the House Master is the will of the House. As Aris saw it, this was all an effort to remove Ty Wu Non from his promotion to House Master. If the Kaifeng SMM took Ty down in combat, so be it. And if not, the accusation that he'd broken a cease-fire, negotiated in the spirit of honoring the Liao Chinese heritage, could just as surely damn him.

Of course, this line of reasoning assumed that Ty Wu Non was not a party to Terry Chan's betrayal and that this was an internal matter, not a part of Kali Liao's recent power plays. It was the best he could do on the limited information. When Aris was finally confident that he'd extracted all useful facts, he'd promised a worried Li Wynn his help in preventing an attack on Kaifeng civilians and then sent the young man off to find them a boat.

Aris looked down to where his strong hands were wrapped about one of the dragon boat oars. This wasn't quite what he'd had in mind, joining the boat crew from out of the Zone. But all other lake traffic had been cleared away in preparation for the boat races, and as near as Aris could figure—trying to triangulate the position using landmarks he'd picked while in the water several days before—his *Wraith* was submerged somewhere out in the middle of the race course.

"Aris," Li said, nudging him from the seat behind. "I think it's about to start."

For a moment Aris thought Li was referring to the 'Mech attack, and quickly scanned the shoreline and into the city for as far as he could see. Then he noticed the preparations among the other boats, and realized that Li

Wynn was referring to the race. All the boats had already made one pass around the buoy placed a kilometer out into the lake. Their honor pass. Now came the race itself. The captain of their boat, a surly-looking man with a shaved, sun-burned head, took up his position at the bow. A drum was fastened to him at waist level by a strap that ran up around his thick neck, and his over-sized hands held two padded mallets for beating out a cadence for the rowers.

"Duanwu!" someone from the beach cried out over a megaphone. *Dragon boats!* It was the call to prepare. There would be three heats, held over the course of the entire day. The three winners, and one boat picked by the crowd's acclamation, would compete in the final race sometime in the early evening. Aris doubted the race would ever be finished, not if the SMM-Chan cabal had their way.

"Saipau!" The same amplified voice from the beach. *Race!*

Aris dug in with his oar. At the boat's prow, the captain hammered out a stiff cadence that was completely ignored during those first few seconds. The boat swung hard to port and starboard before the rowers finally were able to synchronize themselves with the beat. Then the dragon leapt gracefully forward, its slender hull cutting through the placid lake waters.

Aris soon realized that the crew of his boat was very good. They kept their cadence and pulled hard at the water. Soon they were one of the three lead boats, flying along gracefully while the others remained in a rather tight formation behind them. Aris took a moment to enjoy the competition, wondering why he had never participated in such an event back on Randar. Given the chance, that was a mistake he would correct.

Being city-born and raised, Aris knew little of the fertility rites that had originally spawned the festival. From study he knew it was something about the change-over from the positive yang to the negative yin, the midpoint of the growing season. In ancient China, the festival was intended to persuade the gods to provide heavy rain for the rice crops. On this water-rich world that did not seem a problem. But the festival persisted, changing very little over the thousands of years of practice. The boats, the race, the food. All in service of preserving a rich heritage. Aris could understand and appreciate that.

A sudden jolt shocked Aris from his reverie. As the boat lurched to the port, its back end swinging around in roughly the same direction, Aris' first thought was that they had somehow struck his submerged *Wraith*. Then he heard the insults and jeers, and looking around, he noticed that one of the other lead boats had edged closer until finally it had turned sharply to ram them in the stern.

The boat captain barked orders to fall back into cadence, and slowed his beat to allow his rowers to reorganize. Once more the dragon boat slid ahead, now pursued closely by the second. *"Quechuan!"* rowers in the other boat were calling out, trying to goad the first into slowing. *Coward boat.*

The captain's face turned as red as his burned scalp, and he went to a one-armed cadence beat while he brought a small bundle out from under his seat with the other hand. This he threw down the length of the boat to the men sitting at the stern. Positioned roughly toward the boat's middle, Aris could not see what it was.

The rear boat was making another press, trying to angle in from the right and shake up the lead dragon boat again. "Ship oars," the captain called. Obeying, the rowers pulled the oars in to prevent their being smashed by the other boat's prow. But it also slowed them, allowing the attacking boat to hit more broadside than it should have. "Cast," the captain yelled, confusing Aris at the command until he saw what happened next.

At the stern, one man stood up with a casting net held loosely in his hands. With a practiced twirl and cast, he sent it spreading through the air to fall over the other boat's captain and the first several seats of rowers. Then the boats collided, the prow of the attacking boat crushing the rail between Aris and Li Wynn. Several of Aris' fellow rowers were thrown over. Aris managed to hold on, throwing his weight back to the starboard side in an effort to keep the boat upright. Both boats stalled, neither capsizing. Then a second man stood in the rear and let cast another net. This one fell more toward the middle of the other dragon boat, fouling oars and tangling up another five or six rowers.

"Shove us off. Damn rowdies, someone shove us away." The captain of Aris' boat was pounding his drum for attention as insults and curses were swapped.

More than a little bewildered at the attack, Aris finally moved to respond. He and Li Wynn grabbed the other prow and heaved against it. "This happen a lot?" Aris asked.

"Just good healthy competition," Li said. Between the two of them, they managed to shove the other boat back just a bit. Enough for their boat to get its oars back in the water and pull away. The other boat, still fighting against the two nets, fell far behind.

"Last year we sawed halfway through some of their oars the night before," Li said between pulls, laughing. "Most of them snapped during the first heat and they had a heck of a time replacing them before the second."

With one boat fouled, only two now remained out in front of the pack. The boat rowed by residents of the Zone ran second, their encounter having slowed them. The cadence grew faster, though, as each man pulled hard to narrow the gap between them and the lead vessel. Several minutes of hard work paid off, and soon the cadence relaxed long enough for the men to get their strength back. Aris looked over at the other boat, saw them smiling with easy confidence. They didn't look nearly as fatigued, and the race wasn't half over.

Apparently Aris' boat captain thought along the same lines, and decided to even the playing field. He took out another package, what Aris assumed was another two nets, and threw them to the stern. "Hard port," he called. The port-side rowers dipped their oars and back-paddled for an instant, then picked up their stroke on the next beat. Now they were angling for the other craft, and Aris had a good view straight off the stern toward the lake's northern shore.

Two black-and-green painted BattleMechs walked along the northern shore, heading east toward the festival.

"Ship oars!" Aris yelled in his best command voice.

Only those nearest the boat captain failed to respond and the boat quickly bogged down as it shed speed. An instant furor of voices rose, challenging Aris' command, which he quieted by pointing back toward the city and the two bogus Hiritsu 'Mechs. In the sudden silence, they could hear the first salvos of weapons fire as the war machines ripped into lakeside buildings. Sitting in the middle of Lake Ch'u Yuan, nearly three-quarters of a kilometer from shore, there wasn't much they could do but watch.

Wasn't much *they* could do.

Aris checked the landmarks he'd picked out from the water right after leaving his 'Mech. As near as he could tell, they were fairly close to the correct distance from the eastern shore, but a little too far north. Maybe two, three hundred meters. "Captain, a cadence please," Aris called out. "Oars out, hard left, then pull."

The captain blinked dumbly, until Li Wynn called him by name and vouched for Aris. "He can help," he promised, "but he has to get over there." He stabbed a finger in roughly the direction Aris wanted to go.

With a nod, the captain repeated Aris' orders and pounded out a fast cadence. Aris tried to keep track of the BattleMechs' progress as well as constantly checking the three distant landmarks. When he thought they were close, he ordered ship oars and had everyone look for his bottle markers. Forty pairs of eyes scanned the surface.

For a moment Aris thought he'd misremembered, or that his markers had gone down. The thought dried his mouth and throat, and he swallowed painfully against the dryness. If that were the case, then he'd have to start diving and hope the gods of fortune were in a friendly mood. Then someone pointed off the port side and shouted, "There!"

It was one of the sports drink bottles, bobbing lightly in the light chop raised by an easterly breeze. The wrapper had washed off, leaving only the heavy clear plastic, which was nearly invisible against the water. The rowers pulled the boat near. Aris found the nylon rope swollen and algae-covered but still attached.

Aris checked on the progress of the BattleMechs. They were near the point where the northern shore slid around almost ninety degrees to head south. People along the eastern beach were beginning to scatter, but too slowly. There was no sign of any Kaifeng SMM BattleMechs.

Aris paused for a quick handshake with Li Wynn. "Get to shore and get out of the city." The fear behind the other's eyes told Aris that Li understood how much trouble he could be in when Major Bartlett finally put everything together. Then Aris was over the side of the boat, diving past the bottle. He grabbed hold of the rope as it brushed his shoulder, and then, hand over hand, he made his way down into the darker depths of Lake Ch'u Yuan.

24

The *Raven* walked into the middle of the intersection, its hook-nosed head bobbing like the bird that was its namesake. Twin medium lasers mounted to its stubby right arm spat out emerald darts that chewed into a nearby building. Smoke billowed around its right-torso launcher as six short-range missiles flew out and speared into an abandoned automobile, tearing it apart and igniting the fuel tank. The car jackknifed into the air, rising on a column of fire, and then slammed back into the street with fender-crushing force.

An impressive piece of work, Leftenant Kevin Yang thought bitterly. *Maybe there's a threatening ice cream stand nearby that would make a worthy target.*

Yang twisted the *Raven*'s upper torso, searching for a new target far from any people. Panicked Tarrahause citizens were everywhere, most running away from his position, but a bewildered few actually moving toward him as if lost in a maze. Yang swallowed against the constriction in his throat that threatened to suffocate him. "Just following orders," he whispered to the empty cockpit. Now there was an original defense.

It was just as well Yang's communications system had been shut down for this mission. He'd been talking to himself ever since the outskirts of the city, and it wouldn't do for another member of the Kaifeng SMM to overhear him. Maybe it was a secret wish to be caught, discovered, ordered off the mission. Certainly there was no turning back now that he'd actually fired on Tarrahause. He had to play this through to the end.

Actually, it had been too late from the time he walked into that twice-damned terminal with Karl Bartlett and Paul Harris. Yang had always respected Bartlett, and sometimes feared him as well. Kevin Yang was a good MechWarrior. He would never make a living on the game world of Solaris, and he doubted he would ever rise very high in the ranks of the Sarna Supremacy military, the army of a fledgling state. But not everyone was cut out for command positions. No, he was a decent 'Mech pilot and a loyal follower, and for two years he had put his trust in his company commander to make the hard choices while doing the only thing he knew how—pilot a 'Mech.

Now that was all falling apart. He no longer trusted Karl Bartlett. He thought Bartlett was way out of his depth, trying to deal with the Hiritsu traitor without the Leftenant-General Fallon's knowledge, and now he even questioned the man's ability to command. Yang felt lost and alone, and his actions had become like those of an automaton. He wished for something, anything, that could end his misery.

Heat washed over him as he again triggered both medium lasers and his short-range missiles. This time he'd targeted trees standing in K'ung-fu-tzu Park, and they splintered and blew apart under his weapons. He winced, remembering many pleasant evenings spent in the cool of the park. As if in retribution, his 'Mech's sensors screamed warnings at him, and for a moment he feared to see the spirit of K'ung-fu-tzu himself rise from the scarred landscape to confront him.

The *Raven*'s computer painted a red circle on the heads-up display. Behind him, according to the tactical placement, was the BattleMech known as a *Wraith*. The very name of the 'Mech seemed an echo of his thought of the moment before. Yang twisted the *Raven* around, tracking his targeting reticule to the far left-hand edge of the screen and holding it while a combination torso-twist and sidestep brought him to face the lake.

The *Wraith* moved through waist-deep water, wading for the shore. The gun-metal blue of the 'Mech glistened, at once beautiful and deadly. Yang was too stunned to fire on it right away. He thought of the tale of Ch'u Yuan, for whom the lake was named—the ancient poet who'd drowned himself out of despair over the warring Chinese states. It was said the old gods had granted him a form of immortality and that his spirit still continued to walk, trying to bring peace to those who would not lay aside the tools of war.

Kevin Yang's first barely coherent thought was that Ch'u Yuan was packing a large laser.

His last thought, just before the scarlet beam sliced through his cockpit, was a desperate half-formed wish that what the old religions taught was indeed true and that he might hope to be reborn and yet find his true place in life.

The heat levels of Aris' *Wraith* were just edging into the yellow band when he finished off the *Raven*. He left it in the middle of the intersection, a smoking corpse. His first salvo had ripped up the left leg and spread into the center torso. His second had speared directly into the cockpit, melting armor, viewscreen, and the pilot inside. And without any return fire, Aris thought, hoping his luck would hold.

His answer came in the form of two 32mm autocannon slugs that shattered armor plates off his left rear torso and were accompanied by the screaming of warning sensors.

Aris kicked his *Wraith* into a walk, moving past the intersection and the broken *Raven* and around the protection of a nearby building. A glance at his HUD had revealed the *Blackjack* in perfect position nearly a block behind him. Either caution or heat considerations on the other pilot's part had spared Aris the wrath of the *Blackjack*'s four medium lasers, and he wasn't about to chance that again. Not against his weaker—make that nonexistent—rear armor.

When he'd spied the *Blackjack* from the dragon boat, Aris had worried that it might have been the OmniMech he'd encountered at the Jinxiang Bridge. That would have meant fifty tons of state-of-the-art BattleMech; twenty-six point five tons of weapon pods. Enough to gut his *Wraith* in a single, if lucky, volley. The battle computer allayed that fear, though. BJ-1, it tagged the red triangle. Aris knew that meant four medium lasers and two of the smallest autocannon available. Not very fast, but jump-capable. All considered, his *Wraith* held a decided edge.

The BJ-1's first preference would be to fall back to extreme ranges where only the small autocannon could reach. Not very practical in an urban environment, where combat tended to get up close and personal. The next best would be to come in at extremely close range, where its medium lasers would offset the heavy punch of Aris' large pulse laser and rob the *Wraith* of its advantage of mobility. A cautious pilot would choose the former, an aggressive warrior the latter. Aris triggered his jump jets, angling to jump over the building he'd taken refuge behind and straight toward the last known position of the *Blackjack.*

He was betting on the other man being a warrior.

The *Wraith* responded sluggishly, still unbalanced from losing two jump jets at the Jinxiang. But it cleared the building. And as Aris dropped to the other side, his targeting computer reacquired the *Blackjack* moving underneath him, going straight for the same corner Aris had disappeared around. He twisted his control sticks. That and the neurohelmet signals pivoted the *Wraith* in midair like some kind of armored ballerina doing a pirouette. He came down behind the *Blackjack,* his golden targeting reticule sweeping directly over its rear torso.

Regardless of Aris' advantageous position, the *Blackjack* was by no means defeated. The enemy 'Mech swung its arms up and over to fire directly to its rear, calling on the design feature that made *Blackjack*s so popular, the lack of arm actuators. It could bring two thirds of its weapons to bear, the autocannon and two of its lasers. Amber beams worried at the *Wraith*'s leg, melting armor that ran to the ground in fiery rivulets. The depleted-uranium slugs hammered at his left torso and even chipped some armor off his cockpit.

Aris rode out the damage, retaining control of his 'Mech with practiced ease. He tied all three of his weapons into his main Target Interlock Circuit and triggered them. Scarlet beams pulsed into the back of the *Blackjack,* tracking to the center and then drilling deep into its internal structure. He glanced at his tactical readout on the enemy 'Mech and saw a blossom of heat spread throughout its main torso section. An engine hit, and a bad one at that. He knew the *Blackjack* must feel like a walking furnace to its pilot, but the other warrior's quick response to his maneuver told him the battle wasn't over yet.

True to form, the *Blackjack*'s arms snapped back to the front as it turned a tight corner to face Aris' *Wraith*. Aris knew what he'd do if he were sitting at the controls of the other 'Mech—run the heat and try to score deep with the four medium lasers. But he had no intention of putting his *Wraith* through that much damage again. He walked the Wraith backward until it was moving at its maximum walking speed of just over seventy-five kilometers per hour. It was enough to back off almost two hundred meters, placing the medium lasers at the edge of their effective range but still close enough that the *Wraith*'s large pulse laser could score easily.

The *Blackjack* pilot's luck was quickly running sour. Only a single burst of its autocannon fire nipped the *Wraith*. In return, it caught a full stream of scarlet energy in its own left torso and one of Aris' medium lasers dead center. The Kaifeng SMM warrior was faced with unpleasant alternatives. Aris had the best ranged weapon and the mobility to keep at optimum distance for it. A face-off would only lead to a slow death. The pilot's other option was to run for it, but the *Blackjack*'s back was already sliced open. They traded weapons fire again, Aris taking a single laser hit to his right leg and the *Blackjack* losing twice as much armor in the center torso.

That decided matters for the other MechWarrior. Engaging his jump jets, he lifted the *Blackjack* on streams of plasma and banked to place the building between it and the *Wraith*. Aris held his position, lining up for the easy back shot just as the *Blackjack* rotated at the apogee of its flight. His large laser missed completely, surprising him, and one of the mediums only scoured more armor from the *Blackjack*'s left leg. The last medium hit true, however, penetrating the open scar in the back and digging deeper into the fusion engine shielding.

Aris saw the pilot ejection seat blow free of the cockpit not two seconds before the entire 'Mech blew apart. Small pieces of its armor plating struck about the *Wraith*, but none with enough mass or force to damage it. The largest chunk of BattleMech fell on top of the building it had tried to jump over, smashing through the roof and who knew how many floors beneath.

Time to be going, Aris thought. He checked his tactical display. The first Kaifeng SMM 'Mech was just coming on his screen, over a kilometer away along the northern shoreline. There would be more, though. Aris had blown his hiding place in order to save a few civilian lives. Well worth it, as far as he was concerned, providing he could now escape the city.

And maybe he had a few more seconds to spare. Aris located the *Blackjack* pilot, gliding toward the ground in his parafoil. He lined up a careful shot, letting the parachute cross his targeting reticule while it was still a good ten meters above the ground. One burst from his single medium laser left the chute burning, and the pilot fell the last ten meters to hit the ground hard. *That kind of a fall will break something,* Aris thought. *Or at least shake him up bad enough to prevent a fast escape.* Either way, he'd have some questions to answer. Satisfied, Aris walked his *Wraith* back to the lakeshore.

Now there were three Kaifeng 'Mechs, two to the west and one south, all taking advantage of the open shoreline. Traveling through the city was a death sentence waiting to be carried out. That left Aris one last option. He would have to go for cover again, and make his break in a— hopefully—secluded spot. *Over twenty kilometers of shoreline,* he reminded himself, engaging his jump jets and angling as far out over the lake as he could. For the second time since beginning the assault on Kaifeng, Aris readied himself for splashdown.

He was really beginning to hate water.

Jinxiang River Port Terminal 5 South
Tarrahause District, Kaifeng
Sarna Supremacy, Chaos March
25 July 3058

The port terminal lay along the southern stretch of the Jinxiang River, fifty kilometers below Lake Ch'u Yuan. A full company of Hiritsu BattleMechs stood a tight formation in the loading yard. Three others patrolled a healthy perimeter, backing up the infantry posts set up nearly three kilometers beyond them. Two more Battle-Mechs were undergoing routine maintenance in the large hangar-style warehouse while Ty Wu Non and Terry Chan held a private conference in the second-floor office.

The battalion commander stood in front of the air conditioner, eyes closed as the machine's cool flow of air blasted him in the face and chilled the light sheen of sweat he'd gathered by walking to the warehouse. He kept his hands firmly clasped behind his back, knowing they would betray his frustration. *A House Master must always seem to be in control,* he reminded himself. *Even when he is not. Especially when he is not.*

"You're sure?" he asked, keeping his tone carefully neutral. A request for clarification, not a doubt of ability. "It was Aris Sung?"

Terry Chan remained at attention next to the office

desk. He had not invited her to sit, or even put her at ease. Clearly she'd expected it—House Master York had always kept private meetings relaxed. Ty would not be taking such an informal approach to his position. He knew he did not possess Virginia York's matronly charisma, and from the standpoint of discipline he had not always agreed with that policy anyway.

"I've seen Aris in combat," she said. "I've trained next to him. No one else could have been piloting that *Wraith*. It"—she gestured at the air as if searching for the right word—"It *moved* like Aris."

Ty nodded once. "So, Aris Sung is not only alive, but he's been in possession of his *Wraith* all along. And we also have two MechWarriors of the Kaifeng SMM posing as Hiritsu warriors, and attacking their own city. Finally, Aris brings both of them down and disappears again." Ty glanced over at Chan. "You were there. What are your thoughts?"

Terry hedged, shifting uncomfortably from one foot to the other. Her eyes would not meet those of her battalion commander. "Sir, I can only assume that Aris Sung has turned renegade."

Ty blinked his surprise. Terry Chan held no love for Aris, that was certainly true and partially his own fault, but the accusation still shocked him. "Proceed," he said in a level voice.

"Aris has never gotten on well with you, Battalion Commander. And ever since the ambush near the moon Nochen, his assault plan has come under constant criticism. So now he is fighting independent of the House. In his own reasoning, I'm sure he has justified any and all actions. But the truth is that he has broken from standard House doctrine on the conduct of military operations."

Ty set his face against any show of encouragement or discouragement. He wanted Terry's full, unbiased evaluation. She could be right. He didn't want to believe that, not even of Aris Sung, but if it would be anyone, it was him. "And the staged attack against Tarrahause?"

She was ready for that question. Her hesitation had vanished when it became clear that he would hear her out. "Aris is a highly trained operative. I do not believe it beyond his capabilities to recruit local malcontent warriors and turn them against their superiors. His plan is the same as ever, to somehow provoke the defenders into coming out to meet us. It appears to have worked this time, but in doing so he violated the cease-fire."

"And you were able to confirm a build-up of forces in Tarrahause?"

Terry Chan nodded. "It was all over the city that Leftenant-General Fallon is bringing at least a full lance of 'Mechs out of Mahabohdi to Tarrahause. This Major Bartlett is calling the entire affair an Hiritsu ploy to turn Kaifeng's own warriors against each other and violate the cease-fire at the same time. Bartlett's screaming for our blood, but that might be an effort to push the public outrage onto Fallon."

Ty Wu Non turned back to his desk, pacing slowly as he thought. Was this the opportunity they'd been waiting for? Luring the defenders out from the city where House Hiritsu could overwhelm them?

"Aris Sung is to be considered a renegade," he said, dealing with that issue first. "He is to be placed under House arrest upon any sighting. If he resists, House warriors are authorized to use whatever force necessary to bring him in. Pass those orders to the duty officer for transmission." He waited for a responding nod. "So you think they will be coming out?"

"I think they have to, or face a riot."

Ty Wu Non studied Terry Chan with hard eyes. Finally he nodded. "Then we will meet them and crush them. I will order another full lance from Beijing. If the Kaifeng SMM and their mercenary fodder take to the field in any strength, this could very well be the deciding battle for Kaifeng.

"Dismissed."

"Where are they now?"

Major Karl Bartlett flipped on an overhead projector while the general's aide darkened the room by spinning down the dimmer switch. The projector splashed a full-color map of the Tarrahause District onto a blank wall in the major's office. Bartlett, Leftenant-General Cynthia Fallon, and her aide, a Major Cabander, stood in silence for a moment as each studied the layout. The Jinxiang

River was a ribbon of silver running northeast to south-west, opening up at the middle of the wall into the inverted L-shaped Lake Ch'u Yuan. Tarrahause itself was a gray splotch that surrounded the northern and western shore of the lake.

"My scouts say here," Bartlett said, using a laser pointer to highlight a dark spot along the Jinxiang's southern reach labeled Port Terminal Number Five South. "We confirmed that by aerial reconnaissance high fly-overs before that *Overlord* crowded them away. And of course, our Hiritsu friend also verified it." He paused, giving the general an obvious opening to jump into.

"How did House Hiritsu get a BattleMech into this city?" Fallon asked sharply, her eyes never straying from the map.

Bartlett cleared his throat uncomfortably. "We think he entered the Jinxiang River near the northern bridge and walked underwater, south, into the lake. We've never considered that a reasonable threat because of the inherent problems in underwater operations. Especially at anything greater than lance strength."

"Seems that it only took three BattleMechs to throw all of Tarrahause into a panic." Fallon looked over at him, raising an eyebrow. "Two of them your own, piloted by two SMM MechWarriors."

Bartlett could feel a tightness in his chest and swallowed with some difficulty. "As I told the general, I take full responsibility for my men. That Kevin Yang and Paul Harris could be swayed by Capellan bribes or threats or whatever it was Hiritsu used still turns my blood cold."

Cyndi Fallon stared at him, not blinking for longer than Bartlett would have thought possible. "You believe they may have been threatened? With what?"

She had picked up on it. Bartlett shrugged feigned indifference to the question. "I mention it as a possibility only. Kevin Yang has relatives on the southern continent, in Franklin District. Paul Harris' wife is on rotation to the recharge station." He shook his head lightly. "We'll probably never know for sure. We've scraped enough of Yang out of the *Raven*'s cockpit to fill a small box, maybe. I rode in with Paul Harris, hoping to get a statement of any kind, but he never regained consciousness." *I made sure of that.*

Karl Bartlett noticed the general's small shiver when he described Kevin's death. All MechWarriors—himself included—feared burning alive in the cockpit. It probably came from planting your butt on top of a fusion reactor. Engine explosion, inferno rockets, lucky PPC hit to the head—they were the terrifying bane of a warrior's existence. And he had counted on her reaction to help gloss over Harris' death. The last thing he wanted was for her to order a full-scale autopsy, not after the hospital had already ruled shock-trauma.

"Major," General Fallon said calmly, almost as if by afterthought, "intelligence in Mahabohdi has learned of a transfer of four more BattleMechs from Beijing to the Hiritsu forces in the Tarrahause District."

Karl Bartlett nodded and tried to act as if he'd already suspected as much. "They know we'll come after them now. No way around it. There's already a lot of talk about how we're cowering in the city, hiding behind civilian shields." Carefully controlled talk, started by a word or two in the proper place. "Some of those accusations turned fairly nasty when people learned of Yang and Harris. If we don't act, we could find Tarrahause in a state of rebellion." Which also helped explain more of Terry Chan's desire for that staged attack. She wanted them under pressure. He'd missed that possibility, but then he hadn't thought of his people's identities being discovered. Well, he had some trump cards of his own left to play.

"What about our *friend*?" Fallon asked. "Is she still willing to trade information for limited engagements?"

Just what I knew you'd ask, Bartlett thought. "According to her last transmission, she believes that if we come out in force, House Hiritsu will back off again. We can chase them for days."

"But can we keep this up long enough to gain reinforcements?" Fallon said, rubbing at the side of her face in worry. "The blockade around Sarna is going surprisingly well for the Confederation, mostly because no one has recent experience fighting such a tactic involving warships. I mean, what could we do if Sun-Tzu parked that kind of firepower in orbit around Kaifeng? Nothing but sacrifice a few DropShips maybe. The only thing in our favor is that Sun-Tzu has no reserve left either. He stretched himself too thin last year. If not for the blockade, Sarna could reinforce us and take this opportunity to hit Sarmaxa or maybe even Randar." Fallon's face lit up at the thought. "Wouldn't that be a nice gift to our Warrior House friends, to find their homes in ashes and under the Sarna Supremacy when they return?"

Bartlett felt his patience wearing thin. He needed a commitment before Fallon left the room or he might not get it at all. "Such speculations are beyond me, General. But we should be able to hold for a week or more in the field, then we can come back to the city and hole up again. Certainly long enough to get reinforcements onto the planet, and then Hiritsu will have to withdraw."

Actually Bartlett doubted it would last two days, if he could set his plans in motion. Once Terry Chan delivered her battalion commander and a few of his closest supporters, Bartlett would be in the position to crush the Warrior House completely. And he would make sure everyone knew who had done it. Not Cyndi Fallon, that was for sure. Karl doubted the general would even see the end of the campaign.

If Terry Chan could request special targets, there was no reason he couldn't either.

Jinxiang Port Terminal 5 South
Tarrahause District, Kaifeng
Sarna Supremacy, Chaos March
26 July 3058

Aris stood over the unconscious guard, in the moonlit shadow of the port terminal's main warehouse, nursing a bruised knuckle on his left hand. He'd been slightly off on his ridge-hand strike, clipping the base of the infantryman's helmet. It had taken a follow-up kick to finally lay the man out. Aris counted himself fortunate that no alarm had been raised.

Infiltrating the Hiritsu staging area had been easier than he'd thought. He knew Ty Wu Non well enough to assume that the battalion commander would not deviate much from standard House Hiritsu military doctrine. Infantryman posts were set on a perimeter three to four kilometers out, backed up by a roving BattleMech patrol no larger than lance-sized. Once through that, all Aris had to deal with were the port-terminal infantryman patrols.

And the battalion commander's personal security.

For the third time, Aris had taken his *Wraith* under water. Entering the river six kilometers upstream—just to be sure—he'd exited his cockpit just as he had in Lake Ch'u Yuan. Except this time he tied the marker rope to a tree on the bank. Unless a wide-ranging foot patrol literally tripped over the rope, he was confident the 'Mech wouldn't give him away.

The way Aris had been able to second-guess the placement of patrols and standing guards both in the surrounding jungle and once inside the port terminal gave him pause, however. Any competently trained Hiritsu warrior could probably infiltrate standard security every time. It just wasn't considered a possibility that a Hiritsu warrior would ever want to—or need to—act against the House.

The danger of routines and traditions, Aris thought, more convinced than ever that this was what had killed House Master Virginia York. Providing he could convince Ty Wu Non of the threat within his own House, Aris expected much of that to change. He didn't like to think about what this could do to House Hiritsu—to his family. That was the reason behind his stealthy approach. If he could get to Ty Wu Non before an alarm was raised, just maybe there would be a way to heal the wound before it festered.

Aris dragged the guard over to the warehouse wall where some empty barrels had been stacked, and stashed the unconscious man behind them. This was the first major problem of the night. It put Aris on a timetable. He had to reach the battalion commander and persuade him to listen before the guard was discovered, woke, or failed to check in on time.

Aris gave himself ten minutes.

The large doors at the front of the warehouse had been rolled back to open the building to the cool tropical night. Light flooded the loading yard, falling down between the rows of BattleMechs that stood there in silent formation. Aris heard the sounds of welders and hoists and a few shouted orders as techs continued to work in the warehouse. There would be battle tomorrow, just as Aris had thought, which always meant a busy night for the technicians.

He saw what he was looking for at the far side of the loading yard. A long, squat brick building with air conditioning units in every other window. Government-supplied housing for the port-terminal management and workers who didn't relish the idea of a long commute into Tarra-hause every day. And if Aris had any doubts that Ty Wu

Non slept in one of the rooms, the two guards posted at the building's main door erased them. But he had to cross the lighted loading yard to get anywhere near. Circling around in the dark would take too long and was an invitation for another run-in with a guard.

So Aris hid in plain sight, using the same principles of misdirection that had served him in the Gold Pavilion. Served him until Terry Chan recognized him and gave him away, he remembered bitterly.

Slipping around the corner of the warehouse, he moved along the wall until almost to the wide doors. Then he stepped into the light and strolled out toward the Battle-Mechs. He had changed back into the clothes he'd picked up in Tarrahause. They were still wet from his swim out of the river, but no one could tell that at a distance and it looked less suspicious than wearing his only other clothing of shorts and a cooling vest. He even welcomed the cool touch of the wet clothes, though the water-logged shoes chafed at his feet.

It took him less than a minute to cross the loading yard while trying not to pass too close to any technician. The only guards this deep into the port-terminal were those at the building door, and Aris passed in full view of them to tie his shoe and send them a lazy wave. One of them waved back. Shoving his hands into his pockets, he strolled along and even forced himself to whistle until he was safely past the corner of the building and hidden from sight again. It was only then that he noticed the layer of sweat that had broken out on his forehead.

But the demanding part was over. To enter the building, he pried out a screen in the upper half of a window that held an air conditioning unit. By standing on one of many empty crates that lay scattered all over the terminal, he managed to enter without making much noise. His luck was holding; the room was unoccupied.

Five minutes, he told himself, keeping silent track of his time limit. He moved into the hallway and began a stealthy search of the main floor.

Ty Wu Non had a single guard stationed directly outside his door, a man armed with a Nakjama laser sidearm and a radio clipped into a belt holder. It was an interior room, so there would be no open window leading to the outside. The door was midway down a long hallway, giving the sentry ample time to identify and challenge anyone approaching. Smart man. Aris knew the clock was still ticking, and that his luck couldn't hold much longer. It was time to act.

With no way to approach by stealth, Aris decided to hide in plain sight again. He unbuttoned his shirt, giving him access to his own Nakjama, which rode in a nylon shoulder holster. Then he stepped around the corner and into the guard's sight.

Aris immediately looked over his shoulder as if maintaining a conversation with someone back around the corner. "I'll see to it," he called down the empty hallway. "What?" He turned and walked the way he'd come, slowing. *Nothing out of the ordinary,* he thought, trying to impress the thought on the guard. *Would a dangerous person draw so much attention to himself?*

Whether or not his mental cajoling affected the guard, no threatening sounds came from behind him and Aris stole his right hand up into the inside of his shirt. "All right," he called out as if responding to a simple request. Then he spun, laser pistol extended in a classic two-hand grip and pointed directly at the infantryman's left eye. "Think carefully, Leon," he whispered, recognizing the sentry and noticing the man's hand flinch toward his own weapon.

The guard apparently thought better of his position. He relaxed, raising his arms out to either side of him. "What . . ." he started to ask loudly, trying to warn the battalion commander through the door, but Aris thrust his pistol up until the muzzle was only a hair's breadth from the man's eye. When Leon spoke again, it was in a soft, calm tone. "What do you want, Aris Sung?"

"I wish to speak to the battalion commander."

The younger man licked his lips nervously. "You have been declared renegade and ordered arrested."

"I figured on something like that." Terry Chan probably hadn't been able to figure out how to get him ordered shot on sight. Though any member of her little cabal would surely dispose of Aris immediately.

"I cannot allow you to enter armed, Aris Sung. You know that."

Aris saw the tension building in the young man's face, read that he intended to make a play for his own weapon. "Wait," Aris cautioned. "I'll surrender my weapon. To the battalion commander. You call him, but do not say my name or raise an alarm. Just bring him to the door."

The guard thought it over and nodded slowly. One hand reached back cautiously to find the door and knock softly. On the third try, a voice finally called out. "What is it?"

"Sir, could you come to the door please?"

The request, coming through the door, was sufficiently out of place to put Ty on his guard. "For what reason?" he asked.

"You have a visitor," Aris said, speaking clearly and distinctly.

There was a pause, followed by several long uncomfortable seconds. Then the door opened and a third Nakjama joined the party, this one held in Ty Wu Non's small but steady hand. "Drop the pistol, Aris."

Aris let the Nakjama spin down to where he was holding it by the trigger guard. Then he extended it to Ty. "Company Leader Aris Sung reporting to the battalion commander," Aris said quietly as Ty accepted the weapon and the guard drew his own, just to be safe. "I have an immediate report to make on Tarrahause and the death of Virginia York."

Aris almost missed the flash of surprise that flashed across Ty Wu Non's face and then was gone. Ty was getting much better at concealing his thoughts. The infantryman was agog. "Indeed?" Ty asked. "Then perhaps you had better come inside, Aris Sung."

"Sir," Aris said, stopping his commander before he stepped back into the room. "It would be wise if no one knew of my return, at least until after we talk. After that I leave it to your discretion."

"You are hardly in the position to advise me, Aris." Ty Wu Non's voice was frosty. Then he paused, and relented. "Very well. A minor point to grant you, I suppose." He turned to the infantryman. "Leon, you will remain at your post and communicate Aris Sung's return to no one."

"Yes, Battalion Commander."

"And there's an unconscious guard behind the warehouse," Aris informed Ty.

This time there was no mistaking the tension in Ty Wu Non's face. "Get on your radio, Leon. Send a patrol to wake him. Tell him he failed a readiness check by the battalion commander and is confined to his room until further notice. He is under an order of complete silence. No speaking." They waited while Leon relayed the order. "Now get in here, Aris," Ty ordered, straining the very limits of his courtesy.

Aris grabbed Leon's radio on his way through the door, lifting it right out of the holder on the sentry's belt. The younger warrior seemed at a loss, glancing to his battalion commander to see if he should make something of it. Ty Wu Non stepped inside the room and shut the door forcefully. "You had better have a damn good story to tell," he said through clenched teeth, no longer bothering to hide his fury.

Aris did.

Two minutes into the tale, Ty sat down heavily on his bed and except for his facial expressions did not move until Aris had finished. Aris read alternating waves of shock, disgust, fury, and wide-eyed denial that broke over Ty Wu Non's features at irregular intervals during the telling. When it was all over he made Aris repeat the scene from in front of the Gold Pavilion and then sat in stunned silence to consider it all. Aris waited more than five minutes for him to speak.

"If I hadn't been your Mentor, Aris, I doubt I would have believed what you just told me."

"But you do," Aris said quietly.

"But I do," Ty agreed. "It all makes sense, as long as one can accept the idea of outright betrayal in House Hiritsu." He glanced up sharply. "You can prove this?"

"I can."

"And the death of House Master York. How does that fit in?"

Aris shook his head lightly. "I'm not really sure yet," he said, only half lying. "I don't think Terry Chan did it, but I believe these events are related. I only used that to get your attention."

Ty Wu Non shook his head in disbelief. "By the elder gods, Aris, do you realize what this could do to our House?"

Our House. Always before, Ty Wu Non had called it *"my* House" as a way of distancing Aris Sung. That simple inclusion, even if only an oversight due to the shock of Aris' news, warmed Aris for perhaps the first time since Virginia York's death. Right then, Ty Wu Non had made him feel as if he belonged.

"Yes, Battalion Commander," he said. "It would mean inquiries, hearings, executions. And by the time the dust settled, House Hiritsu would be broken. It would take generations to repair the internal damage to the family, and that is *if* the Chancellor did not disband us."

Ty Wu Non blinked rapidly. "You do not try to guild it, do you?"

"I need to be sure we understand each other, Ty Wu Non."

Aris' familiar use of the battalion commander's name shocked the elder man back into a more active state of mind. "Why is that?" he asked cautiously.

Aris drew in a deep breath. "Because I may know a way we can bypass the inquisition and turn the entire situation into an advantage for House Hiritsu on Kaifeng."

Nothing showed on Ty's face or seeped into his voice. "That is a tall order. What will it cost me?"

"You have to be prepared to bury this entire matter, including the death of Virginia York. As far as anyone is concerned, she was killed by a Sarna operative. You would also have to accept my counsel on tomorrow's battle plans, and in a few other areas." *For once in your life, you will have to listen to me and trust me,* Aris thought. *Can you do that?*

Ty Wu Non surprised him. "Let's hear it," he said.

27

Jinxiang Port Terminal 5 South
Tarrahause District, Kaifeng
Sarna Supremacy, Chaos March
26 July 3058

The morning brought a slightly overcast sky, little wind, and an unforgiving jungle heat. By late morning the temperature had already soared past twenty-five degrees Centigrade on the way to thirty. The air was full of moisture and the heavy, wet scent of the tropics. An uncomfortable, sticky heat, but dark clouds piling up over the western horizon promised relief in the form of heavy showers by midday.

Terry Chan walked across the loading yard, the hot, humid air drenching her in sweat. Halfway across she caught up to and passed Company Leader Thom Lindell, who walked along at his usual, sedate pace. Though also covered in sweat and seriously sunburned after so much time on Kaifeng, his composure was as rigid as ever. Terry admired the man's self-discipline, but he also frightened her. One could never be sure what thoughts churned beneath that placid surface. It made someone with as many secrets to guard as Terry Chan self-conscious.

She hurried past, eager for the shade of the warehouse.

Ty Wu Non had spread a large map over the desk in his second-floor office. The two office chairs had been pushed out into the short hall above the stairs, while inside three of the House lance leaders were holding a private conversation right next to the air conditioner. Ty Wu Non stood in silent contemplation of the map. Terry also took to studying the map, trying to guess what her battalion commander would set forth as their plan of battle. She saw many possibilities, but she had to know for sure before contacting Karl Bartlett.

A twinge of conscience over her loyalty to House Hiritsu pricked at her. As she had been doing for several weeks now, she promised herself that she was doing the right thing. The House would grow stronger, and some day she would lead it as Virginia York had. The vision of that day was so clear to her that she could not even imagine events turning out any other way. She would show House Hiritsu and the other Warrior Houses a strength that had been lost in recent years.

Company Leader Lindell and one of his lance leaders were the last to arrive. Lindell shut the door behind him, then stood there, stoically, waiting for Ty Wu Non to begin the briefing.

"I fully expect the Tarrahause defenders to deploy tomorrow," Ty said without preamble. "Leftenant-General Cynthia Fallon has had almost twenty-four hours now to plan a response. We know she hasn't left the city, which means that she will likely lead the assault against us herself. I don't intend to wait here and surrender the initiative. We'll meet them between here and Tarrahause."

"Why wouldn't they deploy today, Battalion Commander?" Terry Chan asked.

Ty Wu Non stared off in the distance, as if trying to organize his thoughts. "Leftenant-General Fallon has been publicly denouncing us for breaking the cease-fire, claiming we used hostages in Franklin and on the recharge station to intimidate her people into betraying her. It's a touchy situation. She will wait for the cease-fire to expire, so she can claim moral superiority."

"Battalion Commander Non." Raven Clearwater's tone was soft and properly respectful as she voiced the first question. "Do we know their full strength?"

Ty turned to Company Leader Lindell, who Terry knew had been given the assignment of ascertaining just that.

The stone-faced warrior spoke directly to the battalion commander. "The DropShip *Lao-tzu* made a high-altitude pass over Tarrahause late yesterday afternoon and again this morning before the city finally put up its own air cover to crowd us off. We now believe that Fallon has brought two lances of mercenaries from Mahabohdi as well as her command lance of the Kaifeng SMM. The mercenaries could be either Ace Darwin's WhipIts or elements of Carlton's Brigade."

"Which brings their total strength to somewhere less than three companies," Ty Wu Non concluded. "Roughly half of which are mercenary. That does not include the Von Luckner tanks, which we know are in Tarrahause. But I expect them to leave the Von Luckners behind. The armored units are perfect for urban defense and they can't leave the city completely open."

"So two to three odds," Terry calculated roughly. "With our edge in equipment and skill, that evens things out, Battalion Commander."

Ty Wu Non smiled thinly. "I hope to tilt those odds backing our favor, Terry Chan." He nodded toward the map spread over his desk and everyone leaned in to watch.

"The Jinxiang River runs more or less southwest from Lake Ch'u Yuan, linking Tarrahause with us at Port Terminal Four South." He traced a finger along the map to indicate the stretch he was referring to. "There's a road that runs along the river—they probably call it a highway—that the Kaifeng SMM is sure to use. The road is bordered to the southeast all the way by a levee and the Jinxiang. Along the other side there's little except rice paddies, flat open ground where an approaching BattleMech would be visible from kilometers away. Little, that is, except for here." He tapped five green splotches.

"These are belts of raw jungle. Kaifeng keeps them partly as windbreaks and partly to prevent a complete destabilization of the native Kaifeng ecology. They also form natural bottlenecks where they run close to the road. They should make Fallon very nervous, since they put a blind spot on her right flank. We will hit her here"—he stabbed a finger down on one of the areas—"at the fourth bottleneck. Only we'll hit along her left flank."

"From the river?" Jill McDaniels asked.

"Exactly. We will submerge our BattleMechs in the Jinxiang and rig floaters for communications. Hidden infantry will alert us when their main body is just opposite our position, and we'll come up over the levee and smash them. We'll use prearranged targets for concentrated fire. With a bit of luck, we'll break them in the first few moments." Ty Wu Non continued to study the map, nodding to himself as if confirming the rightness of his plan. "Comments or questions, anyone?" When no one spoke, he looked to Company Leader Lindell. "Thom?"

"I like it," Lindell said, though by his tone and expression no one could have guessed his feelings one way or another. "It's simple, yet effective. I don't like complicated plans. They're too easily fouled."

When no one else spoke, Ty Wu Non held up a computer disk. "These are the plans. I want someone to take them to the transmitter room, encode and upload them to the *Lao-tzu* for relay to Company Leader James. I want his input. I also want him standing by to lend immediate assistance. This could be the deciding engagement for Kaifeng, and I want all contingencies covered."

Terry Chan had remained silent through most of the short briefing, as had most of the others. Ty Wu Non had come up with a good, solid plan, and the whole time she listened, all she could think of was how was she going to communicate it to Karl Bartlett. Now here Ty Wu Non was handing her the device she needed. "I'll handle the upload, Battalion Commander."

For the briefest second, Terry Chan thought she caught the flash of strong emotion behind Ty Wu Non's eyes. A sadness? Regret? But then it was gone and he held the disk out to her.

"Everyone else brief your lances. We'll reconvene planning at thirteen hundred this afternoon. Any questions or comments can be addressed then. And Terry—." He paused as if to say something, then changed his mind. "Don't be too long. I want your lance briefed within the hour so they have time to study the mission."

She smiled. "More than enough time, Battalion Commander."

*   *   *

Ty Wu Non did not want to ground his DropShips in unsecured territory, so the *Lao-tzu* was currently in orbit above them while the other two ships waited in Franklin and Beijing. But the forces in Tarrahause still needed to maintain communications, so he'd ordered the technicians to bring in a powerful transmitter and receiver. These were now set up in the port terminal administrative office.

The duty technician was quickly relieved and the door locked behind him. The four components of the large transmitter system were still strapped onto their transport, which looked more like a hospital stretcher than a carry-cart. The main unit had two maintenance doors in the back held by a single screw each, making for quick and easy repair. Terry quickly opened one of them. She replaced one of the radio crystals inside with one from her pocket. That altered a low-priority channel to a special frequency monitored by Karl Bartlett or one of his trusted technicians. It was very unlikely that another Hiritsu unit would notice that the station was currently off-line on that one frequency, or if they did, that they would think it worthy of reporting.

Terry Chan reached for the keyboard and quickly typed some instructions. Then she loaded the disk. One copy, encoded and uploaded to the *Lao-tzu*. She earmarked it for immediate relay to Company Leader Jason James in Beijing. Then she dialed in the new frequency.

She paused, looking over the message on the small screen. It occurred to her that with the extra lance recently added to the forces in Tarrahause, there were a lot of duplicated 'Mech designs. She decided to add a more detailed list of the five so-called *friendly* BattleMechs, the ones the Kaifeng SMM were supposed to avoid firing on if possible. She included any variation in weapons configuration or, if necessary, paint schemes. Anything to differentiate between a valid target and her associates. Five warriors, all with a similar vision of what House Hiritsu could be.

Chan also possessed a crystal that would let her communicate with Leftenant-General Cynthia Fallon, but she'd realized days ago that Fallon would never sell out the way Bartlett had. The general might play the waiting game they had started together, but only someone as driven as Bartlett would go along with using SMM 'Mechs and pilots to fake a Hiritsu attack on his own people in Tarrahause two days ago. Bartlett would blunder in, thinking he could control whatever situation developed and in doing so would clear away the last obstacles within House Hiritsu as well as unknowingly condemn Kaifeng. *The next assault,* she thought. After Ty Wu Non was safely out of the way, Terry would feed Bartlett some false information and then would walk him straight into an ambush. And if Fallon could be brought along, the entire assault would be over that much sooner. She double-checked her message and hit the Transmit key.

Nothing happened.

Terry stabbed the key again. And again. The message sat there on the screen, the Ready-to-Transmit light flashed, the key depressed easily—and still nothing.

Then the door opened behind her.

Terry Chan's right hand dropped to the Sunbeam laser pistol she kept holstered at her right side in place of the standard Nakjama as she spun around in the chair. Ty Wu Non stood in the door, his face tightly set against any show of emotion. Aris Sung stood just behind him.

"It won't send, Terry," Ty Wu Non said tonelessly. "Not unless you're on a main channel. And you won't be able to switch back now."

Terry stared at Aris Sung and realized what had happened. He had modified the transmitter, just as he had on the recharge station. They had allowed her access to the room just so she could condemn herself. Then she remembered the list she'd typed in for Bartlett. She'd also condemned her associates! Hand still on the butt of her pistol, she searched her mind furiously for a way out. She couldn't find one.

Aris was ready with some of her options. "You could try to destroy the transmitter," he said. "But if you look to your left you'll see a cable that feeds to an auxiliary memory unit in the next room. We have everything on disk."

"I could shoot you, Aris Sung." Even as she said it, it sounded hollow and petty in her own ears. It was over, and inside she knew it.

"You have never raised your hand, directly, against another warrior of the House," Aris reminded her. "Do you really wish to start now?"

In all honesty, no, she didn't. "Then why are we having this conversation?" She was stalling now, trying to figure out what they had in mind. Something, obviously, or there would be infantrymen here to take her into custody or just put her against a wall to be shot.

"Surrender your sidearm, Terry Chan." Ty Wu Non's voice was hard. "Move away from the transmitter and let Aris in there. Do that, and you will have your chance at redemption."

Terry wanted to laugh, but the moment weighed too heavily on her for laughter. "Redemption? You expect me to believe you would let me live?"

"Did I say live?" Ty Wu Non shook his head. "I said you could redeem yourself. You can die a warrior of House Hiritsu, remembered for your courage and dedication. Or you can die in disgrace here and now. That choice is yours."

There was no choice to make. From the moment they walked in, she'd understood that it was over for her. But to be stripped of her honor and shot as a traitor, that she could not bear to think of. She wondered suddenly if she'd ever really thought about what she might lose in all this.

Terry stood, slowly, and offered Ty Wu Non her Sunbeam, butt first. Ty and Aris Sung stepped fully into the room and closed the door behind them. Aris slid into the seat she had vacated and began to read through her message. "What do you have in mind, Battalion Commander?"

Ty explained while Aris continued to scan through the message and work intermittently on the transmitter. Chan listened intently, offering responses only when directly asked. In one case Aris answered for her. Ty Wu Non had asked how many others were involved, to which Aris responded, "Four. I can identify them from their 'Mech descriptions in the message."

There had been *five* 'Mechs. Had she miss-keyed the message or forgotten one? If so, she wasn't about to tell them. Let the missing person carry the dream further, if able. As for the others, well, Ty Wu Non's offer was generous, considering the circumstances. And in a way it

gave them something they wanted—the opportunity to
show everyone what a House warrior could be. Perhaps
not on the scale they'd imagined, but it was now the only
chance left to them.

She agreed to the terms.

Battalion Commander Non looked to Aris. "Do you
have the transmitter ready?"

Aris nodded.

"Then send the message to Tarrahause. Just as she entered it."

"Send the message?" Terry frowned her confusion.

"Tell her, Aris," Ty said.

Aris turned to her. "We never planned to use that strategy,"
he said with a curt laugh. "But we want Bartlett and Fallon to
think so."

28

Jinxiang River Road
Tarrahause District, Kaifeng
Sarna Supremacy, Chaos March
27 July 3058

The Kaifeng SMM had deployed a full lance of light 'Mechs nearly a kilometer forward as advance scouts, a mixture of regular forces and mercenary. They passed along the edge of the jungle, walking the Jinxiang River Road in single file. One BattleMech, a mercenary *Mercury* bringing up the rear, paused to scan the jungle, but it was only a cursory inspection using standard sensors. The jungle was out of range for the 'Mech's Beagle Active Probe, and the pilot evidenced no desire to leave the easy traveling surface of the road.

After all, they knew where and when the attack was going to take place. Didn't they?

But Aris' plan was to mislead the Kaifeng force into believing the attack would come later and then hit them early with a classic feint strategy. By Ty Wu Non's map, the place where House Hiritsu waited in ambush was actually the third bottleneck between Tarrahause and Port Terminal Five South, not the fourth. The jungle grew to within three hundred meters of the road at this point, the intervening land covered with low-lying, broad-leafed plants.

Over half the Hiritsu force was hiding back inside the dark jungle foliage, their fusion reactors dampened against detection by enemy sensors. It had taken them over an hour to reach their position, pushing through the dense jungle, and another before the usual wild shrilling of birds returned. Over the other side of the levee—submerged in the Jinxiang as per the original plan—Terry Chan and her small cabal of conspirators awaited his signal.

Terry Chan. Lance Leader Jill McDaniels. Brion Lee, one of Raven's warriors. Kevin Larsen, a lance leader under Thom Lindell. Four wayward sons and daughters of the House, yet so much depended on them. If they didn't hold up their end of the plan . . . But Aris promised him they would, and Ty Wu Non had accepted his assurances. Aris knew how to read people, and besides, Ty saw no other way to save the situation without letting the entire story out. Aris was right that the shock to House Hiritsu might well be irreparable. No, it was this way, or not at all.

It twinged his self-esteem just a little, though, to place the fate of House Hiritsu in Aris Sung's hands. Ty had still not fully accepted the young warrior, though he was trying. Aris was his son now, or at least he would be when Sun-Tzu confirmed Ty as the next House Master. A leader of a Warrior House had no business carrying grudges, especially if it was going to prejudice him against recognizing good advice. He hoped that trusting Aris Sung with planning this offensive would be Ty's last step to purging the old jealousies and hatreds.

As long as it succeeded, that is.

Through a carefully arranged break in the vine-strung trees, Ty Wu Non watched as the scouts disappeared beyond a curve in the road and the main body of the Kaifeng defenders appeared from around the northeast bend. An *Atlas* led the parade, its death's head mask surveying the country with its chilling grin. It was one of the largest assault 'Mechs, and Ty was sure it must be Leftenant-General Fallon's machine. Thirty meters behind her walked—Ty would almost say *strutted*—a BJ-O *Blackjack* OmniMech. Major Karl Bartlett. His targeting computer on standby, Ty Wu Non identified as many 'Mechs as he could through field binox.

The range at which the scouts preceded the main body gave Ty an idea. He dialed in an auxiliary channel on his commline. This channel bypasssed the transmitting circuitry and ran directly through a line the House infantrymen had strung between all the waiting 'Mechs. When the action began, the line would tear away, but for now it gave them secure communications.

"They're coming right at us, warriors. Stand ready. Support Three and Auxiliary Two," he called to the two missile-boat BattleMechs in hiding with him. "Those scouts will come flying back around that corner in a hurry once the fireworks start. Drop a welcome for them just this side of the bend. Two full volleys each." He checked the position of the enemy 'Mechs. The lead unit was just passing his position. "Tactical command is passing to Company Leader Aris Sung. Go ahead, Aris."

Aris was the only other BattleMech with full view of the road and the machines moving along it. As Ty listened, Aris ran down the line identifying each BattleMech. He assigned each of the five hidden lances to a particular enemy—the more dangerous enemy 'Mechs on the field—ordering concentrated fire until they were brought down. It took less than a minute, and by then the enemy was in perfect position. "Now," he ordered. "Send the signal to Terry Chan."

Terry Chan had to give it to Aris. He'd timed their arrival extremely well. As her lance of four topped the levee, they found themselves positioned precisely in the middle of the line where the Kaifeng SMM stopped and the mercenary forces began. The line of enemy Battle-Mechs stretched over a half kilometer in either direction, with the two nearest machines not forty meters away down the levee's slope.

At that moment Terry Chan might have radioed Aris Sung from her *Cataphract* to congratulate him except that her radio had been fixed only to receive. So she allowed herself a fraction of a second to admire the view and imagine the surprised expression on Karl Bartlett's otherwise plain face. Then she targeted a nearby Kaifeng *JagerMech* and thumbed her main trigger. Fifty-millimeter slugs of depleted uranium chewed into the *JagerMech,* accompanied by a scathing cloud of LB-10X submunitions. Shattered armor plates crashed to the road around the *Jag*'s feet as Terry Chan claimed first blood.

To her left and right, the other three Mechs of her lance were also engaging the enemy with equal fury, savaging the *JagerMech* and a nearby *Cicada*. Armor melted and ran in some places, flying off as large chunks in others. The *Cicada* crashed to the ground, losing its left leg, and the Kaifeng line of march was thrown into chaos as more than two dozen 'Mechs tried to react to the sudden and vicious onslaught. Some held their position and brought close-range weapons to bear while others spread out into the field on the other side of the road before turning back to engage.

Terry Chan and her lancemates triggered another round almost simultaneously. This time she tied her two forward-firing medium lasers into her main TIC *and* selected the 50mm ultra autocannon to rapid fire, turning the *Cataphract*'s full fury on the hapless *JagerMech*.

I'll be dead before I run out of ammunition, she thought. *Might as well make it a good show.* This time her autocannon slugs smashed their way into the *Jag*'s interior torso structure, followed by nearly half her LB-X submunitions. The *JagerMech* jerked and stumbled forward. Its left side in ruin, bleeding gray-green coolant and black smoke, it crashed to the road without ever having fired off a shot.

As the enemy finally began to return fire, Terry fought her control sticks for balance and screamed a challenge into the tight confines of her own cockpit. The violent barrage shook her like a rag doll in her command couch, but she kept the large war machine on its feet through sheer force of will. Damn Aris Sung and Ty Wu Non and the entire Kaifeng SMM! Before she was done, she would show them all what a warrior of House Hiritsu could do.

Aris watched the battle with more empathy for the doomed House warriors than he would have expected. They were his brothers and sisters. Perhaps they had been misled, but that did not change his relation to them. Aris hoped that each one would now acquit him or herself well.

But he did not order the 'Mechs of the main force forward from their jungle hiding places, which might have saved the isolated lance. The Kaifeng SMM and their bought warriors had been expecting an attack from the river, and Aris had given it to them in the form of Terry Chan and her suicide squad. Now it was his responsibility to make sure their sacrifice was put to the best possible use.

He watched as Terry Chan finished off the Kaifeng *JagerMech* just before her *Cataphract* drew intense counter-fire. At least three fiery PPC streams carved into the 70-ton 'Mech, slashing molten scars across its legs and upper torso. Emerald and ruby laser beams chewed away at her armor until Aris couldn't see a single spot not running molten steel. Autocannons and several flights of missiles bit out large chunks, severing the *Cataphract*'s left arm at the elbow. The greenish smoke of burning coolant poured from several gaping holes.

A flight of nearly twenty long-range missiles struck at the lower legs and feet and tore into the ground around Terry's battered 'Mech, throwing up a veil of dirt and debris. Aris wouldn't have thought that any 'Mech could ride out that kind of damage, and looked for the *Cataphract* to come crashing down any second. Then it stepped through the smoke and the shower of dirt, striding confidently down the side of the levee as it angled toward rear elements of the Kaifeng SMM. The *Cataphract* trailed wisps of green and gray smoke, and pieces of molten armor continued to slough off like some kind of BattleMech leprosy, but on it came.

A 30-ton *Scarabus* tried to stand in Chan's way, its hatchet chopping off more of her BattleMech's left arm while its lasers probed the rents in her armor, seeking critical internal equipment. The *Cataphract* batted the light 'Mech aside with a sweeping blow from its right arm as if the smaller machine was nothing more than a nuisance. The *Scarabus* stumbled to its knees and then sprawled out over the road. Terry turned her lasers and large autocannon on it, switching from cluster ammo to the 180-mm slugs. She then kicked it for good measure. It didn't get up.

Aris winced at Terry Chan's brutal attack against the smaller 'Mech, then looked the battlefield over. All four Hiritsu 'Mechs were still on their feet, though how that was possible Aris couldn't begin to say. He had wanted to wait for the first warrior to fall, but knew if he didn't give the order soon the charade would wear thin. He opened a channel on the secure line.

"Warriors prepare," he said. *One last act to play.* "Chan, fall back to the river now," he ordered, hand hovering near four special switches. He never expected her to do so, but he had to maintain the illusion. "Get out of there."

Of course, Terry Chan could not answer. Aris wasn't really worried that she and her people might try to cause trouble once the battle was joined, but he preferred not to take chances. A flip of a toggle switch on his comm panel and Chan's pre-recorded answer was transmitted over the frequency. "Negative, we're going to stay. Bait Lance, press them hard!"

"Damn," Aris cursed for the audience. "Infantry forces are to concentrate on fallen 'Mechs and taking prisoners. Hiritsu MechWarriors, have at them."

Following his orders, Aris released the safeties imposed on his fusion engine, smiling grimly as it roared to life beneath him. As he coaxed every last bit of speed possible from the 55-ton machine, the *Wraith* broke from the jungle at better than sixty kilometers per hour and accelerating. To his right and left the jungle seemed to come alive as more than a thousand tons of House Hiritsu BattleMechs broke from cover and charged the enemy's rear.

Long-range missiles arced out first, hitting several SMM BattleMechs. The first barrage also included Ty's specially designated targets as two Hiritsu machines spread Thunder mines around the road southwest. Three hundred meters or less separated the Hiritsu force from the scattered Kaifeng line, a void that was suddenly filled with beams and darts of coherent light and azure whips of PPC energy. Autocannon slugs and Gauss rounds went unnoticed in the hellishly bright display of energy, but their damage to the Kaifeng force was no less real.

Reacting to the threat coming from the river, the Kaifeng SMM and the mercenary forces had left their weaker rear armor toward the jungle. They now paid for their reliance on a traitor's report. Armor plates buckled and shattered like eggshells. Lasers cut deep through the thin protection, while the heavy blue-white lances of PPCs passed easily through armor and cored into internal supports and critical systems. Engines and gyros were burned and blasted out, stealing the life from a BattleMech. In one *Archer*'s spectacular case, the ammunition storage for both its torso-mounted long-range missile racks were touched off almost simultaneously. The BattleMech effectively ceased to exist, the explosion knocking over a nearby mercenary *Enforcer* while larger pieces cartwheeled off in bizarre flight patterns.

Aris had targeted five 'Mechs for concentrated fire, and within seconds three of those lay in complete ruin. So did Brion Lee's *Apollo*, Aris noted, recognizing the hunched-shoulders design of a blackened and broken 'Mech. He reached out and flipped up the protective cover on one of four important toggle switches. Each switch could remote-detonate charges planted on the fusion reactors of the 'Mechs of each member of the suicide squad. Just in case they needed help dying a martyr, Aris was ready to give it to them. He hit the switch now, just to be safe.

He turned away from the exploding BattleMech, seeking a target. Two of the five 'Mechs he'd judged most dangerous were still functioning, the *Atlas* and Bartlett's *Blackjack* Omni. As the coordinated assault he'd arranged now broke down into several smaller individual matches, Aris lost visual tracking on both. He decided to use the speed and maneuverability of his *Wraith* to go hunting.

The battle was not won yet.

Smoke stung Karl Bartlett's eyes and burned his throat raw. Autocannon fire had glanced the head of his *Blackjack*, cracking his cockpit open like an oversized egg. Most of his viewscreen remained intact, shielding him from the worst effects of the battlefield such as glare from lasers and the heat wash from his own discharging weapons. But the smoke that leaked in reeked of hot coolant and burning metal and warned him to leave the battlefield.

He wasn't about to flee. Not yet. Rage and a thirst for vengeance drove him on. He was looking for the treacherous Terry Chan and dealt harshly with any House Hiritsu warrior who dared interfere with his quest. The smoldering vegetation, smoking, torn-up earth, and the burning hulks of fallen 'Mechs scattered over the area made the search difficult, but Bartlett only blinked the tears from his eyes and pushed on.

A 75-ton *War Dog* lurched into view, the smoke from a nearby burning *Lineholder* wrapping about its long legs like some kind of creeping black jungle vine. The *War Dog*'s right arm had been half-slagged—by PPC fire, Bartlett thought—ruining its Gauss rifle main weapon. There was nothing wrong with its lasers, though, and ruby darts stitched into the *Blackjack*'s left leg and worked their way up the left side. They found a rent in the armor, just beneath the Omni's left breast, and cut away more of the physical shielding surrounding the 'Mech's fusion engine.

Temperature in the *Blackjack*'s cockpit soared as the atomic fire that powered his mighty war machine leaked past the shielding and dumped raw heat into the internal structure. Flames spewed out of the rent in the left torso, licking up around the viewscreen. But Bartlett's targeting computer had already identified the *War Dog* as one of the four 'Mechs that had launched the ambush, and he triggered his full spread of weapons without a care for heat buildup.

The Inner Sphere OmniMech could hold any of four weapon configurations. Bartlett had selected the "C" class configuration, which mounted an LB-X autocannon and a medium laser in each arm. The autocannon were both selected to fire their 80mm slugs of depleted uranium. One spread caught the *War Dog* in the center torso, the other just to the side of its bulbous cockpit. The lasers merely chewed deeper into an already-ruined right arm, but the hard punches of the autocannons were enough to stop the *Dog* in its tracks and rock it back several meters.

It didn't go down, but the pilot was rattled enough that his or her next salvo of laser fire missed high and to the right. Bartlett grinned savagely, his lips skinning back in a snarl. Heat washed over him in a dizzying wave, pulling his breath from him in a ragged gasp. He ignored the heat monitor, which was edging deep into the red, and selected cluster ammunition for both autocannon. "Time to die," he whispered.

The cluster ammo fragmented just after leaving the barrel, but did not have time to spread over a large area. The concentrated spray of flechettes blasted the *War Dog* across the upper chest and cockpit, some of the submunitions finding their way into the internal structure. The huge machine shuddered and staggered back, almost like a man hit in the chest by a double-barreled shotgun. Bartlett saw a red smear spread across the 'Mech's large, cracked viewscreen, and then the *War Dog* was falling backward.

He did not cheer his victory. He merely accepted it. As his heat levels dropped down out of the critical area to the merely dangerous, he fought to ignore the scent of singed hair and the pain of his heat-blistered knuckles. Peering through the smoke and flame that now belched thickly from his 'Mech's ruined torso, he walked his *Blackjack* deeper into the chaos of the battlefield. Always searching.

29

Jinxiang River Road
Tarrahause District, Kaifeng
Sarna Supremacy, Chaos March
27 July 3058

The *Cataphract* shuddered violently, limbs flailing madly in the air as if suddenly caught in an epileptic seizure. A glance at her 'Mech's damage schematic confirmed Terry Chan's fear; its gyro had been shot out.

"No!" she screamed loud and long, her voice amplified inside the confines of her neurohelmet. She had walked up onto the levee again, scouting for Bartlett, and for a few brief seconds she'd seen his *Blackjack* stalking the battlefield near where the head of the column had been. But as she came down off the rise, a Kaifeng SMM *Gallowglas* had slipped in behind her. Its large laser and PPC had flayed off the last of her rear armor and dug deep, wrecking the large gyroscope that was critical in keeping seventy tons of metal upright and moving.

The *Cataphract* was going down with no way to prevent it. Her controls weren't responding and gravity could be very insistent. Terry refused to let it end so easily, though. A warrior of House Hiritsu did not need a Battle-Mech to be deadly. Aris Sung had proved that many times in the course of his career, and now it was her turn.

Her cockpit ejection mechanism had been deactivated

by Aris Sung, just as her transmitter had. There was nothing Terry Chan could do but ride the large machine down. It fell face-first, but she fought the controls to turn the near-uncontrollable machine so at least it fell onto its side and did not smash her cockpit into the ground.

The cockpit shook hard in the crash, throwing her against the restraining straps and then back against the seat. When it finally stopped she hit the quick-release to her restraints and climbed shakily from the command couch, throwing her neurohelmet to one side. She had little in the way of offensive weapons in the cockpit except a Sunbeam laser pistol stashed under her seat. She retrieved it and strapped it on.

The cockpit hatch was located in the back of the *Cataphract*'s wedge-shaped head. She hit the release and opened it. The caustic smell of the battlefield hit her first. The acrid scent from lasers ionizing the air and metal burning, of smoldering vegetation and scorched earth. The first fat drops of rain were falling from the dark clouds piled overhead, and those that hit Terry Chan's face and trailed down to her lips tasted of the greasy smoke that rose from the battlefield. She shook her head hard, sweat spraying from her face and hair.

"Lance Leader Chan," a voice called out, startling her. She looked down and to her left, toward the ground, and saw four Hiritsu infantrymen crouched behind a small hill her BattleMech's shoulder had plowed up in its fall. They carried grapple rods and demo charges.

Terry Chan smiled, offering thanks to the fates, and started to climb down.

Her *Cataphract* exploded less than a minute later.

From where he fought near the front of the line, Ty Wu Non could not accurately tell how the battle fared. His *Charger,* ancient in comparison to most Hiritsu designs but still the best 'Mech he'd ever piloted, currently limped around the field with a destroyed right hip actuator.

He was hunting for the *Atlas* that had proved so uncannily accurate with its Gauss rifle. The enemy pilot had hit five in six shots so far. Two of the Gauss slugs had cracked open the *Charger*'s right leg up to the hip and destroyed the actuator there. Two more had crushed his center torso armor into small pieces that now littered the battlefield. The final egg-shaped slug had slammed into his left torso, shattering armor plates but leaving him with some protection.

Ty Wu Non's rear armor had been savaged when the forward-deployed scout lance had returned. The *Mercury* he'd noticed before and an SMM *Battle Hawk* had run through the Thunder-mined area near the southwest bend, triggering several of the missile-deployed mines. Their legs had been amputated at the knees and then at the hips, leaving the light 'Mechs rolling through the minefield to be torn apart by even more of the charges. Running slightly behind the first two, a *Spider* and what looked like a factory-new *Jenner* had triggered their jump jets and sailed over the dangerous terrain. They landed less than fifty meters behind Ty's *Charger* and ripped into his rear armor with a flurry of green and blue medium laser bolts.

Ty had wasted precious seconds destroying the *Jenner,* judging it the more dangerous of the two. The *Spider* had escaped on its jump jets, heading deeper into the battlefield, where Ty hoped it would meet its end. But in the meantime, he'd been forced to weather the *Atlas'* sniping Gauss rifle. *No more,* he decided. He would bring down Leftenant-General Fallon himself.

Ty pivoted away from an SMM *Bandersnatch* that was being swarmed by Hiritsu infantry planting charges into its knife-blade hips. It smashed ineffectively at the agile infantrymen with its blocky arms, and Ty Wu Non wrote it off as good as dead.

The first drops of rain spattered against his viewscreen as he found his quarry, the 'Mech's death's head grinning down at a slightly smaller 'Mech that circled it with deadly intent. Aris Sung's *Wraith* cut left and then right, rushing in to snipe with his medium and large pulse lasers and then back out before Fallon in her *Atlas* could get a full lock on him. He used his great speed to dodge from one side or the other to keep the assault 'Mech from bringing to bear its impressive array of weapons. The dance was almost beautiful, an impressive display of skill over raw firepower, and Ty Wu Non felt a sudden stab of pride at having been Aris' Mentor.

But it could only end one way. The *Atlas*, with its twenty tons of armor, had incredible staying power. It reached out with long-range missiles and its Gauss rifle, with large and medium lasers, missing more often than not, but every hit leaving Aris that much more vulnerable. Already Ty could see the gaping holes showing up in the *Wraith*'s protective armor. Soon the *Atlas* would hit something critical—engine shielding or the gyro or possibly a leg actuator—and Aris would be at its mercy.

Ty Wu Non had already lost too many warriors to see Aris fall in front of his eyes. He stabbed down on one of his thumb triggers, sending a full flight of twenty long-range missiles from the *Charger*'s torso-mounted launcher. His right torso kicked back under the sudden thrust of the launching missiles. Before his computer could even register any hits, Ty kicked his 'Mech into running speed and closed on the *Atlas*.

Eighty tons of charging assault 'Mech would give Fallon something to think about.

Over half the missiles found their mark, scattering across the right arm and torso of the *Atlas*. The death's head swung around, as if searching for the machine that would dare engage it, though its sensors undoubtedly told Fallon everything she needed to know. It was the distraction Aris had needed. He slipped in behind the monstrous machine and burned away at its weaker rear armor while Ty triggered his four medium pulse lasers and continued to draw attention to himself.

The Gauss slug caught his *Charger* in the right torso, followed by a large laser hit that chewed through to his internal structure, burning out his Artemis fire-control system and one of his medium pulse lasers. The second large laser missed low, and the emerald darts of the *Atlas'* mediums were ineffective against his left arm. Ty Wu Non fought his control sticks and rode out the damage. The *Atlas* looked large in his viewscreen. Then came the shock of impact, followed by a sickening squeal and crunch as armor plates rubbed and crushed against one another.

Sensors screamed at him for attention, and his damage schematic showed the *Charger* outlined in red all over. Ty held no illusions that he would keep the 80-ton 'Mech upright after such a collision, and surrendered to gravity while working the control sticks to lighten the fall.

The *Charger* bounced heavily against the ground and its cover of broad-leafed plants, which left a green smear across his viewscreen. Ty bounced around against his restraining straps, his head whipping from one side to another. Everything blurred from the violent shaking, and then faded to black.

Running and the constant discharge of his lasers had edged Aris' heat up into the lower part of the red band. Sweat poured freely down the side of his face and ran down his arms and legs. The hot air squeezed at his lungs and scratched his throat. He welcomed the thought of rain as the large drops began to slap against his viewscreen, though locked inside his cockpit he wouldn't be able to take any relief from it.

Ty Wu Non happened by at just the right time. Aris' *Wraith* had only lost a jump jet, but his 'Mech had only about three total tons of armor left, and it was only a matter of time before a Gauss slug or large laser beam put an end to him. He had already hit the other three remote detonators, making sure the cancer within the House died before he did. When the *Atlas* turned away to meet the *Charger*, Aris breathed a heavy sigh of relief and moved around to worry at the assault machine's rear armor.

The collision between the two assault 'Mechs almost caught him unprepared. He had not thought Ty Wu Non would place himself in such jeopardy, going point-blank with the *Atlas'* destructive power and then intentionally slamming his 'Mech into the larger machine. Aris saw it coming only at the last second and managed to move out of the way as both *Atlas* and *Charger* fell and rolled over the terrain where he'd just been standing.

Ty Wu Non's *Charger* hit the ground hard, with less control over its bouncing than the *Atlas*. Aris was concerned for his battalion commander, but he knew that wouldn't help the other man any. He ran his *Wraith* up to the *Atlas*, which was struggling to regain its feet. He jerked repeatedly on his main trigger, pumping the scarlet beams of all three of his lasers into the enemy 'Mech again and again.

The *Atlas* didn't seem affected. Rivulets of molten armor poured from its arms, legs, and torso, and its left side was literally caved in. It rose slowly but steadily to its feet, the death's head grin centered on Aris' *Wraith*.

Then the scarlet darts from Aris' large pulse laser found the smashed left torso of the *Atlas*. Burning its way through the final shards of armor, the laser cut into the ammunition storage for the assault 'Mech's long-range missiles. Fire and gray smoke erupted from the torso as the missiles cooked off. Most of it was channeled out the back of the *Atlas* by the CASE construction, but few pilots could maintain control against the raw force of such an explosion. Not to mention that it would ruin the *Atlas'* bulky extralight engine. The *Atlas* twisted to the left and dove into the ground with its right shoulder forward.

It didn't move again.

"Nicely done," a malicious voice whispered in Aris' ear. "Pity you won't live to enjoy the victory."

Aris recognized the voice of Karl Bartlett, even through the radio filters. He glanced quickly at his control panel, thinking that the Hiritsu commnet might have been breached or sold to the SMM by Chan before yesterday. But the scanner told him that Bartlett was simply transmitting on an open frequency with no scrambling. *Was the man mad, stopping to talk in the middle of battle?*

The *Blackjack* OmniMech stood on top of the levee, barely one hundred meters directly ahead but catching Aris with his *Wraith*'s arms lowered. If Aris tried to bring weapons to bear, one salvo from the LB-X autocannon would rip his 'Mech open like a soldier falling on a grenade.

"The battle is over at this end of the field," Bartlett said. "You may very well own the day, Aris Sung. But you won't see the end of it. I couldn't find Chan, but you will do."

Aris had been tensing up, preparing to make a move that would spoil Bartlett's aim. The *Blackjack* didn't look good. Fire and black smoke poured from three different places on its front. Perhaps it wouldn't be able to track him effectively. He was about to chance it when he noticed the blur of movement against the side of the levee, moving up toward the Omni. *Infantry*, he thought at first, until he realized that the figure wore only shorts, T-shirt, and a cooling vest. He adjusted the image on one of his auxiliary monitors, tightening the shot until recognition sparked. Terry Chan! Alive and moving in with a grapple rod.

Aris hesitated, muscles tensed and screaming for the release of action. If he fired now, Chan would be caught between the two 'Mechs. If he waited, she might not try to intervene until after Bartlett had reduced his *Wraith* to scrap metal. *Time to test your own beliefs,* Aris challenged himself. He had guaranteed Ty Wu Non that Terry Chan's desire to serve House Hiritsu would outweigh whatever animosity she felt for Aris or Ty or anyone else. It had been the fundamental argument for trusting her group as a suicide squad, though Aris had hedged his bets by planting the explosive charges on their fusion engines. This time, though, he didn't have that safety net. *All or nothing,* he told himself. *How much do you believe in the binding force of House Hiritsu?*

Aris released his control sticks and settled back, waiting for vindication or a fiery death.

One of the infantrymen had carried an extra grapple rod, another a second demo pack. Terry Chan had broken from them as they moved off to track a slow-moving *Bandersnatch,* continuing in the direction she'd seen the *Blackjack* heading. The rain increased, now falling in a light curtain of heavy but widely spaced drops. It would soon be pouring hard, cutting visibility down to mere meters, and before then she had to find Bartlett. It was the driving thought that kept her moving, the desire to perform this one last service to House Hiritsu. It warmed her and lent her strength.

She found the Omni as it climbed the levee to preside over the final moments of Aris Sung. She had missed Ty Wu Non's charge, but something stirred inside her at the sight of the *Wraith* standing up to the *Atlas.* She knew that Aris Sung would protect to the death the fallen *Charger* lying sprawled on the ground behind him. And the sight stirred something inside Terry that years of hatred for the young warrior and her secret dissatisfaction with Virginia York's and then Ty Wu Non's rule had been unable to crush. She laughed out loud when the *Atlas* finally fell before Aris' light weaponry.

But now the *Blackjack* stood dominant, ready to tear Aris apart but holding off. Gloating, Terry wondered? Drawing out the one moment of victory in an otherwise obvious defeat? She moved up the side of the levee, readying the grapple rod.

The charge kicked against her shoulder, propelling the adhesive ball almost straight up as Terry angled for the OmniMech's head. It struck what would have been the forehead on a man, sticking fast. Terry slipped her foot into the loop and thumbed the retract button, riding the wire up toward the cockpit.

She remembered the holo of Aris Sung performing a similar maneuver years ago, bluffing a MechWarrior with a first-aid pack. Aris had been willing to risk his life to buy his House Master a few more minutes in which to escape. Now here she was, aping his tactic in order to get that final kill. But where Aris might have been able to flee had the bluff not worked, Terry Chan did not have that luxury and she knew it.

This was a one-way ride.

A wave of heat warned her to curl up protectively as the grapple rod pulled her up past a rent belching flames in the Omni's torso. Pain seared her bare arms and legs, and for a second she was unable to breathe. Terry almost lost her grip then, but ragged determination saw her through. Then there was a jolt as the rod hit its limit switch and stopped reeling in wire.

Terry Chan opened her eyes to find herself bumping up against the cockpit viewscreen. Karl Bartlett stared through the broken screen with a wide-eyed, incredulous expression. Terry reached down and pulled the activation ring on the demo pack that hung from her belt. Smoke teared her eyes and threatened to smother her. Flames still licked at her feet. But Terry Chan was beyond pain and discomfort as she unhooked the demo pack from her belt, drew her arm back, and then rammed the entire package through a broken section of the viewscreen.

Shards of the clear, high-impact plastic broke off, some slicing into her arm, but she held tight until sure the pack was inside the cockpit. Only then did she drop it, the tan-colored pack tumbling off the main control panel and falling to the floor. Karl Bartlett screamed in fear and sudden panic, trying to reach for the package at his feet. Then he straightened up, locking eyes with Terry Chan.

Terry, who had been counting off the seconds, smiled as he reached for the emergency ejection controls. Too late. Fire filled the cockpit and blew out the viewscreen.

30

Hotel Lampur, Mahabohdi Spaceport
Mahabohdi, Kaifeng
Sarna Supremacy, Chaos March
4 August 3058

The Hotel Lampur had been chosen for its convenience to the spaceport, where House Hiritsu had made its headquarters. Li Wynn had recommended it, the suggestion properly advanced through Aris Sung. Li was off packing now, preparing to move aboard the *Lao-Tzu* for safety. The young thief was actually too old to join the Warrior House, but Aris had guaranteed him passage offworld and help settling in one of the larger cities on Randar.

Aris leaned up against the wall just inside the hotel ballroom's open double doors, arms crossed in impatience as he waited for the presentation to begin. Other House warriors sat or strolled about the large room. Two Hiritsu infantrymen stood guard at the ballroom entrance, and two at the large room's only window. Members of the House wore their green and black dress uniforms and either a sidearm or ceremonial katana sword, except for the sentries, who dressed more functionally and carried assault rifles.

A single camera crew had been allowed in, though the signal would be sent to every major network for broadcast. Their equipment was set up at the edge of the large dance floor. Leftenant Ellen Harris stood at a podium on the stage, having been brought down from the recharge station. The gauntlet-and-katana insignia of House Liao and the Capellan Confederation decorated the front of the podium. Somewhere back in the stage wings, Aris knew, another pair of infantrymen watched over Ellen Harris' two children.

Ty Wu Non had privately guaranteed his company leaders, Aris included, that he would never hurt the children. But it wasn't important for Leftenant Harris to know that. Ty wanted the presentation to go flawlessly, which meant keeping a strong hold over her. Aris still disagreed with such tactics, but that was only his opinion and he kept it to himself. Ty Wu Non would be House Master, and the will of the House Master . . .

Just now Battalion Commander Non stood off to one side with Leftenant-General Cynthia Fallon. The battle hadn't lasted much past the death of Major Karl Bartlett. The Kaifeng SMM, decimated almost to the last 'Mech, had never recovered from the initial Hiritsu feint and rearward attack. The mercenary forces, Jacob's Juggernauts and elements of Ace Darwin's WhipIts, had fared better. They'd reacted faster to the changing threats, managing to organize a single counter-attack that Raven Clearwater's lance had blunted. In the end, the mercs had requested standard terms of withdrawal and awarded the day to House Hiritsu.

Aris Sung and Ty Wu Non, together, had pulled Cynthia Fallon from her broken *Atlas*. Initially she thought to be very uncooperative. Then Aris had showed her the accumulated evidence, including some private tapes made by Terry Chan of her conversations with the leftenant-general and Major Karl Bartlett, that would prove conclusively that the Kaifeng SMM—and Fallon in particular—had conspired with members of House Hiritsu. Aris could lay the entire blame for the Dragon Boat Festival attack at her feet. Treason. Violation of the Ares Conventions. It would ruin the Kaifeng SMM, and give the Sarna Supremacy's interstellar relations a black eye as well. Under that kind of political threat, the leftenant-general had calmly folded her hand and agreed to cooperate.

The battle for Kaifeng was over. Only the formalities, and a private vow, remained.

"I have been asked to make a formal statement on behalf of the Kaifeng SMM," Leftenant Harris said. Her voice calm and reassuring, she was the perfect spokesperson.

Aris nodded his approval as the formalities of surrender were begun. Then he shoved himself away from the wall and drifted silently out the door. Statements by Cynthia Fallon and then Ty Wu Non would follow, all aimed at easing the transition to Capellan rule.

Aris estimated he had thirty minutes.

Ty Wu Non noticed Aris Sung taking his leave and the barest trace of a frown creased his brow. It seemed strange that the younger MechWarrior would not stay for the formal surrender of Kaifeng. Aris had been instrumental in arranging the ceremony—indeed, the entire victory—and it was only fitting he be present. But then Ty knew that for all his years as Aris' Mentor he still did not know him as well as he should.

Aris had come to the House with a lot of raw potential, potential that Ty himself would surely have wasted with a single cut of a blade if not for House Master York's protection of his charge. And then Virginia York had assigned Ty as Aris' Mentor, making sure that Aris never got too comfortable within the family structure of House Hiritsu. Ty could now recognize Virginia York's subtle hand in Aris Sung, just as he could see his own harder influence. Insight and action. A good mix. Had this been House Master York's plan all along—to prepare for Ty someone he could rely on to temper his own harsh impulses?

Ty Wu Non would be watching Aris Sung very carefully.

All MechWarrior company and lance leaders, except for the duty lance, had been ordered to remain on hand until after formal surrender. Aris found Senior Company Leader Thom Lindell staring out the window of one of the many second-floor rooms reserved for the use of House Hiritsu officers in the hotel. Lindell was alone, as Aris had expected. Thom Lindell was a man of solitude; in victory . . . or defeat.

Aris let the door shut behind him with a soft snick of its

latch. Lindell never looked around, his attention riveted on the street below. When he spoke, it was with the most neutral of whispers. "I've been expecting you, Aris Sung. Though perhaps not so soon as this."

Aris shrugged first one shoulder and then the other from under his half-cape, then unfastened the clasp to let the cape fall to the floor directly behind him. It did not surprise him that Thom Lindell had guessed his approach. "Your name did not appear on the list of *friendly* 'Mechs that Terry Chan was to transmit to Bartlett."

Lindell nodded once, still looking out the window. "You must have removed it. Terry thought that she'd somehow misskeyed the entry."

"She wasn't that inefficient."

Lindell's voice never wavered an octave. "True. But when faced with the alternative, that you shielded me—." He broke off.

Aris understood perfectly well. It would not have made sense to Terry Chan that Aris would protect Thom Lindell from the same justice meted out to her and the others. "Terry didn't know you as well as she thought. You would have never walked into your death as they did, no matter how honorable an end it was. You would have fought the entire way, and torn the House apart in doing so." Aris felt a flush spread along the base of his scalp as he spoke the accusation out loud.

"What prompts this lack of respect for my personal honor?" Lindell asked. Still there was no deviation from the usual monotone—no anger or curiosity, just a simple question to be answered.

"You killed House Master York," he said evenly.

Still no reaction. "Did I? You must think awfully poor of me to believe that I would turn my hand against the leader of our House."

Aris dropped his left hand to the hilt of the sword he wore at his side. "What did it, Thom? That Virginia York did not protest our exclusion from the attack on Davion's worlds last year? That she settled on Ty Wu Non as her successor and not you?"

Lindell's shoulders hitched, and he gave out a small gasping laugh. It took Aris an extra second to realize that this was Thom's effort to scoff at the charge. He wasn't very good at it. "And for this I strangled her?"

It was all Aris had been waiting for. The katana slid quickly free of its scabbard with a metallic rasp. Aris brought both hands to the hilt and extended the blade so that the tip was against the base of Thom Lindell's throat.

"How did you know she was strangled?" he demanded. "I never even mentioned to Ty Wu Non the bruises I saw. Doctor Hammond's report was sealed. Everyone knew about the slit throat because of all the blood."

Thom Lindell turned away from the window, moving carefully so as not to cut his own throat. Aris could see knowledge of his error on the other man's face. There were no further attempts to turn Aris from his purpose here. He merely regarded Thom Lindell with cool, unrepentant eyes that widened only the briefest sliver upon noticing the blade. "Crescent Moon? You stole it from Ty Wu Non's cabin? You would again violate House tradition just to serve your need for vengeance? A strange way to dispense your justice, Aris Sung."

"Ty Wu Non is not yet House Master," Aris said coldly. "This is Virginia York's sword and Virginia York's justice. And one of the last things I heard from my House Master was a promise that even the smallest instance of defiance would be considered a capital offense."

Aris drew back and slashed, once, with violent force. He let his rage erupt, driving his arm, before he could think better of the execution. The blade cleaved through Lindell's face and continued down to draw a bloody furrow across his chest.

Aris bent over the corpse of Company Leader Lindell. His chest heaved and his stomach felt tied in knots as he cleaned the House Master's blade on Lindell's clothing. "Those were my House Master's last words," he said, partially to the dead man and partially to himself. "And the will of the House Master is the will of the House."

Aris left Lindell there, the blood spreading out in a pool across the floor.

Epilogue

Celestial Palace
Forbidden City, Sian
Sian Commonality
Capellan Confederation
9 August 3058

House Master Ion Rush stood with Colonel Talon Zahn in the Strategic Planning Center of the Celestial Palace. It was the chamber known as the War Room, and few came here. Even fewer knew where it was. The House Master's left arm crossed his chest to support his right elbow, and his right hand cradled his chin. Both men studied the holographic star chart that stretched from floor to ceiling, a two-dimensional representation of the Capellan Confederation and surrounding space.

A prickly warmth tickled at the nape of Rush's neck and he glanced back over his shoulder, searching the shadows of the dimly lit room. Nothing. He shrugged his shoulders to ease the tension pulling at his muscles. No matter where he went in the Celestial Palace, he always felt as if he was being watched, studied. The sensation would come and go, but never had he found any evidence to support the mild paranoia.

It's just that I'd rather be back in the House Imarra stronghold, he thought, looking back to the holographic chart. *Tending the House and walking among warriors.* The Celestial Palace was a place of too many secrets, too much politics, for him to ever feel comfortable. But the Chancellor was absent. He had just completed a diplomatic mission in the Periphery and now headed for a summit meeting on the Lyran Alliance capital of Tharkad, via the Marik capital of Atreus. That meant Ion Rush's place was in the palace where he and the Chancellor's Strategic Military Director, Colonel Zahn, could tend to the business of maintaining the Confederation's state of readiness.

Ion Rush rubbed at the back of his neck, trying to massage away the unease. *That doesn't mean I have to like it.*

"You wanted to lift the blockade at Sarna?" Colonel Zahn asked, though it was more of a prompt. House Master Rush had asked for this private meeting, and he'd remained silent for too long.

The Imarra House Master nodded. "It has served its purpose. Sarna wasn't sure how to react to our warships at first, but they're learning. Soon they'll manage to slip around them, or possibly damage one."

Talon Zahn was young to be named Strategic Director of the Capellan Confederation, though he could boast of being older than Sun-Tzu Liao himself. He was still trim and well-muscled, favoring his right leg and its hip replacement only slightly. Ion Rush considered the man's thirty-odd years an asset. He was old enough to hold the position, young enough that his appointment threatened the older field commanders, and, above all, he was devoted to the Chancellor.

Now the Director frowned, even as he nodded agreement. "Those vessels are too new, too big a chunk of our budget, to risk foolishly. If you believe they may be threatened, I will move them. But what about our people on Kaifeng?"

Ion Rush studied the trio of stars that until only a few days ago had comprised the Sarna Supremacy. Two of them still glowed the turquoise of independent systems—Sarna and Sakhalin. The point of light representing Kaifeng on the star chart was wrapped in a sublime green glow that made Ion Rush smile. "According to the reports from Battalion

Commander Non, Kaifeng has been pacified. He requests an additional battalion to hold Kaifeng against Sarna."

"We have that on Capella," Zahn said easily. "And I will arrange for an adjustment of our shipping routes to take advantage of Kaifeng's food surplus. We can distribute it to several worlds on our border."

Rush cleared his throat to signal a disagreement. "I think we should consider selling the food surplus to Sarna," he said evenly.

"You think what?"

Rush smiled, though it did not quite reach his eyes. "We already have reports of food shortages on Sarna. They relied too heavily on Kaifeng. Sakhalin is even worse off, but then they don't have nearly the same population to support so they'll adapt much faster. If we shut off the supply of food to Sarna, they will have no recourse but to strike hard at Kaifeng and we will lose our advantage. By continuing to sell to them, we buy ourselves time. Once we find adequate reinforcements for our nearby worlds, we slowly inflate the prices and steadily decrease shipments. We put a stranglehold on the entire Sarna Supremacy."

Talon Zahn glanced toward the bottom of the star chart, to the Periphery, where the Magistracy of Canopus rubbed against the border of the Capellan Confederation. "With luck, those reinforcements are not too far off," he said. The Chancellor himself had pulled off the operation that would ally troops of the rich Periphery state of Canopus with the Capellan military.

The problem for the Capellan Confederation was not the taking of worlds, but being able to hold them. Ion Rush had spoken of this to Sun-Tzu when the year began, and the Chancellor had promised to find the troops necessary. Ion Rush had held up his end of the bargain struck that night. Now it was for the Chancellor to hold up his.

"From your lips to the Chancellor's ear," Rush said.

In one of the war room's dark corners, partially screened by a bust of Elias Jung Liao—founder of the Liao dynasty—green eyes peered out from a small square of darkness set into the wall. Like cat's eyes, they trapped the light, almost glowing, and did not blink for long periods. A small piece of wood paneling finally slid back into place to cover the aperture.

Kali Liao stood and stealthily moved down the secret passage. The hidden passages that riddled the Celestial Palace were extensive, and she knew many of them by memory. Her outstretched fingers located the first passage that branched off to the right and she turned into it, only then snapping on the small penlight she carried.

Ty Wu Non still lives, which means Lindell has failed. Houses LuSann and Ijori are beyond my reach, courtesy of Ion Rush. Now my brother returns with Periphery troops. Most inconvenient.

She tossed her head angrily, her wild, dark hair whipping against the side of her face. *Mother should have named me her successor.* Would have, Kali was sure, except for the intervention of her Aunt Candace. Now her brother kept her in the shadows, and those around him worked directly to weaken her. *But it will not matter in the end,* she promised herself. Green eyes bright and fierce, Kali Liao smiled into the darkness. *The death goddess cloaks herself in shadow and has many arms. Only one needs succeed.*

ABOUT THE AUTHOR

LOREN L. COLEMAN has lived most of his life in the Pacific Northwest, an on-again off-again resident of Longview, Washington. He wrote fiction in high school, but it was during his five years as a member of the United States Navy, nuclear power field, that he began to write seriously.

His first year out of the military, Loren joined the Eugene Professional Writer's Workshop and within a few short months sold his first story. He has spent the last three years working as a professional freelancer, writing source material and fiction for game companies such as FASA and TSR. For FASA, he has written for both the **BattleTech®** and **Earthdawn®** games. His first novel, *Double-Blind,* was also set in the **BattleTech®** universe.

Loren Coleman currently resides in Whiteriver, Arizona, where he lives with his wife, Heather Joy, two sons, Talon Laron and Conner Rhys Monroe, and three troublesome cats.

BE SURE TO CATCH THE NEXT EXCITING BATTLETECH NOVEL

EXODUS ROAD

by Blaine Lee Pardoe

Coming in August from Roc!

Racine River Delta
Tukayyid
Free Rasalhague Republic
May 2, 3052

The stark peaks of the Dinju Mountains made a jagged frame for the battle raging in the rolling hills near their base. Star Captain Trent barely noticed them as he piloted his *Timber Wolf* to the crest of a small grassy hill, his 'Mech's enormous feet sinking into the sod as he slowed to a walking pace, searching for targets of opportunity. His Starmate, Schultz, moved to flank him in his *Mad Dog*. The *Dog* was so shattered and mauled that Trent found it hard to believe it could even move, let alone fire. So many warriors had fallen in the fighting. He and Schultz were all that was left of the Binary that had been his command.

The sight of the *Mad Dog,* moving with its lizard-like gait, stirred Trent even after all his years as a MechWarrior. For the past six hundred years 'Mechs had dominated the battles and wars of mankind. Roughly humanoid in shape and rising up to twelve meters tall, a single 'Mech carried enough firepower to level a city block. It could operate in almost any terrain, be it the vacuum of space or the depths of the sea. And animating them were the warriors who sat in their cockpits, using their own neural feedback to help pilot the massive machines of death.

To Trent it was fitting that the cream of Clan technology was here to crush the Inner Sphere's last vestige of hope. There had been some losses, but the might of the invading Clans returning to conquer the Inner Sphere had made the Grand Crusade a stunning success. Planet after planet had fallen to Clans as their armies raced toward Terra.

Then ComStar, the techno-mystical cult that occupied and preserved Terra, had decided to take sides. Using secret intelligence they'd gathered on Clan honor and traditions, they had challenged the Clans to a proxy battle on Tukayyid. If the Clans won, they could claim Terra at last. If they failed, the invading Clans would have to agree to a fifteen-year truce. And for a warrior like Trent that meant he would be too old to take part in the invasion when it resumed. That was why losing the fight here and now was not an option.

"Silver Paw to Cluster Command," he barked, as a series of explosions rippled among the nearby hills. "We are in Sector Five-fourteen."

There was a hiss of static, some from Com Guard ECM, some from damage, Trent's highly trained ears knew the difference and knew the mix as well. The strained voice of an officer—not his own Star Colonel—replied. "Silver Paw, this is Dark Vigil. The command post has been overrun. We are pulling back to the river delta. Elements of the 401st Division are in your area. Link up with Blood Streak Star and pull back as our rear guard. We will reorganize in the delta, *quiaff?*"

Blood Streak Star . . . Jez's command. There was a part of him that hoped Jez had met her fate against the meat grinder of the Com Guards. These were not the untested warriors that Khan Lincoln Osis had led them to expect. The enemy had fought with a ferocity almost equal to that of the Smoke Jaguars themselves. They had hit hard and fast, and then pulled back. The 367th had taken out the two mobile supply bases that his Galaxy had counted on.

Worse, to him, they had nearly destroyed his Star, his combat command. Schultz was all that was left, more by luck than skill. Temper had perished in an ambush by Com Guard infantry. Silvia had died in her cockpit while a Com Guard fighter strafed the battle zone. Winston had died embracing an enemy *Crockett,* letting his fusion reactor go critical as he held his foe in a death-hug.

Trent had to acknowledge the enemy force as true warriors, even if his commanding officers and Clan leaders did not.

It was *supposed* to have been a lightning-fast victory. He let his eyes rove briefly over the surrounding hills and the stark mountains, and in that brief instant understood the meaning of this moment. This was Tukayyid, the largest battle fought since General Kerensky had liberated Terra three centuries before. But that was not all.

Trent was a Smoke Jaguar, and he knew that such a massive battle must surely result in heavy losses. The bloodnames of those who died could now be fought for and claimed by new warriors. The chance of winning a bloodname stirred Trent to his core.

He had met with Star Colonel Benjamin Howell just before this battle had begun, and the Star Colonel had agreed to sponsor him for any bloodnames that became open when the fighting was done. Trent believed it was only a matter of time before he too would stand among the bloodnamed of the Smoke Jaguars and all the other Clans. It was the greatest achievement a warrior could aspire to. His genetic legacy would become part of the gene pool, and he would live on beyond his days.

All that remained was to defeat the Com Guards. He knew that his commanders considered ComStar's effort to end the invasion pure folly. They also viewed the quick strikes of the Com Guards as a waste of resources.

Trent saw the truth, that the Com Guards had played a game of hit and run so hard and fast that the Jaguars of the Beta Galaxy were worn down. Now, the Jaguars were in retreat, no matter how much their commanders called it reorganization. He had tried to tell the Star Colonel what he saw unfolding, how the Com Guards were crippling the Jaguars. But he'd been cut off mid-sentence. The

Jaguar high command believed they had the situation under control. They had ignored him, but he knew that would all change when he could claim the bloodname of Howell as his own.

Just as he was about to signal for Jez, Trent saw her *Warhawk* sweep up the face of a hill a kilometer away. She was following the Com Guard infantry she was routing, mowing them down with a barrage from her large pulse lasers. Or, at least the one that was still operating. He throttled his *Timber Wolf* to a full trot as he raced after her.

He had known Jez since their days in the Mist Lynx sibko. *She will not break off pursuit, no matter what her orders.* They must have already commanded her once. That must be why they were sending him after her. Her willfulness would be her death one day. Perhaps this day . . .

Trent signaled Schultz as he rushed forward, locking on to her signal. "Cover my left flank as we go. We have orders to link up with Jez and pull her back to cover the Galaxy's rear flank."

"Aff, Star Captain," Schultz said as he matched the trotting pace of Trent's *Timber Wolf.*

Trent checked his sensors and saw that Jez was ahead of them, just over the next hill. Her slow movement on the sensor display told him that there was a battle raging there, and he braced for it as he ran through the long green grass of the hillside.

He crested the hillside and was suddenly buffeted by a powerful blast that lifted his *Timber Wolf* off the ground. There were impacts, not from weapons, but from pieces of Schultz's OmniMech as it battered his own.

The short-range sensors told him what was happening. A short-range missile carrier had opened up on Schultz the moment it had spotted him. More than thirty missiles had blown through the remains of Schultz' *Mad Dog* in less than two seconds. There had been no time to eject, no time to fire, only time to die. And Jez was facing two other Com Guard 'Mechs in the middle of what must have been a Com Guard forward command post or repair base. Infantry blasted away with shoulder-mounted missile launchers and manpack PPCs, slowly but surely destroying her *Warhawk*.

Trent was not about to let that be his fate. He locked onto the withdrawing SRM carrier and let go with his long-range missiles. The warheads raced across the smoke-filled base and into the carrier. Digging through its side armor, the blasts ate into the vehicle's magazines, setting off its weapons in a massive explosion.

He pivoted as one of Jez's attackers, a stark white *Crab*, broke off and fired a wild shot in his direction, missing by at least five meters. Trent was hoping for just such a shot, one that let him intrude on Jez's fight without depriving her of any honor. Trent locked on with his last salvo of long-range missiles and let them fly the millisecond he heard the lock tone on the stout *Crab*.

Most of the missiles found their mark on the enemy 'Mech's right side, ripping its arm off and sending a shower of smoke and sparks into the air. At least two of the missiles streaked past the *Crab*, pounding into Jez's 'Mech. *That warrior is good. He has tricked me into doing damage to my own people* . . . The Com Guard 'Mech twisted at the torso under the impact of the blast, but quickly returned fire from its deadly large laser. The shot dug into his left leg, popping off the ferro-fibrous armor in a series of rattling explosions. A flicker of heat rose in his cockpit as he moved to the left of the *Crab*, making it harder for the enemy 'Mech to maintain its weapons lock. Keeping his distance, Trent knew he could optimize his long-range weapons against the injured 'Mech.

He held his fire until he had cleared the distance to the top of another nearby hill, then opened up with his large lasers. The brilliant red lances of laser light reached out for the *Crab*. One hit the ground just past it, sending a streak of smoke across the once green field. The other found its mark, cutting laterally into the hip of the *Crab*. Its armor sizzled for a second, then exploded as the shot sliced deeply into its internal structure. Myomer cabling, the "muscle" fiber that propelled BattleMechs in combat, severed and burned, and a sickening green wisp of smoke rose into the air. The hip joint seized, if only for a second, finally popping loose at the last moment as the *Crab* pilot desperately attempted to put his damaged 'Mech into a better firing stance . . . or so he thought.

Jez's fight with a nearby Com Guard *Thug* was turning into a deadly slugfest as the *Crab* spun back on her, fully exposing its back to Trent on the hillside. He saw the *Thug* drop—its left leg blown off at the knee in an explosion of black smoke and shrapnel that had once been parts of the Com Guard 'Mech. Almost at the same moment the *Crab,* at nearly point-blank range, spun to face her. Jez never saw where the shots came from, and the assault was devastating. The *Crab's* small and medium lasers sent out a wall of pulsating light, gouging into her 'Mech's armpit, stabbing upward because of the *Crab's* lower posture. A secondary blast from within the guts of Jez's OmniMech sent her left weapons pod flying into an infantry trench while the *Crab's* remaining large laser boiled off what was remaining of her rear armor.

Jez pivoted to face her foe, swinging the stump of her mangled arm like a club. In a difficult piloting move, the *Crab* pilot crouched his 'Mech so that the swinging arm missed its mark. Rather than return fire, it moved in close and kept to the side of Jez, giving her a kick that caved in most of the *Warhawk's* leg. Trent was impressed. To dodge, turn, and still attack at such range was the mark of a warrior worthy of a Jaguar in combat.

Trent could not let Jez die. They both were Smoke Jaguars, no matter how he felt about her. If he didn't leap to her defense, she would die. Like his own OmniMech, hers had been in the field long enough to have taken quite a bit of damage. Then he saw what the *Crab* pilot had done and smiled to himself. *A worthy foe indeed.* From the way the 'Mechs were positioned and their close proximity, Trent would hit Jez's dying *Warhawk* if he fired at the *Crab* and missed. The choice was his. Hold his fire and move to her flank, possibly allowing Jez to die, or open fire.

For Trent, a Smoke Jaguar as surely as if its heart beat in his own chest, there was no choice.

As his targeting cross hairs arced down on the *Crab* and his weapons hummed with preheat energy, he hoped that the *Crab* pilot would somehow survive attack. He or she would make a fine addition to the Smoke Jaguar Clan as a bondsman. Anyone willing to place him or herself between two foes and take both of them on at the same time was a worthy prize of battle.

Trent held his stance and fired with everything he had, hitting the rear flank of the *Crab* with a horrific blast of laser fire. The bright red and green laser beams sliced into the armor deep and brutally, sending slabs dropping and spraying into the sod of the hillside. None of his shots had missed . . . Jez lived for now. The *Crab* warrior held his own, firing steadily at Jez as she finally turned her 'Mech so that she could retaliate. The Com Guard MechWarrior stayed with his 'Mech long enough to see Jez's *Warhawk* shred two tons of his armor in a wracking series of laser blasts doled out at devastating range. The superior Clan technology held. The *Warhawk* stood its ground, readying for a kill.

Trent's shots ensured that Jez would not have the honor of dying on the field. He had locked onto the *Crab*'s damaged hip region and his lasers had done their job well. A burp of black smoke and green coolant spilled from the area of his impacts. There was a flash of flame as the hip actuator superheated and exploded violently, knocking the *Crab* down and out of the battle. Its pilot knew that the 'Mech was all but finished. Trent saw the cockpit blast clear and the ejection seat rise up on a white wisp of smoke over the battlefield. *Punch out.*

Jez swept the retreating Com Guard infantry with her lasers, hitting only one trooper, but pressing the others deep into their foxholes and trenches with the fiery display. Trent opened a broad-band signal to the entire area. "Pilot of the Com Guard *Crab,* I claim you as *isorla* in the name of the Smoke Jaguars."

His communications channel came to life as Jez spoke to him. "You dared violate my honor by firing on that *Crab, quiaff*? I shall face you and kill you for your actions."

"The *Crab* fired at me first, Jez. No honor was lost. We have orders to fall back to the river delta and act as rear guard. You will accompany me," Trent replied curtly.

"Orders to fall back? That is not the way of the Jaguar warrior."

"It is the way of all warriors to follow orders of superiors, and yours come from Galaxy command. We must leave now."

Jez did not get a chance to respond. From the top of a distant hill a swarm of Com Guard BattleMechs rose and took firing stance, lighting up Trent's short-range sensors. He saw the count of enemy targets on the display and felt his mouth go dry. *Ten!* Trent instantly understood why he had been ordered to withdraw. Apparently the 401st Com Guards Division had managed to rally, and were heading straight at him. *Clan honor places victory above wasteful death. Standing and fighting here means death.*

The closest, a racing *Hussar,* was locking onto Jez at the same time Trent opened up with his extended long-range lasers. He reopened a channel to Jez. "Pull back now, Jez!" He began to move his *Timber Wolf* along the hill and was preparing to break into a full run.

"Damn you," she said, finally conceding and moving toward him. "When this is done, you will die at my hand in a Circle of Equals . . ."

"Later, then. For now, do your duty and move out!"

His sensors showed a Star of Smoke Jaguars closing in, rushing in to reinforce them, but they were still precious seconds away. Jez's 'Mech cleared the hill in front of him and he mentally cursed. No matter what he did or said, she would bend it to her purposes, twist the truth to fit her vision of the events. He did not need this, not with his chance at a Bloodname so close at hand. *Perhaps she will die before we can settle this matter. No question of honor can taint me when I am presented for the Trials . . .*

Suddenly the ground seemed to erupt all around the *Timber Wolf.* Sod and fire, grass and death splattered against his *Timber Wolf* as if the very surface of Tukayyid was coming apart under him. As the 'Mech pitched, he compensated, flames licking upward at him from the ground.

His targeting computer demanded his attention as he rocked. *Artillery—and Arrow missiles.* They were not confronting him in a direct fight, but wanted him dead without honor. Jez raced past him as he turned his 'Mech to try to get free. It was a move he would never complete.

The second barrage did not rip at the soil but found its mark on the already-battered *Timber Wolf.* Artillery rounds shattered his shoulder-mounted missile racks, turning them into debris in a matter of an instant. A blast of warmth seemed to wrap his body as he saw the image of a ComStar *Hussar,* still racing straight at him, its laser blazing at him as his 'Mech staggered like a drunkard. One of the Arrow VI missiles went off on his foot, then another dug deeply into his shoulder, ripping his left weapons pod away from his 'Mech's torso with a thunderous blast. His 'Mech was dying, but Trent knew he had to survive. Somehow.

There was no time to fire or move, as if the fates themselves had taken control of the universe around him. His *Timber Wolf* began to tumble as countless artillery rounds rained down on him. The 'Mech quaked under each impact, and Trent's brain shrieked as the battle computer sent a stream of neural energy back into his neurohelmet. Trent wanted to scream and may have, but the deafening echoes of explosions drowned out every sound around him. His secondary display lit up as jump infantry suddenly appeared all round him. The display imploded and cracked, its plasma crackling like green and orange lightning. Other controls popped and smoked. His mind sped like a wild horse, trying to find a way out of the disaster around him. *It is too late.*

He reached forward for the ejection control when suddenly the cockpit glass in front of him blew inward. A wave of flames roared to life before him. *Infernos!* The missiles were filled with gelled petrochemicals that could generate incredible heat in a 'Mech. Given his crippled status, the use of inferno weapons meant a burning death for him. Trent felt his body tense against the restraining straps as the flames engulfed his arms. His neurohelmet visor popped off from the blast, and flames lapped inward at his eyes. The smell of cooking meat filled his nostrils and he understood that the smell was his own flesh.

Pain, deeper and darker than anything he had ever felt before. Every cell of his skin seemed to sear with a burning pain that cut deep to the bone. A bright white light seemed to take him, and the sounds seemed to disappear. *Death. It had to be death. If only the pain would go as well* . . . Blindly, he reached into the light, groping either for the visage of death or for the ejection control, whichever he could find first.

Wraith

Hatchetman

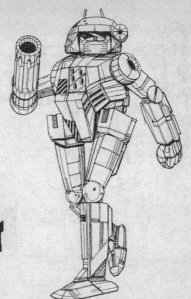

Vindicator

Huron Warrior

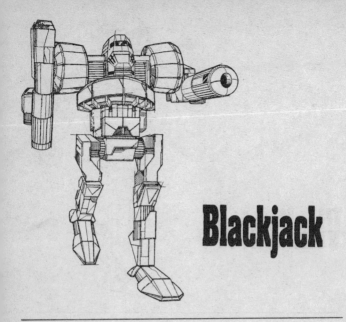

Blackjack

Lineholder

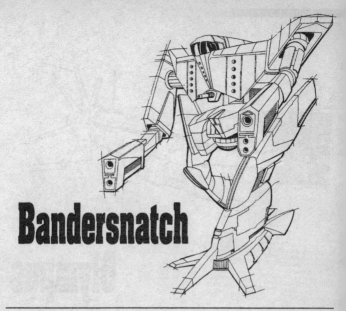

Bandersnatch

Scarabus

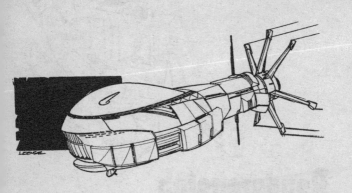

Olympus

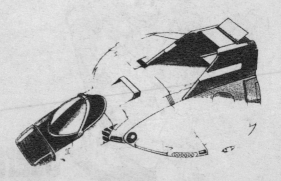

Thrush

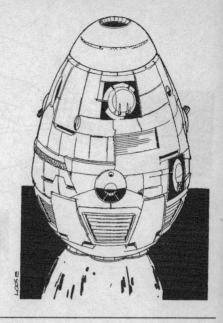

Overlord

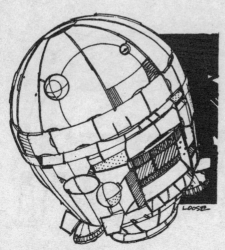

Intruder

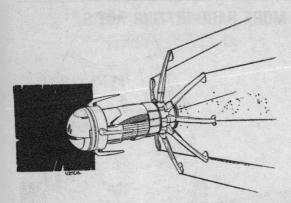

Merchant

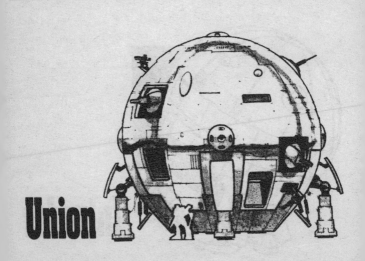

Union

MORE HARD-HITTING ACTION
FROM BATTLETECH®

☐ **CLOSE QUARTERS** by Victor Milán   (453786—$4.99)

☐ **BRED FOR WAR** by Michael A. Stackpole   (453794—$5.99)

☐ **I AM JADE FALCON** by Robert Thurston   (453808—$4.99)

☐ **HIGHLANDER GAMBIT** by Blaine Lee Pardoe   (453816—$4.99)

☐ **TACTICS OF DUTY** by William H. Keith, Jr.   (453824—$4.50)

☐ **LETHAL HERITAGE** by Michael A. Stackpole   (453832—$4.99)

☐ **BLOOD LEGACY** by Michael A. Stackpole   (453840—$5.50)

☐ **LOST DESTINY** by Michael A. Stackpole   (453859—$5.99)

☐ **STAR LORD** by Donald G. Phillips   (453867—$5.50)

☐ **MALICIOUS INTENT** by Michael A. Stackpole   (453875—$5.50)

☐ **WOLVES ON THE BORDER** by Robert N. Charrette   (453883—$5.50)

☐ **HEARTS OF CHAOS** by Victor Milán   (455231—$5.99)

☐ **OPERATION EXCALIBUR** by William H. Keith, Jr.   (455266—$5.50)

☐ **HEIR TO THE DRAGON** by Robert N. Charrette   (455274—$5.99)

☐ **BLACK DRAGON** by Victor Milán   (455282—$5.99)

☐ **IMPETUS OF WAR** by Blaine Lee Pardoe   (455290—$5.99)

☐ **DOUBLE-BLIND** by Loren L. Coleman   (455975—$5.99)

*Prices slightly higher in Canada

Buy them at your local bookstore or use this convenient coupon for ordering.

PENGUIN USA
P.O. Box 999 — Dept. #17109
Bergenfield, New Jersey 07621

Please send me the books I have checked above.
I am enclosing $_____ (please add $2.00 to cover postage and handling). Send check or money order (no cash or C.O.D.'s) or charge by Mastercard or VISA (with a $15.00 minimum). Prices and numbers are subject to change without notice.

Card #_____ Exp. Date _____
Signature_____
Name_____
Address_____
City _____ State _____ Zip Code _____

For faster service when ordering by credit card call **1-800-253-6476**

Allow a minimum of 4-6 weeks for delivery. This offer is subject to change without notice.

FASA

RELENTLESS ACTION FROM BATTLETECH ®

☐ **WAY OF THE CLANS** by Robert Thurston   (451015—$5.50)

☐ **BLOODNAME** by Robert Thurston   (451171—$5.50)

☐ **FALCON GUARD** by Robert Thurston   (451295—$5.50)

☐ **WOLF PACK** by Robert N. Charrette   (451503—$5.99)

☐ **NATURAL SELECTION** by Michael A. Stackpole   (451724—$4.50)

☐ **DECISION AT THUNDER RIFT** by William H. Keith, Jr.   (451848—$5.50)

☐ **MERCENARY'S STAR** by William H. Keith, Jr.   (451945—$5.99)

☐ **THE PRICE OF GLORY** by William H. Keith, Jr.   (452178—$4.99)

☐ **IDEAL WAR** by Christopher Kubasik   (452127—$4.99)

☐ **MAIN EVENT** by Jim Long   (452453—$5.50)

☐ **BLOOD OF HEROES** by Andrew Keith   (452593—$5.99)

☐ **ASSUMPTION OF RISK** by Michael A. Stackpole   (452836—$5.50)

☐ **FAR COUNTRY** by Peter L. Rice   (452917—$5.50)

☐ **D. R. T.** by James D. Long   (453663—$4.99)

*Prices slightly higher in Canada

Buy them at your local bookstore or use this convenient coupon for ordering.

PENGUIN USA
P.O. Box 999 — Dept. #17109
Bergenfield, New Jersey 07621

Please send me the books I have checked above.
I am enclosing $_____ (please add $2.00 to cover postage and handling). Send check or money order (no cash or C.O.D.'s) or charge by Mastercard or VISA (with a $15.00 minimum). Prices and numbers are subject to change without notice.

Card #_____ Exp. Date _____
Signature_____
Name_____
Address_____
City _____ State _____ Zip Code _____

For faster service when ordering by credit card call **1-800-253-6476**

Allow a minimum of 4-6 weeks for delivery. This offer is subject to change without notice.

THE WORLD OF SHADOWRUN®

☐ *NEVER DEAL WITH A DRAGON:* **Secrets of Power Volume 1 by Robert N. Charrette.** In the year 2050, the power of magic has returned to the earth. Elves, Mages and lethal Dragons find a home where technology and human flesh have melded into deadly urban predators. (450787—$4.99)

☐ *CHOOSE YOUR ENEMIES CAREFULLY:* **Secrets of Power Volume 2 by Robert N. Charrette.** As Sam searches for his sister, he realizes that only when he accepts his destiny as a shaman can he embrace the power he needs for what awaits him in the final confrontation. . . . (450876—$5.50)

☐ *FIND YOUR OWN TRUTH:* **Secrets of Power Volume 3 by Robert N. Charrette.** A young shaman unwittingly releases a terror from the ancient reign of magic. (450825—$4.99)

Prices slightly higher in Canada

Buy them at your local bookstore or use this convenient coupon for ordering.

PENGUIN USA
P.O. Box 999 — Dept. #17109
Bergenfield, New Jersey 07621

Please send me the books I have checked above.
I am enclosing $_____ (please add $2.00 to cover postage and handling). Send check or money order (no cash or C.O.D.'s) or charge by Mastercard or VISA (with a $15.00 minimum). Prices and numbers are subject to change without notice.

Card #_____ Exp. Date _____
Signature_____
Name_____
Address_____
City _____ State _____ Zip Code _____

For faster service when ordering by credit card call **1-800-253-6476**

Allow a minimum of 4-6 weeks for delivery. This offer is subject to change without notice.

YOUR OPINION CAN MAKE A DIFFERENCE!
LET US KNOW WHAT *YOU* THINK.

Send this completed survey to us and enter a weekly drawing to win a special prize!

1.) Do you play any of the following role-playing games?
   Shadowrun _____ Earthdawn _____ BattleTech _____

2.) Did you play any of the games before you read the novels?
   Yes _____ No _____

3.) How many novels have you read in each of the following series?
   Shadowrun _____ Earthdawn _____ BattleTech _____

4.) What other game novel lines do you read?
   TSR _____ White Wolf _____ Other (Specify) _____

5.) Who is your favorite FASA author?
_____

6.) Which book did you take this survey from?
_____

7.) Where did you buy this book?
   Bookstore _____ Game Store _____ Comic Store _____
   FASA Mail Order _____ Other (Specify) _____

8.) Your opinion of the book (please print)
_____
_____
_____
_____

Name _____ Age _____ Gender _____
Address _____
City _____ State _____ Country _____ Zip _____

Send this page or a photocopy of it to:
FASA Corporation
Editorial/Novels
1100 W. Cermak Suite B-305
Chicago, IL 60608